© Fred Gary

About the Author

Ann Herendeen, a native New Yorker and lifelong resident of Brooklyn, has worked as a researcher for an urban planning consultant; an advertising media planner; a public and academic business reference librarian; a trademarks monitor for an intellectual property law firm; and a cataloguing librarian specializing in natural history. She is a graduate of Princeton University, where she majored in English while maintaining a strong interest in English history.

PHYLLIDA
and the
BROTHERHOOD
of
PHILANDER

HARPER

NEW YORK • LONDON • TORONTO • SYDNEY

PHYLLIDA *and the* BROTHERHOOD *of* PHILANDER

A Novel

Ann Herendeen

HARPER

HarperCollins books may be purchased for educational, business, or sales promotional use. For information please write: Special Markets Department, HarperCollins Publishers, 10 East 53rd Street, New York, NY 10022.

FIRST EDITION

Designed by Jamie Kerner-Scott

Library of Congress Cataloging-in-Publication Data is available upon request.

ISBN 978-0-06-145136-2

08 09 10 11 12 OV/RRD 10 9 8 7 6 5 4 3 2 1

To the first readers of *Phyllida*,
John Atchison and Rita Scholl:
for your enthusiasm and gentle criticism
as the chapters came out of the computer;

to the readers of my earlier work,
I.B., Roxanne Brie, and Kevin Gillespie:
for your devoted reading, your praise,
and your encouragement, which inspired me
to write something purely my own;

to my mother,
Jane:
for having the honesty and love
(as you always did) to speak the truth,
that your only child's work wasn't perfect
. . . yet:

my heartfelt thanks for making *Phyllida* a better book.

And to my perspicacious editor, Rakesh Satyal,
and the select few who recognized *Phyllida*'s worth
when she was just a POD (you know who you are),
my undying gratitude for bringing about her metamorphosis
into glittering publication.

Acknowledgments

I WILL BE ETERNALLY GRATEFUL to HarperCollins for giving this Cinderella her chance to go to the ball. Specifically, I wish to thank my editor, Rakesh Satyal, for believing in *Phyllida*, and for his support and encouragement that helped me through the long prepublication process; his assistant, Robert Crawford, who dealt cheerfully and expeditiously with the mundane tasks of getting and sending (sorry, Wordsworth), and answering my many ignorant questions; the artists who created the gorgeous cover image and the stylish interior designs that complement it so perfectly; and my meticulous, conscientious copy editor, Olga Galvin Gardner, who corrected all my misused "which"s and "that"s and worried over every historical detail that I had cavalierly assumed wouldn't matter in a lighthearted comic novel. Any errors of fact (or lost glass slippers) that have escaped her vigilance are mine, and I take full responsibility for them.

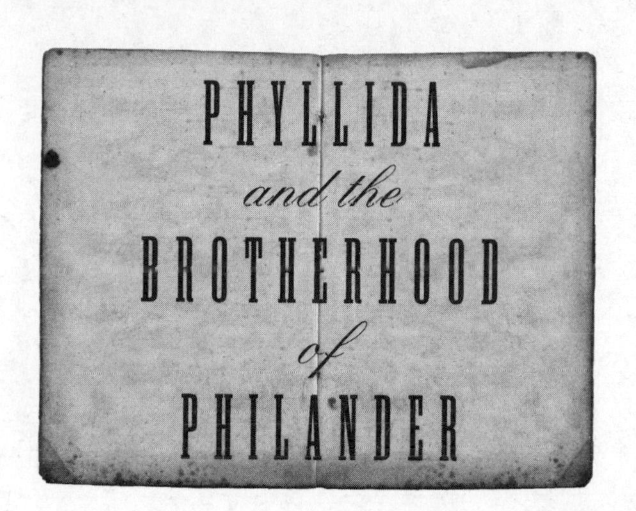
PHYLLIDA
and the
BROTHERHOOD
of
PHILANDER

LONDON, MARCH 1, 1812

ANDREW CARRINGTON AWOKE WITH a headache, no memory of the previous night, and a sneaking suspicion that he was not alone. He opened his eyes and groaned. Daylight—bright, intrusive, accusing daylight—was peeping through the chinks in the hastily pulled drapes covering the windows of the bedroom in his Grosvenor Square town house. "Damn," he muttered.

"Mornin'," a cheerful voice assaulted him. "Back in the land of the livin'?"

Andrew turned his head a fraction of an inch. The pain was excruciating, stabbing. "Not exactly living, no," he said. He studied the irritatingly pert face a couple of inches away. "And just who the hell are you?"

The face lost some of its good humor and took on what Andrew imagined was a more habitual look of ill-usage and distrust. "Don'tcha remember?" he asked. "Covent Garden, White's, the Brotherhood of—of—Phil somefink or other?"

Andrew focused his tired eyes. His companion was young, little more than a boy, although his voice had broken, thank goodness. He had a pretty face, but pinched, scrawny, as if he'd never had a full meal in his entire life. Which, Andrew reflected, he probably hadn't. His body, perhaps as a result, was possessed of a certain whipcord muscularity—the reason, no doubt, Andrew had been drawn to him in the first place. Andrew snorted. "White's?" he said. "I doubt that very much. Covent Garden, I'll accept. As to the Brotherhood of Philander, I imagine they'd throw us out."

"Yeah, well," his companion admitted, "you're right there, guv'nor. Bruiser at the door took one look at me and said we'd 'ave to *find other accommodation*. White's—" he grinned, showing an alarming, gap-toothed smile, "—worth a shot, just to see what you recollected. But you done me right. Took me 'ome wif you. Most nobs wouldn't let me near a mile o' their place."

"Always was a soft touch," Andrew said.

"Nah," the boy argued, "you ain't soft. 'Ard as steel you was, don't you worry. Just tight as a tick, that's all."

Andrew groaned again. Worse than he thought. No, he decided, exactly as he had feared.

"You gonna be sick?" his companion asked. He looked around for the slop jar, couldn't recognize so utilitarian an object in the elegant furnishings of the large room, and brought forth the full, reeking chamber pot.

That did it. Only mildly nauseated before, Andrew, confronted with the effluvia of a night's worth of two drunken male bodies, coughed up the remainder of his stomach contents, retching and heaving over the side of the bed.

The boy held the pot until Andrew appeared to be finished, touched his dark, pomaded locks in a tentative caress, and said, "Feel better then, love?"

"No," Andrew growled. "I feel like death warmed over."

The boy shrugged. "Some breakfast'll put ya to rights. Betcha serve a real spread."

Andrew lay back on the pillows and took a few deep breaths. At least his headache had abated. "Wouldn't you like to know?" he teased.

The boy's face fell. "You wouldn't kick me out wifout breakfast, guv?"

"Why not?" Andrew asked. "I paid you well enough to buy your own."

The boy sniffled. He looked about twelve years old like that, with his tousled hair, badly in need of a wash and a cut, falling over his eyes, and with his narrow face and hollow chest. "Ain't the same," he said. "Thought I was gonna eat like a lord."

"Well, you won't," Andrew said, as the boy's face hardened and closed, his eyes narrowing into shifty, veiled slits. "Because I'm not a lord. I'm just Mr. Carr—" That's all he needed, he thought, his lips clamping shut. Why not tell this little whore where he banked and direct his man of business to open a draft account for him? Must be losing his mind. *If only Harry hadn't been sent away. . .*

The boy's face relaxed, just enough that Andrew stopped worrying where he'd left his pistols and whether they were loaded. "You pullin' me leg?"

"No," Andrew said. "I am not a member of the peerage. Never said I was."

"No, I mean, you told me your real name," the boy said on a note of wonder. "Nobody done that since I started working." He stuck out a grimy hand. "I'm Kit."

Andrew shook the offered hand automatically, both embarrassed and touched by the human gesture intruding on the sordid commercial transaction. "Kit," he said. "Short for Christopher?"

"Dunno," the boy said. "Everybody calls me Kit."

"I shall call you Marlowe, then," Andrew said, smiling. "Kit Marlowe. How does that sound?"

"I'm just Kit," the boy protested.

"Ah, but you see, Christopher—or Kit—Marlowe is one of our patron saints."

The boy scuttled a few inches away in the wide bed. "You a Papist?"

"Ha!" Andrew abandoned himself to humor for a few seconds. "No, Marlowe, I am a Protestant and a sodomite, much like you. Christopher Marlowe was a poet who had the admirable good sense to proclaim his two greatest loves to be tobacco—and boys." Andrew slid his eyes sideways to see how his nervous companion took this. "Although I can't abide the noxious weed myself."

Kit didn't look happy at this revelation. "Ain't a sodomite," he muttered. "Just do it fer money. And I ain't a boy, neither. Almost eighteen."

"Indeed?" Andrew said, pleased to learn that he had not been so far gone last night that he need accuse himself of robbing the cradle. It was difficult to stretch his mind around the fact that the last time they had been together, Harry had been the same age as this waif. Kit was more than a foot shorter and doubtless half Harry's weight—and that with a good breakfast inside him. "Most of your fellows pretend to be younger."

"Ya see, guv, I'm old enough to know I oughta be gettin' out of this life while I can."

Andrew threw the covers off and prepared to get up. "And you're hoping I'll be your new protector, is that it? Now listen here, Marlowe. I may have been foxed last night, and careless enough to bring you into my house, but I am not the complete flat you take me for."

Kit, unfazed by this speech, grinned, rolled over in the bed, and knelt, turning his head in a flirtatious manner that made Andrew think he was going to be sick again, if there were anything left in his hollow guts. "Want some Greek before breakfast, Mr. Carr?"

"No," Andrew said.

"Yer rod says yes."

Andrew looked down at himself. By God, the boy was right. Inconvenient, the male body, sometimes, with its indiscriminate tastes. No point in fighting nature, though. "So he does," Andrew agreed. "Tell you what. We'll enjoy *le petit déjeuner*—"

"Wot's that?" Kit asked, evidently afraid he was about to be introduced to some new perversion, probably painful.

"French," Andrew said. "You give me a good French breakfast here, then we'll have a real English breakfast downstairs."

Kit flinched again. "That'll cost you extra."

"Roast beef and ale. Eggs. Ham," Andrew elaborated.

Kit laughed through what Andrew suspected were genuine tears of relief. "I knew you was a right one," he said. "The minute I set eyes on you, I knew you was a real gent." He set to work with renewed and hearty appetite.

And that, Andrew thought, was the lowest he'd ever sunk.

SEVERAL HOURS LATER, ANDREW SAT in the heavily curtained back parlor of the Brotherhood of Philander and made an announcement. "I've decided to marry."

A moment of stunned, uncomprehending silence was succeeded by the voices of several men exclaiming at once. "Thought your Harry was still in the Peninsula." "He means a woman, idiot." "No, he doesn't. Doesn't know any women. At least not the sort one marries." "Who is he, then?"

"As Pierce has so astutely pointed out," Andrew said, raising his hand for silence, which was instantly obtained, "I mean a woman. A lady. In the Church of England. Marriage. An institution some of you may have heard of."

After an awkward pause, Lord David Pierce stood and held out his hand. "I think I speak for all of us when I say I shall be damned sorry to lose your friendship."

Andrew stared. "What the devil are you talking about?"

Sir Frederick Verney cleared his throat "Vere Street scandal got to you at last, did it? Can't say I blame you, although it will be a shame to see one of our most, ah, active members dwindle into a husband."

"I thank you for the compliment," Andrew said, inclining his head to Verney, where he sat, naked to the waist, at the card table, "but I am in no immediate danger of a decline. Just thought it was about time for me to do my duty to my family."

The Honorable Sylvester Monkton gave a raucous laugh. "That gloomy old butler of yours been putting the bite on you because of his nephew, eh? I say, Carrington, I never figured you for the sort to knuckle under to blackmail."

"Nothing like that, Monkton," Andrew said, "though trust you to think the worst. Yardley has suffered a great deal of needless mortification over his nephew's connection with the Vere Street house. The poor man has assured me that he has broken off all communication since the disastrous events of two years ago, out of a rather touching desire to protect both of his families, as he terms it." Andrew shrugged. "No, it's really quite simple. I'm almost thirty, you know. Been neglecting my responsibility as the eldest. Last night merely brought it home to me."

"Last night?" Monkton said. "Now we have it. Come on, Carrington, tell all." The other men drummed their hands on the tables and stamped their feet to cheer him on.

Andrew grimaced. "Nothing much to tell. Had a run of luck at White's, thought I'd celebrate with stronger drink and a stroll by Covent Garden—" jeers and catcalls were interjected at this point, "—picked up some ganymede, actually brought him to my house. Nearly told him my name in a fit of early-morning delirium. Boy ate enough provisions for a week. Probably should have had the footmen search him for the silver before he left."

The others nodded, sympathetic. "Don't see what all the fuss is about," Monkton said. "We've all done that, or something like it. Doesn't make us want to retire into defeated matrimonial respectability." He shuddered, his willowy frame in his dandified coat with its padded shoulders swaying elegantly. "Although once he knows where you live, no use concealing your name. Have to expect some repercussions, old fellow."

"Don't I know it," Andrew said. "A pathetic attempt to salvage some security after my ruinous lack of discretion. Why they call gin 'blue ruin,' I suppose."

"Yes," George Witherspoon said, daring to open his mouth after following the conversation with difficulty. "Next time, just bring the boy here. That's what the club is for, isn't it?"

"Are you mad?" Pierce turned on his friend. "A whore from Covent Garden? Why not invite an entire regiment of Guards to bivouac in here?"

"Might be interesting," Witherspoon said, the dreamy look in his eyes enhancing the effect of a fair, angelic countenance.

"As it happens," Andrew intervened, "our man on the door was vigilant and refused us entrance."

"Oh, dear," Monkton said with a sigh. "I hope you didn't give him the sack, as they say in France. It's hard enough as it is to find the right sort of people to work here."

"No," Andrew said, "I did not dismiss him. He did what he was hired to do. As Pierce says, we can't start bringing in trade or we won't have a safe haven, which is, despite Witherspoon's amusing conjectures, what this place was designed to be."

"Was it?" Verney said. "I thought it was a place where we could behave honestly, without pretense."

"That's just it," Pierce said. "We can only afford to remove our masks, so to speak, if we're safe, if we don't have to worry about informers and blackmailers on the one hand, and thieves and rough trade on the other."

"Then what are all those rooms upstairs for?" Witherspoon persisted.

"For respectable couples," Pierce explained. "Men like us, those who lodge here or who can't go to their own lodgings, or prefer not to. Not for married men deceiving their wives."

"It may have escaped your attention, Pierce," Andrew drawled, "since I don't suppose you've ever lifted your face out of Witherspoon's lap long enough to notice, but Lord Isham, the founder of this club, is married. I have no intention of deceiving my wife, and if I were you I would be careful about making offensive insinuations."

Pierce stood up, his hands balled into fists. The little redhead, younger son of an obscure Anglo-Irish duke, was fierce as a wasp. "Would you?" he said. "It may have escaped your attention, Carrington, as your brain is obviously preoccupied by your prick's *fundamental* mission to penetrate every underage bumhole between here and Whitechapel, but there are two founders of this club, Isham and Lord Rupert Archbold. Just how do you propose to have it both ways?"

Andrew shook his head, conceding the verbal contest. "I don't know. Why shouldn't I? Most married men have mistresses, after all. How does Isham do it?"

Through a chorus of snickers and strangled guffaws, Monkton answered, "Ever had a good look at Melford, Isham's eldest, and Archbold, side by side? Don't think that's exactly what you have in mind."

Andrew grinned. "Point taken. But I don't believe Isham intended this club to be merely an exclusive madge house for single gentlemen with independent fortunes. And if he can stay happily married for fifty years while living his life the way he pleases, then I'm damned if I'll let wedlock turn me into some sort of fugitive in my own country."

"Hear, hear." "Well said." There was a smattering of applause.

"Well, then," Pierce said, "after that fiery manifesto, you'd better tell her the truth. She'll only find it out anyway and you'll drag out the rest of your miserable existence under the cat's paw."

"No," Verney said, "I think it depends on the woman. Some of 'em don't want to know. Happier living in a delusional world of their own."

"True enough," Monkton said, "but if he don't tell her, she'll think he's in love with her, and she'll expect him to *make* love to her, and she'll pester him to death until he'll be ready to shoot her and swing for it just to get a little peace."

"I certainly don't intend to lie to her," Andrew said.

"So," Witherspoon said, "who is she?"

"I don't know," Andrew said. "I told you, I only got the idea this morning."

The others stared at him as if he were the lunatic he felt he was in danger of becoming.

"Here," Monkton said, approaching him with a glass of brandy. "Have some of this and you'll feel more yourself."

Andrew waved it away. "That's the root of the trouble," he said. "Woke up sick as a dog this morning, audacious little ganymede chumming it up as if I'd proposed to *him* during the night, which, given my complete lack of memory after my last hand of faro, is quite possible. Made me think. My brother Tom is serving in the Peninsula, and Richard is no more likely to marry than I am. Very fond of women, is Dick, so long as they already have husbands. My uncle Newburn has nothing but daughters. So really, when you look at the situation, it's up to me to ensure the continuity of the line."

"But that's dreadful," Monkton said. "I had no idea. You poor man. Surely there's a less drastic solution. Perhaps a natural son."

"Don't be absurd," Verney said. "A natural son can't inherit."

"A title," Monkton said. "Can't inherit a title. No reason Carrington couldn't father a bastard and leave him his property."

"You forget," Andrew said, "that when my uncle dies, I'll inherit the earldom as well. No, if I'm going to do this at all, I want to do it right. Marriage to a lady from a decent family."

"No offense," Witherspoon said, "but do you think a respectable lady will have you? And what about her parents?"

Andrew raised his eyebrows. "I assure you, Witherspoon, the Carrington name and fortune are more than enough to purchase the acquiescence of the starchiest puritans in England."

"So long as they're poor," Pierce said. "An heiress from a titled family might stick at sharing your bed with ganymedes."

"More likely demand to share the boys," Monkton said.

"Not all titled families have the morals of yours, Monkton," Andrew said. "Or lack of them. Anyway, I don't need to marry an heiress, or a peer's daughter. I do need a virgin, sophisticated enough not to raise a fuss about my way of life, but brought up as a lady. There's no point in subjecting myself to this if I have to worry whether the brats are mine. And pretty. I can't afford to go limp at the sight of her on our wedding night."

"You don't actually mean to bed her!" Monkton was aghast.

"And just how do you propose I father the heir?" Andrew said.

"Lord! I wasn't thinking about that," Monkton admitted. "You are in a tight spot."

"Not so bad as all that," Verney said. "He'll just have to go to Almack's, and *ton* parties and society balls, and put himself on the marriage mart."

"Oh, my God," Monkton shrieked. "It's worse!"

Andrew almost shuddered himself. "I admit, the prospect is singularly unappealing. If any of your unmarried sisters or cousins might be interested, or know someone—"

"Are you seriously suggesting," Pierce said, his voice icy, "that I, or any of us, would allow you within a hundred yards of our sisters?"

Andrew stood up, his fluid movement belying the nervous, hungover condition in which he had arrived. His height was suddenly noticeable, threatening, even in the high-ceilinged first-floor parlor of the modern town house on Park Lane. "Care to rephrase that, Pierce?" he said, his voice smooth as velvet. "I haven't lost my aim, you know, however rashly I behaved last night."

"Oh, keep your shirt on," Pierce said. "Pardon the expression, Verney." He inclined his head to the half-naked baronet at the card table before turning back to Andrew. "Think about it. Would you let any of us marry your sister—assuming that she wasn't already shackled to Fanshawe?"

Andrew's eyes widened in shock. "One of you marry Elizabeth? I'd plug the man who tried and spend my life abroad without regret."

He heard the words, and his fury drained out of him as quickly as it had boiled up, replaced by rueful humor. "What a mess," he groaned as he sat down, shaking with laughter. "What the devil am I to do?"

"I think," Verney said, "I may have a solution."

THELMA LEWIS READ THE NOTE again, for about the hundredth time, and shook her head. Sounded too good to be true, no doubt about it. And anybody with an ounce of sense had learned long before reaching her years that if something sounded too good to be true, it was. Still, Sir Frederick Verney was a trustworthy man. No vices, a considerate landlord, excellent manners, and he had honored his father's wishes in looking after Thelma and her family admirably over the last years. If only he spent more time here in Sussex managing his estate and less time with his sodomite friends in London—well, that brought her back to Verney's letter.

> *A friend of mine, Mr. Andrew Carrington, is looking for a wife. His uncle, the Earl of Newburn, has no son to inherit, and Mr. Carrington has expressed the admirable intention of doing his duty by his family. He needs a sensible young lady, one who won't interfere with his way of life but who will respect the rules of marriage on her side. Mr. Carrington is possessed of an independent fortune, and he is prepared to be most generous in the terms of the settlement. His wife will enjoy every luxury—a town house in Mayfair, summers at Brighton, a set of jewels appropriate to her position, and a substantial gift on the birth of each child. On the birth of a healthy son, the assignment of the rights of a small estate in Northumberland.*

Mrs. Lewis had read it so many times she had it memorized, and the edges of the paper were becoming frayed and dirty. All the disappointments of the past few years—Phyllida's rejection of Lord Hearn, her determined refusal of Mr. Coulter—were on a way to being rectified. Mrs. Lewis had begun to worry about her eldest daughter. Although she had inherited her father's good looks and her mother's brains, it sometimes seemed that Phyllida lacked both passion and cunning. Now the perfect solution seemed to have fallen into her lap.

If only Phyllida were not so independent, and had not got this notion for writing into her head. Still, the first book had sold well for the debut of an unknown author, far better than either of them had expected. Mr. Edwards, the publisher, had offered a very tidy sum indeed for the rights to the second one, already in galley proofs, and there was every reason to expect a decent profit in addition, from the sales. But it was nothing—nothing—to what she could expect from this Andrew Carrington. And, by extension, her mother and sisters would share in the bounty. Mrs. Lewis squared her shoulders and prepared to do battle to the death, if necessary.

Phyllida, as always, was seated at the cramped boudoir table she was forced to share with her two sisters, sheets of printed proofs annotated in her scrawling hand spread around her, a bottle of ink set precariously near the edge of the table, broken pens scattered across. Her pots of face cream and powder, her combs and brush, and her sisters' similar accoutrements had all been pushed aside or tumbled to the floor. She looked up at her mother's entrance and frowned. "Is it important, Mama?" she asked. "Because these are due back tomorrow and it's my last chance to make any corrections. I'm at a crucial place, where Ludovic is about to encounter his nemesis, whom he's been pursuing across the Carpathians, and—"

Mrs. Lewis waved a plump hand. "No time for that folderol, Phyllida," she said. "And no, it's not important. Not unless you think that marriage to the heir to an earldom with a fortune of half a million pounds is important."

Phyllida smiled. "That's funny, Mama," she said. "Because I was just debating with myself whether to change the ending. Perhaps, instead of marrying Ludovic, who is penniless but in love with her, Melisande might actually marry the nemesis, who is filthy rich, and exceedingly handsome in a saturnine way, and—"

"I'm not trying to be humorous, Phyl," Mrs. Lewis interrupted the flow of words that would otherwise have gone on unchecked until an entire volume's plot was summarized and analyzed. "I am completely serious. I have been informed that a Mr. Andrew Carrington, a man of great fortune, and heir to the Earl of Newburn, is in the market for a wife. And our dear Sir Frederick has promised to make the introduction."

"A friend of Sir Frederick's?" Phyllida said. "That means he doesn't care for women, any more than Sir Frederick does. Probably less, since he's making his friend find a wife for him. No thank you, Mama. I have no objection to men of that sort, but I would rather remain a spinster than be tied for life to a man who doesn't really want me. Perhaps Harriet might be interested." She turned away, picked up a fresh pen, dipped it in the ink, and settled down to check the description of the nemesis.

Mrs. Lewis grabbed her daughter's hand, forcing her to sit still so as not to overturn the ink bottle or the table. "No, Phyllida," she said. "You listen to me. For once, you will do as I say and as I think best. 'No objection to men of that sort?' By God, girl, for an offer like this, I should hope not. Don't you understand? This is the chance of a lifetime. He doesn't want a flibbertigibbet like Harriet, but a sensible girl like you. He wants to *marry*. He wants an *heir*. He's not offering you a sham, but genuine, respectable, in the church, marriage. And you will receive him, wearing your best gown, and with your hair curled, and you will listen to his proposal, and when he's finished you will curtsy and say, 'Yes, thank you kindly, sir,' and then I will come in and hear the good news." She heaved a great breath after her long scold, set her arms akimbo, and waited for the counterassault.

It didn't come, or not in the form she was expecting. Phyllida, her wide brown eyes and round fresh face the picture of maidenly innocence, studied her mother's flushed countenance and heaving bosom. "Andrew Carrington," she said. "What does he look like?"

"Oh!" Mrs. Lewis was ready to wring her daughter's neck. "Like a man, I suppose. I don't know any more than you. Honestly, Phyllida, what does it matter? For a fortune like this I'd—"

"You'd marry someone as fat as the Prince Regent or as ancient as Methuselah or as debauched as Lord Hearn—and poxed into the bargain. Well, I'm not you, Mama. I'm twenty-two, which is not yet on the shelf, and I may not be a beauty, but I'm no antidote. We're not rich, but we have a roof over our heads, and a manservant and a maid. And now that my books may be catching on, we can afford to indulge ourselves occasionally. You know I haven't grudged a penny for you or for Harriet and Maria."

"I know that, Phyl," Mrs. Lewis said. "I've never accused you of being less than the generous, dutiful child you are. And you don't have to be modest with me, love, you're the prettiest girl in the county, if I say so myself. But you could go to London and spend five seasons there and never get an offer like this, for all your beauty and virtues. I never blamed you for turning down Hearn, you know. Seems like it was for the best."

Phyllida sat in silence, sucking the tip of her pen, a habit Mrs. Lewis found both distasteful and disturbing. But Mrs. Lewis said nothing, knowing that her daughter had reached the place of decision, and to admonish her now might mean pushing her over the edge, in the wrong direction. Her patience and self-control were rewarded.

"You're right, Mama," Phyllida said at last. "It's very possible I could spend my entire life in London and never receive a suitable offer at all. I didn't do very well in my one season, did I?"

"There, now," Mrs. Lewis said, appeased by the apology, "you did your best. It's not easy having such a small portion, and dependent on friends." Again she waited.

"There's no reason not to receive Mr. Carrington," Phyllida said. "And I certainly intend to look my best when I receive a gentleman, no matter what his inclinations."

Music to a mother's ears. "I knew I could rely on your good sense." Mrs. Lewis dared to breathe.

"May I see the letter?" Phyllida held out her hand and Mrs. Lewis reluctantly passed it over, noticing with another pang of revulsion that her daughter's fingers were stained dark with ink. The girl was too sharp by half, bound to discover some flaw or other. But she would never agree to anything without knowing the full particulars.

"It is most remarkable." Phyllida looked up from the letter, which she had scanned twice, going over the most interesting parts carefully. "But I can't promise to accept his offer. Not without seeing him for myself and hearing his manner of expressing it. I won't say yes unless I think it will work."

"That's all I ask," Mrs. Lewis lied. Just let him come into the house, she swore to herself, and he would not leave a free man, even if it meant marrying him herself. Which, from all accounts, she wouldn't mind in the least. Pity that, at forty, she could no longer claim to be at the height of her childbearing years. "All I ask is that you receive him and hear what he has to say."

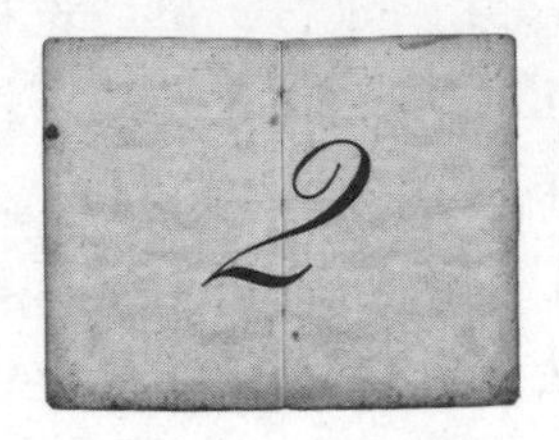

THE DRIVE DOWN TO Verney's estate was surprisingly pleasant. Andrew hated traveling enclosed, even in his well sprung and luxurious coach, drawn by his matched team and covering some of the easiest roads in the kingdom, but he would need the vehicle to convey his bride back with him. It was Verney who thought of the solution.

They took turns driving Andrew's curricle, while his coachman drove the larger vehicle with the luggage, Andrew's secretary, and his valet. "Can do the same thing on the way back," Verney said. "No law you have to ride with a woman just because you've married her."

The weather held up nicely, considering the time of year, and Verney told Andrew more of the girl's background. "Her mother kept my father company for a year or so after Mama died. Made him very happy, far as I can tell, but when she met her young Captain Lewis and he offered marriage, Papa didn't stand in her way. Gave them the cottage, no hard feelings. I suppose everybody loves a love match."

"And the daughter?" Andrew asked. "Phyllis? Sure I won't be marrying your half-sister?"

"Phyllida," Verney said, laughing. "Lord knows where Mrs.

Lewis got that from. But no, she's the image of her father. A fine-looking man."

Halfway through the journey, Andrew realized he had left his pistols at home.

"Not planning to fight a duel, were you?" Verney said by way of comfort when he heard the explanation for Andrew's sudden and violent outburst of expletives.

"Not anymore," Andrew said.

"Weren't going to force the girl at gunpoint?"

"Don't be absurd."

"So what's the trouble?"

Andrew shrugged. "I like having my pistols with me. Like to practice every day. Keeps the aim true."

"Use my fowling piece," Verney said. "Pulls a little to the left. Or is it the right?"

Andrew rolled his eyes. "You're too kind," he murmured.

They reached Verney's home in time for an early dinner, country hours, and then there was the debate whether to pay an evening call or wait until a more conventional hour the following day.

"I'd prefer to get it over with," Andrew said, "but I don't want to spook her."

"Not a nervous filly," Verney said. "Really a very levelheaded girl. My sister took Phyllida up to town, sponsored her for a season a couple of years ago. Cathy became very fond of her. Said it was a pity she had so little money and so much brains."

"Bluestocking, is she?" Andrew asked with alarm. "Don't want her holding a salon and bringing a lot of curst anarchists and radicals into my house."

"No, no," Verney assured him. "Nothing like that. I think she writes."

"Writes?" This was even worse. "Poetry? I will not be subjected to flowery verses in my own home, not if Lord Byron himself were to read them to me naked." Verney raised a satirical eyebrow. "All right, maybe then. But not from my wife."

Verney shook his head. "I don't think it's poetry. I don't really know. She don't use her own name, so it's harmless."

"I wouldn't go that far," Andrew said, secretly relieved. He had an out. If the girl had a squint or bad teeth or giggled or was a chatterbox or any of a hundred irksome little things that a man in his situation should overlook, he could object to the writing with no fear of being thought finicky. No man of sense wanted an authoress for a wife.

In the end they followed the standard custom. Verney showed Andrew around the house and grounds during the remainder of the daylight hours, and they played piquet after supper like an old married couple. Andrew won every hand, until Verney was stripped naked. Literally. They played by the rules of the Brotherhood of Philander, in which gambling for money was forbidden. Men who ruined each other became enemies, fought duels, wounded and killed each other. Men who got naked together merely laughed or went to bed and got it out of their systems.

"That's it, Carrington," Verney said. "Will you try a last hand?"

"What have you to stake?" Andrew said. "Your favors in bed? I think I've already won that."

"No," Verney said, smiling, "you have to win again to earn that."

Andrew shuffled the deck. "You'd better make it worth my while. Cut."

"I will, Andrew," Verney whispered. "But you have to win first. Deal."

Andrew threw down his cards shortly afterward. "You weren't even trying to win," he complained.

Verney stood, his smooth skin gleaming in the candlelight, his chiseled profile and handsome body limned with muscles like a Greek statue. "Oh," he said softly, "I won all right."

Andrew laughed deep in his throat. "No," he said, "I think we both won." He took Verney in his arms and the men shared a deep kiss. *Not really my sort*, Andrew thought, but he was Verney's friend and guest, and he owed him this much for his hospitality. If the girl turned out to be a dog, he still owed his friend something for trying; if the girl was a winner, he really would be in Verney's debt. And the man was handsome, hot, a strange mix of showy sexuality beneath the stolid country squire exterior. A most intriguing combination.

"I would think you'd have a friend," Andrew whispered, his hand moving slowly down Verney's hard body.

Verney shook his head. "Not the marrying kind," he said. "Not even with men."

THE LEWIS COTTAGE WAS A solid, pretty little place, well kept, with flower beds in the garden and boxes on the windowsills, brown and empty now in early March. A maidservant answered the door and showed the two men into a snug parlor. "Miss Lewis will be downstairs directly," she said and offered them cider, which Andrew accepted with thanks. He'd had enough trouble from strong drink.

There were whispers and giggles in the corridor, and a high, girlish voice exclaimed, "But I want to see a real sod—" before a sharp slap cut her off and a deeper voice said, "That's enough, Maria. You will see him at the wedding, and not before."

A stout, middle-aged woman appeared and was greeted warmly

by Verney, who introduced her as Mrs. Lewis. The woman gave a little gasp as she took in Andrew's height and elegance. "Such a pleasure to meet you, Mr. Carrington," she said. "Please do be seated. I promise you, Phyllida won't keep you waiting long."

Andrew, thankful that his intended was not the girl in the corridor, was tempted to pull out his watch but refrained. A punctual female was a rare breed; he had not expected it. Still, he dreaded having to make conversation with a woman who looked both vulgar and mercenary.

He was in luck. Just as Mrs. Lewis began to regale the men with an account of the mad social whirl of this part of Sussex, the legions of suitors for her daughters' hands, footsteps were heard descending the stairs, and a young woman entered the room. She was a little below average height, although no one would describe her as short, and she had a round, plump figure, in excellent proportion, shown off to advantage in a tight gown more suitable for a ball than the parlor of a country cottage in early afternoon. Her hair and eyes were an undistinguished light brown, but her rosy complexion and the sparkle in her eyes prevented the least suggestion of mousiness or drabness. Andrew found himself smiling in surprise.

The young woman stopped in the doorway and curtsied to her visitors as introductions were made. Mrs. Lewis lost no time in shepherding Sir Frederick out, offering him a stroll in the garden. "Best to leave them to get acquainted," she said.

"Surely," Verney protested, "Miss Lewis should be chaperoned."

Mrs. Lewis's laugh was loud and grating. "Don't you trust your friend?" she said. "He is offering marriage, isn't he? Come, Sir Frederick, tell me if you think the crocuses will be *coming up* in a day or two."

Andrew cringed in sympathy, as if he shared Verney's sensation of the elbow nudging his ribs. Verney's attempts to defend Andrew's character while continuing to argue in favor of observing propriety drifted away in the direction of the garden and became inaudible.

"Please, Miss Lewis," Andrew said, still standing since her arrival, "do sit down. I promise not to pounce."

Phyllida startled and moved to a straight-backed chair. She had been rendered speechless since she first raised her eyes from her curtsy and saw a vision of manhood that she had not thought existed outside her imagination and the world of her fantastical fiction. "Forgive me, Mr. Carrington," she said. "I suppose I find this situation a little strange."

"Well, then," he said, "that makes two of us." He smiled again, and any last vestige of hope that she could decline his peculiar offer out of hand died.

He had a long, lean body and a long, lean face to go with it. He had dark, curly hair cut fashionably short, and dressed in what Phyllida guessed was the latest style. His eyes were pale gray, piercing, and his nose was narrow and prominent, curved, almost a beak. His mouth was wide, with mobile, thin lips, and there were already deep creases forming between his nose and his chin. He looked dangerous, predatory, and completely, deliciously masculine. When he smiled, he looked like the fascinating villains in her books, whom she always ended up falling in love with, try though she might to make them wicked beyond redemption.

Phyllida sighed. "Sir Frederick wrote that you are looking for a wife?"

He nodded. "I woke up the other morning with the uncomfortable realization that as the eldest son, and approaching the dismal age of thirty, I am neglecting my obligation to carry on the line."

Phyllida returned the smile, but her eyes widened in a quizzical look. "Forgive me, Mr. Carrington, but surely, considering the generous terms of your offer, there must be dozens of young ladies in London who would be more than happy to assist you."

Andrew's face closed in on itself. Phyllida was reminded of a wounded animal, a fox surrounded by hounds. "Did your mama or Verney not tell you? I have a somewhat daunting reputation, beyond the pale for many of the best families."

"My mother and I understood only that you— that you prefer men to women," she said. "We did not know of anything else."

Andrew let out a bark of laughter. "Is that not enough?"

Phyllida shook her head. "I don't know," she said. "I thought— it seemed to me— in London—"

He laughed more gently. "In London, you thought, sodomy is too common to be a serious obstacle to matrimony."

"Is that not the case?" she asked.

He was captivated. A levelheaded, sensible, plain-speaking young lady, living in a cottage in a Sussex village. Impossible to believe such a creature existed, if he were not sitting right here in the same room with her. "Yes," he answered her question, "in essence you are right. But by the rules of the game, I would be required to pretend, to keep my lovers hidden, to act the part of a ladies' man, never to speak openly to my wife of my activities and not to associate with my friends at my club."

The girl nodded. "I see," she said, smiling as if she had heard good news. "And so you would rather purchase a wife with whom you can live honestly."

Andrew raised an eyebrow. "This amuses you?"

"It is more of a relief," she said. "I worried that if you were traveling so far out of your way to find a wife, there must be a sinister reason."

"And the truth does not worry you?"

"No. I had rather have a marriage based on honesty."

"Speaking of which," he said, his voice harsh, "are you really a virgin?"

Phyllida went bright red and stood up. "Sir," she said, her voice choking with distress. "That is offensive."

Andrew stood up also, as manners required, towering over her, and put a tentative hand on her arm. He was amazed at the soft warmth, the immediate sense of connection he felt. "And not the behavior of a gentleman," he said. "Please, sit down again and bear with me. I knew no other way to be certain than the direct question."

"And you think I have answered it?"

"Absolutely. A woman who was shamming would have been indignant, loudly proclaiming her virtue, whereas you blushed and looked embarrassed. Proof of unsullied maidenhood."

"Any woman who wishes to can act the part," Phyllida protested.

"Few can blush bright red on cue," Andrew said. "Now, let us have a truce and see if we can come to terms." The girl sat, mollified but nervous. "Has your mother told you the conditions?"

Phyllida frowned. "I can read, you know. I studied Sir Frederick's letter myself." She paused, saw his patient, sardonic expression, and decided to let go of her indignation. "I am to be a faithful wife to you, although you will not be a faithful husband. I am to try to give you an heir. There is a house in town and I—or we, it was not clear—can spend summers in Brighton. On the birth of a son, you will make over to me a small estate in Northumberland." She looked up from her lap, where she had been staring as she recited from memory. "That seems most unfair. It's not as if one can choose to bear a son."

Andrew exploded with laughter. "It is a standard arrangement. And that is your only objection?"

"No," Phyllida said. "I think it unfair that you are allowed to have lovers but I must be virtuous. Although I understand the reasons, so I cannot honestly say that I would reject your offer because of it."

Andrew was feeling mellow after these intriguing revelations. "It is unfair, of course. It is the way of the world, is it not? It is to ensure that your children are mine. And that, you see, is the sole reason for my coming here and making you this offer. Besides, think—you will have the pleasure of knowing that I will not betray you with another woman."

Phyllida laughed. "You're right!" she exclaimed. "I hadn't thought of that. It is lowering to one's pride to discover how much like other people one is, isn't it?"

"How so?"

"Why, the desire for wealth and a young, attractive husband who enjoys no other lady's favors seems to be a universal feminine trait."

"I see that I am taking a philosopher for a wife. Are we agreed then?" He held out his hand.

Phyllida stood up in alarm, forcing him to rise yet again. "Just like that?" she asked. "Don't you think we should spend some time together, see if we suit?"

Andrew smiled down at her. Obviously virtuous, he thought, despite the frank manner. A little too prim, perhaps, but far, far better than a worldly, cynical lady of fashion who would attempt to manipulate his every waking moment and most of his sleeping ones. "You forget, my dear," he said, "that I am a man for men. I have seen you, spoken to you, and I have learned that you are pretty, intelligent, chaste, and much more interesting than I had hoped. That is all I need to know." He stepped closer. "Please, Miss Lewis, will you give me your hand and allow me to inform your mother and Sir Frederick of the good news?"

Phyllida backed up until her legs hit the seat of the chair. "And you forget, sir," she said, "that I am a maid. It is frightening to me to sell myself to someone I have only met ten minutes ago. If I say yes, I am tied to you for life. I would prefer to know if you are as kind and generous and sympathetic as you are handsome before I make my decision."

"Oh," Andrew said, waving his hand at the compliment to his appearance and attempting a joke, "that would be beyond even the ability of a saint. But I promise you will not find me to be a brute."

Phyllida laughed, but her face showed her wariness. "Any man can say he is good. It takes time for others to learn his true nature. Please, I ask only a little while—a month."

"A month!" Andrew forgot manners and sat down. "No, damn it. I did not purchase a special license only to waste the same amount of time on this tedious business as having the banns read. I traveled down here, when I detest the country, and spent a dull night at Verney's"—he offered up a silent apology to his accommodating friend and host for the lie—"with the express purpose of getting it over and done with as soon as possible. You must give me your answer now. And if you say no and come to regret it, you will not have another chance. I will find someone else."

"But we are not living in the Middle Ages," Phyllida said. "Even in an arranged marriage the man is expected to woo his bride."

Andrew shrugged. "Very well," he said, patting his knee. "Come here."

"Sit on your lap? That is not what I meant."

"Hmmm," Andrew said. "It seems that although I am the one going against my nature, you are the one acting reluctant."

Phyllida saw he was laughing at her, daring her to take him up on his offer. And although this was not the kind of courtship she had had in mind, it was also an important fact to discover, whether they could share intimacy comfortably. It would be more for him to worry than for her, she supposed, but still, good looks did not always lead to the desire for lovemaking. Sir Frederick was just as handsome—more so, really, in a conventional way—and Phyllida had never felt the least bit tempted to sit on his lap. Not that he had ever offered.

She walked over to where Andrew sat with his long, slender legs slightly spread, lifted her skirts just enough not to wrinkle them by sitting, and settled herself on his thighs. She was surprised at how firm the muscular flesh felt, harder than the horsehair sofa, and at the warmth exuding from his embroidered waistcoat and clean, starched shirt, with the rest of that solid male body under it. "Now," she said, trying to keep the fear and excitement from showing too obviously in her voice, "what happens next?"

Andrew almost pushed her off before she landed. He had not for a minute expected her to respond to his dare. But it would not do, when she was already skittish, to make her feel that he found her repulsive. And as soon as he got his breath back and put his arm around her waist to hold her in place, he knew that he did not. In fact, her soft, round body was most appealing. Not as stirring as a chiseled hunk of man like Verney, but far safer than that starved little ganymede from the other night. He smiled at her provocative question. "This," he murmured, and kissed her on the lips.

It was not a hard kiss or a deep one, but that of a man who has had a great deal of practice and knows that a kiss is but the beginning of a long, intricate process. He brushed his lips over hers, then pressed against her mouth and drew back several times, to encourage her to open her lips. She complied easily, naturally. He sucked on her lower lip, nipped at the upper one, and licked at each corner in turn. His clean breath sighed into her, and she whimpered as his tongue entered her mouth and plunged toward her throat.

She flung her arms around his neck, kissing him in return with clumsy eagerness. "Oh!" she cried as he separated their mouths at an opportune moment. "Oh, that was lovely."

Andrew pulled himself free. The girl was breathing very hard, her skin was flushed, and she was quivering. It was worse than he had feared. He had found a virgin, all right. He had found an untouched, amorous young lady, and had awakened the sleeping tiger of her considerable passion. It was just what that dandy Monkton had warned him of. She was in danger of falling in love with him, and she would be all over him, expecting his marital attentions all the time.

He opened his mouth to tell her—what? That he had rescinded the offer? That now that he saw they did suit, he was reneging? He was a brute; he could have done it, and he almost did, except for one overpowering and deciding fact. He was hard, as hard as he had ever been for any man. As hard as he had been for Harry, the greatest love of his life. "Yes," Andrew drawled, "that was very lovely indeed. See what you have done?" He guided her hand to feel the bulge in his tight breeches.

Her eyes widened in the unconsciously theatrical way she had, and she snatched her hand away as soon as he released it. But she stayed on his lap, nestled in against his chest. "Really?" she asked. "Kissing me caused that? Oh, I am glad."

"That is not the answer a virtuous maid should give," he said, again in his drawling, supercilious voice, the one he used not on his inferiors, who had no weapons to defend themselves, but on those of his own milieu who attempted to control him or judge him or change him. He had another use for it, too, a far more enjoyable one, although he had never thought of trying it with a woman . . .

She did not flinch at the tone. She seemed, if anything, to grow redder and shorter of breath. "But I am not to be a virtuous maid much longer," she said. "And I see you are a brute after all. Would you like to kiss again?" She didn't wait for his answer, but planted her lips on his, wriggling her body against his and moving perilously close to his stiff and by now painful member.

"Stop it," he whispered, pushing at her, trying to move her away from his sensitive flesh. By the worst of bad luck, his hand almost completely enclosed one of the firm globes. The tight ball gown provided at best inadequate cover, having been designed to expose the breasts down to the very edge of the nipple. And that was when it fit the wearer perfectly. It was obvious that the girl had grown quite a bit since this dress had been made, and all her energetic writhing had brought her breast free of any filmy wisps of cloth. The little nub of nipple, already puckered, grew hard and engorged with the touch of Andrew's hand. Despite his good intentions, he could not resist pinching it between his thumb and forefinger. Just to see what happened.

A mistake. She moaned and moved closer, put her hand squarely on his erection, and squeezed. If a week ago anyone had suggested Andrew would be on the verge of ruining a perfectly good pair of breeches while a woman sat on his lap and his hand clutched her breast, he would have sued to have the person locked up for slander—or lunacy. It was worse than his hungover awakening the other day.

Andrew groaned and forcibly removed her hand, just sparing himself the ultimate humiliation in the nick of time. He was still holding her breast, and he rubbed the rosy bud of the nipple gently, as if to apologize for the rough handling before he released it, with something like regret.

"You mustn't do that," he explained. "Not until we're married."

Phyllida opened her eyes and lifted her head, which appeared to have been flung back in the throes of delight. "I don't believe you're a sodomite," she said. "I think there's something very wrong about you that you're afraid to tell."

"I am most definitely a sodomite," he said. "And if you believe there's something wrong with me, there's only one way to find out. Marry me."

THE SETTLEMENT WAS DRAWN UP that same day. Verney, the local magistrate, oversaw the negotiations. Mrs. Lewis, as sharp and beady-eyed an old procuress as Andrew had ever seen, seemed more than capable of driving a hard bargain, and Phyllida herself was no simpering idiot, but to be fair, he asked Verney to act as their representative.

Andrew's secretary, a diffident but intelligent young man named Philip Turner, was put to work drafting the appropriate documents and discussing any last-minute demands or differences of opinions with the ladies. A pity he would have to end the man's employment soon, Andrew thought, momentarily forgetting the matter at hand. Despite being untrained to the work, Turner had shown himself to be efficient and diligent.

The process was quick and without serious difficulties, until the end. Miss Lewis had one unexpected and curious request. "I want it in the contract that I am allowed to write," she said, when asked for any last stipulations.

Mrs. Lewis clucked her tongue. "Don't be silly, Phyl," she scolded. "What can it matter now, with such lavish allowance and pin money?"

"It's not the money," Phyllida said. "If Mr. Carrington is allowed his freedom, it does not seem so very much to ask."

"What do you write, Miss Lewis?" Mr. Turner asked.

"Novels," she said.

"Has your work been published?" The young man seemed most impressed.

Phyllida smiled. "Oh yes," she said. "The second one is in galley proofs."

Andrew turned to stare at her. "Do you mean to say you have written and sold two works of fiction, and not breathed a word to me? Don't you think, after boasting of your desire for a marriage based on honesty, I deserved to be told that much?"

Phyllida blushed, looking as abashed as if discovered in adultery. "I'm sorry," she said. "I didn't think you'd be interested. They are women's novels, you know, romances. Men hardly ever read that sort of thing. And I don't use my own name. Nobody knows that I am the author, except my publisher of course."

"Fanny Burney," Andrew said.

"What?" The others looked at him in confusion.

"Fanny Burney," he repeated. "Now called by her married name, Mme. D'Arblay. Miss Burney has published 'women's novels,' to great acclamation, under her own name. I do not care to be *Mr.* Fanny Burney, nor even the Chevalier D'Arblay."

"Does this mean, sir," Mr. Turner asked, "that Miss Lewis will not be permitted to write?"

"No," Andrew said, "Miss Lewis may write to her heart's content.

It is Mrs. Carrington who will not be permitted to write—or publish. You may put that in the contract."

"Then Miss Lewis will remain Miss Lewis, thank you very much," Phyllida said, jumping up from the table and looking around for her wrap. "I am only glad that I discovered my mistake in time."

"Phyllida! Sit down!" Mrs. Lewis's voice was loud, harsh, and more vulgar than Andrew had imagined possible, more like a drill sergeant ordering a green recruit into line than the deferential mother of a young woman contemplating an advantageous match. "Forgive her, sir," she said to Andrew. "Young girls get odd notions before they know the pleasures of marriage. You won't hear a word about it, I assure you, after the honeymoon, if you catch my drift." She had the effrontery to wink at him.

Before Andrew could think of a suitable reply, Verney, of all people, came to Phyllida's defense. "I say, Carrington," he said, "I think you're making too much of this. After all, she said she don't use her own name and nobody knows she's the author." He looked at Phyllida where she stood, hands clenched, eyes flashing fire. "Now, Miss Lewis, are you prepared to agree, in writing, to continue to remain anonymous, and not reveal your identity?"

"Yes," she said. "I don't want people to know." She glanced sideways at Andrew's forbidding frown. "My novels aren't as good as Mme. D'Arblay's."

"If you don't want fame, and you don't care about the money, why do you do it?" Andrew couldn't contain his curiosity.

Phyllida shot him a challenging look. "Why do you take men for lovers?" she said by way of reply.

"Phyllida!" Mrs. Lewis's roar nearly brought the roof down on their heads, and Mr. Turner had to smother nervous laughter, disguising it as a cough. "How dare you speak to Mr. Carrington so brazenly!"

Andrew felt the blood draining from his face, a sign of extreme temper. But when he met Phyllida's fiery look, the humor of it all took over. "For pleasure," he answered, perceiving her meaning. "Not for fame, exactly, and certainly not for money," he murmured in a suggestive purr.

She laughed, putting her hand to her mouth, not from anxiety but from sheer, exuberant joy in their newfound understanding, and not wishing to shout like her mother. "You would rather I had something to keep me busy, and not have me gallivanting about town meeting men on the lookout for a neglected young bride," she said, still behind her hand.

"You will not be neglected," he said, continuing in a muted tone, "I promise you."

"Perhaps not, " she whispered, "but you will not wish to spend all your evenings in domesticity."

"God, no."

"Well then, doesn't it make sense to allow me my innocent pastime?"

Andrew looked up and saw all the others pretending not to listen, leaning in toward him and Phyllida, hoping to catch a word. He raised his quizzing glass. "Dear me," he said, "can't a man enjoy a tête-à-tête with his betrothed? Mr. Turner, you may put it into the contract that, so long as she uses a nom de plume, Mrs. Carrington will be free to pursue her career as an author."

THEY WERE MARRIED BY special license the following day. Andrew had purchased it before he left London, in case all went well. Easy enough to tear it up if it turned out not to be needed. Verney offered to marry them—"I am a justice of the peace," he said—but Andrew insisted on a church wedding. "Didn't lay out all this blunt on a special license just to get the blessing of the Brotherhood of Philander," he teased.

The ceremony was short and simple, the vicar obviously troubled by the suddenness of the request and the aristocratic stylishness of the groom. "Didn't know dear Miss Lewis was betrothed," he said.

"Wanted to keep it secret," Verney explained. "Mr. Carrington was a friend of Captain Lewis's and promised to Miss Lewis from childhood, but he wanted to wait until Miss Lewis was of age and could choose for herself."

"Indeed?" The Rev. Cecil Portdown, nobody's fool, had his own opinion, but would not gainsay his patron, to whom he owed his living. Captain Lewis had been dead seven years. What kind of "friend" could this Mr. Carrington have been when he was barely out of his teens? Well, if Verney vouched for the fellow, he must be all right, however dubious his appearance. It was only in stage plays and silly romances that villains were tall and dark and saturnine. Still, he wished the whole thing hadn't such a rushed, spontaneous feel. He supposed the damned man had got Miss Lewis with child, although when he'd had the opportunity, he couldn't imagine. And Phyllida had always been the soul of rectitude. Why, as recently as a week ago, he could have sworn her own mother was still pushing her into compromising situations with Leighton Coulter, a rising young solicitor with a reputation for taking his pleasure where he found it, but the girl had always managed to rescue herself unscathed. . .

Andrew pulled out his watch and flipped open the case. "Eleven o'clock already?" he drawled. "I was hoping to enjoy the wedding breakfast while the term was not yet a paradox."

Mr. Portdown roused himself, snorted, and opened the Book of Common Prayer, not that he needed it. "Dearly beloved," he began.

The rest of the day passed maddeningly slowly. Verney offered to provide the feast, and in this, at least, Andrew was more than willing to acquiesce. "More intimate than an inn," Verney said. "Phyllida will feel more comfortable in familiar surroundings."

Familiar, indeed. Andrew, fresh from the battles over the contract, was learning the miseries of in-laws. One did not, it seemed, merely marry a woman. No, one married her whole family, from the loud, insinuating mother to the giggling, nubile eighteen-year-old Harriet, and the even more giggling and bouncy fifteen-year-old Maria.

Apparently, the Lewises were well known in the village, and well liked. Scores of visitors began to show up, a few at the front door, many more at the back, in the kitchen, requesting to be allowed to wish Phyllida the best. Verney, affable and aware of the importance of openness and hospitality to his position, invited them all in. The housekeeper and staff, who might have been expected to raise a fuss over such an invasion, must have been tipped off well ahead of time, perhaps when Verney extended the invitation to Andrew. The house was clean, a substantial meal ready, which was more than adequate for the numbers.

There were toasts and congratulations to be answered, and an oily young man named Mr. Coulter glowered at Andrew all through the meal until Andrew began to wonder if he had heard something of his reputation.

Only one way to find out. He waited until the last course, when the few guests who had not stuffed themselves into immobility were discussing the possibility of dancing, and strolled over to where the young man sat. The man never took his eyes from Andrew during his progress all the way around the long table, bravado that Andrew found both admirable and touching. "Well, Mr. Coulter," Andrew drawled, "have I offended you in some way, or are you merely envious?"

"What do you mean?" Close up, the man was more menacing than he at first appeared, with the self-satisfied expression of the unchallenged cock on his own little dunghill. "Envy you?"

"No," Andrew said. "I rather suspect you envy the bride." He stood, his body tense, waiting for the reaction when his meaning sunk in.

It was lucky he had drunk little. The fist shot out so suddenly he barely had time to block it. Instinct took over then, and he planted a facer on the snarling jaw, bringing the inebriated man down with a crash. Women screamed, men exclaimed, and pandemonium appeared about to break loose.

Andrew shook out his fist. Like most young men of the fashionable world, he practiced boxing, not only to maintain his athletic form but also to make possible the freedom of speech and action that was his birthright. "I do beg your pardon," he said, raising his voice to be heard over the hubbub. "Mr. Coulter was not watching where he was going. He walked right into my fist before I had the chance to warn him how unpleasant that could be."

A few men laughed. There were mutters—ugly, low-voiced. The young man groaned and tried to stand up. Andrew extended his hand in assistance. "Bloody sodomite," Coulter growled, loud enough for the nearest people to hear. "Wouldn't touch your hand for a hundred pounds. Don't know where it's been."

Phyllida was suddenly beside Andrew, holding on to his arm, glaring down at Coulter, who was about to stand and, if Andrew was not mistaken, take another swing at him. "Don't be absurd, Leighton," she said, deliberately using his Christian name as if he were a child. "I'm sure Mr. Carrington will accept an apology, if you offer it immediately."

Coulter glared at Phyllida, as if he'd just now noticed she was in the room. "Ought to be me," he said. "Ought to be me in bed with you tonight. Do better by you than this limp-dick cocksucker—"

Phyllida let go of Andrew's arm and stepped back, as if she knew what was coming.

Bloody hell. A rejected, jealous suitor. Why hadn't Andrew thought of that? Lord knows she was pretty enough. Perhaps because the distance between himself and this village tough was so immense, he couldn't consider the man serious competition.

Andrew waited until the man was fully on his feet and had thrown a couple of wild, easily dodged punches, before knocking him down again. The audience, torn between defense of their own and admiration of technical skill, proclaimed the bridegroom the victor on all counts.

"You were magnificent." Phyllida had resumed her place at his side during the ensuing commotion.

Andrew raised his eyebrows, his mouth turned down in a quelling sneer. "For striking a foolish boy who had too much to drink? I hope you are not one of those abominable females who enjoy the sight of men beating each other to a pulp."

Phyllida tightened her hold on his arm. "Don't go all supercilious," she said. Her face was glowing, alight with love. "It's only that I've been wanting for years to do what you did to Mr. Coulter just now. It's really the nicest wedding present you could have given me."

One good result of the fistfight was that it brought the wedding party to an abrupt end. Mrs. Lewis's commonness had its uses, too. "Might as well go to bed early," she said, winking and tittering and making eyes at everything in breeches between the ages of fifteen and sixty. "Ready to get down to it, I should think, eh?"

In a very short time, before it was even dark outside, Phyllida was undressing, helped by her household maid, Jenny Porter, and listening to a talk by her mother that was apparently meant to hearten her but was having the opposite effect. "Please, Mama," she said when there was a pause in the stream of advice. "It will be all right."

Mrs. Lewis eyed her daughter in her lush nakedness with gloating admiration. "With any ordinary man, yes," she said. "Enough to make the saints in heaven stand and salute. The thing is, you don't know how your Mr. Carrington will feel. So all I'm saying is, there are ways to put a man in the mood, even if he—"

"Please, Mama," Phyllida said, near tears. "Don't spoil things for me tonight."

"Hmph!" Mrs. Lewis shrugged in irritation. "Don't blame me if you rise in the morning as much a maid as you are now."

"I won't," Phyllida said. "I'm sure everything will be fine."

Jenny listened openmouthed to the conversation before daring to put forth her opinion. "Mr. Carrington looks to be a right strong 'un," she said. "The way he dropped that Mr. Coulter—twice." Her eyes shone with admiration and hopeless longing.

Mrs. Lewis rounded on the girl. "Marriage isn't a sparring match, Jenny," she said, "however much your poor mama was knocked about by that gallows-meat ruffian Josh Porter."

Jenny flushed and stared at the floor.

"Leave me, please!" Phyllida took the opportunity to push the other women out. She stood for a moment, calming herself, studying her reflection in the mirrors that seemed to cover every surface in the master bedroom Sir Frederick had so generously insisted they use for their wedding night. The multiple reflections showed her from almost every angle, on every side, so that she could see her back, both profiles, and her front, replicating and disappearing into the distance.

She had to admit, with almost any other man there should be little to worry about. Her full breasts were firm and high, twin globes that needed no corset or stays to raise them to a pert position. The small nipples were already stiff and beaded from anticipation. Her skin glowed translucent pearly pink in the soft light and her long hair rippled down her back, shiny with its recent washing and brushing and forming natural corkscrew curls. A narrow waist set off the flare of wide hips, and the patch of hair between her thighs was a neat triangle, clipped short. Phyllida had almost cried from embarrassment when her mother had trimmed it with the sewing scissors after her bath.

"A man like Mr. Carrington won't want a big dirty bush down there," Mrs. Lewis had insisted over her daughter's protests. "I'd shave it smooth, but we don't want him to think you're no better than you should be, neither."

What *would* he think? Phyllida wondered. She shivered, hugged herself, and debated whether to put on her old, serviceable linen nightgown, definitely a virginal garment, or await her groom naked. She remembered their kiss, the hardness he had claimed she caused. Surely the situation was not so desperate. But she would not take any foolish chances. Leaving the nightgown hanging over the back of a chair, she climbed onto the high bed and arranged herself to what she hoped was best advantage. She tried flat on her back first, and nearly leaped out of the bed in fright at catching a sight of yet another reflection, from the mirror on the underside of the canopy. Imagine Sir Frederick, she couldn't help laughing a little under her breath, with his men friends in this room, in this bed. She wondered if he and Andrew had—no, she decided, that was just being silly—although it was a stimulating image all the same.

She turned halfway on her side. This way she had only a partial glimpse of herself, her breasts askew from the leaning position, her hips making a large S-curve. Not bad, she decided. Almost artistic.

There was a knock at the door. "C-c-come in." Phyllida hadn't realized how dry her mouth was.

Andrew entered, a silk dressing gown belted loosely around his narrow hips. The fabric, a deep charcoal gray, shimmered with his movements as he walked toward the bed. Phyllida had never thought gray was a color at all, much less a rich one, full of highlights and hints of blue, of burgundy, of green and gold.

Andrew stopped a few feet from the bed, taking in her naked body and suggestive pose. "What a beautiful sight," he said. The words were polite, perfunctory. He untied the robe, removed it, and flung it on top of Phyllida's nightgown.

"Yes," Phyllida said in a whisper. "Beautiful." She couldn't help staring, knew she was devouring him with her eyes. He was all long, slender limbs and solid muscle, as sinewy and graceful as a thoroughbred. His legs seemed to go on forever. They were rather hairy, actually, ropy with knotted muscles. His forearms were equally hairy; a few veins stood out sharply delineated. His chest was, thankfully, completely smooth, an odd contrast when she thought about it. She wasn't thinking much at all, though, just looking and dreaming. His male member was as long and lean as every other part of him—and soft, hanging limp over his balls.

Phyllida almost cried with despair. She had never seen a naked man, but her mother had told her how to judge. "If it doesn't point straight out or stand up, and if it isn't big enough to scare you, then you won't be Mrs. Carrington this night."

She might never be truly married, never produce an heir for him, never earn her estate in Northumberland. Not that that mattered. But she wanted to know the feel of him, the taste of him, that thick hardness inside her that she had felt with her hand through the leather of his riding breeches. She sniffed as a teardrop formed, ran down her cheek, and stained the satin pillowcase.

Andrew sat on the side of the bed and touched a finger to her wet cheek. "You mustn't be afraid, my dear," he said. "You know I must hurt you a little tonight, but I will be as gentle as I can. After that it will be easier."

"I know," Phyllida looked up into his eyes at the soft touch and kind words, and burst into tears. Worse and yet worse. He would be gentle all right. He probably wouldn't even attempt to make love to her. She bawled louder, unable, after the anxiety of the past days, to control the sobs that wracked her body. "I'm sorry," she gulped and cried. "I'm sorry."

"Oh, dear." Andrew sighed and gathered her into his arms. "Poor child." He hadn't expected this, had not thought the authoress who had stood her ground over the wording of the contract, and the bold wench who had sat on his lap and grabbed him, would turn out to be a scared little nun after all. It certainly didn't match the lush, ripe body or that whorish clipped patch of hair at her crotch.

He tightened his arms inadvertently and kissed her open, gulping mouth. His lips closed over hers, his tongue snaked in automatically, and the skin of his chest, oversensitive from the regular shaving, reacted with a strange, primitive feeling of lust at the firm, full breasts with their little buds of nipples mashed so forcefully against him. He was erect, hard in a couple of seconds, when only a minute ago he had been feeling the dread of having to perform on demand, suspecting the whole idea had been a huge and humiliating mistake.

"Oh," Phyllida sensed the change in him before she had a chance to discover it directly. Her tears dried instantly. "Please, Andrew. Make love to me."

"You are braver now?" he whispered.

She had her mother's good sense, at least, not to confess the truth. "Yes," she murmured, lowering her face to hide her smile. "You don't have to worry. I won't cry anymore."

Andrew, too, tried to disguise his relief. "Thank goodness for that," he said in his patrician drawl. "Never made a woman cry before. Men, now. I've made hardened war veterans weep for fear at sight of my beef bayonet." His lips curled in a half-smile.

Phyllida caught her breath. The effect of his voice, his look of hauteur, was astonishing. She could feel herself growing wet between her thighs just from the sound of that aristocratic, drawling tone. She lay back, ignoring the unnerving reflection above, and stretched out, arching her spine and spreading her legs.

Andrew frowned. The transition into sexual invitation was so sudden, he would have thought the tears faked if he hadn't felt for himself the violence of her convulsions. Still, there was no point worrying over nothing. If the girl was by any chance not a virgin, he should be able to tell. He could wait until her courses came before bedding her again, or send her back to her mother. In the meantime, tonight, better to go through with it, and he had far rather a willing, even an eager bride than a terrified, crying victim.

He moved up the bed until he could put his hands on her, and toyed with the hard little nipples. She accepted his touch easily, almost happily. Her breathing grew ragged as he continued to play, and she began to buck and writhe with excitement, odd little whimpering sounds emerging from her throat. Definitely a passionate woman, although based on what Andrew heard from his friends who enjoyed the female sex, the frigid, unresponsive woman was more a myth created by clumsy, inept men than by any flaw in her nature.

Which brought him back to his own predicament. What was he to do now? Oh, he knew the mechanics well enough. He'd been initiated into the female mysteries by an upstairs maid when he was fourteen, and had gone on to sample the wares at a couple of London's most luxurious brothels a few years later. Just enough to see that it was not for him. He had made no attempt to discover exactly what it was that was supposed to bring a woman to that peak of ecstasy his friends with mistresses boasted of producing, several times a night. Merely sticking one's cock in and thrusting in and out a few times was not the way to success, apparently. From what he gathered, women required far more time and effort to please than men.

Well, he wasn't with a mistress, who might expect some attention to her sexual gratification. He was with his wife, and all he really had to do was take her maidenhood. If he gave her little pleasure, the feeling would be mutual. The arrangement was all spelled out. He could get her pregnant easily enough, assuming she was fertile, and that he was. He took it for granted he was, how not? But that was a gamble all men took.

Enough, he told himself. Get on with it. Indeed, Phyllida was mouthing the same thought, pleading with him, pulling his hand, reaching, with that same disingenuous desire of the previous day, for his erect member. "Wait," he said, forcing a smile. "Let's see if you're ready for me."

"Please, Andrew," she said. "I'm ready."

He knew this fact, too. A woman who was ready for a man to enter her produced her own natural lubrication. Although how he was supposed to tell what was sexual readiness and what was merely ordinary female sliminess was beyond him. At least he was prepared for this eventuality. If she wasn't ready soon, or never got there, there was a pot of Verney's expensive odorless grease on the night table. Andrew always traveled with a similar jar. So there was nothing to hold him back now. He put his hand between the spread thighs and dabbled his fingers. When he brought his hand away, his fingers were dripping with clear mucus. "So it appears," he drawled.

She moaned and lifted her hips as if begging for his penetration. "Please," she said again, her voice breathy.

She probably really did want it. He was used to being desired, by men and women both. He had become jaded—spoiled, really. It was an unattractive thought. Just because his bride was no different from all the others did not make her desire any less of a gift.

"If you're quite sure, my dear," he murmured. Her moans almost frightened him with their intensity and he laughed to disguise his nervousness. He knelt over her, positioning himself between her thighs. Her firm, round buttocks raised her sufficiently that he did not need to place a pillow under her, another friendly piece of advice he had received somewhere over the years. He was still hard, thank goodness, her cries for some reason having quite a powerful effect on him. It was like being someone else, someone in a dream, or a play, acting out an imaginary character's part, not one's own desires. But it was his desire, he discovered. Very much so.

He guided himself into her tight little opening with one hand. There was no doubt she was a virgin. She was as hot and snug as any little ganymede's bum, and the wetness was an added bonus. He pushed in as far as he could without forcing. This time her moan was one of pain, not pleasure. He knew that distinction very well.

He held back with difficulty. He liked this, wanted this. The roaring of the blood in his ears, the heat, the wetness, the tightness, her moans and sighs—God!—even the smell of her was an aphrodisiac. "I'm sorry, my dear," he said as he lost control, thrusting into her to the hilt. She cried out, then went rigid, her eyes wide open. He tried to stay still until she had a chance to adjust, but it was no use. He was beyond restraint, oblivious, caught up in the most unusual sexual encounter of fifteen years of wide-ranging experience. He drew back to the edge of her stretched opening and plunged back in, repeated the motion, over and over, increasing the rhythm, pounding her mercilessly, her cries only spurring him to greater force. He felt himself coming, exploding, driving his seed up into her, and he finished in a frenzy of rapid, deep thrusts that left him spent and panting, lying with his full weight on her, his member slowly softening inside her. "My wife," he whispered, and fell into a stupor.

Phyllida lay quietly when Andrew finished. He was still inside her. She was idiotically pleased at that. At least he had done it, had been fully as vigorous and virile as she had hoped.

The pain had been severe, but so brief she was already forgetting it. She dared to sigh, to heave a deep breath, having to lift his body with her own expanding chest. He had promised to be gentle, but he hadn't been, not once he got going. Still, better than not doing it at all. And her mother and everybody all said that after the first time it wouldn't hurt. Of course, there was supposed to be pleasure, too. She had loved it when he touched her breasts, and that one moment when he put his hand between her legs, she had thought for a second that something really wonderful was going to happen. But then he had simply fucked her. She knew she wasn't supposed to say that word or even think it, but that's what it was. There was no other word.

He hadn't made love to her. He had started to, with his kissing and his touching, and his drawling, teasing words. She wished she knew how to encourage him to do more of that. Maybe, next time, or whenever they became more familiar with each other's bodies, she could tell him, or show him, before it all degenerated into fucking.

She laughed silently to herself. Listen to her complaining, when any other girl in her position would be euphoric. A wealthy, handsome, kind husband, one whose touch she wanted. How many women had old, disgusting husbands whose pawing, drooling fumbling had simply to be endured, assuming they could fuck at all. At least Andrew didn't have any problem there. And her mother's honest concern had prepared her for the possibility that he might not be able to. No, she was a very lucky woman and she would thank him when he woke up.

Andrew snorted, blinked, and lifted himself off and out of her. The sound of him pulling out was so funny, a sucking, farting sound, she had to bite her lip not to laugh. "Did I hurt you very much?" he asked.

"No," she said, stroking his dark hair. "No, it was wonderful. Thank you, Andrew, for a beautiful wedding night."

He stared into her wide brown eyes. Thanking him? For that sorry performance, as bad as a fifteen-year-old boy's with the village slut? If he didn't know better, he'd swear she was a practiced, lying bitch of a whore. "You mustn't thank me," he drawled. "It will make me vain."

She couldn't help teasing him a little. "That's all right then," she said. "The damage has already been done."

He raised himself on one elbow in surprise, stared into her flushed face, the eyelids puffy and red, her mouth looking bruised, although he had kissed her very little. The glimmer of laughter was unmistakable, behind the residue of tears and the pain of lost virginity. "Why, you little shrew," he said, amused, delighted with her spirit. He gathered her in his arms again, held her close, laid a soft kiss on her tousled brown curls, and drifted to sleep with the feeling that he had found a new kind of love, in the strangest place.

THEY WOKE NEAR DAWN AFTER their early night. Andrew roused first, sat up with a start when he saw the strange feminine reflections all around, and lay back down when he remembered. How different it had all been from his imaginings—better in many ways, worse in others. One thing was certain. He was a married man, with a wife whose maidenhood he had taken. There was even the telltale stain on the satin sheet. Oh well, Verney's sheets had seen far more than a girl's virgin blood. He grinned, recalling his first evening here. The funny thing was, he wasn't at all sure he would wish to change partners now, even if the offer were made.

He let his hand roam softly, slowly, over the form of his sleeping bride. She was, he realized, a beautiful woman, with the sort of body that could drive men to ridiculous lengths to win her favors. And he had purchased her, almost as easily as he had obtained his team of matched bays or his hunting box in Leicestershire.

She stirred as his hand explored her secret places. "Mmm," she purred in pleasure, or at least an excellent imitation, yawning and stretching. "Good morning, Andrew."

He removed his hand and rolled over to kiss her. "Good morning, wife," he said. "Shall I worship you with my body, as I promised?"

"Yes, please, Andrew," she said. "Are you sure you really want to?"

He steered her hand, with no fear now of embarrassment, to his hard member. "One thing you will learn, Mrs. Carrington," he said, "is that even on his deathbed a man always wakes up hard."

"I wish," she said, "you'd call me by my name. Don't you like it?"

"Phyllida," he said, nibbling at her breasts. "A very romantic, silly name for a passionate, beautiful woman. But Phyllida it shall be, if it is your wish." He was feeling quite silly and romantic this morning.

"My mother was reading poetry when I was born," she gasped out between his nibbling and kissing.

"I suppose," he drawled, "it made the pangs of labor seem as nothing by comparison." He knelt between her thighs and positioned himself, like last night. She laughed at his remark, but her expression was guarded. "What is it, my dear?" he asked. "Are you still sore?"

"No," she said. "I don't know. Would you mind, please, touching me some more? The way you were doing when you woke me?"

Ah, here it came at last, the well-deserved criticism. Well, he could hold back more easily this morning, in his dreamy dawn languor. And perhaps he could actually learn something, although he doubted she would know what to teach. "Tell me, Phyllida," he said. "How shall I please thee?"

She blushed. "I don't know. Just touch me."

He tried, suckling at her breasts—all women liked that—and poking and prodding around with two fingers in the maze of folds and crevices between her legs. It was, on the whole, a middling success. She did seem to enjoy the suckling, going so far as to clutch his head to keep him at it when he was ready to move on, and there were times when whatever was down there between her thighs was being pleasured, because she would lift her hips and grind against his hand and moan and whimper. But he couldn't keep this nonsense up forever, and before he lost his hardness he tore himself loose from her grasping hands and thrust in.

He had more control now, and he was able to give her the full benefit of his expertise that had escaped him last night. Indeed, he knew he'd find it difficult to climax without the right sort of male body to motivate him, so he simply rode her, letting her feel his potential, his stamina, his hard, thick rod that could hold an erection forever, it sometimes seemed, if he concentrated.

When he was ready, he thought of Harry—that gorgeous blond hunk of man, even at seventeen a man's body, at the height of his sexual vitality, and always gratifyingly, endearingly eager to accept Andrew's lovemaking whenever and however and wherever he wanted it. *Harry*, he thought, hoping he had the decency not to say the name aloud, but lost to everything now except the throes of his desire, and he spent himself in her with even more force than last night, just from the image of Harry on their last night together, when they had vowed to make love the entire night long. "So's to have a year's worth before I go," Harry had said, knowing it might be longer than that before they would see each other again. If ever.

He opened his eyes where he lay a few inches from her face. He was shocked by the frustration and pain he saw before she realized he was awake and watching her. Then a false smile of lazy satisfaction was brought up from the depths of her considerable repertory of pretense. "Oh," she breathed, "you are such a stallion. You will soon wear me out."

He did not leap out of the bed in horror, mainly because he was still catching his breath from his exertions. "Don't talk like a whore," he said. "Just because your mother is—"

"Don't you dare say one word against my mother," she said. She sat up and for a minute he thought she was going to hit him. "She may not be *refained* enough to suit my lord Carrington"—she used, sneering, the fake genteel pronunciation of the pretentious arriviste, the nouveau riche—"but she did her best for me, for all of us. She can't help her origins."

He groaned. Rule number one, he had known all along, was never to insult a girl's mother, however great a harridan. "I do beg your pardon," he said. "The heat of the moment."

"But why?" she asked. "What have I done or said?"

He was certain now. She wasn't acting. She was merely doing as her whore of a mother had instructed her, pretending pleasure no matter how wretched she felt, however abysmal his performance. And the hell of it was he had no idea how he had failed, or how to put it right. In town he would have to seek out knowledgeable people, admit his ignorance, and ask their help. Or he could simply ignore the situation. Once she was with child, he wouldn't have to do it with her for almost a full nine months, if she told him early. Afterward she'd need weeks, maybe months to recover. And if, please God, it was a boy, he might never have to do it again . . .

"Nothing," he answered. "I am just a grumpy old bear first thing in the morning, even after a delightful coupling with my beautiful and charming bride." He growled and made his hands into claws, hoping to raise a laugh. She obliged, again with patent falseness. He sighed. "Shall we go down and scrounge a sandwich instead of waiting for breakfast?"

"Yes, please," she said. "I'm so hungry I could eat a bear."

They were laughing with genuine good humor as they went to their separate rooms to wash and dress.

VERNEY, EVER THE PERFECT host, had managed to clear the house of guests the night before. It had been, after all, a purely local affair. So there was no jovial set of country wits to face, winking and nudging and asking sly questions, but only Sir Frederick, who left the two of them alone for their improvised breakfast. He and Andrew said their good-byes in the corridor. "All went well, my dear?" Verney asked, drawing his friend into a loose embrace and cradling his head.

Andrew rubbed his cheek against Verney's, enjoying the feel of freshly shaved masculine skin, the smell of clean male body. "Very well, Fred," he said. "Excellent, in fact. I am in your debt."

Verney laughed. "I shall hold you to that, Andrew," he said. "I will enter it into the book at the club."

Andrew drew back in alarm. "At White's?"

"No, no," Verney said. "Can't put that sort of thing in the betting book at White's. Ain't really a wager. No, at the Brotherhood."

Andrew squeezed his friend's firm buttocks. "You are a slut and a whore," he said with a grin. "Exactly what I like in a man. Don't worry—I'll pay up, with interest. Just give me a chance to do my duty by my bride."

Phyllida cleared her throat from the door of the breakfast room and the two men recoiled with comical force. "I am in your debt, too, Sir Frederick," she said, coming up to the men and holding out her hand as if she had observed nothing unusual. "You have been such a good friend to my family over the years." She smiled at her husband. "I fear it will take a number of entries in your interesting club's book, Andrew, before we have fully paid Sir Frederick back."

The two stared at her in horror. Was this how it would be? Andrew had a moment of despair. His wife spying on him, blackmailing him?

"Oh," Phyllida said. "I see how it is. We had a perfectly straightforward agreement. We were to be honest with each other and I was not to interfere in your life. I did not understand that I am now the one who must pretend, to act as if I see and hear nothing." She shook her head. "I can't do it, Andrew. It is not what I agreed to."

Verney stared down at her, his eyes narrowed. "You don't realize the dangers, Miss Lewis—Mrs. Carrington. It is one thing to be honest here, in my own house, surrounded by friends and my household that has been with me for years. It is another thing entirely in town. Society is not honest, and it punishes—brutally—those who are."

"What do you mean?" Phyllida asked, dreading to hear the answer yet unable to hold back the question.

"Surely, even down here, you have heard the story of the White Swan, the Vere Street scandal," Verney said. Seeing her nervous nod, he added softly, "That was a group of men, and a house, not so very different from the Brotherhood of Philander. The kind of club often called a madge house."

There had been no escaping that story. The papers had been full of lurid details for weeks. Phyllida, prompted by Verney's reminder, was assailed by a dreadful vision. *Andrew, his glossy hair, his entire elegant and manicured body covered in filth, his fine-boned aristocratic face held in the pillory, choked and broken—blinded, perhaps—pelted with rocks and dung and fish guts . . .* Her face paled and she swayed where she stood, leaning on the wall for support. "But surely, men like you, with money and from good families . . ."

"Unfortunately," Verney replied, "that factor weighs little in public opinion, which is where so much of the rough justice in these affairs is meted out."

"It can rather weigh against us," Andrew said, then wished he had held his tongue. He was struck by the crushed look on his wife's face. She had been so sparkling and vivacious when he met her, so full of innocent vitality. Now she looked like one of those poor women punished by being whipped at the cart's tail, near collapse, trembling and faint. He no more wanted that for a companion than he did an extortionate, scheming whore.

"Phyllida," he murmured, his heart turning over as she lifted wide, tearful eyes to his face. "Listen to me. Sir Frederick is right, so far as it goes. But it is for that very reason that we are careful in the Brotherhood. We do not let in anybody off the streets. We accept as members only those that two or more of us can vouch for. And our wealth does count for something, after all. If worse comes to worst, we can at least buy our escape." He looked at Verney. "Remember Ferrars, Lord Leicester? Chartley, as he was then. Living abroad now."

"Not the same," Verney said, a note of warning in his voice. "Man wore pink ribbons in his shoes, for God's sake. No need to worry Mrs. Carrington over an odd fish like that."

"It was his wife, you see, who brought the charges," Andrew said.

Phyllida looked from her husband to Sir Frederick and back again. "I would never—"

"I know," Andrew said. "And I have no intention of committing the sort of offenses that caused Ferrars's wife to take legal action against him. But that is precisely why I insisted on honesty between us from the start, and drew up so strict an agreement." Seeing her still worried, he put his arm around her, concerned at her fragility. "There is no reason to feel constrained within our own household and amongst our own set of friends. My butler, Yardley, is the uncle of one of the White Swan's founders, although you mustn't let on I told you. A very correct and discreet man, with my family over thirty years. I think it almost broke his heart when his nephew had to disappear."

Andrew blinked away the sad memories. "No, it is only when we are in public we must play the game. Surely you did not expect to go to Almack's and society balls and proclaim to everybody you meet that your husband is a notorious sodomite and that he pays his debts to his friends with unnatural sexual practices at his club?"

Phyllida laughed at his words, her face slowly brightening. "No, Andrew," she agreed. "I had not expected to go to Almack's at all. Is that why your club is called the Brotherhood of Philander? As a disguise? I thought a philanderer was a man who pursued women."

Andrew and Verney exchanged a look. "It's a fair question," Andrew said. "Yes, Phyllida, the founders wanted an ambiguous name, one that could be interpreted in different ways. Although 'philander,' from the Greek for 'love' and 'man,' is usually construed to mean a 'loving man,' in the sense of a lover of women or, more generously, a lover of mankind, it can just as well mean a lover of men. And so Philander in that sense is the eponym of our society."

"But why call the club anything at all?" Phyllida asked. "Why not just refer to the house by its number and street?"

"Because it is a brotherhood," Verney said. "Lord Isham was adamant that it would not be just another molly house, as they were called in his day, but an assembly of uncompromising men who would fight rather than give in to informers, to blackmail and extortion. Warriors, if you like. A band of brothers."

"A very select band," Andrew said. "What we lose in variety, with our expensive dues and restricted membership, we gain in security."

"Thank you, Andrew, Sir Frederick," Phyllida said. "That is very enlightening. I had not given much thought to the dangers you face." She nodded and turned back down the corridor.

"Andrew," Verney whispered, "I'm so sorry. I don't know what to say. Her father was a gentleman. Imprudent, no doubt, and with deplorable taste in women, but an honorable man from a reputable family. I thought his character had made more of an impression on his daughters, at least on the eldest."

"Don't be such a stick," Andrew said. "It will be all right. Just a matter of getting away from noxious influences and acquiring some town polish."

ANDREW REALIZED HOW MUCH HE dreaded facing Mrs. Lewis's avid curiosity when he felt the familiar headache coming on. Phyllida, noticing his wince and grimace at her mother's greeting, handled the situation with admirable tact, nodding briefly and holding up her hand, two fingers showing. "Mr. Carrington does not enjoy conversation before noon," she said, forestalling the burst of congratulations.

Nothing was too good for him after that. Mrs. Lewis, her fondest hopes realized—twice—was prepared to indulge her wealthy son-in-law in any peculiarity, even silence. She contented herself with whispering to her two younger daughters and the one overburdened maidservant while Phyllida's few belongings were brought down and stowed in the coach. The family's good-byes, loud, tearful, and excited, were finished within a quarter of an hour and Phyllida, tearing herself out of her mother's embrace, was soon seated beside Andrew, the door shut and the coachman given the order to move.

Andrew actually enjoyed the drive back to town. Phyllida was all sympathy when she understood his dislike of closed carriages, and urged him to drive his curricle with Sir Frederick as planned, saying she had a great deal of work to do, and would be delighted to have time to read over the proofs and note any errors. That settled it. He knew he had agreed that she would be allowed to write, but that didn't mean she had to be given unnecessary opportunities to indulge her vice.

"You are very kind," he replied, "but fond as I am of Verney I have not married him. We must use the journey to become better acquainted so that when we get back to town we will seem as familiar and bored with each other as any other married couple."

Once under way, she requested that the windows be opened. "It's the stuffiness that makes you sick," she said. "Fresh air is all you need."

It was a typical March day, blustery and damp, and Andrew was afraid the moisture might ruin the interior, but it worked. He felt barely a twinge of nausea, and not the least hint of a headache. "I have married a physician," he said, "as well as a philosopher."

Phyllida smiled. She had been gratified by her new husband's insistence on riding inside, but suspicious of his motive. He had been on the point of wavering, and only when she explained about the work she wanted to do had he become firm again in his purpose. Oh well, there wasn't really a lot she could accomplish in a coach, rattling along at high speed with Andrew's prime horses probably setting a record for covering the distance in the least time. Although it was so well sprung it rode smoothly and comfortably enough that she could almost have written out a fair copy.

"Better than a physician," she said, "because my remedies actually work, and I don't charge a fee."

"No," Andrew drawled, "only half my entire fortune, my name and—" He stopped, the joke seeming cruel and not in the least humorous.

Phyllida was unperturbed. "I think you will grow accustomed to having a wife," she said in a placid tone. "Just as I will *acquire town polish* once safely away from the *noxious influence* of my mother and sisters."

"I'm sorry, Phyllida," Andrew said. "It seems I must learn discretion also." Into the grudging silence, he asked, "Will you miss them very much? You shall have Maria to stay in a month or so, and you may go home for a visit any time, once you are breeding."

"Harriet," she said. "My second sister is Harriet, who will be coming out this season." She broke into honest, happy gurgles of laughter. "Oh, Andrew, don't be angry with me, but I was never so pleased in my life as when we got it settled that they would not come to town and would not live with us."

He stared, his face growing cold. "Then why, my dear," he said, "did you drive such a hard bargain, making me pay them an allowance and insisting that—Harriet—must be sponsored for a season?"

"Don't you see?" she asked. "I couldn't let Mama know how eager I was to leave home. And I do think I owe them a share in my good fortune. But all I wanted was to get away, with my husband, have my independence as a married lady. And the surest way to achieve it was to push so they'd get as much as possible. That way it would look as if I had tried my best, and had come to grief on the rocky shoals of your masculine hardheartedness. I knew you'd never agree to letting them come and live with us in town."

"You betray yourself as a writer of low female romances," he said. "And you put a great deal of faith in my masculine hardheartedness."

"Not really," she said, perfectly innocent. "I knew I could rely on your selfishness, if nothing else. All men are fundamentally as selfish as cats."

"And women are not?"

Phyllida grinned. "We hide it better."

Andrew reached for her and brought her to sit on his lap. "You are a baggage. A scheming, calculating wench. You deserve a kiss." He obeyed his own suggestion. He felt well, not sick at all, able to make love to a woman in a moving vehicle instead of hanging his head out the window and gagging. "I really am sorry for what I said about your mother," he said, magnanimous now that he felt so safe.

Phyllida, too, was feeling gracious. "Forget it, Andrew. Let us start fresh."

"I'm curious, though," he said. "Was it she who had you trim your hair below?"

"Yes," she whispered, blushing. "Please, will you let it go?"

"Phyllida." The word was a command. "Look at me. You are my wife. I chose you of my own free will, and we are honorably married in the church. I would not marry a woman who was less than a lady. Your mother's failings are not yours. I simply wanted to know whose idea it was to trim your hair."

"I suppose it makes me look like a whore," she muttered.

"Let us rather say," Andrew corrected gently, "a woman who has had more experience with men than a virtuous bride should have." He took her hand and kissed it. "I shave my chest, you know—or, to be completely truthful, my man does."

She was diverted, as he had hoped. "Do you really?" she asked, her eyes lighting up with interest. "I did wonder at how hairy your legs and arms are, and how smooth your chest." Again she broke off in embarrassment.

"We are married," he said. "There is no need for modesty. You may comment on my body, ask questions—when we are alone, of course. I will not be offended."

She met his eyes, took him at his word. "Why?" she asked. "Why do you shave your chest?"

"Because I like the way it looks and feels. That is, my lovers do."

"Oh." She pondered this answer. "Then why not shave your legs, too?"

"Why not, indeed? The Greeks did. The simple answer—too much bother. And men don't seem to mind the hairy legs. I think they prefer them." He kissed her mouth again. "Which reminds me. Promise not to go on shaving yourself down there."

"Gladly," she said. "But don't you want me to be clean?"

"You must bathe, obviously," he said. "But I like it hairy. After all, if I didn't like a hairy tail, I wouldn't be much of a sodomite, would I?" He shouted with laughter as she pretended to slap his face, grabbed her hand, and forced an easy surrender to his fervent kisses. "Shall I introduce you to the pleasures of making love in a coach?" His hand was already moving to unbutton the flap of his pantaloons.

Phyllida shook her head. "No, Andrew," she said. "I'm sorry, but I would prefer to arrive at your house *looking* respectable, at least."

Andrew sighed. She was right, of course. He was as much at fault for her indiscreet behavior as any member of her family. Used to the effortless, hasty, and uncomplicated couplings of men, he was going to have to start attending to the myriad differences when a woman was involved—or, more precisely, a wife. He could just imagine the shock and dismay of his so very correct and acquiescent staff if he appeared with a disheveled, voluptuous woman in a stained and rumpled gown and introduced her as their new mistress. "As always, my dear," he said, "you prove yourself a far better wife than I dared hope for—or deserve."

THE TOWN HOUSE IN GROSVENOR Square was so grand, Phyllida's first reaction was to request an annulment or a divorce and run back to Sussex. The front of the house appeared twice as wide as any of the others, with tall windows and a massive wooden door more appropriate to a castle. A liveried footman opened it before they had a chance to knock, and a staff of at least twenty people was on hand to greet the returning master and his bride. The rest of the household, she was informed by the butler, the dour Yardley, would pay their respects the next morning. Just in case, Phyllida thought, she felt the need to hire more people, enough to fill the first tier at the opera.

A nervous young girl was assigned to assist Mrs. Carrington. "The master wrote as how you wasn't bringing your own maid," Nan said. "We din't have time to find a proper one, but I said I'd give it a try. If I don't suit, you are to hire someone yourself."

"And what will happen to you?" Phyllida asked.

"I'll go back to the scullery," Nan said. She saw Phyllida's frown. "Don't worry, madam, I'll still have a place. I won't tease you, I promise. Just give me a chance. My mam was a real lady's maid, for the master's mam, and she taught me summat."

Phyllida saw she had freed herself from the needs and ambitions of a family of four only to assume those of a household of five times that number. Perhaps, she told herself, it would be five times easier as well, for having the wherewithal to gratify them. She doubted it. "Well, Nan," she said, "then you know more about it than I do. You do your best and I expect I will be more than satisfied."

Nan thanked her new mistress profusely but stared with suspicion at her admission of ignorance. Phyllida wasn't sure if her generous speech had helped or hurt. She had married Andrew with the proviso of total honesty on both sides, but she was beginning to see that it might not be the best policy with the rest of his household.

Phyllida had expected Andrew to take the first opportunity to dash out to freedom, and was disconcerted when he expressed his intention of staying home after dinner. "Don't look so alarmed, my dear," he said. "I shan't become overly uxorious. But the sooner we get you in the family way, the easier for us both, don't you agree?"

On that romantic note, she retired early, had Nan brush out her hair and lay out a nightgown, and settled herself in the majestic bed. The master bedroom was much like Sir Frederick's, only with fewer mirrors and a more pronounced, airy elegance in the furnishings. Very much a man's room, but she had her own lovely boudoir, she had been pleased to note, although sparsely furnished and, what there was, in the graceful but outdated style of thirty years back. Andrew had mentioned that, as the house had naturally been a bachelor establishment for years, the wife's apartments had been neglected. "Feel free to decorate, refurbish, purchase as you require," he'd said. "I expect to be consulted if you wish to change the downstairs, but your own rooms are your domain."

Andrew entered, apparently deep in contemplation, and stopped in surprise halfway across the room. "Good Lord," he said, "did I not make myself clear? I will visit you in your bedchamber. You will not come here. This is where I will bring my lovers." He laughed. "I shudder at the thought of some of my acquaintance finding a woman—

worse, my wife—in my bed. They would get the oddest notions of my practices."

"Of course," Phyllida said. She felt horribly embarrassed. "I did not understand."

"No," he said. "There is a small bedroom on the other side of your boudoir. That is where you will sleep. When I wish to have marital relations, you will await me there."

Phyllida sat up and looked for her slippers. She was red-faced, her bosom heaving.

"Now," Andrew said, "what have I done? It is not unusual for husband and wife to have separate bedrooms. All the titled families use that arrangement."

Phyllida shook her head. "It is the way you said it. As if—as if I was just one of the servants. A particularly stupid girl who could not obey the simplest commands."

"Oh, for pity's sake." The sensibilities of the female sex were beyond Andrew's fathoming. He sighed and shrugged. "It will do no harm tonight. You might as well stay here. But you will dispense with that odious nightgown. Makes you look like an overgrown schoolgirl." He snapped his fingers.

Phyllida's eyes widened until Andrew thought they were going to pop out of her head. She leaped from the bed and hurled herself at him, scratching and clawing at him and windmilling her arms when he tried to catch hold of her.

"What the bloody hell is the matter with you?" he shouted when he had caught her at last and held her pinioned, her arms behind her back, writhing and twisting in his grasp but unable to free herself.

"The matter with me?" she screamed, turning her head to shout in his face. "It's what's the matter with *you*! You are a brute, and an overbearing, odious tyrant, without the manners of a— of a—" She couldn't think of a comparison. "My *mother* has better manners than you."

He released her in shock. "That is a low blow," he drawled. He held his hands up, palms out, prepared to ward off any more of her attacks.

Phyllida stood in front of him, sadly defeated. She hung her head, sniffling, her arms limp at her sides. "Yes," she said, "but only because it is true."

Not defeated, after all. He grinned. "What a little cat," he said, stepping back as she came at him again. "Enough of this. Phyllida, please." He tried a new tactic, embracing her in a sudden bear hug, immobilizing her this time face-to-face, or face-to-chest. He pressed her against him until she could hear the beating of his heart, loud in the slender frame and narrow ribcage, and she became aware, to the exclusion of all other sensations, of his erection leaping against her belly.

She raised her face to his, barely had time to register his eyes dark with strong passion—Was it lust, hatred, anger?—before he kissed her so hard and so unexpectedly he crushed the breath out of her. He plundered her mouth, as he had ravished her body the night before, sucking and thrusting with his tongue, until she thought she was going to pass out if she did not soon have a chance to breathe. Just when black spots were bursting like dark fireworks in the depths of her vision, he released her, but before she could fall in a swoon, he had lifted her lightly in his sinewy arms, carried her to the bed, and laid her down.

She gasped in long, wheezing breaths.

He was on top of her, pushing up her nightgown over her hips, lifting her buttocks with his hands, feeling roughly in her cleft and arranging her legs over his thighs.

"Andrew," she said. "Wait."

"Don't talk," he said. He sealed her mouth again with his, making sure she could not utter an intelligible word, and entered her with one smooth motion. He kept his mouth over hers the entire time, allowing her to breathe as necessary, but taking her cries and moans into his, so that little noise escaped.

He rode her as before, but this time there was the beginning of a response. At her initial, indignant realization of what he was doing, she lay back in helpless surrender, but after the first few thrusts, she began rocking her hips in rhythm with his, pulling back as he withdrew and lifting up to meet him when he pushed in. Her legs came up, she locked her ankles around his waist, and she pumped against him in a primal, pounding physical duet.

He was groaning after a couple of minutes, dimly aware of the strange noises she was making directly into his mouth. Whimpering, high-pitched yelps and screams. He almost stopped, taken aback by the unusual feminine sounds, in danger of losing the great hardness after all. Then it started—powerful contractions of her inner muscles, clenching and releasing around him. He groaned louder, lifting his mouth from hers at last, and surrendered in turn to her amazing, stimulating grip.

When he collapsed at the end, she was panting, weeping and moaning, her lower body still gripping and relaxing, gripping and relaxing. He felt as if he might not be able to have another erection for a week, so depleted he was. So gloriously, satisfyingly drained.

He kissed her flushed cheek. "My dear," he whispered.

She turned her head away. "Don't."

He pulled out of her, staring in dismay at her teary face and trembling lips. "Phyllida," he said. "What is the trouble?"

She sat up, pushed his out-flung arm away from her, and stood up. "I know I am your wife and you are within your rights to use me whenever and however you wish. But I beg you, if there is any pity or decency in you, leave me alone for the rest of this night, at least."

"Phyllida!" he called, the torpor of his great release making him slow to react. She was gone, the door shut carefully behind her, to her own room.

PHYLLIDA MADE SURE TO LOCK the door, grateful it had a lock and a key, then threw herself onto her own smaller, narrower bed, in a paroxysm of tears she had not known since childhood—the fall from the tree, the broken arm, the agony of the setting and splinting. She felt the same dreamy languor as then, too, but with a difference, one she could not make sense of at first.

Then she understood. Breaking her arm had been a child's pain. And only pain. The great warmth and comfort, the lazy pleasure that had followed, had been from the cessation of suffering, after the worst with the doctor was over and the laudanum had taken effect.

Tonight's events were a woman's pains—the lot, she supposed, of most of the world's female half. And what bothered her more than anything was that it hadn't really been painful—just humiliating, frightening, and bewildering. The way she felt now tranquil, almost happy—was the effect, not of the easing of pain, or of a drug, but apparently the aftermath of that truly astonishing series of waves or contractions—like a small explosion inside her—produced, it seemed, from Andrew's raping her!

She had been furious with him, the way he spoke to her, the things he said, but equally furious at herself, for responding as before with desire to his sneering, supercilious manner. Her attack on him had been instinctive, an attempt to deny this unnatural reaction. Surely men and women should speak lovingly, kindly, sweetly to each other. Certainly a married couple ought to make love gently, considerately, as an expression of the sacred bond they shared. Even an arranged marriage was blessed, if both consented.

How could it be instead that a husband could take a wife in anger, or in contempt, and she would derive some pleasure anyway? It was apparently true, and appalling, that a man could force a woman and make her like it. What a system! What a strange way to design people. It made one wonder if God truly had anything to do with it, or whether, indeed, there was a god at all, at least one who cared about his creation.

She stopped weeping. It wasn't like her to let so preposterous a thing defeat her. She put her hand between her legs, sticky with Andrew's seed leaking out of her, and attempted to find that place that had so betrayed her, making her whimper like a whipped dog, surrender to Andrew's bruising riding, and shatter into pieces with such abandon. There, she could feel it easily, had fingered it often over the years in the way that uninhibited, curious children touched themselves. But she had never brought this sensation on herself, perhaps because it was so far beyond her imaginings she had not known to try.

She wished she was as heartless and inconsiderate as her husband, that she could wake poor little Nan and have a bath. But she wasn't. She washed herself instead as best she could in the cold water left in the pitcher, changed into another nightgown, clean and unstained, and went back to bed, falling instantly into one of the soundest, deepest sleeps she had enjoyed in years.

ANDREW LAY AWAKE FOR OVER an hour after Phyllida left. What had happened? *How* had it happened? One thing was clear—he had hurt her very much. Maybe not physically—she had, after all, appeared to have experienced that climax that had eluded her before. But surely, if she had enjoyed what had occurred between them she would have been happy afterward. Drowsy, satisfied contentment, as Andrew had been feeling until she told him not to "use her" again this night.

Is that what he had done? Used her?

He thought of the conversation, such as it was, that had led up to his extraordinary arousal. He had been so astonished to see her in the master bedroom, his most masculine retreat, that he had been put immediately on the defensive. Seeing her there, warm and soft and curvaceous, was like a slap in the face to his image of what the room and the bed represented. Not a malicious slap in the face. No, more of an amusing, start-things-off-with-a-wallop slap in the face.

That was it, of course. She had accused him of speaking to her like a servant. But Andrew would never address a servant in that tone. He used it only with equals—men—when he wanted to play the game. Dominance and submission, teasing, name-calling, the preliminaries to the rough, forceful sport that men like Harry enjoyed. That most men enjoyed.

Perhaps it worked with women, too. Phyllida had certainly reacted to it, throwing herself at him like a warrior queen against an invading Roman legion. He remembered their first meeting, in the sunny parlor of her mother's cottage, the way she had reddened and grown short of breath when he resorted to the drawling tone at her surprising eagerness for his kiss. Then why was she angry now that they had followed the promise of the overture and played out the full symphony?

Probably it was just as men of his kind said. Women—ladies—were frail creatures, requiring delicacy of handling like a wild falcon or an unbroken horse. It took an enormous amount of time and care to teach them to enjoy the sexual act, and even then not all were capable of it. For the first time in his life, Andrew felt a grudging admiration for rakes and libertines, men who had a reputation for pleasing ladies. Lord, they must work very hard!

Andrew rolled onto his back, hands clasped behind his head. He thought longingly of Harry, how they had taken every opportunity to enjoy each other, in coaches, in secluded walks in Vauxhall Gardens and St. James's Park, even on the stairs of this town house, when they hadn't been able to make it all the way to the bedroom in time. After the household had gone to bed, of course. In fact, Andrew suspected that he could count on one hand the number of times they had actually done it in a bed, behind closed doors.

How long had it been since Harry's last letter? Weeks? Months, more like, since before the victorious assault on Ciudad Rodrigo that Andrew's brother Tom had described so vividly in his recent letter. Surely, if Harry had been killed or badly wounded, his name would be printed in the lists in the newspapers. His father's disowning him could not change his rank—when last heard from, he had been recently promoted from lowly second lieutenant to first—nor could it undo the fact that he was a son, albeit the younger son, of a peer.

No, it was all too clear that Harry, gone to war for close on three years now, had forsaken his lover at home, besieged as he must be on all sides by sex-starved men in uniform. Andrew was a fool for hoping otherwise. It was the way of things—of men, of sex, of the world. A damned commonplace, immortalized in the army's favorite marching song, played and sung whenever they left a town for the next posting.

Andrew hummed a few bars of "The Girl I Left Behind Me." He had never thought to see himself in that role.

He had not, of course, expected sexual fidelity from Harry, any more than he had promised it for himself at home. It was just that he had somehow hoped Harry felt as he did, that they were more than simply sex partners, but lovers, that when the war was over, or Harry had leave, they would come together again, resume their life as a couple. In the beginning, it seemed, it had been so. Harry had corresponded faithfully, although he was not much of a writer, having not been much of a scholar. His letters had been fervent, brief, and explicit, much like their physical lovemaking, and they had been sent regularly, gladdening Andrew's heart, inspiring him to compose long, equally explicit but more elaborately expressed sentiments in return.

Then, early this year, they had stopped. Even before that, they had become less frequent, less passionate. Andrew had attributed it to the dampening effects of absence and distance. He had continued to write, hoping he was keeping the memory of their love alive, that the one-sided correspondence would lead eventually to the same joyous, hard—very hard—reunion he had dreamed of. Now it was clear that it was simply over.

Andrew touched himself, taken unawares by the sudden hardness. He had thought, half seriously, after the amazing session with Phyllida, he would not be able to rise again this night. And here he was, stiff as a poker, just from remembering Harry. Even knowing it was finished between them, the image of Harry still had him up and ready to go.

Go where? he thought in a sour pun. It was late by now, irksome and fatiguing to get dressed to cruise the parks and the streets. He could walk to the Brotherhood, he supposed, see if anybody halfway decent was there and free for the evening, or he could take a hackney to a boy brothel or a madge house, but damn it, what was the use of having a wife if she could not ease his needs?

He put his dressing gown over his shoulders for decency, not bothering to belt it, and glided out into the corridor. He knocked softly on the door to her room. "Phyllida?" he whispered. "May I come in?"

No answer. Perhaps she was asleep. No point in waking everybody up. He turned the knob slowly, quietly, and pushed. The door didn't budge, the bolt merely catching in the lock with a clunk, agonizingly loud in the still, dark house. She had locked it, locked him out. Her husband!

He went back into his room, slamming the door with a report like a clap of thunder, and flung himself onto the bed. Bugger her! Bugger them all. He almost felt up to buggering the whole damn household. He grinned. Wouldn't that be the scandal of the season? He turned on his side, took a firm grip on himself, and thought of Harry. Harry, with his wide mouth and red tongue, with his breeches open and his erection, the largest Andrew had ever seen, standing to attention. He relieved himself efficiently into a towel and was asleep before five minutes had passed.

PHYLLIDA WAS TEMPTED TO have breakfast in bed the next morning rather than face her rapist of a husband, but she was not about to hide in her boudoir for the rest of her life. Maids brought water for the desired bath, and Nan helped her into a morning gown and dressed her hair. Phyllida could tell, from the look on the girl's face, that even to a humble scullery maid her clothes and linen were not up to the standards of Mrs. Andrew Carrington.

She was not going to start out by pretending. "I will have to buy my wedding clothes now," she said. "There wasn't time before."

Nan's face brightened. "Yes, madam," she said. "The master will want you to look as elegant as him."

Phyllida laughed. "I mustn't aspire to the unattainable," she said.

Yardley himself intercepted her at the foot of the stairs. "Mr. Carrington wished me to inform you that he has gone out," he said, in tones that implied Andrew was attending a funeral or taking part in a duel or perhaps hearing the announcement of the end of the world. "Lady Fanshawe is in the breakfast room."

Filled with trepidation, Phyllida entered. "Now, don't be offended," a woman's voice drawled. "I know it's unconventional, but when I heard Andrew had married—*married!*—I just couldn't wait for proper visiting hours. Besides, I was sure you'd need a friend, a female friend, moving into this horrid bachelor establishment."

Phyllida advanced more confidently. "Lady Fanshawe," she said. There could be little doubt of the woman's identity, even without Yardley's warning. Andrew had only the one sister, and this lady was a female version of him, tall and slender, almost angular, with the same dark hair and aquiline features. Even the voice and manner of speaking were much the same. The interesting thing was that, while she could not, even by generous standards, be described as beautiful, Lady Fanshawe was fascinating—an attraction comprised equally of charm and erotic allure.

"And you are obviously the beautiful and ladylike Phyllida," Lady Fanshawe said. "And no, don't look at me like that. My brother wrote to me, you know, and he called on me this morning, at the most absurd hour, so I know all about you—especially that you seem to have achieved the impossible." She laughed, obviously awaiting some response to her gay prattle.

"Forgive me," Phyllida said, "I have just arisen, and—"

"And you would like some breakfast," Lady Fanshawe said. "Or at least a cup of coffee. But you have, you know. You have made my brother, an irredeemable, perennial bachelor, fall in love with you. Oh yes, I see all the signs."

Phyllida shook her head at such absurdity and sat down. The footman was at her side immediately, filling her cup with coffee after giving her the choice of chocolate or tea as well, and directing her attention to the selection of dishes on the sideboard. She ate in fuming silence while Lady Fanshawe never stopped talking except to draw the occasional breath or take the odd bite of toast.

"Fanshawe—that's my husband, you know—nearly fell off his

chair when I told him that my brother had married. 'Dick married?' he said. 'Gave one of his doxies a slip on the shoulder and got caught, eh?'" She let out an unnerving deep laugh, so much like Andrew's that Phyllida looked around, expecting to see him standing in the doorway. "He thought it was our youngest brother, you see. Dick is quite the handsomest of us all, and the ladies do love him so, I'm sure it's not his fault the way they throw themselves at his feet. But I had the greatest pleasure in telling Wilt—that's Fanshawe, you know—that it was Andrew who was married. And do you know what the man was so provoking as to say? Said he hoped it really was a female he had married and not some conniving ganymede in skirts." She went into peals of that deep laughter. "Well! I just hope I'm there to see Wilt's face when he gets a look at you and your hourglass figure. As if Andrew wouldn't examine the goods before proposing marriage."

Phyllida stared at her plate and made no comment. So these were the manners of the *ton*, the standard of behavior she was to emulate. What a joke. But it would make excellent material for future books. Just think of the world of experience opening up to her. She could probably sell hundreds more copies to the real-life models of the new characters she could create, aristocratic types drawn convincingly from life.

She finished her meal, stood up, and held out her hand. "It was a pleasure meeting you, Lady Fanshawe," she said. "Do call as often as you wish. You must forgive me, but there is so much to do, what with just arriving yesterday."

"You must call me Lizzie," Lady Fanshawe said. "And of course there is much to do. That is why I am here. I am to take you shopping. Andrew expressly desired me to see that you have a whole new wardrobe. I declare, just when he is the most annoying, infuriating man, he turns around and comes up with the one thing that will make me forgive him every past offense and a score of future ones."

Phyllida could only look blank.

"Now, please, don't be coy or embarrassed," Lady Fanshawe said. "I know all about the arrangement and that you have no suitable town clothes. It will be such a pleasure to go to the very best modiste, and be able to fling out one's arms and say, 'Spare no expense, but dress Mrs. Carrington in the height of fashion from head to toe—and underneath.' Something lacy and diaphanous that'll drive Andrew to break down that locked bedroom door."

Phyllida blushed deep crimson. "How did you—" she choked out.

"Oh!" Lady Fanshawe said. "Servants hear things, after all. And say things. I grew up in this house, so they know me as a friend. You must give up this missishness, my dear, if you want Andrew to do his duty as your husband. Nothing so disgusts a man of his inclinations as the appearance of reluctance or a dislike of the male sex."

Phyllida opened her mouth to explain, then swallowed her indignant words. What did she care if this overbearing female Carrington had things totally wrong? It was none of the woman's business anyway, no matter how she considered herself rightfully privy to every intimate detail of her brother's life. Phyllida thought of the way she had felt obliged to apologize for her mother's behavior, to intervene and protect Andrew from her intrusive vulgarity, while he had not scrupled to leave her to the mercy of his odious sister. Lady Fanshawe was every bit as rude as Mrs. Lewis, but no doubt Andrew wouldn't see it that way. Just because she was a Carrington, one of the *ton*, and had married a peer, her manners were simply assumed, by definition, to be perfect.

"Yes," Phyllida said, giving the faint, closed-mouth smile that only her family recognized as a declaration of war. "You are quite right—Lizzie. I appreciate your taking the trouble to help me."

"No trouble at all," Lady Fanshawe said, adding, in an artless way that quite made Phyllida forgive some of her worst lapses. "If it were trouble, you know, I would not do it. That's the way all of us Carringtons are—you will find out soon enough. Which is why we were so bowled over by Andrew's news. For what could be more trouble for a man like him than marriage?"

"Just let me get my bonnet and pelisse," Phyllida said.

MR. RICHARD CARRINGTON FOUND HIS brother on the first try, at Manton's shooting gallery, where it was Andrew's practice most mornings to murder a substantial number of wafers.

"Andrew!" Richard chose his moment after Andrew had fired all ten loaded pistols laid out for him, hitting a bull's-eye nine times and cursing and examining the tenth pistol to see why he had only clipped the edge of the last wafer. "Allow me to congratulate you and to thank you from the bottom of my heart."

Andrew laid down the offending pistol and turned to his brother, raising one eyebrow. "Thank me, Dick?" he drawled. "I rather think you should kneel down and kiss my boots."

"Just so long as you don't ask me to do what your ganymedes do on their knees," Richard said. "Although considering the fate you've spared me, I'd accept it as a fair trade."

Andrew laughed and held out his hand. Richard was a rogue, the baby of the family, spoiled but easygoing and amiable. "You astonish me," he said. "I may have my vices, but incest isn't one of them."

"Now that you've got me off the hook like this," Richard said, "I'll call the man out who says you have any vices at all."

Andrew clasped his hands at his chest. "I have a champion," he said. "Come on, what do you say to breakfast at White's? On me, of course."

Richard looked uncharacteristically twitchy. "No, Andrew," he said. "Can't let you do that. Not after all you're doing for me."

"Can't let me buy you breakfast?" Andrew said. "Dick, I've married, that's all. And yes, I did have to pay the girl's family an exorbitant amount, but I can still manage to spring for breakfast at White's."

"Tell you the truth, Andrew," Richard said, looking sicker by the minute, "I'd rather not be seen at White's just now, if you know what I mean."

"Oh, for God's sake, Dick," Andrew said. "Have you run through this quarter's allowance already?"

"I'll come about," Richard said. "Just rather not go to White's."

"You know better than that," Andrew said. "If you owe a debt of honor, I'll bail you out. Won't have my own brother under the hatches, skulking around town avoiding people. How much?"

Richard shrugged and gave up. "Look, Andrew, now that all those pistols are discharged, might as well tell you. There's a bet on."

"A bet at White's? You don't say. And this concerns me—how?" He understood, the minute the words left his mouth. "Bloody hell. I'll murder the lot of them. And how did you think I wouldn't find out?"

"I just hoped you wouldn't find out around me, that's all," Richard said. "And I swear to you, it wasn't my idea. Not that far gone."

"Then who?" Andrew asked. He snapped his fingers. "Fanshawe! I knew I shouldn't have told Lizzie, but I'd never hear the end of it if I didn't." He brooded in silence for a minute before muttering, "And the devil of it is, I can't in good conscience call out my own brother-in-law."

"Not when he shoots as badly as Fanshawe," Richard agreed.

"Just what is this wager, anyway?"

"Not so bad, really," Richard said, brightening. "In fact, you may want to get in on it yourself. I mean, can't officially, of course, but I could place it for you." He paled at Andrew's homicidal gaze. "It simply is a question of whether you'll get your wife in whelp by the end of the season. And the joke of it is that while we in your family know you're *up* to the task"—he nudged his brother in the ribs— "the rest of the world is so ignorant about these things the odds are running ten to one against you. Ten to one! Can you believe it? So we stand to make a real killing." He gasped as his arm was grasped tightly enough to cut off the circulation.

"And just how," Andrew drawled in his quietest, most dangerous voice, "is the truth of Phyllida's condition to be determined? Can't imagine the sporting gentlemen of White's are prepared to wait a twelvemonth to settle their wager."

"Phyllida? That her name?" Richard gulped, stalling for time. "Not sure. Bribe her maid, perhaps."

Andrew released his brother's arm. Richard massaged the bruised flesh as Andrew spoke softly to himself. "No," Andrew said, "I think it's worse than that. And here I thought Lizzie was eager to take Phyllida shopping simply because it's her favorite pastime and only real accomplishment."

"You mean you let Lizzie loose on your bride when you've just been married a couple of days?" Richard stood back, aghast at his brother's callousness. "Damn it, Andrew, if I'd known how things were between you and your wife, I wouldn't have staked the entire next quarter's allowance on you."

BY THE END OF THE morning, Phyllida was quite in charity with her youngest brother-in-law, even if she hadn't yet made his acquaintance. Lady Fanshawe kept up her barrage of verbiage the entire time, during the ride in the coach to Mme. Argonne's and all through the long, confusing, and tedious business of choosing fabrics and patterns.

Phyllida had dreamed of having enough money to buy fashionable gowns, as many as she wanted, and not to have to continually make over last year's, or the year before that's. Now that her dream was coming true, all she wanted to do was escape to peace and quiet, and work on the proofs of her book. She had sent off the last batch from Sussex with a note informing her publisher of her marriage and enclosing her new direction, and a new batch had already been waiting for her upon her arrival at the town house. Mr. Edwards had promised to try to bring the book out before the end of the season, but only if she was diligent about returning the corrected proofs.

The fitting began disagreeably when the French modiste did not seem to believe that Phyllida really was Mrs. Carrington. She stared at Phyllida's left hand, empty of rings, and Phyllida opened her mouth to explain about Andrew's having given her his signet until he could get a ring made to fit her, and that she had taken to keeping the large ring in her pocket because it was impractical to wear on her thumb, the only finger big enough to hold it.

But before she got a word out—indeed, she thought, if she spent too long with Lizzie, she might lose the ability to articulate sounds at all—Lady Fanshawe winked and shook her head and spoke rapidly in French, a language Phyllida had studied from books but had rarely heard and had never spoken herself. "*Monsieur Richard?*" Mme. Argonne said, eyes narrowed in suspicion.

"*Non, non,*" Lady Fanshawe said, with her fascinating laugh, "*c'est vraiment Monsieur Andrew.*" Phyllida was unable to follow the conversation beyond that point, although she caught the words *innocente* and *paysanne*.

The gesture Lady Fanshawe made, rubbing thumb and forefinger together to indicate a substantial cash transaction, was universal.

Mme. Argonne nodded and smiled at Lady Fanshawe's speech, but in a most unpleasant, insinuating way that reminded Phyllida of nothing so much as her own mother when she was trying to get her daughter to agree to something revolting, like submitting to Mr. Coulter's advances.

At least things moved along more easily after that. Phyllida's measurements were taken and she was given pattern books to study and swatches of fabrics to choose from, although every time she picked something out, she was told that it was outmoded or meant for a girl in her first season, not a married lady who would want something more sophisticated. "And with madame's exquisite figure," Mme. Argonne gushed, "we must show you off properly, not hide your charms behind the high necks and the long sleeves and the so heavy material." Even the fabrics seemed flimsy, almost transparent, but when Phyllida expressed any reservations, she was told emphatically by both women that she was betraying her country ignorance, that in town only the lightest of gauze and muslin would do.

In the end, Phyllida gave up and let the other women choose. She liked clothes well enough—what woman did not?—but she did not care for the process of acquiring them, it seemed. She knew her figure was good and she supposed that in town, married to the notorious Andrew Carrington, it would only make her a laughingstock to be seen wearing clothes more suitable for a debutante.

"Well! Wasn't that a treat!" Phyllida blinked as Lady Fanshawe prepared to bundle her back into the waiting coach, clutching the box with the one ready-made gown for Phyllida to wear until the rest of the purchases were finished. "I wish I could be there when you show Andrew all the fruits of our labors."

"Your labors," Phyllida said dutifully. Typical that the woman had finally shut her mouth just in time to receive a compliment. "I really didn't do anything, except make bad choices and accept corrections."

Lady Fanshawe laughed in her low voice. "The fate of all country girls, my dear. You will learn soon enough."

"I'm not a complete novice, you know," Phyllida said. "I did have one season."

"Indeed?" Lady Fanshawe raised her eyebrows, just like Andrew at his most annoying. "And how did that go?"

"Dreadfully." Phyllida was forced to admit defeat in an uneven contest of spite. "I only received one offer, from the old Earl of Hearn. And even a poor country girl like me could not be taken in by a man of his reputation."

"Pity," Lady Fanshawe said. "Hearn died over Christmas. Too much plum pudding and mistletoe. You'd be a wealthy widow now, besieged by every handsome rake and buck in town."

"Believe it or not," Phyllida said, "that is not every woman's idea of happiness."

Lady Fanshawe sniffed. "Don't think you can keep up this charade of innocence forever," she said. "You'll have to unbend a little if you want Andrew to win—" She clapped her hands over her mouth while her eyes darted back and forth in comical and, Phyllida was convinced, feigned dismay.

"What do you mean, win?" Phyllida asked.

"Oh!" Lady Fanshawe cried, writhing on the seat of the coach as if in the agonies of torture. "I promised not to say anything, and look what you've made me do. There's a bet at White's, that's what. You know, the most exclusive of gentlemen's clubs, where they wager on everything. They write them down in a book, you see, so there's no pretending afterward the terms have changed. And if you don't start behaving like a real wife to Andrew I'll lose all my pin money and Wilt will never forgive me." She burst into loud, racking sobs, covering her face and fishing in vain for a handkerchief until Phyllida, more out of defense of her own hygiene than from any real sense of charity, gave up hers.

ANDREW CAME HOME AT MID-AFTERNOON to find his wife wearing her new gown but hiding in her boudoir, while Nan fussed about her with lace and pins. He took one look at the low-cut bodice that exposed the top of the nipples, the net tunic over the sheer underskirt through which the dark triangle at the top of her thighs showed as a dim shadow, and exploded in wrath. "Leave us," he said to Nan, who squeaked, dropped a quick curtsy, and fled. "If that is a sample of your mother's idea of decent attire, you will pack it all up and send it home. Or throw it out. Or donate it to a charity for down-at-heels courtesans, if there is such a thing. Damn it all! Didn't Lizzie take you shopping this morning?"

"Yes, Andrew," Phyllida said. "This is the ready-made gown. Indeed, I did not think it proper, but Lady Fanshawe and Mme. Argonne insisted that it was what all the ladies of fashion are wearing."

"The fashionable impures," Andrew scoffed. "Mme. Argonne sold you that? Did she not know you are my wife?"

Phyllida shook her head. "I think at first she thought I was one of your brother's mistresses. But Lady Fanshawe explained about our marriage. She spoke all in French, you see, so I don't know everything that was said."

Andrew squeezed his eyes shut and counted slowly to ten. When would he learn, he asked himself. When would he accept that Lizzie was no more to be trusted than any female—less, because she knew so much more about him. He opened his eyes. *"Parles-tu Français?"* he asked.

Phyllida shook her head. *"Un petit peu,"* she replied.

"Un très petit peu," Andrew said. "Your accent is atrocious. Didn't you study French? Verney insisted you were educated like a gentleman's daughter."

"I studied from books after I left the village school," Phyllida said. "Sir Frederick was kind enough to let me use his library. We could not afford a governess. I learned the grammar, but there was no one to speak it with."

"What about Verney's sister?" Andrew asked. "He mentioned she sponsored you for a season."

"Mrs. Rathbone was very kind," Phyllida said. "But she was not a close friend. She was married and moved away by the time I was fifteen. She only invited me up for the season because Sir Frederick asked her to, although I think she enjoyed having a protegée."

"And what did you wear during your season?" Andrew asked, returning to the problem at hand. "Surely not that disgraceful and outgrown ball gown you were wearing when we met. In fact, if you brought that with you I demand that you produce it now so it can be disposed of." He snapped his fingers.

Phyllida thought she was going to faint, but she wouldn't leave herself so vulnerable. She bowed her head, bending over from the waist to keep the blood from draining. When she felt more in control, she straightened up to see Andrew observing her with a quizzical smile on his face. "Get out!" she said.

"What?" He raised his glass to his eye.

"You heard me. You will not come into my domain and snap your fingers at me and order me about. Get out."

Andrew stood, transfixed by the sight of his splendidly enraged wife. Bending over and standing up had brought her breasts completely out of the bodice, more suitable for a harem than an English lady's boudoir. Her exquisite body was quivering, flushed with rage, deceptively similar to arousal. He was hard, suffused with desire for her, stronger even than last night, because he was beginning now to understand the intriguing dynamic between them. He stepped closer and reached for her. "Come here, wife," he said, gruff, imperious. The game, just as he liked it. As she obviously did, despite her denials. "Take off that whore's garment and come here, or I will take it off you myself."

"Brute! Fiend!" Phyllida came barreling at him, prepared today for his attempt to seize and overpower her, as she had not been last night. She sidestepped, slipping easily out of his reaching arms, and pushed him with both hands against his chest. "Get *out. Out. Out.*" She emphasized each word with a forceful shove until he was knocked off balance. He staggered to keep from falling, heading inexorably toward the door. Phyllida continued shoving him, her strength remarkable for one so much smaller. The moment he was in the corridor, she slammed the door in his face and locked it.

Andrew was so nonplussed he actually kicked the door, leaving a scuff and scratches on his boot that would mystify his valet for days. "Phyllida!" he roared. "What is the meaning of this appalling behavior?"

"Go to hell!" was the ladylike answer he received.

ANDREW FLUNG HIMSELF OUT OF the house in such a towering rage his valet, Mr. Pumfry, didn't dare ask him a question. So it was with his dark curls disarranged, his cravat askew, and his coat creased, that Andrew enjoyed, if that is the word, a lengthy and emphatic discussion with Mme. Argonne on the proper attire for his wife. It was only when the dressmaker came to understand that the young lady with the curvaceous body and fresh-faced country looks was truly wedded to Mr. Carrington, and not the object of a perverse wager perpetrated by his sister and brother-in-law, that she apologized profusely, fluttering her hands and begging to be permitted to retain the privilege of dressing Mrs. Carrington. She would be delighted, she claimed, to make a gift of the interesting garments so unwisely sent home with the lady. Perhaps Mr. Carrington would enjoy them in the privacy of the boudoir, yes?

"*Non!*" Andrew roared, before recollecting that his every public utterance on the subject of his wife would from now on be noted by some interested party and handicapped by the bookmakers at White's. "*Oui, peut-être,*" he corrected with a sickly grin.

Confused by the unconvincing reversal, Mme. Argonne launched into a sharp-eyed inquisition of Andrew's preferences—colors, styles, fabrics, even the degree of trimming, laces, and ribbons—until Andrew almost demanded merely enough to hang himself. He raised a hand to stop the flood of questions.

"*Je ne sais pas,*" he said. "I don't know and I don't care. Phyllida—Mrs. Carrington—is a beautiful woman. Surely it cannot be difficult to clothe her decently, as befits my wife. It is your job to know what colors and styles suit her best. Just do it. If she is satisfied and I am not scandalized by the results, I will pay the bills without question." He turned and ran out before he became any further entangled in the minutiae of feminine attire. Another session like this and he'd be in danger of turning into a mincing, effeminate man-milliner.

Mme. Argonne, a speculative smile creasing her plump face, waited a few moments to make sure her wealthy new client was safely gone. Then she went into the back room, unlocked a small steel strongbox, withdrew a substantial sum of notes, and called for a messenger. She had a number of clients whose husbands or protectors were members of White's. One or two of these men could be trusted to place a bet for her discreetly, especially since she held the secrets of both wife and mistress as a surety.

A HALF HOUR LATER, ANDREW barged through the doors of the Brotherhood of Philander, collapsed onto a sofa, and demanded a brandy. Having drained it, and a second one, he was able to meet the fascinated and dismayed gaze of his friends. "Never marry a woman," he said. "Never."

"Sorry, old fellow." Monkton was the first to brave the fortress of wrath. "Can't say we didn't warn you."

"Bugger off," Andrew said.

"Oh, I will," Monkton replied in dulcet tones. "Pity you can't."

Verney looked up from the card table. "Leave him alone, Monkton," he said. "What's the trouble, Carrington? Thought things were going well."

Andrew rubbed his eyes and ran a hand through his hair, ruining what few good effects remained from the morning's barbering. "Care to guess where I just came from? A modiste! Can you believe it? I foresee the rest of my days mired in a slough of trivia until I end up in Bedlam."

Pierce dared to sit on the same sofa, although maintaining a prudent distance. "Extravagant, is she?" he said. "Seems to me it's easier to simply pay the bills. So long as she's not about to bankrupt you, I mean. She'll think you're indulging her and you'll win her gratitude along with some peace and quiet."

Andrew shook his head. "Nothing like that. Really can't talk about it."

"Can't talk about it!" Monkton's outraged voice rose at least an octave. "Then why did you come here and practically announce a lecture on the perils of marriage?"

"Yes, really, Carrington," Witherspoon was emboldened to enter the fray. "It's not fair to whet our appetites like this and then withhold the final favors, so to speak."

"Well, you've hit the nail on the head," Andrew said. He let loose with a frightening bellow that might have been demented laughter or a battle cry.

The others stared. It was Monkton, as usual, who was quickest on the uptake. "Are you serious?" he asked. "*You're* courting *her*? *She's* rejecting *you*? Oh, it's too delicious." His voice oozed sham commiseration; his face was a picture of delighted, triumphant gloating.

"I would take that smirk off my face and change my tone if I were you," Andrew said. "Unless you wish to be looking down the wrong end of my pistol."

"Ooooh," Monkton said, "I thought you'd never offer. But you mustn't show me your pistol at all now, you know. You're a married man." He clutched his slender waist, bending over with whoops and giggles.

"Oh, do shut up, Monkton," Verney said. "This is serious. If Carrington's marriage isn't working out it's something that concerns all of us."

"How do you mean?" Witherspoon asked.

"The wager, of course," Pierce said.

There was a moment of complete stillness, like the commemoration of a death.

"Damn it all to hell!" Andrew broke the silence. "I will not be wagered on like a racehorse or a prize bull."

"Too late," Monkton said. "Already laying odds against you ten to one the minute Fanshawe let it out you'd tied the knot. This news will probably raise it to twenty to one. Maybe even fifty."

Everybody stared at his shoes, shuffling his feet. The room was like a Quaker meeting awaiting inspiration.

"Don't fall all over yourselves trying to cheer me up," Andrew said. "Although if any of you know how to murder one's sister and get away with it, I'll be grateful for the information."

"Look, Carrington," Pierce said, "of course we're sympathetic. The thing is, we all have a lot riding on the outcome."

"Do you mean to say you bet on me? My own friends?"

"Of course," Witherspoon said. "Because we are your friends. Got to stand up for the honor of one of our own. Besides, *we* know what a stud you are. Seemed like a sure thing."

"You know, I could barely keep the smile off my face," Verney reminisced innocently, "when they were exclaiming at White's, setting the odds. And there I was, just come up from the country, after Andrew's successful nuptials—"

"Wait a minute," Pierce interrupted. "Are you saying the marriage was consummated? That changes everything."

"Hell and damnation!" Andrew exclaimed. "Fred, I thought we had an agreement—"

"Well, was it?" Monkton demanded.

"Yes, damn your eyes," Andrew said. "So you can all find another victim to torment."

"But I don't understand," Witherspoon lamented. "If she let you in already, why is she shutting you out now?"

Andrew raised a fist. "I'll shut you out, you little twit—"

Pierce stood up. "Don't you threaten him, you bad-tempered, overbearing bully. Just because your legendary prowess doesn't extend to females is no reason to take it out on George."

"Gentlemen, gentlemen," Monkton said. "You can all go upstairs later and thrash this out amongst yourselves. The important thing is to protect our investment. Now, Carrington, enough of this coyness. Just what is the trouble between you and your reluctant bride?"

Andrew groaned. "That's the hell of it," he said. "I don't know. I just don't know."

AFTER A GREAT MANY USELESS suggestions involving various discredited aphrodisiacs, black leather undergarments, consultation with Mme. Amélie, the proprietress of the most exclusive and luxurious brothel in the West End, and the simple expedient of force, Andrew was ready to put the wrong end of his pistol in his mouth and pull the trigger.

"That's it," he said, rising to leave when Monkton recommended tying Phyllida to the bed and keeping her there for the next two months ("Her maid can feed her with a spoon and see to her other needs, you know"). "I'll do better asking Dick."

"That's a splendid idea," Pierce said. "Didn't like to suggest it myself. Not the easiest thing, asking a younger brother for help."

Andrew merely glared at him.

"I say!" Witherspoon sat up very straight, the light of inspiration in his eyes. "That's the answer."

Everybody turned to stare. Witherspoon, while blessed with angelic sweetness of temper and looks to match, was not the brightest light in the house.

"Don't you see?" he asked. "They say Dick Carrington can get any woman he wants just by snapping his fingers. And with the family resemblance, no one will ever be able to prove Andrew ain't the father."

There was a stunned, awed silence.

Andrew loomed over Witherspoon, his face as dark and ominous as an approaching hurricane. "Repeat that disgusting thought anywhere, anywhere at all, and I will hunt you down and put a period to your existence. Do you understand?"

Witherspoon gulped and swallowed. "Really, Carrington," he stammered. "I only wanted to help."

Pierce took Andrew by the arm. "You are out of line, Carrington," he said.

Andrew flung the offending hand off with a wide, violent gesture. "And you, sir," he said, "are a dead man. Name your second."

"Don't be ridiculous," Pierce said. "George meant no offense. And if and when you sober up, you'll see that it was actually quite an ingenious suggestion." He nodded encouragement at his nervous friend, smiling his approbation and winking.

The others spoke up hurriedly, hoping to divert Andrew's attention and avoid an affair of honor. "Yes, really, Carrington," Monkton said. "It sounds like the perfect solution. Should have thought of it before."

Andrew glowered at his erstwhile friends. "I am only going to say this once. After this, if any one of you, Witherspoon included, has the effrontery to mention this loathsome idea, either in my hearing or where it gets back to me, I will call the man out and I will not delope." He waited until everyone was watching his face, silent and attentive. "Only one man will father my heir. Me. Not my brother Richard or anybody else. If Mrs. Carrington is blessed with a child, there had better not be so much as a whisper that it is not mine."

He stood, elbows bent, fists at the ready, just in case someone—God! he hoped it was Monkton—was imprudent enough to crack a joke or make a sarcastic comment, so he could smash the man's face in. Nobody said a word. "Good day, gentlemen," he said, turning to the door, where he retrieved his hat and gloves and was bowed out by the same man who had refused him entrance that fateful night with the street boy. The man was as expressionless as the rest of the club's members. At least, Andrew thought, he hadn't lost his touch with men, however he lacked skill with women.

Once the door was safely shut behind Andrew, the rest of the Brotherhood erupted in a cacophony of conjectures, nervous laughter, and after-the-fact proposals for what should have been said.

"*Delope* means to fire in the air," Pierce explained to Witherspoon, "which is what a *gentleman* would do."

" 'Blessed with a child'?" Monkton repeated, shaking his head in disbelief. "The deprivations of marriage have turned him into a mealy-mouthed curate."

Only Verney was silent. He stood up, stripped to his drawers from his endless, losing games of cards, and cleared his throat. "I think we're overlooking an important fact," he said, his strong profile and burnished skin giving him an air of authority at odds with his state of undress. "It seems to me that Carrington's in love."

WITH THE INEVITABLE BAD luck that comes in threes, Andrew ran into Richard, idling not two feet from the door of the Brotherhood. "Interested in joining, Dick?" Andrew drawled. "Gone through every female under sixty and ready to start in on the men?"

"Don't be an ass," Richard said, linking his arm through Andrew's and hanging on against his brother's forcible and angry attempts to disengage. "I wouldn't dare enter into competition with you on that field."

"It's not a sport, damn it," Andrew said, "no matter that every blood and buck seems to have nothing better to do than concern himself with my private activities."

"As to that," Richard said, "it seems high time for me to be introduced to the latest addition to our family. Can't make an informed wager on a pig in a poke. Lizzie claims she's nothing but a round, jolly country wench, but I can't imagine you'd go for that. And our sister, let's face it, is not the most reliable judge of feminine charms."

"Unlike you," Andrew said, recognizing that the meeting between his brother and his bride could not be put off forever, and perhaps ought not to be. "Come on then and see just how far off the mark Lizzie was this time."

Phyllida, when summoned from her boudoir, was clothed in a simple, tasteful gown, clearly not in the latest mode but well fitting, neither too tight nor hanging like a sack, and her hair was arranged in a similarly plain style that emphasized its luster and luxuriant curls. The two appeared to take to each other. Richard, after one look at Phyllida, staggered dramatically, clutching his chest and saying, "A hit. A very palpable hit," making Phyllida laugh in a natural, captivating voice that Andrew remembered from the drive home. It seemed like a distant year ago, not a mere day.

"You did not tell me, Andrew," Richard said, "that you'd found a genuine, out-and-out beauty." He bowed to Phyllida. "When you tire of my brother, and you're bound to quite soon, please know I am always, forever, hopelessly at your service."

"Why should I tell you," Andrew replied to his brother, "what you have far more pleasure discovering for yourself? Anyway, you would not have believed me."

Richard leaned over Phyllida and stage-whispered in her ear, "The fool probably doesn't even recognize his good fortune. The only kind of beauty he appreciates is found in Jackson's Boxing Saloon."

"A hit," Andrew drawled. "A very palpable hit. Although I doubt you would notice Venus herself unless she was safely married to a complaisant husband. And I am not complaisant."

"No," Richard said. "I should damn well hope not. Not with this business at White's." He turned to Phyllida to beg her pardon for the language.

"It's all right," she said. "I know about the wager."

"Hell," Andrew swore and slammed his fist into his palm. "Lizzie, I suppose?"

Phyllida shrugged. "Better to hear it from her straight out at the beginning than after I've been in society for a month, thinking I'd been accepted."

Richard was all solicitude. "Really, Andrew," he said. "Oughtn't to use language like that in front of a lady. Mrs. Carrington—may I call you Phyllida? It really is the most beautiful name, suits you perfectly. You mustn't worry about being accepted. Beauty like yours can overcome all snobbery and pretension. And don't let the wager trouble you. They always bet on the most intimate things at White's. Why, just last year they bet on whether Lady Finchley's youngest was fathered by her late husband or somebody else. Your wager is nothing by comparison."

"Thank you," Andrew said. "That is all very edifying. Please don't let me keep you from dinner."

"Ain't you going to invite me?" Richard asked. "I'm quite free tonight, no pressing engagements."

"What about—forgive me, I've been out of town for two days—Lydia Swain, is it?" Andrew asked, flicking an invisible speck of lint from his coat sleeve.

Richard shook his head in a hopeless attempt to deflect his brother's relentless attention. "I told you, Andrew. No engagements."

"Swain at home tonight, is he?" Andrew said. "Pity. These invalid husbands do have a tendency to curtail their wives' freedom. By the way, who was the father of Lady Finchley's child? I can't recall offhand."

"That wasn't the wager," Richard said, pushed to the limit. "All that mattered was they knew it wasn't Finchley's. Born ten months after he stuck his spoon in the wall."

"Yesss," Andrew said. "I remember now. Handsome child. Saw it at the christening. Funny how all the unmarried ladies ask me to be godfather. Big. Dark hair, prominent nose. Looked a bit like you, Dick, when you was an infant. And Finchley, poor fellow, was a rather reedy, sandy blond. Wonder how Mrs. Swain would like to hear about that?"

"Oh, come off your high horse, Andrew," Richard said. "Lydia is a very sensible woman. Understands a man's failings. No reason to upset her with old gossip. Don't really see why you have it in for me anyway. *I* didn't start this wager about you."

Andrew glanced at Phyllida and was shocked by the avid gleam in her eyes. He supposed, like all women, she thrived on gossip and scandal. "What an appalling introduction to London society you've had," he said.

"Oh no," she said. "It's far more interesting than I expected."

Richard laughed. "A treasure, Andrew. You've found buried treasure in Sussex." He lifted Phyllida's hand and kissed it, turned it over and kissed the palm, touching the tip of his tongue to her warm flesh. "Don't let my brother turn your pure gold into just another brazen town idol," he whispered.

Phyllida shivered at the sensuous touch, snatching her hand back as soon as Richard freed it and shaking her head at Richard's words.

Andrew's eyes narrowed. "I'm serious, Dick," he said. "Try anything with Phyllida, anything at all, and I won't hesitate to put you out of commission."

"Is that a threat?" Richard said. "I've had just about enough of your tyrannical—"

"No," Andrew said, "it's a warning, pure and simple. Interfere with my wife, and I'll cut off next quarter's allowance, staked or not."

"You can't," Richard said. "I'm of age."

"You forget," Andrew said, "I'm the head of the family. This branch, at any rate. And you don't actually come into your majority until you're twenty-five. So, yes, Dick, I hold the purse strings."

In the end, properly chastened, Richard stayed to dinner. The conversation was stilted at first, the mood soured by the brothers' argument and inhibited in the presence of that most exotic of species, a lady. But slowly, over the various courses, the ambience relaxed until Phyllida was sorry to see the evening draw to a close. After a series of cryptic winks and throat-clearings and coughs, she remembered that she was supposed to leave the men alone to their port, and rose with reluctance, bidding them good night.

"NOW," RICHARD DEMANDED, "OUT WITH it. The true story of how you met Sleeping Beauty, or Cinderella, or whatever her real name is."

"Phyllida Lewis," Andrew said. "Her real name is—was—Phyllida Lewis. Her mother was reading poetry when she was born."

"You know what I mean," Richard pleaded. "D'ye know, if I'd met her first, I'd have been damn well tempted to marry her myself."

"No, you wouldn't," Andrew said. "You'd have been tempted to ruin her. And her whore of a mother would probably have helped you to it."

"So that's it." Richard nodded wisely. "Bought her off a bawd—" He choked as he found himself pulled nearly horizontal, the legs of his chair bending precariously, his neck-cloth twisted in his brother's implacable grip.

"Why," Andrew complained, "does everybody persist in starting false and hurtful rumors about my wife?" He released Richard, who tore his cravat loose and coughed, reaching for water.

"Damn it, Andrew," Richard said, after gulping a tumblerful. "*You* called her mother a whore."

"I'm sorry," Andrew said. "It's true. I'm becoming sensitive, you see. First the mother, then this trouble between— then this wager. Can't it be stopped?"

"What trouble?" Richard asked.

Andrew explained at length, with much recitation of detail and many amusing phrases in French, about the misunderstanding with Mme. Argonne.

"That's very interesting," Richard said when Andrew had finished. "But what's the trouble between you and the beautiful Phyllida? Please don't choke me again or shoot me or throw me out. I can see it. Every time you looked at her over dinner I thought you were going to tear her clothes off and ravish her right here on the table. And she seemed to be both scared that you would and rather more scared that you wouldn't."

Andrew sighed. "I wish you were right," he said.

"About what?"

"That she wanted me."

Richard took the bottle of port and poured another glass. "You'd better tell me everything," he said. "If you want to put it right, whatever it is, you'll have to tell me the truth."

PHYLLIDA SAT AT HER BOUDOIR table, her hair tied back loosely, just to keep it out of her face. She realized the men might emerge from the dining room and expect more conversation or a game of cards before tea was brought in, but she had the impression the brothers were holed up for a long talk—probably about her. So she had come upstairs and taken out her work, the first time she had had a chance since her mother had told her of Andrew's "proposal."

She was wearing her old chamber robe, tattered and frayed, ink-stained and grubby. Nan had been near tears when she pulled it out of the trunk and Phyllida had insisted on keeping it. It was her writing costume, the only thing she could feel comfortable in to think, to formulate sentences and paragraphs, pages and chapters. She had had to sneak it into her trunk, as her mother's reaction to the hideous object had been similar to Nan's but more forcefully expressed.

Phyllida sighed with contentment, took a sip of wine, and dipped her pen in the ink. This was why she had accepted the arrangement. Not to be married and away from home, nor even to be with her ideal man—after all, look at what a disaster that had turned out to be. No, it was to have this luxury, to lock herself in her room, sip a ladylike glass of expensive wine, just enough to lubricate the creative juices, and write. No interruptions, no distractions. No sisters wanting to sleep, no Mr. Coulter pawing her and trying to get under her skirts while her mother deliberately left the two of them alone in the room. No housekeeping chores to be shared because there was only Jenny and old Ned Hurriman, whom they all used to joke about, poor man, because he was so gnarled with arthritis that "Hurry, man" was more of a constant command than a description. Poor old fellow. Having to work for his few shillings a year when he ought to have been at home by the fire with someone to wait on him.

Well, it was all in the way of being remedied now. Her family could hire someone younger. They could hire an extra maidservant as well, and Ned could have a pension with some of Andrew's money.

She had a moment of blinding tears, thinking of her brief moment of infatuation, the tall, elegant figure who blew into her life and so quickly changed her virginal dreams into a woman's cynical disappointment. But she wiped her eyes on the sleeve of her robe.

She could use the experience. That was the ultimate reward. These past two days had given her more material than her entire twenty-two years of country life. The shock of the wedding night and last night's rape, the bet at White's, the spiteful sister, like something out of a fairy tale, and the handsome, kind younger brother who was considered a rake because he genuinely liked women. Exactly like a story.

Her pen had dried and she dipped it again, although she would not be doing any real writing tonight. It was a ritual, a pleasurable ceremony, to sit and suck on the nib of her pen, letting the thoughts come; but for now and over the next weeks, she could only proof-read. If she wanted to free herself to start a new work, she had better get this one off to the printer as soon as possible.

She read the words of the section, finding them both curiously prescient and laughably naïve. It was as if someone else had written them a long time ago. Which was true, of course. Two months ago, when she had finished her final draft, she had been a very different person—a girl, a virgin, and with little chance of ever meeting someone she could love and hope to marry.

> "Please, sir," Melisande said. "I beg you. Do not force what should be given in love."
>
> The tall, elegant man smiled in a way that reminded Melisande of nothing so much as a wolf at the kill. "Oh," he drawled, "what a pretty speech. Don't behave like a child, Melisande. Your dear Ludovic cannot rescue you now. But if you please me, I am prepared to be generous. In fact, I may stoop to the ultimate sacrifice, and make you my wife, if your charms live up to their promise."
>
> "I would rather die," Melisande said, "than be subjected to your hateful lust, no matter how great the reward."

Lord Iskander laughed, his shoulders shaking with his barely contained mirth. "A woman of spirit, I see," he said. "Just the sort I like, to have the pleasure of breaking it. You will beg for my touch, Melisande, when I am finished with you. You will be the one to come to me, eager for the favor of my lust. It will not be hateful to you after tonight."

"I will never surrender to you," Melisande said. "If you do not let me go, it will be only my corpse you will enjoy, its pale, bloodless lips and clouded eyes, its shrunken, withered form."

"A poetess, as well as a beauty," Iskander said with a chuckle. "You will be writing verses of praise to my manhood soon enough."

"You are disgusting," Melisande said. She backed away as he came toward her, so tall and slim, his dark curls and aquiline profile strangely compelling against the pale mountain light that filtered through the one barred window of her prison.

"What are you afraid of, my dear?" he asked. "Afraid that I will ravish you? Or afraid that you will like it?" His wiry arms caught her and imprisoned her like steel bands. She twisted and writhed, unable to free herself, aware only of the unusual hardness of his flesh, the heavy breathing from his chest—and hers. When his mouth closed over hers, she was powerless to fight. She sank down under his weight, falling onto the narrow bed with a sense of inevitability, trying to cry for help but breathless, unable to form coherent sounds. "You may cry out," Iskander whispered. "No one will hear you but I. You will cry out. You will cry again and again, begging for my attentions."

Then the darkness descended, and she knew nothing more.

Well, that was a laugh. But she could barely get away with even this much. If she tried to describe the rape in detail, her book would no longer be "gothic" or a romance, but obscene, and she could be arrested. No, not even that, because Mr. Edwards would not publish it, for fear of being prosecuted. He had explained it all quite carefully in a letter accepting her first book. He was a businessman, not a clergyman or a member of Parliament. He had not lectured her on her morals, only made the important distinction between what was acceptable to print and what would bring an action for lewdness.

Phyllida lingered over the scene. People did like reading shocking, scandalous tales. Look at how something that was banned by the authorities always made a hit and was passed around surreptitiously. Two months ago she had had no choice. She hadn't known any lascivious details with which to embellish the scene, at least none that she was certain would be credible. She didn't want her story to end up in court, the target of lawsuits, but surely there was a way to imply the worst while writing only the suggestion of it. Mr. Edwards might even welcome a few minor changes if they promised to increase sales.

Once again she dipped her pen. This time she set it to the paper.

"WAIT," RICHARD SAID, DEEP INTO the second bottle of port between them. "Let me see if I follow this. You took her once on your wedding night, once the following morning, and once last night. Only the third time did she appear to enjoy it. That's when she fled to her room and locked you out and hasn't let you in since. Have I got it right?"

"In the bare facts, yes," Andrew said. "Thought I might make some sense of it by reciting it aloud, but I still don't see what went wrong."

Richard took a long gulp of the excellent port. "You truly value my help, Andrew?" he asked. "Because I'm going to have to ask you some rather pointed questions, and I don't want you ripping my head off."

Andrew sighed. "Better you," he said, "than the gossipmongers at the Brotherhood of Philander."

"You asked *them*?" Richard's eyes goggled. "You *have* taken leave of your senses. Those madge culls wouldn't know what to do with a woman if she was tied naked to the bed with instructions printed on her waist."

Andrew guffawed. "That, in fact, was one of the suggestions I received. Tying her to the bed, I mean."

"Phyllida? Those bastards said that about Phyllida? And you let them live?" Richard was on his feet, prepared to do battle.

"Sit down, brother," Andrew said. "That was when I left. Knew I wasn't getting anywhere. And yes, I let them live. Friends of mine, after all. Not their fault they don't have any idea what to do. I don't either."

"Well, then," Richard said. "Bear with me. Have to ask. First, you do know which place to put it in?"

"Oh, for God's sake, Dick!"

"Now that's what I mean," Richard complained. "Biting my head off as soon as I open my mouth. Lots of fellows, not just your sort, try the backdoor delivery, think they can get away with it. Let you in on a secret. Women hate it. There's not a woman alive who likes it, and if she says she does she's either lying, or drunk to the point of insensibility, or getting paid enough to claim she'd enjoy being hanged, drawn, and quartered if the client wanted it."

Andrew took a deep breath and closed his eyes. "Thank you," he said, "for making that matter so clear. But I have not been using the back door, as you so quaintly call it. I want an heir, remember? Now, do you have any useful ideas?"

"Got to ask more questions first," Richard said. "Still don't know where the problem is. Oh, Lord. Got another touchy one. Bound to murder me, but I can't help you if I don't know." He looked imploringly at his brother, half hoping Andrew could read his mind before he had to commit himself to words. Andrew stared implacably back at him. "You ah, that is, I assume you were able to, you know—"

This time Andrew was calm. "Oh, don't look so sick. It's a reasonable question. Although I thought the answer was obvious. Yes, Dick, I was more than adequate in that respect. In fact, I'm afraid I hurt her quite a bit the first time, but it's my understanding that's inevitable."

Richard's face lost some of its tension. "Yes, you did sound as if you performed up to your usual standard, but men tend to lie about these things, as I'm sure I don't have to tell you."

Andrew merely smiled.

"All right," Richard continued the interrogation. "What else did you do?"

"What do you mean?" Andrew asked, looking somewhat sick himself.

"You know," Richard said. "Did you kiss her? Did you suckle her breasts? Was she ready for you when you took her?"

"Yes, yes and yes," Andrew said, waving his hand. "I am not a complete ignoramus."

"Never said you were," Richard said. "I expect you'd find me far more ignorant if I wanted to take up with boys."

Andrew raised an eyebrow. "Do you, Dick? Is that what this is leading up to—payment in the form of advice in my area of expertise?"

"No, of course not. Just meant—know it ain't easy having to ask for a brother's help, however well-meaning. Want you to know I admire your grasp of other subjects."

"Yes," Andrew said, "I do have a rather firm grasp of other, related subjects. Much good it's doing me." He laughed, his voice harsh.

Richard's eyelids, which had been drooping toward half-mast, snapped open. "The little man in the boat," he said. "Did you find the little man in the boat?"

Andrew's face softened. "You are rather cup-shot, my dear," he said in gentler tones. "Time I saw you safely home."

Richard struggled to sit up straight. "Wait, Andrew. Listen. This is important. I think I know what the problem is. You didn't find the little man in the boat, did you?"

Andrew rolled his eyes to the ceiling. "No, Dick. But I did find the tall man in the coach and the medium-sized fellow on horseback."

"Stop being so infernally clever and pay attention," Richard said. "I know. I'll draw you a picture." He looked futilely around the dining room for a few seconds. "Don't you have any paper and pens?"

"A picture of what?" Andrew asked.

"No good at drawing, anyway," Richard muttered. "How about a peach? Do you have a ripe, juicy peach?"

"It's March," Andrew said.

"You must have smutty books, though. Erotica. Where do you keep— Oh. No pictures of women, I don't suppose."

Andrew had a moment of insight. "Are you trying to tell me about female anatomy?"

"Isn't that what this conversation is *for*? Well, I'll just have to describe it. What did you see when you looked up Phyllida's cunt?"

Andrew's jaw tightened and his complexion developed a strange, mottled look as most of the blood left his face. "Do you know," he said through lips that barely moved, "if you were not my brother, my spoiled youngest brother, you'd be stumbling around right now, searching for your head, which would be difficult to find because it would no longer be attached to your body."

"Oohh," Richard groaned. "I'm sorry. I don't know how else to say it. What did you see— Wait, did you even look?"

"Why would I look?" Andrew asked. "There's nothing to see. It's just a lot of mucky flesh around a hole."

"Oh. My. God," Richard exclaimed, giving each word equal emphasis. "Your poor long-suffering wife. If you had the least bit of natural curiosity, you'd have looked between your beautiful bride's legs. And what you would have seen looks sort of like a rowboat. At the front, the top of the boat, there's a little red lump. The man in the boat." He paused and leaned precariously across the table to drive home the force of his argument, speaking in loud, slurred tones when he resumed. "This is the secret to women's pleasure. Once you make friends with the little man in the boat, your wife will be so eager for your attentions you'll spend the next three months in bed. Probably expire from overexertion in a week, but it'll be worth it."

Andrew grimaced. "This has all been very educational, Dick. But as I've already said, the last time I lay with Phyllida—the time she objected to afterward—she reached the peak of pleasure. Whether her boatman was enjoying himself, I have no idea."

"How do you know?" Richard demanded. "Lots of men think they're genuine Don Juans while their poor conquests are just thrashing about hoping to get it over with."

Andrew, his eyes closed and his fingertips steepled against the awkwardness, described in detail his every recollection of Phyllida's amazing responses and his own resulting satisfaction. When he was finished, he opened his eyes to see Richard listening intently, mesmerized, a dreamy smile on his face. Andrew snapped his fingers under his brother's nose.

Richard jumped and blinked. "Have to admit, that sounds surprisingly authentic," he said. "Lady like Phyllida, a virgin the day before, wouldn't know how to act. Not convincingly."

"So," Andrew said. "That explodes your nonsensical theory."

Richard shook his head in slow motion, attempting to clear it. "Nooo," he said, "just means you were very lucky that time. Hit the spot by accident."

Andrew shrugged and rose. "Possible, I'll admit. I don't have the experience to argue it either way. But we're no closer to a solution than we were before, although we're a couple of bottles of port nearer to a splitting head. Come on, Dick. It's late, and I'd rather not waste any more time downstairs."

Richard leaned back in his chair and stared up at the blurry form of his brother. "You mean to say you're going to try again? Right now? Don't you think you ought to wait until she invites you?"

"She's my wife, Dick. I married her to have an heir, not so I could learn the finer points of rowboats and oarsmen. She can't keep me out forever. It's my right."

Richard struggled out of his chair and held on to the back as the room spun slowly around him. "No, it ain't," he said. "Ain't right. Too good for you. Won't stand by while you mistreat a beautiful, sweet lady."

"Then don't," Andrew said. "Go home. I'll have Yardley call you a chair. You're in no condition to walk."

Richard, hearing the word, settled back into his seat and closed his eyes. "Good idea," he mumbled. "I'll just close my eyes for half an hour and be on my way."

"Oh, good Lord," Andrew said. "In half an hour I'll be finished mistreating my long-suffering bride and rising for a second bout."

Richard lifted his heavy eyelids like the laborious raising of the sails on a tall-masted ship. "You what?" he said. "My God, that's it."

Andrew leaned over to help his brother back on his feet. "Yes, yes," he said. "You go home, get a good night's sleep, and tell me all about it in the morning."

Richard pushed his brother's hands away and fought for consciousness. "Look, Andrew, be honest. How long did you spend playing with her before you took the plunge?"

"How long? Damn it! I wasn't watching the clock."

"Take a guess. Fifteen minutes? Half an hour?"

"Half an hour? Are you mad? My God, even with Harry Swain I'd go soft after half an hour of fooling around for nothing."

Richard shook his head and clicked his tongue several times. "That's the price you pay, old man. Women like it slow. Very, very slow. And if she's new to the game, you have to go even slower than that."

"That's absurd," Andrew protested. "I don't believe it." He thought back to that last time, the way taunts and flailing arms had led directly to the final act, and his face grew more thoughtful. He walked to his chair and sat down.

Richard planted both elbows on the arms of his chair, rested his chin on his folded hands, and stared earnestly into his brother's face. "Going to tell you a story," he said. "First time I made love to Caroline."

"Lady Finchley?" Andrew said, curling his lip. "Must I be subjected to this?"

"Yes," Richard said. "Do you good to hear this. She taught me things—things I'd tell you, but there's no point in learning to run before you can walk. Anyway, she told me we were going to spend the entire first half of the night doing nothing but kissing. Not just on the lips, you know, but kissing." He paused to gauge the effect on his audience, but received no clues of any kind from his brother's impassive stare. "Best night I ever had. With anybody. See what I mean? Made me wait for it. But it was worth it."

Andrew fought a heroic battle to keep the smirk off his face and lost. "I felicitate you, Dick," he said. "When may I wish the two of you happy? Oh, but I forget. You are no longer spending entire nights kissing the divine Caroline, are you? And what does this have to do with me?"

"Don't you see?" Richard said. "That's what you have to do with Phyllida."

"That's impossible," Andrew said. "Even if I wanted to, I'd never keep it up all that time."

"No," Richard agreed, "most men can't. But you have to stretch things out as long as you can. Really watch the clock. Spend at least half an hour just on her breasts. God! I wish I could spend half an hour on Phyllida's—"

"Watch it, Dick." The voice was cold sober and deadly calm.

"Sorry, Andrew. Got carried away. What I wanted to say was, the most important thing is, *be gentle*." He sat back and put his hands behind his head with the air of a man who has succeeded in a dangerous but crucial enterprise. "You can kill me now if you like, but just remember, in nine months' time, it'll be thanks to me you have your heir."

Melisande awoke in the dark. She did not at first remember where she was. Then, like the new pain in her secret place, it came back to her—the feel of his hands on her, the violation, the touch of his lips. She wept, mourning the death of the innocent Melisande who had been brought here a prisoner. She was a different person now, no longer the virtuous maiden but a woman. A ruined woman.

She searched in vain in the darkness through her meager possessions, the few things Iskander had allowed her to keep. No weapon, no way to restore her good name. And the worst of it was she knew that although she did not lack the courage, she lacked the will to take her life, to do what she ought. Because Iskander had been right. She knew now what it was to lie with a man. And she wanted it. She wanted him. She was ruined, but she wanted to live.

There was a knock at the door. "Phyllida," Andrew said. "Are you awake?"

"I was just about to put out the candle," Phyllida called through the closed and locked door. "Can we talk tomorrow?"

"Please, Phyllida," Andrew said. "Talking was not exactly what I had in mind."

"I'm sorry, Andrew," Phyllida said. "I'm much too tired tonight. Perhaps I'll feel better tomorrow, after a night's rest."

She waited, wondering if she should extinguish all the candles so it would look as if she were telling the truth. It would be difficult to light them again, though, with no fire in the grate, and she was not going to start running around like a scared rabbit just because she didn't dare stand up to her husband.

She watched, fascinated and horrified, as the doorknob turned and the bolt was pushed against the lock. "Phyllida," Andrew said, louder, while trying to keep his voice to a whisper that would not be heard by the servants. "Phyllida, you are my wife. You must let me in."

"What's that, Andrew?" Phyllida called in a normal speaking voice, suitable for talking outdoors on a windy day. "I can't quite hear you through the door."

Andrew bumped the bolt against the lock, rattling the door until Phyllida was afraid it would splinter. It held, for now. "Damn it!" he shouted. "God damn it."

"Good night, Andrew," Phyllida called, keeping her voice high and cheery, although it was an effort to prevent it from shaking. "Perhaps we can talk over breakfast."

Not if I stay inspired, she thought to herself. What a luxury, to be able to work all night if she chose. She supposed she'd have to surrender to her husband eventually. It was, after all, his right. But she would hold out as long as she could. If he would only admit his fault, promise to be gentle, she was prepared to submit. Tonight, though, she wanted to jot her ideas down while they were fresh.

A door slammed down the corridor and she jumped. Was Andrew still angry or was he going out? She hoped he was leaving to find his pleasure elsewhere, like frustrated husbands the whole world over, from time immemorial. Perhaps if he found himself a friend of his own kind he would satisfy his craving for roughness and be able to make love to her tenderly the next time. She wondered what kind of men he liked. Young, she supposed. All men liked youth. But did he have a particular preference, like tall and blond, or did any handsome young man attract him?

Suppose, she mused, that when Ludovic came to Melisande's rescue and was imprisoned in turn, he too was subjected to Lord Iskander's lustful passion. Could she possibly get away with writing that? She would have to be very, very careful. Give only the slightest hints; let the reader wonder if she was really saying it. At the end, perhaps something of the truth could be revealed, but it would have to end tragically. Oh, dear. She always liked a happy ending. Putting her characters through such terrible ordeals almost required a happy ending to make the reader tolerate what came before.

She looked at the clock. Goodness! How could it be so late? She actually was tired now, ready for sleep. As she nestled into her snug little bed and blew out the last candle, she felt happy and excited at the prospect of this new direction for her work, something to pursue in the days ahead, a reward for her sacrifice.

If only, she thought.

What? her practical self inquired.

If only, the romance writer answered, *Andrew cared for me.*

PHYLLIDA ROSE LATE THE next morning, sparing herself the confrontation with Andrew she knew she could not avoid forever. After a mercifully solitary breakfast, she was waited on by first the housekeeper, then the cook, wanting to know her instructions. "Whatever you've been doing in the past should be acceptable," Phyllida replied to both formidable parties. "Mr. Carrington won't want his life turned upside down just because he's married."

Mrs. Featherstone, the housekeeper, accepted such weak-mindedness with a disapproving sniff, but the cook, a Mrs. Badger, with manners to match her name, put her hands on her hips and prepared to argue the point. "But that's just what he's done, madam, begging your pardon," she said. "Turned his life upside down. No getting around it. Now, all I'm asking is that you tell me what you want for the menu each day, and when you're having guests, and how many and—"

Phyllida held up a hand. "Did Mr. Carrington tell you all this?" she asked.

Mrs. Badger looked ready to bolt for her earth. "When he remembered," she muttered, lowering her belligerent gaze.

Phyllida laughed. "And you hoped I would be more amenable.

The fact is, Mr. Carrington hasn't confided any of these details to me, either. But if and when he does, you'll be the first to hear the news."

Mrs. Badger stared at such forthrightness. "Don't you at least want to look over the accounts?"

"Who looks them over now?" Phyllida asked. "Isn't it the housekeeper's duty?"

"That there secretary, Mr. Turner," Mrs. Badger said. "The master said he particularly wanted Mr. Turner to keep the books. But it's a woman's job, by rights. And seeing as how there's a missus now—"

"Is there a problem with the accounts?" Phyllida asked.

"Not what you'd call a problem," Mrs. Badger said. "It's just that a man, and a young one at that, don't really understand how a kitchen works."

"And you think I do?" Phyllida said with a sigh. "Well, you're right, I do. But I was hoping to forget." She smiled into the woman's red face and received an unexpected wink and smile in return.

"Hoping to live the soft life, was you, madam?" Mrs. Badger said. "Can't say I blame you. But there's no escaping some work, after all, not in this life, at any rate."

"And looking over accounts is so little compared with running a kitchen," Phyllida agreed. "Very well, I'll take a look." She accepted the proffered greasy, curled sheets with a shrug of resignation.

Mrs. Badger, delighted to find a mistress both appreciative of her labors and not too high and mighty to say so, left the interview well satisfied. "Don't know where she come from," she informed the other staff members, "nor how the master come to marry her, but she's a lady all the same."

"A real lady," Mrs. Featherstone said, "would take more of an interest in the household, instead of locking herself in her room and puttering about with pen and ink. Did you see her fingers? All over ink stains. Disgraceful. No wonder the master keeps his distance."

"Now, as to that," Yardley said, "it's my opinion the master is sore put upon. Ought to have seen his face this morning, and the day before." He shook his head. "Terrible business, this matrimony. Never thought to see the day when our Mr. Carrington fell into the snare of a scheming female."

Mr. Pumfry, Andrew's valet, who rarely mixed with the lower servants, felt bound to stand up for his master's abilities. "Mr. Carrington was not ensnared. He has merely accepted the responsibilities of being the eldest."

"Yes," Mrs. Featherstone said, "by letting himself be caught by a gold-digging, lazy wench who's no better than—"

"You mind your tongue, Betty," Mrs. Badger said. "The missus may not have been born with a silver spoon in her mouth, but she's a pleasant-spoken, friendly, decent sort, and we should be right thankful the master chose one like her instead of what he could have brought home."

"You mean that piece of street trash last week?" Mrs. Featherstone said. "For all we know, this woman is his sister."

"Oh!" Nan forgot her shyness in defense of her new mistress. "She couldn't be! Ain'tcha heard her talk? Right ladylike. I don't believe it." She gasped and hung her head after her outburst, aghast at her own boldness, forgetting that, in her new position, she had more right than most to put forth her opinion.

"I meant in spirit," Mrs. Featherstone replied to Nan. "Of course she's not actually sister to a street boy, but her motives for marrying the master, and her conduct since, bear too great a similarity, if you ask me."

"Mrs. Featherstone," Yardley said. "You forget yourself. Mr. Carrington is a man, not a plaster saint. Mrs. Carrington is his wife, and our mistress. It is not your place to be commenting on either of them."

"Hmph," Mrs. Featherstone sniffed. "All I know is, a woman who *writes* when she ought to be minding her needle or overseeing the kitchen is not my idea of a lady."

"Surely she must send letters to her family at home," Mr. Pumfry said.

"It's more than letters," Mrs. Featherstone said. "Mr. Turner told me she's writing a book, a novel."

There was general consternation. "A *what*?" "No!" "How'd *he* know?"

"Had it put into the marriage contract," Mrs. Featherstone said, the thrill of holding inside knowledge leading her to forget her status and sink to the level of gossiping chambermaid. "Said if she couldn't write her books she'd rather stay *Miss Lewis*."

Yardley shook his head in his dour manner. "The master would never permit anything so improper," he said. "You must have misunderstood."

"I know what I heard," Mrs. Featherstone insisted. "Mr. Turner said she doesn't use her real name, so the master agreed to it. But it makes you wonder all the same."

"Indeed it does," Mr. Yardley said.

PHYLLIDA, IGNORANT OF THE DISCUSSION taking place below stairs, took a quick look into the kitchen accounts, just enough to see that the expenses for one month for this household of twenty were enough to have fed, clothed, and paid the rent for her family of four for a year. Produce and meat were certainly far more dear in

London than in the country, but even so, there were some very odd sums tacked on at the end of each week, in a different hand from the listings for flour and tea, butter and eggs, fruit and veg, milk and cheese. She stuck her tongue out at the accounts and shoved them under a pile of proofs. She had not contracted this marriage merely to become a housewife on a grand scale. This tiresome business would have to wait until the more important matter of her book was concluded.

Happily ensconced in her boudoir, Phyllida was again engaged in the questionable and regrettable practice of her art when Andrew knocked at the door. He was in a surprisingly good mood.

"Feeling better today?" he asked, entering at her nod.

"Yes, of course," Phyllida answered, remembering belatedly she had claimed to be too tired to accept Andrew's husbandly overtures last night. "That is, so long as I keep to my chamber."

Andrew accepted the correction without comment. "How have you been occupying yourself?"

Phyllida smiled up at him. "As you see. Writing. Or at least proofreading." She resisted the impulse to stash all her incriminating prose under the blotter. Nothing would more pointedly call attention to it, whereas leaving it out in the open would arouse little suspicion. Still, it took the greatest willpower to leave the scenes describing rape, scandalous pleasures, and deadly passions lying face-up. She rested one elbow on the worst of them, as if pausing in the act of editing.

Andrew frowned. He had disliked the idea of marrying an authoress from the start, and had hoped that with her dawning awareness of the change in her circumstances, Phyllida would no longer be driven by the compulsion. Whatever her claims to enjoy writing for its own sake, surely, as the duties and, with any luck, pleasures of married life became routine for her, they would supersede this masculine and plebeian obsession. "Yes, I do see," he said. "Your fingers are as black as a chimney sweep's prick."

Phyllida laughed off Andrew's shamefaced apology for the simile and held up her hands with a sigh. "Mama was always scolding me. I've tried vinegar, and lemon juice is so hard to come by. The only thing that really works is lye soap, and that takes the skin off along with the ink."

"Never mind," Andrew said. "Perhaps this will provide an incentive to cleanliness. I ought to have given it to you before." He held out a worn leather box.

Phyllida opened it. Inside was an antique gold ring, plain and unadorned. A wedding band. Phyllida picked it up and examined it in the palm of her hand. "It's lovely," she said, running the tip of a finger around the smooth outer surface. "Are you sure you want me to have it?"

"It was my mother's," Andrew said. "It was meant for me to give to my bride. I simply forgot. Go ahead, try it on. Let's see if it needs to be adjusted."

Phyllida slipped it over her ring finger. It slid easily, needing only a little push over the inner knuckle. "It's perfect," she said. "Thank you. Let me return your signet." She went into the bedroom to find her pocket, where she had left the large ring. Andrew followed her, still talking.

"Funny," he said, his eyes focused far away. "My mother was about six inches taller than you, but with the slenderest limbs and fingers. That ring had to be tightened for her so as not to fall off, or so she claimed."

"I suppose you all take after her," Phyllida said. "Were you very close?"

"Good Lord, no," Andrew said, coming out of his dream with a start. "She handed each of us over to the wet nurse at birth, and allowed us a ten-minute visit once a day, if we were good. I was always very naughty indeed."

"Poor Andrew," Phyllida said, trying for a light tone but feeling her heart bleed for the neglected little boy.

"Nonsense," he said. "Don't start getting romantic notions and putting me into those novels of yours. I had an excellent nanny. Millie loved me like her own child. It's the way of the fashionable world. You'll do the same."

Phyllida stared in horror. She had not thought this far ahead. "No," she said. "I won't hand my child over to a stranger."

Andrew laughed. "When you have a child, you'll see. You won't want to spoil your figure and ruin your gowns. And you certainly won't be able to write with a howling infant at your breast."

Phyllida shook her head. No point in arguing about something that might never happen, and was months away even if it did. "I shall want help, of course," she said. "But I could never just ignore my own child."

"Assuming, of course, that you intend at some point to allow me the opportunity to give you one," Andrew said, moving to the bed and sprawling his long body the length of it. "What do you say, wife of mine? Am I forgiven for my sins? May I hope to live in your good graces once more?"

"Of course, Andrew," Phyllida answered without thinking. "What, do you mean now? In the daytime?"

"Why not?" Andrew said, lifting an eyebrow. "The door, as has been demonstrated most thoroughly, has a secure lock."

Phyllida blushed deeply and charmingly. "Oh, dear," she said. "I never thought myself prudish, but—"

"But you are embarrassed to make love with your husband when there is light enough to see each other. This from a woman who allowed—nay, encouraged—me to take her virginity in a room lined with mirrors, including on the ceiling. No, my dear, it won't wash." He stretched out a hand. "Come. I will not hurt you. We will go very slowly." He might actually enjoy this, he thought. An interesting experiment. See what all those theories of his brother's added up to.

Phyllida approached the bed as if it were a Hindu funeral pyre and she the widow. Andrew looked so formidable, lying with his long legs extending beyond the end of the bed, his boots resting on the footboard. He dominated the bed as he did her, as he did everything. As she moved closer, staring despite her best intentions at his groin, where a visible swelling was growing, he deliberately moved his hand over it, stroking. "You see, my dear?" he whispered. "I want you more than ever, now that you have denied me twice. Can you honestly say you don't want me just a little, hmm?"

Phyllida shook her head. He read her thoughts, she was sure of it. She felt that he looked right through her head, or was it her heart, or someplace lower down, and knew her mingled fear and longing for a repetition of that great pleasure of the other night. "I'm afraid," she said, yet all the time moving closer.

His hand grabbed hers and pulled her to the bed. "Was I rough with you before? I am sorry. You will find me a slow, gentle ride today, I promise." He was undoing his cravat and loosening his pantaloons all the time with his free hand as he cajoled and soothed. His hand on hers gripped like a vise, pulling her in until she was sitting beside him. He sat up and nibbled at her earlobe. "If I hurt you, you must tell me. In fact, I won't do anything until you tell me you want it. How's that?"

His hand traveled over her breasts with the lightest of caresses through the fabric of her gown. Phyllida felt her nipples stiffening. That place between her legs grew tight in some way, as if it were swelling like Andrew's member, engorged with blood. She let out her breath in what was supposed to be a silent exhale but turned without control into a low moan.

"Do you like that?" he asked. "Do you want more?"

"Yes," Phyllida said. "No. Oh, Andrew, why do you do this to me?"

The strange question broke the mood. "Why? Why do you think? You are my wife. I want you to bear my child."

"Then why not just—"

"What? Take you without pleasure?" He lay back on the pillows, his hands behind his head. "Because, my dear, you seem to have developed a habit of locking me out. And I rather thought, correct me if I am wrong, that you had some pleasure in our last time together, despite your subsequent rejections."

Phyllida stared at her lap. "I did," she said, her voice so low Andrew had to strain to catch the words. "But I don't believe that justifies rape."

"Rape?" Andrew shouted. "There's no such thing as rape between husband and wife."

"Not in law, I know," Phyllida said. "But when a man forces himself on a woman, whether his wife or a stranger, it is the same to her."

"Forces himself?" He caught himself repeating her words, and sat up again, as if the vertical posture would clear his head. "When have I forced myself on you?"

"The other night," Phyllida muttered. "I was not ready."

Andrew bit back the words he was about to fling at her. What did *she* have to do? he wanted to ask. *He* was the one who had to get hard—

for a woman—and maintain the erection long enough to penetrate, and keep going until he came and spilled his seed in her. All *she* had to do was lie back, spread her legs, and let him do the work. But what did he know? Hell, he was the one who had never even heard of the little man in the boat. He sighed. "Forgive me, Phyllida," he forced the false words out. "I see I have much to learn about women."

Phyllida jumped up from the bed and moved back toward the boudoir. "I am sorry, too, Andrew," she said. "But please, can you give me a little more time to prepare myself?"

"It will not be so agonizing an execution," Andrew murmured. "The sword, at any rate, not the ax or the rope."

His tone made her laugh. "You really are very kind," she said. "I promise I will try to be brave. Just let us wait until tonight."

"You shall have a reprieve," Andrew said, "if not a full pardon. I shan't disturb you tonight. I will be attending the theater."

Phyllida turned from the door. "Oh yes?" she said. "What a treat!"

"Do you wish to accompany me?" Andrew asked. "Perhaps you have another engagement?"

"How could I?" Phyllida said. "I don't know anyone here except Sir Frederick and his sister, Mrs. Rathbone. And your sister and brother of course, and I understand you don't wish me to become overly friendly with Richard." She frowned. "Do you not want me to come with you?"

Andrew, used to making his plans without the need to consult anyone else, had not considered the changes that a wife would entail. He had his own motive for going to the play tonight, one that did not involve Phyllida. Yet always, in the background, was this curst wager, and the reasons for marrying in the first place. It would do him good to show her off to the fashionable world, or that small portion of it that might choose to go to a performance of a dull tragedy by actors most of whom were unknown.

He relented at her wistful look. "Of course you're welcome to come with me," he said. "It's only that it's a rather tiresome play—Shakespeare."

"But you see," Phyllida said, "I am not so jaded by years of town life. It would be of interest to me whether it is high tragedy enacted by a classically trained troupe or low farce by traveling mountebanks. Shakespeare is a rare delight. I have read all his plays, and the sonnets."

Andrew dared to come closer. He ran a casual finger down her cheek. "A scholar of English," he murmured, "if not of French."

Phyllida blushed at the tone and the touch. "I studied both, you know. It's not my fault I had no one to practice the French with."

Andrew blinked. "I intended no criticism," he said. "Most young women wouldn't have bothered to study anything but gossip and husband-hunting, if left to their own devices."

"I suppose you think young men would do better," she said in a challenging tone.

"Not at all," Andrew said. "It's why we need an army, with or without Bonaparte. No, I meant you showed admirable discipline in your situation."

"It was not discipline," Phyllida said. "I enjoyed it. Even though I cannot write on Shakespeare's level, or even close, I still appreciate great literature."

Andrew laughed to cover his inconvenient sympathy. "You won't be seeing great literature tonight, I'm afraid. Merely *Romeo and Juliet*. But the actors are superb. Now, what have you to wear?"

THEY MADE QUITE AN ENTRANCE. The theater was full, despite Andrew's deprecating remarks. The troupe was on the cusp of fame, and the leading pair, a brother and sister team, were both handsome and talented. Andrew and Phyllida arrived fashionably late, well into the first act. The audience, once the newcomers were recognized, turned around to watch the rather more diverting spectacle of the appearance of, until recently, London's most notorious and entrenched bachelor and the woman who had managed to capture his heart, or at least his name and his purse.

They were not disappointed. Andrew, at his most elegant, wore the pale pantaloons and glossy black Hessian boots that had recently become de rigueur for men of fashion at all but the most formal of gatherings. His dark blue coat of superfine cloth fit him to perfection. Phyllida had already noted how, despite his lanky frame, there was no need to pad the shoulders of his coat or flesh out the calves of his tight pantaloons. His muscles were clearly defined through the tailored garments, and his appearance was one of lithe, potent masculinity. His dark curls, too springy for the "Brutus," cropped too short for the "windswept," brushed into a perfect compromise between the two styles, caught the light and gleamed.

Phyllida, lost at first in the shadow of her husband's brilliance, was passed over. But when people comprehended that the small young lady on Andrew's arm had to be the new bride, they declared themselves captivated by her mix of country freshness and youthful grace. In consultation with Nan and Andrew, Phyllida had determined that the sheer net overdress of Mme. Argonne's diabolical efforts could be worn with perfect modesty over one of her old opaque underskirts. The color, a soft pink, set off her rosy complexion perfectly, and blended well with the light brown of her hair. This latter, dressed in Grecian style, bound in place with a pink ribbon wrapped twice around her head, curls tumbling down from a topknot, gave her an inch or two of height and added greatly to the modish effect. Nan had wanted to cut it, but Andrew insisted she leave it long. "It is lovely hair," he said, "and there is no point in chopping it off just to blend in with the town beauties. You will stand out this way, and begin to make your reputation as a lady who is not afraid to set her own style."

As they took their seats in Andrew's box, heads nodded in their direction, quizzing glasses were raised and lowered, and a buzz of conversation quite put a stop to the action onstage. The players, deciding not to compete with a greater entertainment, merely held their positions until the hubbub had died down. In the expectant pause before resuming, the man playing Romeo bowed ever so slightly in Andrew's direction. Phyllida would not have been sure of what she had seen except that Andrew, catching the gesture, raised his fingers to his lips and kissed them, then stretched his arm out in the direction of the young blond actor.

Phyllida settled in happily to enjoy the show, and was surprised by the swift arrival of the first interval. "Will you walk with me, or let visitors come to us?" Andrew asked, standing up.

"Walk, I think," Phyllida said. She wished only for the play to resume, but acknowledged that stretching her legs would be beneficial.

It was not to be. "Oh, if I had known you were to be here, we would have sat with you instead of enduring the tedium of Uncle Francis." Lizzie Fanshawe rushed in, all lace and silk, rustles and flutters of her fan. "But Wilt swore you would not be so naughty as to neglect Juliet's charms for Romeo's so soon."

"Now Lizzie, my love," a rotund young man a few inches shorter than his wife protested, "don't go repeating every remark I make in the privacy of my own home."

"Oh, pooh," Lady Fanshawe retorted, "Phyllida is not such a ninnyhammer as to misunderstand the nature of her marriage."

"Oughtn't to talk like that in front of Mrs. Carrington," Fanshawe muttered, accustomed to having his opinions ignored and disregarded, but intent on stating them anyway, perhaps for his own self-respect. "Oughtn't to talk like that at all. *We* don't know the nature of the marriage." He bowed to Phyllida. "Mrs. Carrington? Pleased to make your acquaintance. As you may have surmised, I am the fortunate swain who captured the heart of your husband's beautiful sister."

"Not the way I would have put it, old fellow," Andrew drawled, "but a most diplomatic turn of phrase. Phyllida, my dear, allow me to present Wilton, Lord Fanshawe, to whom I will be eternally indebted for relieving me of the necessity of enduring Lizzie's chatter."

Lady Fanshawe appeared delighted with the respective views of her husband and brother. "Andrew loves to play the stern head of the family," she said. "And all the time he criticizes us for indulging ourselves, he does exactly as he pleases. Why, even in marriage he has moaned about duty and obligations, until we were quite sure he would bring home a superannuated, dried-up spinster, instead of— Well, as you see."

"Indeed," was Fanshawe's sole comment. As if only his wife's encomium had caused him to notice Phyllida's considerable physical allure, he raised his glass and began a slow perusal of his new sister-in-law, starting not at her face but at her bosom, which tonight, while decently covered, compared to the original design of the outer garment, managed to expose a great expanse of round, smooth pink-and-white flesh in the accepted style for evening wear. "Indeed," he repeated more enthusiastically.

Andrew raised his own glass and glared with the magnified eye at his brother-in-law. "I will thank you, Fanshawe," he said, "not to ogle my wife as if she were a mare at Tattersall's." He paused while Fanshawe slowly looked up. "But I forget that you are accustomed to treating my entire family as mere off-season extensions of the races at Newmarket."

"What?" Fanshawe said. He blinked, his attention caught somewhere between Phyllida's cleavage and the distinctly menacing tone of Andrew's voice. "What's that you say?"

"Just this," Andrew said. "I can't help it if you start improper and disgusting wagers about me. But I will not permit you to make Mrs. Carrington the object of your sordid and repellent amusements. And brother-in-law or not, I will enforce my wishes, if not with the pistol then with the whip. Do I make myself clear?"

"Now see here," Fanshawe said. His face grew an alarming shade of deep red and his chest swelled as the offensive tone sank in. "*I'm* not the one with the reputation for—"

"Think very carefully before you complete that sentence," Andrew said. "Much as it would pain me to be forced to call you out, it would pain me more to have Lizzie back on my hands as a widow. But I will do whatever is necessary to protect my wife from the scandal-mongering of loose fish and town wits."

"Andrew!" Lady Fanshawe interjected. "*Please* don't start a quarrel with Wilt. Indeed it was not his fault about the wager. All he did was tell them about the marriage. *He* couldn't help it that they wrote it in the betting book. *You* know what it's like at White's. All one has to do is mention the most innocuous thing and right away they're betting on it, at least that's what Wilt says. And you *must* realize that your marriage is *not* innocuous, but so *very* interesting to everybody. Indeed, I was all set to wager on it myself until I found out—" She thought better of this line of conversation and broke off, contenting herself with a warning: "And if you do call Wilt out, you won't have me on your hands, because I will shoot you myself for being so provoking."

Fortunately, the play resumed at this moment. Phyllida watched enthralled. Although the drama enacted by her new family was perhaps more heartfelt and spontaneous than the pallid story onstage, the players had the edge when it came to style, except perhaps for her husband. But she could see him anytime. She had been to two professionally acted plays in her life, during her season four years ago, and she had never seen something performed that she had read and studied. The two principals, the brother and sister, were young enough to be convincing in the title roles, while possessed of the eloquence that gave their speeches a poignancy rarely projected by untrained youths. Despite the contrived story, the strange Renaissance-style costumes, and the creaky plot machinations, Phyllida found herself near tears when the curtain came down for the second interval.

"Enjoying yourself?" Andrew noticed her rapt expression.

"Oh, yes!" she looked up at his face. "Juliet makes me remember just what it was like at that age—assuming one were brave enough to disregard all conventional morality. And the actor who plays Romeo—he makes me believe he loves her so much he would die rather than live without her."

"If you like," Andrew said, "I will introduce you after the play is finished."

Phyllida expressed her delight and, at the conclusion, once the actors had taken their final bows and the curtain had come down for the last time, Andrew led her by a circuitous route to the dressing room, knocked, and said simply, "It's me." The door was flung open at once and a hard young male body, shirtless and with a towel wrapped around his head, threw himself into Andrew's open arms. The young man pressed his lips to Andrew's and twined one leg around Andrew's hips, and seemed intent on completing as much of the sexual act as two men could while wearing breeches and standing up. The other actors in the room went about their business quickly and drifted out.

Phyllida watched, the blood rushing to her face and her breath coming in short little gasps. She should look away, she told herself, or say something, but she did neither. She was only vaguely aware that her secret place, the one Andrew had brought to so frightening a peak of ecstasy, was again engorged, almost throbbing, just at the sight of her husband and the handsome actor embracing.

The young man wiggled his hips against Andrew's. "Ouch!" Andrew pulled away an inch or two. "Now I know why they call it a prick."

"Oh, my love, I'm sorry," the actor said. "It's this blasted codpiece. You know, I was never so grateful for this ridiculous costume until tonight. When I saw you come in I was that pleased, the front rows would have seen more than they bargained for if it weren't for this contraption."

"Ought to play without it," Andrew murmured. "You could sell out the house for months. Of course you'd have all the madges and mollies and high impures sitting in the pit with their tongues hanging out."

Phyllida tried to smother her laughter, but too late. The two men broke their embrace and turned to her, the younger man's mouth forming a perfect circle.

"Rhys, my dear," Andrew said, stroking the man's cheek and tucking a wisp of hair under the towel, "allow me to present my wife. Phyllida, this is Rhys Powyl, who plays Romeo so credibly. Rhys, say hello to Mrs. Carrington."

The young actor found himself, for the first time he could remember since infancy, speechless. Once he recollected his training, however, he came through like a trouper. "I heard rumors that Andrew had married," he said, smiling and bowing in his best stage manner—the broad, toothy grin and the outstretched hand. "But if I had known that Andrew had captured Venus herself for his bride, I would not have welcomed him so warmly. Say you forgive me, dear goddess."

Phyllida laughed and held out her hand. "There is nothing to forgive, Mr. Powyl. I am delighted that Andrew has such an interesting friend. You are a wonderful Romeo. I cried at the end, even knowing it was all pretense." Her eyes shone, and a soft smile curved the corners of her mouth.

Rhys turned to Andrew, put his hands on his hips, and confronted him like a scolding fishwife. "What are you doing," he demanded, "exposing this goddess to the profane stares of every rake and wastrel in the town? God, Andrew, take her home before she finds her own Adonis." He leaned back toward Phyllida, winked, and said, "You must know, I spend my life in delightful vacillation between the rival delights of Venus and Mars."

Andrew sneered. "That's the first I've heard of it. Never knew you even to flirt with your leading ladies—other than Gladys, of course."

Rhys laughed. "Let me say, then, that meeting Mrs. Carrington has led me to reconsider. You are a very lucky man and a very wicked one, to marry such beauty and such charm and not to value her as she deserves."

"How do you know," Andrew said, "that I do not value Phyllida as she deserves?"

"If you did," Rhys replied, "you would not kiss me like that in front of her."

"But, my dear," Andrew purred, "*you* kissed *me*."

A connecting door opened and the young woman who played Juliet came in, also with a towel around her hair and wearing only her shift, exposing a surprisingly sturdy body compared to the waiflike Juliet that Phyllida had wept for. "Hello, Andrew," she said. "Rhys and I did not expect to see you again." She smiled at her brother. "You go on, then, enjoy yourself. I'll have supper with the others." She looked Phyllida over with unconcealed interest before turning to go.

"Gladys," Rhys said. "You should pay your respects to Mrs. Carrington." He added something in a guttural language.

The young woman stood, like her brother, temporarily amazed, as the introductions were made. "Mrs. Carrington?" she said. "I heard the gossip, but we all thought—" She completed her remarks in the same odd language her brother had just used.

"Don't," Rhys warned his sister. "Whatever we thought, we had no business to think it. Mrs. Carrington is most gracious."

"Miss Powyl," Phyllida said, hoping to bring the subject back to the more manageable one of theater, "I told your brother, but it's just as true for you. You were so real, it made me cry. Even though I know the story is silly. You both have an extraordinary gift."

"You are very kind," the woman said. Her voice, like her brother's, was warm and resonant, lilting with a singsong quality. "We shall be doing *Henry V* next, if we do well enough with this play to earn a second week. Our contribution to patriotic fervor."

"Oh!" Phyllida clapped her hands and bounced up and down like a child. "Oh, Andrew! May we come? Please?"

Rhys and Gladys caught each other's eyes and smiled. "A connoisseur," Rhys said. "Have you seen much theater, Mrs. Carrington? Sarah Siddons? Edmund Kean?"

Phyllida blushed and shook her head. "No, this was only the third play I saw in my life. I'm sorry. I suppose all these extravagant compliments don't mean much when I have no basis for comparison."

"It is the greatest compliment of all," Gladys said, "that we moved you. If you enjoyed our performance so much that you came back here to tell us so, and expressed genuine desire to see us in one of those tedious and bloodthirsty history plays, that is high praise indeed."

"Tedious?" Phyllida was aghast. "How can you say so? How can you wish to act in it if that's what you think?"

"You must know," Andrew said, "my wife may not have had much opportunity to attend the theater, but she is definitely a connoisseur of Shakespeare."

"A muse as well as a goddess," Rhys said. "I warn you Andrew, I am in danger of falling very hard."

"Rhys," Gladys said in a low voice. "Be careful."

"Yes," Andrew drawled, "be extremely careful. If you wish to come to supper with us you will have to be very cautious and discreet."

Rhys backed away, his eyes widening in genuine fear. "I'm sorry, Andrew. You know I talk a good game, but that really is not my style at all. Forgive me, Mrs. Carrington. You are a lovely lady and I shall hope to see you next week when I change from lovesick Romeo to Harry the King, but I prefer to entangle myself with but one lover at a time."

"I fear you have misinterpreted the situation, Rhys," Andrew said, his deep voice ominous. "Mrs. Carrington and I have an understanding. I did not invite you to anything more or less improper than our previous evenings."

Rhys laughed, his relief giving it the sound of a sob. "God, I do keep putting my foot in it." He turned to Phyllida. "Are you sure you don't mind?"

Phyllida held up her hands and removed the glove from her right. "As you see, Mr. Powyl," she said, "I am not a goddess, nor even a muse, but an ink-stained wretch. A writer—not of tragedy or lyric poetry but gothic romance. I would be delighted if you accepted our invitation to supper. Afterward I intend to work."

"Yes," Andrew said, "now you know the true scandal. I have married an authoress. With luck, marriage will cure her eventually."

"There is no cure for art," Rhys said. "Only death."

"Then I'm safe," Phyllida said. "I don't write art."

"Perhaps in that case," Gladys said as she bade them good-night, "you are a playwright."

"God help me," Andrew said.

THE SUPPER WAS MERRIER even than yesterday's dinner with Richard. Rhys, relaxed and cheerful now that the state of affairs had been made clear, was as entertaining on the small stage of the Carrington dining room as he had been at the Drury Lane playhouse. Over the course of the simple meal, made longer and convivial by a copious flow of wine, he told of the tour the troupe was embarking on, regaled them with scandalous tales of the intrigues of the other players and their suitors, would-be lovers, and internecine amours, and recited many famous speeches and others less well known. Phyllida was in transports, clapping and shouting bravo at his every turn.

Softened by wine and admiration, Rhys encouraged Phyllida to shine. "Surely, Phyllida," he said, the two of them having long since agreed on the use of first names, "such a scholar of the Bard has committed some speeches to memory."

Phyllida admitted shyly that she had, turning her eyes to Andrew, who nodded, a fond smile on his lips. "Go ahead, my dear."

Phyllida stood up, pushed back her chair, raised one arm, and launched into a loud declamation of Henry V's St. Crispin's Day speech, taking the two men so by surprise they laughed until the tears ran. Phyllida stopped in mid-exhortation. "Now I see," she said. "You were mocking me."

Rhys took her hand and kissed it. "No, no, dear lady," he said, wiping his eyes with his other hand. "It's just—the contrast, you see. So gentle and sweet you are, such a soft, rounded beauty, and the speech is that of a warrior, a king, battle-worn and desperate."

"And the delivery was so poor I could not make you forget the body to hear the meaning," Phyllida sighed. "I was not meant to be an actress."

"Thank God for small mercies," Andrew muttered.

"Now, now," Rhys said. "Even the most talented of us do not start with so challenging a role, or expect to prevail at Agincourt on our first performance. Perhaps you know something more feminine—Ophelia, say."

Phyllida shook her head. "I never liked that part," she said. "I like the fighters, not the pitiful ones."

"Kate the Shrew?" Andrew drawled. "Must know that by heart."

"Andrew," Rhys chided, "we all know you are the perfect Petruchio, but let us have harmony in the house tonight."

Andrew raised his little finger, kissed it, and gestured at Rhys, but smiled and said nothing.

"How about Lady Macbeth," Rhys said. "You already have the stained hand."

Andrew groaned. "I thought we wanted peace, not bloody murder."

"I know," Phyllida said. "Not a play, but a sonnet." She stood with her eyes shut for a long minute, breathing slowly, recalling the bitter words in their graceful phrasings. She had the audience to appreciate it tonight, at least one man who would comprehend the poet's acrimonious views, as she had not been fully able to until her marriage. She opened her eyes, focused on a piece of wood paneling, held her arms loose at her sides, and began in a controlled, slow intonation, pitched noticeably lower than her speaking voice, "Th'expense of spirit in a waste of shame / Is lust in action."

There was a surprised and harsh intake of breath, a gentle shushing. She did not look up or break her rhythm to see how the men reacted. She did not care. She would see if she could carry it through to the end. "All this the world well knows; yet none knows well / To shun the heaven that leads *women* to this hell." She changed the one word, to see how Andrew took it. The silence was so profound she thought she had put her audience to sleep or that Andrew was so angry he could not show it in front of his friend. She bowed her head, nodded once, and sat down.

Rhys burst into applause, and Andrew followed suit. "Magnificent," Rhys said at last. "Absolutely magnificent."

Phyllida turned to Andrew to see if he shared this opinion. He was staring at her, an odd look in his eyes. "Yes, my love," he said when applied to. "You were extraordinary. I never imagined a woman to say it with such conviction. To say it at all. And you changed the ending—did you catch that, Rhys?" The actor shook his head. He knew plays, not private verses. "I will tell you later. But Phyllida, what made you commit *that* poem to memory?"

Phyllida shook her head. "I don't know. I was fascinated by it the first time I read it, as a young girl. I didn't understand it, but I was struck by its resentful, angry quality, so different from a simple lovers' quarrel. And now that I am married, it seemed somehow appropriate."

Andrew's voice cracked with what might have been laughter. "There, you see how I am put in my place?"

The clock chimed midnight and they startled. "The witching hour," Rhys said. He looked meaningfully at Andrew.

Phyllida took the hint. "Goodness! I lost track." She stood and held out her hand as the two men rose. "Forgive me for overstaying, Andrew."

Andrew took his wife's hand and bowed over it. "No, my dear," he murmured. "Do not think that. I never expected to so enjoy an evening with my wife. It is a pity you must leave us."

Phyllida shivered. It was almost, she thought, as if Andrew really did want to keep her here along with Rhys, as if, despite his protestations, something about the situation excited him. She looked to the blond young man where he stood in front of his chair, waiting for her to leave the room so he could be at ease again. "Good night—Rhys," she said. "Thank you for the most enjoyable evening I have had in my life. I do hope I will see you as Henry V." She removed her hand from her husband's strong grip and fled to the door.

Andrew stood staring after her a long minute. "Oh, God," he groaned. "I thought I would explode under the table." He beckoned to Rhys.

Rhys put his hand over his lover's erection. "You *are* ready," he said, admiration in his voice. "Can you make it upstairs or—"

"No," Andrew said. "And yes. Right here. Now."

Rhys sank to his knees and gently, deftly, opened the flap, releasing the long, swollen cock. "Beautiful," he said with a sigh. He kissed and licked for a few pleasurable moments but, mindful of Andrew's urgent need, he soon took the length in his supple throat.

PHYLLIDA PAUSED OUTSIDE THE DINING room door before moving to the stairs. She knew she shouldn't listen, must not become the kind of wife who spied on her husband. But she couldn't seem to help it. Something about the whole evening had left her agitated, more than the entertaining conversation and the rousing recitations. Her heart was pounding, her breath was rapid and shallow, and she was sweating, although the house was kept quite cool.

There were no sounds from the dining room, at least nothing resembling speech. A low noise that might have been a groan, a faint gulping or swallowing. She forced herself to turn away and walk upstairs to her room. It was late, but perhaps she could do an hour of work.

Nan, tousled and bleary, woke from her doze in the chair by the boudoir door. "Had a good evening then, madam?" she asked.

"Wonderful!" Phyllida said. "But you mustn't wait up so late. You'll be exhausted."

"I don't mind," Nan said. "I'd like— Would you tell me about the play?"

Phyllida outlined the bare bones of the plot as Nan helped her out of the improvised gown and let down her hair.

"They killed themselves?" Nan asked. "For love?"

"Silly, isn't it," Phyllida agreed. "But the way the actors did it, you believed it. You felt that they had no choice, that their passions were that strong."

"Italians," Nan said.

Phyllida laughed. "That's true. But I think it's meant to be universal. To show us a side of ourselves that might emerge if we were in the same situation."

"I never would kill myself for love of some boy," Nan scoffed.

"No, I can't imagine doing that either," Phyllida confessed. "But it was beautiful to watch. Made me cry."

"Over a story?"

Phyllida shrugged. "That's the point of stories. To move us, whether to tears or laughter. If they don't, the writer has failed. Of course, some people think *Romeo and Juliet* isn't supposed to make us cry for the young lovers, but make us feel as you do, that they were foolish children who disobeyed their parents and reaped the reward of sin. But when you watch it performed as this troupe does it, you forget everything except the love."

There were footfalls in the corridor, male voices murmuring too loud and shushing each other emphatically, making even more of a racket. "Who's that, then?" Nan asked, eyes agog.

"Oh, Mr. Carrington invited the lead actor to supper. That's why I'm so late. We had such a good time, and he was so clever, reciting speeches from all the plays, and telling us—a lot of things he probably shouldn't."

Nan stared at her mistress. "He's staying the night? With the master?"

"Yes, of course," Phyllida said. "They're old friends, it seems. You must have seen him here before."

"No," Nan said with regret. "I never saw nothing before, in the scullery."

ANDREW AWOKE A COUPLE OF hours later, soft blond hair tickling his nose, a man's arm draped over his chest. For one painful moment he thought, *Harry*—then remembered. He smoothed the hair down and ran his hand along Rhys's bristly cheek, already needing the morning shave. The greasy remains of the cream the actor had used to remove his makeup were congealing at the hairline. Rhys really was very sweet, he thought. Pity the troupe will only be in town another week or so.

He didn't feel sad, though. It seemed just right. A week's interlude of pleasure while Phyllida prepared herself for the ordeal of having him make love to her. *Th'expense of spirit in a waste of shame.* Was that really how she saw it? He stroked the young man to the beginnings of arousal and slid slowly down in the bed until he could take the cock in his mouth.

Rhys fluttered his eyes and came to life. "Boyo," he said, "the nicest way to wake a man of any I know, it is." The Welsh came through rarely, as when half-awake, or at the height of pleasure. "Although I imagine you'll be wanting one of your rough rides after. Try to leave me capable of strutting the stage, love. An athletic part, it is, Romeo."

Andrew took his mouth from Rhys just long enough to say, "You know you want it, slut. You'll take every hard inch and beg for more."

"I will that," Rhys agreed, lying back and giving himself up to Andrew's ministrations.

PHYLLIDA FOUND IT HARD TO concentrate on her work. She caught herself daydreaming, if one could call it that after midnight, recalling the image of Rhys in her husband's arms, the deep kisses, the obvious physical passion they felt for each other. The young actor was handsome, certainly, and charming and witty—really the ideal of masculine attractiveness. But Phyllida felt certain it was seeing him with Andrew that made her notice him in this way. If she had met him socially, and had seen him only in a conventional setting, perhaps escorting a lady, would she have felt so drawn to him? She did not think so.

She forced her attention back to the printed sheets, an earlier section than the previous night's work.

"Get out," Melisande said, drawing herself up and pointing imperiously to the door. "If you are a gentleman, get out and leave me virtuous, as you have found me."

Lord Iskander grinned. "Magnificent. But I prefer the suppliant attitude." He snapped his fingers. "Kneel and try again, Melisande. Perhaps I will leave you pure, for now, if you please me with your mouth."

Melisande startled at the click of the man's fingers. It enraged her far more than the drawling, wicked words. "How dare you?" she said. "How dare you assail my maidenhood with your filthy perversions?"

Iskander laughed in his infuriating way. "But my dear," he drawled, "it is not your maidenhood I am assailing. Only your sensibilities, it seems, and your red lips and slender throat."

Was that too obvious? Phyllida wondered. How much did London society know about deviant sexual practices? Probably a lot more than she did. All she knew was the little her mother had told her before her wedding, the ways a woman could stiffen a man if he did not get hard on his own. And of course the word—*cocksucker*. That was another word a lady should never say, or admit to knowing. But people said it, more often than the polite world might wish. Mr. Coulter had called Andrew "cocksucker" before Andrew knocked him down . . .

She put the nib of the pen in her mouth as she did when she was revising her work. For a long time, while the candles burned themselves to stubs, and the boudoir clock ticked softly, she played the scene over in her mind—Rhys flinging himself into Andrew's embrace, pressing his hips against his lover's. And later, after supper, when she had felt the tension in the air, the three of them suddenly conscious of the awkwardness of their odd-numbered group. What had possessed her to listen outside the door? Andrew had married her so that he would not have to change his way of life or lie about it. But he had not intended to have his bride participate in his affairs.

The alkali taste of ink brought her mind back to the boudoir table and the late hour. She removed the pen from her mouth, wrinkling her nose and taking a few generous sips of wine to cleanse her palate. She would leave the episode in for now and let Mr. Edwards decide how far she could go.

THE MEN LAY AT PEACE for half an hour before Rhys dared speak his mind. "A real prize you've found, your Phyllida," he said.

Andrew sighed. "I know."

"You are unhappy?"

"You heard her recitation. The last line should be, 'that leads *men* to this hell.' She's afraid of me."

Rhys lifted himself on one elbow and studied his lover's face. "She's not a timid soul. What have you done to her, Andrew?"

Andrew sighed again. "I don't know. She claims I made love to her before she was ready. But she had pleasure in it. She admitted it. Still, she's wary of me, locks me out."

Rhys snorted. "Don't tell me you rode her the way you do me?"

Andrew stared. "How else? I want a child. It's why I married."

"Oh, my dear," Rhys groaned. "You can't treat a delicate female like a man, not if you want her to like it."

"And what would you know of it?" Andrew's voice was icy.

"On my own account? Nothing. But I talk with Gladys. How do you think I play Romeo and Benedick and all the other lovers of women? How will I play King Harry wooing French Kate? By knowing what women like. And they like gentleness. Not on the outside, perhaps, but in the bedroom. A woman can't give herself freely if she's worried that you'll hurt her."

"I would never—" Andrew stopped, his mouth turned down in disgust at the thought of causing even the slightest harm to that soft flesh, of bruising that translucent skin. "She can't think I'd want to."

"She doesn't, love." Rhys saw Andrew's anxiety and tried to soothe. "Not in her mind. But she's been wounded in some way and it shows. You must have patience."

"It's not my forte, patience," Andrew said.

"Lord, don't I know it. But cheer up. You won't have long to wait. She's mad for you. Anyone can see it."

"Do you really think so?"

"I saw it, not just downstairs, but at the theater. And that's another thing, Andrew. I never thought you the sort to like performing for an audience."

"What do you mean?"

"Surely it's why you chose her over all the society belles and peers' daughters? Because she likes seeing men together."

Andrew sat bolt upright. "What? Are there such women?"

"Oh, yes, boyo. There are indeed. When we were kissing, before I knew she was there, and I looked up, she was watching us like—like a cat watching a bird in a cage, licking its whiskers and waiting its chance."

Andrew's eyes narrowed. "That's my wife you're talking about."

"Aren't you the lucky sod, then?" Rhys said. "But how did you find her?"

"Friend of mine introduced us," Andrew said.

"Ah," Rhys said, as if that explained everything.

"No," Andrew said. "It's not like that. Her father was a gentleman, an infantry officer."

"Which is it, then?" Rhys teased. "A gentleman? Or a murdering Anglish-Saxonish soldier?"

"Welsh savage," Andrew said, stopping for a kiss and a caress, but not to be swayed from his concerns. "I decided I should marry, and my friend, a baronet, a respectable man, said he knew of a suitable girl."

"You have a respectable friend?" Rhys said. "Do tell."

"Do you want to hear this or not?"

"Yes, me lord. Beggin' your pardon, me lord." Rhys tugged at his forelock.

"Anyway," Andrew ignored the performance, "I explained my situation and my requirements, and Verney said he thought Miss Lewis might suit. So I bought a special license and we went down to his place in Sussex the next day. Mother's a real piece of work, had to have made her living on her back, but the marriage was valid, and Verney swears Phyllida's the spit 'n' image of the father. I liked her at once, and she was agreeable, so we drew up a contract and took our vows and—here we are."

Rhys cogitated for a while. "Verney," he said. "Sir Frederick Verney? Mirrors all over the bedroom? Likes to play cards and shed his clothes?" He laughed at Andrew's surprised nod. "Oh, me boyo, and you claimed he was respectable. Damned nice fellow, strong as a blacksmith and game for anything, but respectable?"

Andrew tried for a quelling look. "In his country seat, Rhys, he is a justice of the peace, a good landlord and a pillar of society. And he's a friend of mine."

"And he discovered the beautiful Phyllida. And he didn't tell you about her—tastes?"

Andrew scowled, remembering that peculiar moment, the morning after the wedding, Phyllida coming along the corridor while he kissed Verney good-bye. "I'm sure he would have said something, if he'd known."

"Perhaps *she* didn't know," Rhys said. "She was a maid when you married?"

"Of course."

"Well, then," Rhys said. "Fate, it is."

IT WAS ONLY AS PHYLLIDA lay in the dark, in her comfortable nightgown in her solitary bed, furtively touching herself, that she began to see the truth. She was—she wanted—she did not have the vocabulary to express it, even to herself. She wanted a man to make love to her. It was a wish that a virtuous young lady, even a married one, was not supposed to express openly, although it was conceded that she might feel it on occasion.

It was so very complicated. If she married for love, a woman was expected to welcome her husband's attentions and it was understood that she would enjoy them. But she was not supposed to say so, out loud, in plain language, or to show it by looking too eagerly or explicitly at her husband.

If she did not marry for love, she was considered to have made a bargain, that in return for the benefit of his wealth and position, or simply for the security of a home and children, she was giving her husband the right to do something unpleasant with her body. These arrangements were respected, sometimes even admired, as the acts of prudent, sensible women. At other times they were disparaged. A lot depended, it seemed, on just how unpleasant the thing was the woman had agreed to, and how much she had gained in return.

Worst of all were unmarried women who were known to have lost their virtue, and married women who had adulterous affairs. Lord!

Then it was dreadful. Women like that were called whores and sluts, sometimes even by respectable ladies who would allow the most vicious words to pass their lips in vilifying members of their own sex. Not that men were kinder. It's just that they spoke roughly about everything, so the contrast was not so great.

And where did Phyllida fit into all this? She was clearly in the second category, the arrangement. People who did not know Andrew's reputation, and the few, like her mother, who did not care, would applaud her marriage. To grow up in a small village, the impoverished daughter of a soldier, and to marry a wealthy young man, heir to an earldom, was the stuff of fairy tales. It was almost as good as that nauseating book, *Pamela*, of the last century. Whatever went on between her and Andrew in the privacy of the bedroom, people would judge it a fair trade. No, they would think Phyllida had the better side of the bargain, no matter what, because of the disparity of their circumstances before the marriage.

But what about the reality? That Andrew liked men? That he made love fiercely, forcibly, as to another man, because that's all he knew? And that Phyllida wanted him anyway? In fact, it was seeing him with a lover—a man—that had brought on all these inconvenient desires. No, Phyllida shook her head in the dark, correcting herself. She had always wanted Andrew. Seeing him and Rhys together merely heightened the desire that was already there, gave it added dimension and weight. How would the world judge that, she wondered, smiling despite her sinking heart. It was something, she was quite sure, the world had no idea of but would muddle into incomprehensibility, given the least chance.

Phyllida remembered the other night's musings, the unfairness of the ways of men and women. She cringed, even alone, recalling the bizarre events of the previous day, the scene over the improper clothing. Andrew appeared to have forgotten it by now, as if nothing had happened, but for Phyllida, every glance at his forbidding profile, every drawling word from those thin, sensual lips was a reminder of the hopeless situation in which she had placed herself.

Truly, she had no one to blame but herself for her predicament. She had agreed so readily to this bargain with the devil, simply because she had known, from the moment of setting eyes on him, that she desired Andrew Carrington beyond reason. An hour's careful reflection might have warned her that basing so important a decision on a feeling that went beyond reason was a recipe for disaster. But she had not once reflected, from the minute he walked into her parlor and smiled.

That was the worst of it. She had not been honest with herself just now. With the knowledge of three less than perfect encounters behind her, she could say with certainty that she did not want just any man, not even a kind and gentle one. She wanted only the rough, careless *fucking* of her sodomite husband.

Well, not exactly. She didn't want him to be rough or careless. She wished he would be gentle and sensitive and slow. But she wanted it to be Andrew doing it, nobody else.

The next time he demanded his conjugal rights, she would acquiesce.

FOR AN ENTIRE WEEK, Phyllida had no chance to prove her willingness for wifely submission. Rhys continued in his role as Romeo, and Andrew, uninterested in seeing his lover perform the same part night after night, merely sent his carriage to pick up the actor afterward and bring him to the town house. There was no better place for their assignations, as a club like White's would not admit an actor; a madge house was sordid and potentially dangerous; and Andrew had no desire to advertise to the Brotherhood of Philander that he was less than assiduous in pursuing their interests. Besides, Andrew argued to himself, wasn't that why he had purchased a wife in the first place, so as not to disturb his usual style of life? Phyllida was made welcome at the suppers, but they were not so lively as the first night, nor so late, and she was always careful to leave immediately at the end of the meal and retire to her bedroom.

At least she accomplished a great deal of work on her book. The first two volumes were, with any luck, rolling off the press. As to the third volume, Phyllida was still working on the last additions and amplifications. She had tried to word as many of the changes as she could so as to fit them within the existing pagination. The printer would not have to reset the whole thing, merely make the alterations on individual pages. She had written to Mr. Edwards to explain, and she was sure that when he saw the direction the work was taking, he would be willing to accept the slight inconvenience and delay in anticipation of increased sales.

There were no callers, and with no escort other than Andrew, to whom it did not occur to take Phyllida anyplace she would be permitted to go or interested in seeing, she had no outings. She didn't care. It was like a calling, this book, a compulsion to put down all her new thoughts, all her new ways of looking at the world. Only thus could she make sense of what seemed to be the gothic story of her married life. Even if Mr. Edwards rejected her changes or refused to alter the proofs, she would be glad to have written it all out to her own satisfaction.

When her new clothes were delivered, Phyllida actually felt a moment of vexation at the interruption.

"Ain't you going to try them on, madam?" Nan asked.

"I suppose I'd better," Phyllida said. "Have to make sure they're decent." She shivered, thinking of Andrew coming in, perhaps seeing her in her shift, or the new ball gown, snapping his fingers at her and ordering her to remove it or he would do it himself. She thought, perhaps, she would tell him to do it himself, and see what happened.

"Are you cold, madam?" Nan asked. "I'll build up the fire. No, that's right, I'm to get a chambermaid to build up the fire." She laughed at the wonders of her elevated status. Nan had risen in the world, several rungs all at once. She was supposed to be called by her surname, Crowder, although she and the mistress had agreed that when they were alone they could revert to their former friendly manner. She was promised some of the mistress's old gowns, and there was a new scullery maid starting today. If Mrs. Carrington asked her to cut her little finger off, Nan thought she would do it. But that was the beauty of it. Mrs. Carrington was the type of mistress who would be more likely to cut her own finger off before asking another to do anything so wicked.

"No, Nan," Phyllida said. "I'm quite warm. Come, you'd better help me with these gowns. Oh! Have you ever seen anything so stylish?"

A good half hour was spent before the looking glass, oohing and aahing. Mme. Argonne had taken Andrew's ranting to heart and produced a wardrobe of clothes that blended the fashionable with the demure in a perfect style for the equal contrast of Phyllida's robust beauty and delicate coloring. There were the pinks that best suited her pale skin and rosy cheeks, along with the more sophisticated sage greens and ivories to complement her light brown hair and eyes. Everything fitted perfectly, showing off her curves without exposing her like a street bawd. Phyllida whirled and swayed in the ball gown, a fantastic confection of pale pink muslin and cream lace trim, which managed the seemingly impossible task of making such a combination not look insipid, and imagined herself on Andrew's arm at a ball, being led out onto an empty dance floor . . .

There was a knock at the door. "You have callers, madam," Joan, the downstairs maid, said, out of breath from running. "Mr. George Witherspoon and Miss Agatha Gatling. Also Lord David Pierce. Shall Mr. Yardley tell them you ain't at home?"

That was Phyllida's first reaction. She had never heard of these people. But that was wrong, she felt. It was obviously some kind of courtesy call, no doubt because of her marriage. In fact, she ought to have received a great many such calls. Whoever these people were, they must be Andrew's associates, and it was important to make their acquaintance. Andrew would want her to welcome his friends and be a gracious hostess. At least, she assumed he must. It would shame him if his wife hid away in her boudoir as if she were so disreputable she could not show her face.

"No, Joan, tell Yardley to show them into the drawing room and offer them refreshments. I'll be delayed coming down. I'm just dressing."

Phyllida had never dressed so richly and so quickly as she did now, scrambling into one of the new morning gowns, a sober but pretty ecru with amber-colored ribbons. She ran down the stairs then caught herself outside the drawing room door, composing herself.

It was fortunate she did. The three people who awaited her were the grandest, most elegant people she had ever seen, other than Andrew himself. At least the men were. One was a very young man with golden hair and a face like that of a Renaissance angel. The other was quite short, with carroty hair. Phyllida knew little of men's clothes, and guessed only that if a small man with hair that color looked as if he could be a model for a fashion plate, his tailoring and style of dress must have something to do with it.

The woman was less frightening from the standpoint of beauty. She was not tall, but solidly built, square and thick, with not much neck, and a face that Phyllida couldn't help thinking resembled a pug dog's, with prominent eyes and a squashed little nose. But she more than made up for any lack with an aggressively aristocratic manner.

It was she who spoke first. "How do you do, Mrs. Carrington? I apologize for barging in on you like this, but if we were to wait for your husband to remember to put a notice in the paper, I'm afraid we might not meet until well into the season, if then." She stared pointedly at Phyllida's midsection and brayed a loud, horsy laugh at which the blond joined in and the redhead merely lifted his eyebrows. "Now, I am Miss Agatha Gatling, and this is my brother, George Witherspoon. Half brother. As you see, he got our mother's looks." She smiled as she said it, thrusting out her receding chin.

Phyllida discerned the bravado behind the brusque manner and warmed to the little pug lady. "How do you do, Miss Gatling?" she said. "Indeed, you are not intruding. You are most welcome. And yes, now that you mention it, I have had no callers beyond the immediate family."

The redhead moved forward. "I am Lord David Pierce. I do hope we did not interrupt your letter-writing." He frowned over the ink stains as he took her hand to kiss.

"No," Phyllida said. "I was just finishing. Have you been given refreshments?" She remembered to sit at last, noticing that the two men sat close together on the sofa, while Miss Gatling chose one of the harder chairs. Phyllida turned to point out a softer one, but the lady forestalled her.

"Like a hard chair. Good for the spine. Sitting is quite bad for the posture. A hard chair prevents too great a curvature or slumping. Do you ride, Mrs. Carrington?"

Phyllida had already noted and admired the lady's ramrod bearing. "Not really." She felt as if she were confessing a crime. "In the country, of course, one must learn to amble along on a carthorse or be housebound, but I would not call it riding."

"No," Miss Gatling agreed with a grimace. "I ride every day, rain or shine. Be delighted to teach you, although it is perhaps not the ideal thing for a female in a delicate condition, or hoping to be. Best exercise there is for ladies. Men can box and fence and swim without drawing comment, but we poor females have so few choices for outdoor activities."

"Indeed," Mr. Witherspoon spoke at last in a soft, engaging voice, "Agatha has the best seat of anyone I know. Except for you,

Davey." He smiled so warmly into the other man's eyes that Phyllida blinked and lowered her eyes, as if she had come upon her husband in an intimacy with Rhys. *Of course,* she thought. *Friends of Andrew's.*

The redhead caught her discomfiture, if that's what it was. "Forgive us, Mrs. Carrington, for not introducing ourselves more thoroughly. Mr. Witherspoon and I are friends of Carrington's, through the gentlemen's club we belong to. And Miss Gatling is *our* good friend, as well as our entrance ticket here." He winked at Miss Gatling and the woman colored and looked away, but hiding a smile.

"How do you mean?" Phyllida asked.

"Would look rather fishy, two men calling on a lady," Miss Gatling explained. "Need a respectable female to get in the door. Best these two could get is me." Again the braying laugh.

Phyllida joined in the laughter. "I am sorry Mr. Carrington is not home right now, or I'm sure he'd want to look in and thank you for calling."

Pierce waved a freckled white hand. "Please don't apologize, madam. Of course he's not home. Probably out popping away at Manton's or sparring at Jackson's. It's you we came to see."

"Wanted to see the lay of the land, you know," Witherspoon said and laughed at the weak pun.

"Hush, George," Miss Gatling said in a fierce whisper. "Didn't I go over and over this with you? You are not to breathe a word of it."

Witherspoon's angelic countenance crumpled like a whipped child's. "I'm sorry, Aggie. I forgot. Please don't scold."

Pierce shook his head at Miss Gatling, rolled his eyes, and put his arm around Witherspoon. "There, there, George," he said. "No great harm done." He looked up in a speculative way, met Phyllida's glance, and looked down again, his face flushing in angry blotches.

His fair skin gave it away, Phyllida thought, for all his poise. "If this is because of the wager," she said, "I know all about it. So, please, Mr. Witherspoon, you needn't feel bad. You didn't give up a secret after all."

Witherspoon lifted his head from Pierce's shoulder at the kind words and broke into the most heartbreakingly sweet smile Phyllida had ever seen on an adult. "Oh, I'm glad," he said. "Everybody's been so worried, you know, because we all bet so much on Carrington, and we heard things weren't going well. But if you know about it, and are not put out, then it's bound to be all right."

"George!" Miss Gatling jumped up and advanced on her brother, looking ready to whip him in earnest. Phyllida was glad to see the lady had not actually brought her riding crop with her. "Come, we are leaving. Mrs. Carrington, all I can do is offer you my deepest apologies. George doesn't mean any harm. The mind of a child in some ways. But I don't suppose you'll care to see us again and I quite understand. Good day to you, madam. We wish you well in your marriage. Come along, George. I swear, when we get home—"

Pierce had risen also and placed himself in front of his taller friend. The effect was comical yet somehow touching. "Agatha, my dear," he whispered. "He really doesn't understand. Let me handle it."

Phyllida had been biting her lip to keep from laughing. "Please," she said. "I wish you would stay a little longer. I am not so thin-skinned as to take offense at a mention of what appears to be the talk of the town."

"You are most generous." Miss Gatling allowed herself the luxury of being forgiven. "Most fashionable ladies would pretend to have the vapors in public, and gloat in private to their confidantes about their notoriety."

"Well, as you see," Phyllida said, "I am not fashionable."

"Not yet," Pierce said, "and only because you are unknown." He raised his glass. "That is a very fetching gown. From Mme. Argonne, I understand. You should try her, Agatha."

Phyllida, not at all disturbed by the mention of the wager, was horrified to learn that Andrew had apparently not hesitated to share with his friends all the details of the affair with the modiste. She blushed and stared at her lap, unable to control her fury but not wishing to vent it at relative strangers. Unlike her betrayer of a husband—*perjured, murd'rous . . . not to trust*. The words of the sonnet ran in her mind.

"Oh, don't be absurd, David," Miss Gatling was saying. "Even a French dressmaker can't turn a sow's ear into a silk purse."

"You must stop undervaluing yourself, my dear," Pierce said.

"I beg your pardon for interrupting your visit." Phyllida looked up. "I appear to have developed the severest headache. Pray excuse me." She stood and moved toward the door, the others rising in confusion.

It was Pierce who caught on. "There, you see, Agatha? It is I who should be horsewhipped. Mrs. Carrington, I don't know what is the matter with me. It was most improper to have mentioned Mme. Argonne, but I assure you, Carrington spoke only of the fact that there was some problem with her work and he had to go around and straighten everything out. Because of the language. Whatever quarrel or disagreement may have preceded that, he said nothing he should not."

Witherspoon came over and took Phyllida's hand. "We have upset you very much. I am sorry. You are such a beautiful lady, and so sweet and kind. If we had known how lovely you are, we would not have had to come, but I'm glad we did, to see for ourselves."

Phyllida stared, still not quite comprehending.

"Well, if you didn't have a headache before, I'll wager you have a migraine now," Miss Gatling said. "George, let go of Mrs. Carrington."

Witherspoon did not immediately obey his sister. He clung to Phyllida's hand, looked earnestly into her eyes, and said, "The way Carrington spoke, you see, we thought you were a very different sort of person. You won't lock him out anymore, will you?"

There was no help for it. Phyllida staggered to a chair, poured herself a glass of ratafia, gulped it down, and burst into tears.

The others stood around helplessly, wanting to leave but feeling that, since this fit was all their doing, they ought to stay to offer assistance.

Eventually, Miss Gatling discovered that the tears had turned to laughter. "There, that's the spirit, Mrs. Carrington," she said, putting a solid, meaty arm around Phyllida's shoulders. "Don't let the men get us down, eh?"

"That's right," Witherspoon said. "We say the horridest things to each other in the Brotherhood, but we're all good friends, really."

"Thank you, George," Pierce said. "The truth is Carrington had no business to talk as he did. Now we see the result of such imprudence. I'd like to call him out, but one can't call a man out on behalf of *his* wife."

"No!" Witherspoon stared in alarm. "You mustn't do that, Davey! Carrington's the deadliest shot. I saw him shoot Verney's hat off his head at fifty paces. At twilight."

"Yes, yes," Pierce said. "We all saw that. Damn fool thing. Could have killed him. Don't worry, my love. Can't call him out even if I wanted to. Not my affair."

Phyllida forgot her own trouble for this moment of perfect idiocy. "Sir Frederick Verney?" she asked. "But why? I thought they were friends."

"What else?" Miss Gatling supplied the answer. "Too much to drink and a wager. Sir Frederick's always literally losing his shirt—and more—from what I hear."

"Oh no, Aggie," Witherspoon said, "Verney was completely dressed, in addition to the hat, of course, to go outdoors. Very cold day that was."

IN THE END, THE GUESTS, after much pleading on Phyllida's part, stayed a full half hour, twice the requisite term of a morning call. When they left, Miss Gatling urged Phyllida to return the visit. "I should welcome the company of a sensible female, and enjoy the ease of conversation with one who will not need to dissemble and prevaricate." Phyllida, despite her better instincts, felt moved to accept.

But when Andrew came home, Phyllida had had time to reflect, and was in a foul temper. "I did not understand," she said by way of greeting, "that I am such an embarrassment to you."

"What the devil are you talking about?"

"You did not even put an announcement of our marriage in the newspaper."

Andrew snapped his fingers in annoyance. "I knew I had forgotten something. I am sorry. I will correct it first thing tomorrow." He smiled down at her as if everything were fine.

"I have had no callers all week, you see," Phyllida said, unwilling to let her grudge go so meekly and fighting to maintain control of her seesawing emotions.

"You had Pierce and Witherspoon today," Andrew said.

"And Miss Gatling, Mr. Witherspoon's sister," Phyllida said. "Or didn't your club mates remember to mention a mere female in the course of dissecting all our conversation? Tell me, Andrew. Do they give you advice on what to do in bed? Do they write you out a plan? They will have to come up with something better than what they have produced so far if you are not to lose everybody a great fortune, it seems."

"Actually, it was Yardley who informed me of our visitors," Andrew said. He walked to the door and shut it quietly before turning and saying, "And how dare you speak to me that way?"

"How dare I?" Phyllida said. "How dare you tell them all about me, about us, about Mme. Argonne, and locking the door."

"Witherspoon," Andrew said. "I might have known that little featherbrain would—"

"No, it was not Mr. Witherspoon," Phyllida said. "It was your perfect gentleman, Lord David Pierce. Apparently our every intimate act is common talk at your club. Don't you have anything better to do? Oh, but I was forgetting. The height of wit and sophistication is shooting at one another and taking one's clothes off."

Andrew shrugged and laughed. "At least it works both ways. It seems they didn't hesitate to tell tales of our doings to you."

"I didn't ask to hear it," Phyllida shouted. "I agreed not to interfere in your life, but I expect my life to be my own in return. If everything that happens between us is to become grist for the rumor mill at your club, I can promise you one thing. There will be nothing between us from now on. Nothing. And if your friends lose their despicable wager, so much the better."

"Oh dear," Andrew said with a sigh. "You see, these are my friends. My closest friends. Men like me, gentlemen who enjoy the company and favors of other men. We are accustomed to sharing everything—preferences, histories, and yes, even the most indelicate particulars of the bedroom. It is impossible to keep secrets in such an ingrown society, and we have given up trying. I never considered how different it would be with a wife."

"You don't consider me at all," Phyllida said. "You don't even think of me as a human being. I am nothing but a possession to you, a vessel for breeding your heir."

"And how is this different from the views of any other ninety-nine men out of a hundred?"

"It isn't, I'll allow," Phyllida said. "I suppose I thought you would be the one in the hundred."

"Why?" Andrew said. "Because I'm a sodomite? Because I'm expected to be sensitive and poetic and sympathetic to the feminine mind?" He snorted in disgust. "You have a lot to learn about men, my dear."

Phyllida, embarrassed at the way in which her deep-seated assumptions had been exposed as banalities, fought back with rancor. "I have learned enough about men in a week of marriage to last a lifetime," she said.

"Pity you feel that way," Andrew said. "I don't intend to let you give up your lessons after one week. I am very much afraid you are doomed to become an authority on the subject, at least on one man." He put a hand on her arm. "Come, let us try to be friends. I promise not to discuss you with anybody from now on."

Phyllida shook off the hand, moving away and turning her head so as not to betray how his touch had seared her flesh, all the way to the heart. "How can we be friends, Andrew? You have just admitted you don't see me as a person."

"I did not," Andrew said. "I said that what you accused me of was an opinion shared by the majority of my fellow offenders. I did not actually confess to the crime."

"Oh!" Phyllida was near to screaming. "You are a master of sophistry."

"I thank you, my dear." Andrew bowed as if he had been complimented. "Now, here is my proposal. Tonight you will accompany me to the theater to see *Henry V*. Rhys will be in town for another week, so there will be no need for you and me to reach an understanding until the end of that time. But after the week is up—and I am most serious about this, Phyllida—you will receive me in your bedchamber. And if you lock the door I will have the footmen break it down."

Phyllida stared. "You wouldn't!"

"Try me," Andrew said. "But I warn you, I will not be denied."

THE PRODUCTION OF *HENRY V* was memorable, but somehow not as extraordinary as the lesser play Phyllida had seen first. It was the newness, she supposed. One's initial experience of something, even if imperfect, was bound to stand out in some indefinable way, exceeding all subsequent occurrences, no matter how technically superior.

Of course, the company in the box may have had something to do with it. Andrew's sister and her husband made it a point of honor to accompany their new sister-in-law, and the party in the next box—Lord and Lady Swain, their eldest son and daughter-in-law, and their daughter—displayed a tenuous and fraught connection with Andrew's brother.

Richard Carrington, slinking in behind the family groupings, managed, after a set of maneuvers that Lord Wellington, in command of the forces in the Peninsula, would have admired, to snag the seat on Phyllida's free side, next to the divider that separated the Carringtons' box from the Swains'—more particularly, Lydia

Swain. Phyllida spent the better part of the drama fending off furtive brushes of the young man's hand, not quite catching whispered remarks, which obliged her to bend her head to hear what invariably turned out to be vapid and overdone compliments, and enduring the equally fulminating stares of her husband and his brother's neglected and jealous inamorata.

At the end of the evening, Phyllida was so grateful to be whisked away to the actors' dressing room that she bore in stoic silence Andrew's lecture on the proper conduct of a lady in repelling the advances of a man not her husband. Only when Andrew had reached the door and was about to knock did Phyllida say, "Why don't you tell this to Richard instead of me? Or does your nerve not extend to male members of your family? I did not ask him to sit next to me."

"But you permitted it," Andrew said. "You encouraged him in his familiarities, turning your head and whispering with him. If he were not my brother I could call him out for less than the disgusting display I was subjected to tonight. And as for you! Most husbands would beat a wife who behaves as you do and then has the audacity to answer back." He knocked on the door.

The door was opened, not by Rhys but by an older actor, who said casually over his shoulder, "Rhys, your gentleman friend is here," before bowing and leaving by the connecting door. Rhys, naked to the waist, bent over the washstand, rinsing his face. Andrew could not resist palming the firm buttocks so temptingly offered.

Rhys sputtered and stood up, whirling around with his fist in the air. Andrew blocked the blow with his forearm and pulled the actor into a kiss, unconcerned with dripping water. "Oh, it is a brute you are," Rhys murmured after a long silence. He looked younger and far more vulnerable without the heavy makeup. "How did you like Harry the King?"

"Superb," Andrew answered. "I am looking forward to tonight, my dear. I have never fu— had royalty before. Unless that rather plump guardsman last month was Princess Caroline in disguise."

Rhys, shocked by Andrew's crude speech, and feeling somehow that the kiss was the expression of a passion that had arisen in a different context, cocked his head at Phyllida. "What a swine you have married."

"Yes," Phyllida replied. "He just now threatened to beat me, merely because his brother sat next to me in the box. I'm sorry, Rhys. I wasn't able to concentrate on the play as I would have liked. I would ask Andrew to bring me another night, except he would assume I was meeting my lover."

"I am flattered, beautiful lady," Rhys teased. "But I am terrified of your husband's beatings also." He grinned at Andrew's scowling countenance. "And you swore you had no inclination for violence. See how your lies have found you out."

"I have a temper," Andrew said. "I say things. Of course I would never actually strike a woman. As for an encroaching, viper-tongued *actor—*"

"So you discussed me with Rhys, too," Phyllida said. "I ought to have guessed. I hope your footmen have strong shoulders, Andrew. They will need them in a week."

"Shrew," Andrew said. "I will break the door down myself."

"I'm glad to know that solid blockhead of yours is good for something," Phyllida said. "But it will take more than brawn to win my surrender."

Rhys stared openmouthed at the squabbling pair. He was suddenly aware of a strange feeling, of being the unnecessary third in the company of an aroused, amorous couple, very much in the way. But it was his dressing room, after all. He watched the developing drama, alternately enthralled and repulsed.

"No," Andrew answered Phyllida's last insult, "all I'll need is the brawn in my breeches. Just the way you sluts like it, hard and rough."

"I'm sure you know all about sluts," Phyllida said. "You haven't the least idea how to make love to a lady."

"Probably not," Andrew agreed. "But since it's you I'll be tumbling, you little strumpet, I don't expect to have any trouble. You'll be on all fours, waving your tail in the air like a bitch in heat before I'm halfway through the door."

"Round one goes to the lady, round two to the gentleman, and there will be no third round." Rhys had decided it was time to intervene. "As the designated referee, I am calling this match a draw, as all good marriages must be."

"Stay out of it, Rhys," Andrew growled. He was breathing heavily and his color was up. He pushed Rhys away and advanced on Phyllida.

"This is my room, this is—" Rhys protested. "In your own house, you may screw each other senseless for all I care, but in my room behave yourselves you will."

Andrew turned his head at the nervous voice. "How dare you speak so of Phyllida, you impudent Welsh whore?"

The connecting door opened and Gladys came in, looking flustered. "Whatever is the matter?" she said. "Oh, it's you, Andrew. Hello, Mrs. Carrington. Is everything all right?"

"Perfectly," Phyllida said. "Andrew was merely demonstrating masculine hypocrisy, blaming Rhys and me for his own faults. I warn you, enter the room at your peril. You'll likely be accused of provoking whatever horrid thing Andrew says next."

"Round three to the lady," Andrew whispered to Phyllida, holding out his hand. "Regardless of marital propriety." He raised his voice to greet the other woman. "Gladys, your entrance, as always, was perfectly timed. The victory goes to your sex, and we poor men must grovel in ignominious defeat. Will you join us for supper?"

Phyllida took the offered hand without conscious thought. Andrew's long fingers closed over her hand, crushing it in a death grip. She winced but did not try to disengage. If Gladys had not come in just now, if they were in their own house, she very much suspected they would at this moment be screwing each other senseless. Here it was again, the mystery of the poorly designed system of men and women.

"Thank you, but I must decline," Gladys said. "I have a prior engagement."

"Who is that?" a soft, well-bred voice called from the next room. "Gladys, dear, are you coming?"

"Yes, Priscilla," Gladys said. "I was just saying good-night to my brother."

"Lady Priscilla Upton," Andrew said with a grin. "I'll be damned. I felicitate you, Gladys. Quite a coup. Never heard she spread her legs for anyone, except her horse."

Gladys smiled back at Andrew. "Kiss my arse," she said, turning and throwing her skirts up to flash her rump for an instant before closing the door behind her.

The carriage ride home passed in smoldering silence. Andrew rode with Rhys nestled beside him, his arm around the other man's shoulders, but all the time his clear eyes bored into Phyllida's, where she sat across from the men. Phyllida began to wonder if she were still fully clothed or if Andrew's stare had stripped shawl and gown from her shoulders and was even now peeling shift and stays from her waist. A slow, deep flush began somewhere down in her lower half and moved by degrees up her body until she was hot and breathless.

When they arrived at the town house, Phyllida could hardly wait for Andrew to hand her down, and tried to rush ahead into the house. But the death grip caught her again and held her in restraint. "Will you receive me now, before supper?" he whispered, bending over her hand as she descended the stairs of the carriage.

Phyllida shook her head, tore her hand loose, and ran to the welcoming light of the entrance, Yardley bowing her in and the footmen upstairs ready to put the cold supper on the table and retire. "I seem to be unusually fatigued tonight," she said. Her husband and Rhys followed close on her heels. "I think I will have supper in my room and an early night. I'm sorry, Andrew. Forgive me, Mr. Powyl," she added for the benefit of the listening servants.

IT WAS A LONG TIME before Phyllida was able to do any work. She stared abstracted at the fire while Nan helped her disrobe, and later as she picked at her tray of supper. "They do say," Nan ventured hopefully, "that when a woman's expecting, she don't have no appetite at first."

"What?" Phyllida was roused from her meditations. "Don't be silly, Nan. I've only been married a week."

Dressed in her ratty robe, her papers and pens in front of her, Phyllida stuck the nib of her pen in her mouth, puzzling over the license that men had to indulge their every preference, every whim, while women were blamed even for the mere appearance of straying.

Was that the answer? Did she secretly want a lover of her own, and could Andrew tell? Richard was very sweet, certainly. A dreadful flirt, but safe. He clearly found her as beautiful as he claimed, but Phyllida sensed he was fundamentally honorable and would not really want to compromise his own brother. And he seemed, for all his air of a rakish man of the world, a little young for her. She suspected he was just about her age, twenty-two. Andrew's seven-year advantage in age was far more appealing.

Phyllida knew one thing only. She had no desire for a lover, even were it worth the risk. Although she did not feel the reverence she should for the laws of church and society, she was uncomfortable with the idea of adultery and faithlessness. Look at all the trouble it caused. Look at that Lady Finchley, widowed and bearing her lover's child, the object of a demeaning wager at a so-called gentlemen's club. And Lydia Swain, so jealous and possessive in her glares tonight, her name bandied about as the synonym for "whore," while her only crime was taking a lover, a man who boasted openly of having had scores of mistresses of his own.

Still, it could be nice to have a suitor, someone to compliment her on her clothes and laugh at her jokes, to pursue her with ardent, hopeless admiration. If Rhys were only slightly interested in women, and were not leaving in a few days to go on tour . . . The fact that it was all playacting would make it perfect, except for Andrew's overheated and unnecessary jealousy. And she was afraid of that triangle, suspecting that Andrew was both excited and disgusted at the thought of sharing a lover with his wife. Or would he see it as sharing his wife?

Andrew had goaded her on purpose. Phyllida saw it now. He *knew* how she responded to his drawling insults and acrimonious accusations, and deliberately provoked her. Was she unusually perverse and wicked? Or did other people have a similar reaction? If Andrew truly disliked quarreling, why would he pick a fight over something so trivial as his younger brother's flirting?

It would serve Andrew right if she did have an affair with his brother. She could imagine that Richard wouldn't force her, would know exactly how to make that sensitive little nub of flesh between her legs melt with delight. The thought didn't excite her in the least. She was very much a part of this messed-up system. With an ideal lover practically hers for the asking, she knew there was only one man she wanted—her arrogant ravisher of a husband.

In less than a week the reprieve would be over. Phyllida wondered what would happen. Would Andrew be polite and quiet and simply assume that Phyllida would receive him? Or would he snap his fingers at her and order her to leave her bedroom door unlocked? What if he precipitated another spat to get himself in the mood? How could she make him understand her willingness and at the same time persuade him to treat her more gently?

A solution came to mind, but it seemed the imaginings of a lunatic—to goad Andrew first. Perhaps, Phyllida thought, if *she* confronted *him* she would gain the upper hand. Did she dare? Phyllida was no coward, but she had never faced an opponent like Andrew. And she had never loved before. It would be an interesting experiment, if she had the courage.

ANDREW LAY AWAKE THAT NIGHT, going over and over the conversation with Phyllida. What had possessed him to speak to her so? The business with Richard was only a pretext, he admitted now to himself. The boy was harmless, a flirt, but not a threat. And even if he were dangerous, Andrew knew by now he could trust Phyllida. He could sense it, with his instinct for attraction, that she felt nothing for any other man.

No, he had played the jealous husband because it gave him an excuse to start up the game with her that he so enjoyed. They had been sparring since that afternoon, the argument over the notice in the papers and the lack of callers. It had been Phyllida who had prolonged the discussion, no doubt frustrated by Andrew's tame capitulation at her original complaint.

He knew for certain now, if he had ever doubted it, that she responded to the game. Look how she had not cried, or whined, or begged, but had answered him back at every turn, every flung accusation. She was not afraid of him, not in the least, although she had claimed to be when explaining the locked door. No, she must merely be uneasy at the novelty, and needed time to grow accustomed to having a husband. God, she was a prize!

Rhys stirred beside him, muttering in his guttural language. Andrew kissed him to half consciousness and said, "I'm sorry I put you in the middle of that, my dear. May I have another 'little touch of Harry in the night'?"

Harry—the name rang in Andrew's head, yet for some reason without its usual force. The lovemaking was fierce, intense, as it was so often when an affair was approaching its natural end, neither man willing to admit to the other the waning of passion.

Rhys, sensing the change, said, "Go carefully with her, Andrew. One wrong move and you will spoil it. But do it right, and you will gain a love in a thousand."

"No," Andrew murmured, near sleep, "one in a million."

THE NEXT DAYS WERE the slowest Phyllida had spent in her life. She had expected the time to fly by, dreading the encounter that was to occur at the end of it, but that was not the case. Mrs. Badger asked once or twice after the household accounts and Phyllida, ashamed at her negligence, made a serious effort to find the book. After burrowing fruitlessly under a couple of the stacks of proofs, she gave up. She loathed hunting for lost objects. One could knock oneself out tearing rooms apart, only to have the dratted thing turn up in a logical place when one wasn't looking. Better to wait and let it come to light when it would.

Even Andrew's secretary asked about the accounts, waylaying Phyllida one morning after breakfast. Phyllida could not easily admit her carelessness. "Don't worry, Mr. Turner," she said. "That millstone is off your neck now."

"If it is such a burden, madam," he said, "I would be happy to relieve you of it."

"I warn you," Phyllida said with a laugh, surprised at his eagerness to resume so irksome a task, "if you press me too hard I will certainly yield. But it would not do to let Mr. Carrington think I am unwilling to fulfill the duties of a wife. In a month or two, I can give the job back to you with less damage to my reputation."

The man looked as if he would persist, but was thwarted by the arrival of visitors. Phyllida tore herself away from Mr. Turner's importuning at the maid's welcome interruption and hurried downstairs. "No need for that," a booming male voice overrode Yardley's attempt at announcement. "We'll introduce ourselves, as family ought."

The self-proclaimed relative burst into the drawing room. He was a tall, portly, red-faced man, accompanied by a matronly but smartly dressed woman, to whom he was saying, "Depend on it, my dear, it will turn out to be a sham. Just let me get a look at her, and I'll— Oh!— How d'ye do, Mrs. Carrington? Newburn. Your husband's Uncle Francis. And this is Lady Newburn, Aunt Mabel. Now, what is all this talk about Andrew's marrying?"

"As you see, my lord," Phyllida answered, attempting to keep her temper, "I am Mrs. Carrington, as you have guessed. Will you be seated?"

"Won't be staying long," Newburn said, glancing around the room with interest. "Haven't seen the inside of this place since Ronald was alive. My brother, Andrew's father. My God! Wouldn't recognize it to save my life. So this is what the young sod—ah—young gentlemen—consider modish, is it? Looks like a damned brothel."

"Frank," his wife said, laying a restraining hand on his arm, which he shook off with irritation. "Mrs. Carrington is no doubt unused to your familiar way of speaking. He doesn't mean any harm." She looked sardonically over to Phyllida. "My husband expressed surprise when he learned that his eldest nephew had decided to do his duty to his family. But I warned you, Frank, that one cannot truly assess a young man's character before his thirtieth birthday."

Lord Newburn seated himself on a chair near Phyllida, the better to study her through his glass. He seemed, on one level, pleased with what he saw, but in some way unable to credit the evidence of his eyes. "Known Andrew long?" he inquired.

"No," Phyllida answered. "It was an arranged marriage." She had decided ahead of time to pursue a policy of honesty with Andrew's relations, and this interview had so far not given her any reason to change her course of action.

"I dare say," Newburn said. "Nasty shock, eh?"

"I beg your pardon?" Phyllida said.

"Finding out the truth."

"Frank," his wife cautioned him.

"Better have it out now," Newburn said. "No point in having somebody else's brat inheriting the title when it's too late to do anything about it. Better a divorce now than the entire estate passing to the by-blow of an actor or a libertine."

Phyllida stood up. She was trembling with the effort to stay calm, and her voice shook as she spoke. "My lord, that is going too far. Whatever your opinion of your nephew, you have no right to say such things of me to my face. If Andrew were home, he would throw you out. As it is, I will ask Yardley to show you the door." She pulled the bell rope.

"There, Frank," Lady Newburn said. "I hope you're satisfied. Another estrangement in the family. One less set of acquaintances to call on." She grimaced, but did not seem unduly upset when Yardley knocked and entered at Phyllida's command.

"Yardley," Phyllida said, "Lord and Lady Newburn are leaving. They discovered they were mistaken in the address. It seems they were looking for a house of ill repute."

Yardley choked at the words, trying not to laugh, contorting his features in a way that made his resemblance to a prune even more pronounced.

"What's that? What's that?" Lord Newburn said.

"A set down," Lady Newburn said. "And about time someone had the courage to give it to you. Mrs. Carrington, I wish you well. Another time, may I call on you alone?"

Phyllida merely raised her eyebrows and gave a slight lift to her shoulders, not quite enough to qualify as a shrug. "It will depend on Mr. Carrington," she said.

"That's fine," Lord Newburn said, finding his voice again. "You tell that unnatural young nephew of mine exactly what I said—and you too, you little hussy. It's my land and my money that'll be coming to you, unless I change my will. And don't think I won't."

Again Phyllida shrugged. "Good day. I will tell Mr. Carrington you asked after him." Her voice no longer shook, but she was feeling drained, as after a fright—or a fight.

"You oughtn't to have said that, madam," Yardley said after the callers had left and the footman had shut the door firmly behind them. "But I'm glad you did. Never once set foot in the house since the old master died, Mr. Carrington's father."

"But why?" Phyllida said, not quite able to credit the answer. "If Mr. Carrington is his heir, shouldn't Lord Newburn be pleased that he's married?"

"Don't be asking me," Yardley said. "It's not for me to comment on my betters."

Andrew, when applied to later in the day, merely scowled. "I hear you did yeoman's service today," he said. "I am as usual in your debt. It is another penalty of marrying into a titled family. It seems the higher the rank, the worse the manners."

"You are not angry with me?"

"After what he said to you? No, I'm only sorry I wasn't here to throw him out on his fat arse, as you so accurately predicted."

"But I still don't understand," Phyllida said. "Why is your own uncle so annoyed that you married? I should think he'd be relieved."

Andrew's mouth turned down in an unpleasant and unhappy reverse smile. "There you have it, my dear. The sodomite's dilemma. Some men hate us so much that when we do what society requires it only intensifies their detestation. It's as if we have defeated them by succeeding at the one thing in which they consider themselves superior and unassailable—marriage and fatherhood."

"But what if he changes his will?" Phyllida said. "He threatened to."

"Stupid old fart," Andrew said. "He can't disinherit the legitimate heir to the title except by making, and proving, the kind of accusations that would heap such opprobrium on the entire family I think even he would stick at them. All he can do is leave the property in such a muddle that I end up selling it off to rid myself of the trouble. If he wants to destroy generations of careful husbandry to spite me, I can't stop him, and I won't crawl to him. Even if I needed the money, I wouldn't. But I don't need it, and I don't need him, either."

GRADUALLY MORE CALLERS CAME TO the house, although they were not so numerous as Phyllida had hoped. She had not thought herself a social butterfly; her life in the village had been necessarily narrow in acquaintance and repetitious in its activities. It seemed she had emerged from a cocoon, flexing her new, glittering wings and wishing for a garden in which to test them. But it was still March, after all, not yet the season. Not everybody was in town, nor was there the multiplicity of balls and parties that would be offered after Easter.

As Andrew had no female acquaintances—at least, no respectable ladies of the sort to pay morning calls—the visitors were members of his club, bachelors who managed to scare up a female connection or two to keep appearances correct. Sir Frederick Verney was the next to call, accompanied by his sister, Mrs. Rathbone. The woman was delighted with the house, unable to sit and talk, flitting around the room, admiring the modern furnishings and the large windows, the silver and the porcelain. Sir Frederick gave up attempting to include his sister in the conversation and, letting her roam at will, leaned close to Phyllida. "You are content?" he said in a low voice.

"I have no reason to complain," Phyllida said.

Somehow, Mrs. Rathbone heard this. "Complain?" she exclaimed, turning from fingering the rich material of the drapes. "I should think not! When I remember your season, all those years ago, and your turning down your only offer—Lord Hearn, you know, Fred, the old earl—I should rather expect you would not be *complaining* at your unexpected good fortune."

"It was a figure of speech," Phyllida said, looking to Sir Frederick for support.

"Honestly, Cathy," Verney said, "you do have a way of taking a person up short on the most innocent remark. I was inquiring into Mrs. Carrington's well being, since it was I who engineered the match."

"And a fine thing you did, to be sure," Mrs. Rathbone said. "I imagine Mrs. Carrington considers herself to be very much in your debt."

"Actually," Verney said, "I consider Andrew to have benefited equally, if not more."

"What?" Mrs. Rathbone stood still and raised her eyebrows. "A man who could have the pick of society girls? A man who is heir to an earldom? Come, come, Fred. I know you are fond of the girl, but that is absurd."

"You forget, Cathy," Verney said, almost choking with the difficulty of chiding his older sister, "Mrs. Carrington is sitting right here, our hostess."

"Nonsense," Mrs. Rathbone said. "Phyllida won't have put on airs or gotten above herself in a week or two of marriage. Always was a sensible girl." She nodded pleasantly in Phyllida's direction without actually looking at her. "Understand there's a bit of a wager going on. Don't want to promote that sort of thing, you know. Not good for your reputation."

Phyllida, stung beyond endurance, stood up. "I can't help it that men wager on things they ought not," she said. "As a female, I am not eligible to be a member of White's, nor of the Brotherhood of Philander. Perhaps you should ask your brother how these wagers start, and how to stop them. It is certainly not within my control."

"Well!" Mrs. Rathbone colored angrily. "Plain speaking indeed." She turned to her brother. "The Brotherhood of Philander, Fred? Is that what I think it is? You ought not to encourage Mrs. Carrington to mention such things in polite society. Her husband will be greatly displeased if he finds he has tied himself to a shameless country wench instead of a lady of refinement."

"Andrew?" Verney laughed. "The last thing he wanted was one of these swooning, delicate debutantes. Why do you think I suggested Miss Lewis?"

"I thank you for the compliment, Sir Frederick," Phyllida said.

"I only meant—" Verney began.

"I know you mean well," Phyllida said, softening toward the man. She was stuck, probably forever, with a mental image of Sir Frederick, naked but for a top hat, shivering in Hyde Park while Andrew aimed a pistol at his head and shouted at him to stand still. "And I do thank you for arranging my marriage. I think Mr. Carrington and I will suit very well, once we become accustomed to each other's peculiarities."

"Peculiarities?" Once again Mrs. Rathbone was incensed. "A lady ought not to have any, and a married lady ought not to mention her husband's, or imply that he has any, either. You know, Phyllida, I don't remember you being such a brazen, outspoken sort of person. I suspect all this independence has turned your head."

Phyllida nodded. "I think perhaps it has, Mrs. Rathbone." She bowed, a slight inclination only of the head. "Sir Frederick, Mrs. Rathbone. I will wish you good day. It is one of my peculiarities that I do not encourage morning calls beyond the standard length." To her guests' astonishment, or at least the lady's, she rang the bell and had Yardley show them out.

Sir Frederick winked at her as he took his hat and gloves. "I, for one, am confident in the outcome of the wager," he whispered as he bowed over her hand.

SYLVESTER MONKTON, THE NEXT VISITOR, appeared alone in Phyllida's drawing room. Indifferent to the rules of society, and secure in his independent fortune and his lack of responsibilities, with a married older brother whose wife had just announced her delicate condition, Monkton brought no female companion to smooth his way. He had realized just this morning that, so far from being in the vanguard of those up on the latest gossip and who had seen all the new faces, he was in danger of being the very last person of consequence to set eyes on Andrew's reluctant bride. Overcoming with difficulty his utter lack of interest in the opposite sex, he dressed with his usual flair for fashion and presented himself to Yardley.

Phyllida needed all her newfound confidence for this visitor, although there was nothing overtly intimidating in Monkton's appearance. He was a willowy man of average height, with soft brown hair and unusually prominent green eyes. The shoulders of his coat were padded into absurd unnatural peaks, his collar points reached dizzying heights up to the line of his jaw and beyond, held in place by a wide, heavily starched cravat tied in the most elaborate confection of a knot Phyllida had ever seen, and it was obvious that more than good posture accounted for the nipped-in wasp waist of his coat.

But there was an air of menace about him all the same. He stood when Phyllida entered the drawing room, raised his quizzing glass immediately, and when Phyllida was about to sit, shook his head and held up a chiding finger. "Not quite yet," he said in a soft but penetrating voice. "In a moment." After subjecting her to a lengthy and insulting examination, the distorted image of his magnified green eye blazing at Phyllida like a bilious sun, he allowed her to take her seat.

"Well, Mr. Monkton," Phyllida inquired, "have I passed your inspection?"

Monkton was silent, continuing to command obedience with his raised hand as he moved the glass down to view Phyllida's feet. "Shoes," he said.

"I beg your pardon?"

"Your dress is admirable, Mrs. Carrington, and your hair distinctive. But your feet are shod abominably. Did you think people would not notice?"

"You are impertinent," Phyllida said. "I must ask you to leave."

"Must you?" Monkton said with languid unconcern. "I shan't go until I am ready, however. And I shan't be ready until I have decided whether you will do."

"If you think I am going to discuss my situation with Andrew for your benefit, you are quite out," Phyllida said. "And I don't care a fig about your disgusting wager. In fact, I hope you all lose."

Monkton laughed in an artificial but genial tone. "Oh, I see," he said. "That does put a new perspective on things."

"What are you talking about?"

"Carrington has always liked, shall we say, spirited companions. It had not occurred to me, and nobody so far has seen fit to mention it, that you are of that breed. I imagine most of your visitors hadn't thought that a female could attract him. I certainly did not. But seeing you, and especially conversing with you, gives one hope."

Phyllida was left momentarily speechless.

"But you must do something about the shoes," Monkton continued, unperturbed by her lack of response. "You will need sandals, dancing slippers for balls, and half boots for walking and visiting. Those excrescences on your feet should be burned. I would not advise passing them on to your abigail or even the scullery maid, as she will inevitably tell where she got them, and it will be almost as bad as wearing them yourself."

"You are the horridest man I have ever met," Phyllida said. "Are you really a friend of Andrew's?"

"Not a bosom bow, no," Monkton said. "In fact we seem to get on each other's nerves."

"I can't imagine why," Phyllida murmured.

"*Brava*, madam, *brava*," Monkton said. "You do that very well. No, Carrington and I are not close, but we are members of the same club, and I do have a substantial sum invested in his success."

"And you think my acquiring new shoes will ensure it?"

"Hardly. No, madam, I am merely doing what little I can to help, by fitting you for your role in society. Whether you and Carrington can reach a rapprochement is up to you. But I know Carrington well enough to say that he will never be happy with a wife who cannot hold her own in his world. If your dress is shabby or your manners lacking, you will not last long enough to have a chance of being, ah, how did Carrington put it? Oh, yes. 'Blessed with a child' was his revolting phrase."

Phyllida couldn't help smiling, even as some of Monkton's predictions seemed all too likely. "I see. So now you're saying my husband is some sort of Bluebeard? Just how will he get rid of me? He won't want a divorce. The scandal."

Monkton shrugged. "What's scandal to men like us? Divorce is practically an encomium compared to unnatural vice."

"And he would divorce me over shoes?"

"Of course not. No, Carrington would no doubt merely wonder why you were not taken up by the *ton*, would hurl a great many wild accusations at your head, most of which, if not all, would be irrelevant and incomprehensible, and finish by drawing up divorce proceedings, no doubt naming himself as the erring party. Which reminds me. Has he been seeing a lot of that greasy Welsh actor?"

Phyllida shook her head. The accuracy of Monkton's description of Andrew, humorous as it was, had unnerved her. "No, Rhys—Mr. Powyl—has not been here lately."

"Ah," Monkton said. "You do that rather less well, Mrs. Carrington, I'm afraid. You will have to work at it. The social whirl would come to a jolting halt in five minutes' time if everyone were to lie as badly as you."

"Mr. Monkton," Phyllida said, relaxing for the first time in this bizarre interview. "I think I have misjudged you. The resemblance to your father is misleading."

"Hearn?" Monkton said with a shudder. "Surely you are mistaken. You can't have known him."

"Yes, I did," Phyllida said. "He made me an offer during my season four years ago. The only proposal I received."

"Marriage?" Monkton said, his eyes nearly popping out of his head. "Oh, you poor thing. I am sorry. But you had the good sense not to accept, at least."

"Anyone with the intelligence of a flea should have that much sense," Phyllida said. "But there is a similarity between you, a glossy surface protecting a vulnerable heart. In him, I am afraid it had all rotted into wickedness; in you, I suspect there is a hidden core of decency."

"I doubt it, madam," Monkton said, recovering his poise. "I am not an amiable person. The only difference between me and most others is that I don't try to hide what I am or wish to change."

"But that," Phyllida said, "is most refreshing."

"So is falling in the ocean," Monkton said. "But one drowns all the same."

"Mr. Powyl goes on tour with his troupe in a couple of days," Phyllida said, deciding that, perverse at it seemed, Monkton was the one visitor so far to whom she felt perfectly safe in divulging the truth. "To the west—Wales and then Dublin, I think. So nobody needs be concerned about that. As for my shoes, can you recommend a good establishment for ladies' footwear?"

Monkton raised an eyebrow. "Do I appear to be the sort of man who knows things like that? Of course I can't. But Carrington's sister will know. And come to think of it, ought you not to be seeing more of Lady Fanshawe? I have not heard anything of the two of you visiting since the no doubt disastrous affair of Mme. Argonne."

"That's just it," Phyllida said. "Lady Fanshawe did it deliberately, led Mme. Argonne to believe I was Richard's mistress instead of Andrew's wife. So her first contributions to my wardrobe were—inappropriate for a respectable married lady. That's what made Andrew so furious. And I can't like her—Lady Fanshawe, I mean. She's like a female Andrew without the charm."

Monkton laughed naturally for the first time in almost ten years of his adult life. "Mrs. Carrington, you are a delight. Although I must question the notion that a male Andrew has any charm, I do see your point. Nevertheless, you must bite the bullet and force yourself to endure her company once in a while."

"For Andrew's sake?"

"In a way. For society's, more exactly. And bear in mind, a fact that ought to make the whole process much less painful—the woman must be insanely jealous of you."

"Of me? Why?"

"Have you looked in the glass lately? I mean within the last five years? You are beautiful. Not perhaps in the current ideal, but in the much more meaningful way, a carnal way, which men find irresistible, even men like me, to an extent. For the majority, those who are closer to the middle of the spectrum, like Carrington, you must appear as a very dainty morsel indeed."

Phyllida was unsure whether she was pleased or repelled by the notion. "But Lady Fanshawe is fascinating. That voice and—"

"Yes, she has allure. But you have true beauty, and wit and intelligence. And while you are neither spiteful nor cruel, you have not allowed your natural kindness and generosity to cloud the shining purity of your malice. There is a remarkable openness in your conversation, with just the hint of acid that makes for a perfect bouquet, like a dry wine of superior vintage." He took her hand to kiss in conclusion of the visit. "No, my dear, attend to your feet and—my God!—what are those stains on your fingers?"

"Ink," Phyllida said. "I write."

"So I see. You must not, you know."

"But it's in the marriage contract. I insisted."

Again Monkton was nonplussed. "Carrington allowed that? He must be absolutely besotted. You know, I almost envy him. And that, coming from me, is the greatest compliment any woman will ever receive."

THE FINAL CALLERS OF THE long week were the same family group that had ruined Phyllida's last visit to the theater. The Swains—thankfully, only the female members—were waiting for Phyllida when she returned from a trying but successful visit to a shoemaker's with Lady Fanshawe.

"Please forgive the intrusion," a petite middle-aged lady said when Phyllida peered into the drawing room. "But your man said you had gone out quite early and were bound to be back soon, and we thought we would take the chance and wait a few minutes. We are so sorry not to have called before, but without any notice in the papers, and not being properly introduced at the theater—"

"Oh, come, Mama," a beautiful dark-haired woman said. "Mrs. Carrington does not appear to be an idiot or a green goose. Be honest and say we did not know how to approach the wife of the brother of the man who is making James jealous, and all for naught."

Phyllida recognized the lady who had looked daggers at her all during the long performance. "Mrs. Swain?" she said, remembering Monkton's instructions, and attempting to do a more credible job of lying. "Yes, Mr. Richard Carrington has mentioned you to Mr. Carrington and me, purely as an example of innocent friendship."

"Yes," Lydia said with a knowing and approving smirk, "we have often lamented the way the world cannot see a friendship between a man and a woman but must turn it into a dishonest romance."

Phyllida had had quite enough by now of this conversational thin ice. "It is difficult, is it not," she said, "to find a way to call on the wife of a man who had no hostess before his marriage to make the introductions. I am glad you decided to be brave. Mr. Carrington wants me to mix with society before the season begins, so that it will not all be new to me."

"But I heard you had been out for a season, Mrs. Carrington?" the youngest lady, an enormous blonde, asked.

"Yes, Miss Swain," Phyllida said. "Four years ago. Sir Frederick Verney's sister, Mrs. Rathbone, sponsored me. As you can imagine, as a country girl from an unknown family and with no portion, I did not do very well."

"Charlotte has been out for two seasons," Lady Swain said, whether boasting or lamenting it was hard to judge. "Of course, she received a number of reasonable offers, but we are holding out for something much better, aren't we, my dear?" She nodded her head at her daughter and smiled in an encouraging way.

Charlotte blushed and shook her head. "Please, Mama," she said in a low voice. "I cannot believe it right to speak of such things."

The girl was ill at ease in society, Phyllida saw, no doubt because of her great height and voluptuous figure. Phyllida imagined that men must be so overwhelmed by her, a statue of Juno come to life, that they were either unforgivably rude or hopelessly shy. "I know what you mean," Phyllida said, smiling at the large girl. "If you say it out loud, it's bad luck." She wondered who the man was who was hoped of so desperately.

"Yes, Mrs. Carrington," Charlotte said with a smile of gratitude. "It's a silly superstition, but one is afraid to go against it."

"For one who did not do well in her only season," Lydia Swain returned to the earlier conversation, "you have redeemed yourself now."

"It was all Sir Frederick Verney's doing," Phyllida said. "I can't take any credit."

"He certainly has been generous," Lydia said. "What exactly is the tie between you two?" She opened her lazy bedroom eyes wide and round in feigned innocence, all the while Phyllida guessed she knew Verney's tastes very well and was merely making mischief for its own sake.

"Lydia!" Lady Swain spoke sharply. "You are married to my son and I insist that you behave as a daughter of mine would."

Lydia lifted a shoulder as if to ward off the little lady's wrath and smiled her unpleasant, closed-mouth smile at Phyllida. "Well?" she said.

"Friendship," Phyllida said. "The tie is between our two families—a long friendship, going back to the time of my father and Sir Frederick's father, I believe. It's a pity, isn't it, as you were saying, how quickly the world assumes the worst of what is so often an innocent situation."

Lydia blinked at the pointed sarcasm and smiled a genuine grin. "Dick said you were something out of the common way." She held out her hand. "Truce, Mrs. Carrington?"

Phyllida took the offered hand in the tips of her fingers. "Truce, Mrs. Swain," she said, dropping the hand as soon as politely possible. There was something reptilian about the woman, like a venomous snake with brilliant colors and patterns of its scales, and a coiling, sinuous body, poised to strike with deadly fangs. Whatever ailment Lydia's husband suffered from, Phyllida suspected that marriage to such a wife was a sorry remedy.

Charlotte lowered her head from her great height to speak to Phyllida. "I understand your father was a military man, Mrs. Carrington?"

Phyllida looked up at the girl with gratitude. No one in London seemed to care in the least about her dear papa and all the others who had gone off so cheerfully to every posting, looking so handsome in their red coats, and had died in France and the Low Countries and the Americas—and, like her own father, in India, of fever. *Just wasted away*, Mama had said when she got the letter, although how she could actually know . . . "Yes, Miss Swain," Phyllida answered. "He was a captain in the Fifty-first Foot. He was the second son, and was destined for the military career."

"My brother Harry is a lieutenant in the Ninety-fifth Rifles in the Peninsula," Miss Swain said. "For more or less the same reason. Perhaps Mr. Carrington has mentioned him?"

Phyllida shook her head. "I am sorry. I do not recall his mentioning a Harry Swain. But we have not spoken of past acquaintances. I will ask, if you like."

"Oh, no! Please!" The girl was horrified. "I only wondered. Harry is like most young men, not a diligent correspondent, and we have not heard from him since the taking of Ciudad Rodrigo—"

"Charlotte!" Lady Swain was so angry Phyllida was afraid the little woman was going to explode. Her soft gray hair seemed to rise from her scalp and expand under her frilly lace cap, and two big spots of red covered her cheeks in blotches, turning an interesting shade of purplish red as Phyllida watched. "I thought you had better sense than to mention that name in company."

"But Mama," Lydia intervened, delighted at the embarrassing turn the conversation had taken, "Mrs. Carrington is surely an exception." She turned to Phyllida. "You would not have known, of course, but three years ago Mr. Carrington and our Harry were the *best* of good friends. It *is* interesting, as we have remarked, how the world puts such unpleasant interpretations on the purest of friendships."

So, Phyllida thought, amused. Another attempted spoke in the wheel of her marriage. And Lydia must have found a way to have a bet placed for her at White's—against Andrew's success. She was tempted to ask Andrew, but for poor Miss Swain's mortification.

"Yes, it is interesting," Phyllida replied to Lydia's last barb, but looking at blonde Miss Swain. "Fortunately Mr. Carrington and I have promised to be honest. It was a condition of our marriage, one might say, so there is no reason for us to hide our true feelings or otherwise dissemble."

"Well!" Lady Swain let out her breath with a whoosh. "There's a recipe for a failed marriage if ever I heard one."

"Indeed," Lydia said with a hiss of laughter, "imagine if the rest of the world adopted such a scheme. Nothing but murder, divorce, and scandal."

It was to be hoped, Phyllida thought, as the conversation wound down into less contentious topics, that adherence to the terms of honesty, and her plan for bringing her relations with Andrew to some kind of resolution, did not culminate in the ending of her marriage in all three of these calamities.

THE MORNING OF THE day that was to end in Phyllida's capitulation began propitiously enough. Phyllida made a point of coming down to breakfast to put her plan into action, instead of taking the usual tray in her boudoir. However nervous she felt, she was determined not to let herself off the hook.

"Good morning, Andrew," she said, seeing him engrossed in the newspaper. "I was testing the lock on my bedroom door last night. It sticks sometimes, you know. Do you think Yardley can get someone to loosen it?"

Andrew seemed to stiffen behind the paper. He lowered the sheets and peered over the top. "I beg your pardon?" he said.

"My bedroom door, Andrew. The lock is hard to turn."

Andrew put the paper down. "Hail Caesar," he whispered. "We who are about to die salute you." He beckoned to a footman. "Have Jamie and Kevin attend us here, please."

"Now, sir?" the man asked.

"As soon as possible," Andrew said.

In about ten minutes two enormous young men, obviously called from other duties, one smelling strongly of horse, the other wiping hands encrusted with garden soil on his grimy breeches, came slouching into the breakfast room. Andrew apologized for interrupting their work and turned to Phyllida. "You see the size of these two?" he remarked. "I don't think a jammed door would stand up to one gentle push from their shoulders, do you?" He nodded at the two bewildered men. "That will be all, thank you."

The two bowed, as mystified as before, and moved to go. "Be you needing a door opened?" the bolder one said.

"We'll see," Andrew said. "If it gives me the least trouble, I'll send for you."

"Ought to do it now, sir," the man said. "Don't want the missus to be stuck inside and everyone out or downstairs."

Andrew raised his eyebrows. "Your zeal is commendable—Kevin, is it?" The man nodded. "But I doubt very much there's a problem. I only called you in so that Mrs. Carrington could see there was nothing to worry about."

The men went out and Andrew smiled at Phyllida. "Round one to me, I think," he said.

Phyllida bit her lip and tried to hide her answering smile. She had been unprepared for that gambit. She wasn't sure what to do next. There really was no reason for her to quarrel with Andrew. Perhaps she could claim it was the wrong time of the month. But what if he believed her and wouldn't come to her bed? No, that was too risky. "I can promise you one thing, Andrew," she said. "If you snap your fingers at me I won't answer for the consequences."

"What?" Andrew abandoned the paper he had taken up again. He snapped his fingers. "Like this?"

"Not now," Phyllida said. "Later." She flickered her eyes to the liveried footman standing by the sideboard.

"Ah," Andrew said, beginning to comprehend. "I wish I'd known before." He snapped his fingers again. "Interesting. I never thought."

"The post, sir." Yardley came in, bearing a few letters and invitations on a tray, plus one large wrapped parcel. He was surprised to see Phyllida at the table. "Good morning, madam. A pleasure to see you downstairs so early."

"Thank you, Yardley," Phyllida said.

"Yardley." Andrew's voice was cold. "Mrs. Carrington's habits need not be commented on, by you or anyone."

The man's face became stern and set, the eyes veiled. "I beg your pardon, sir, madam. I meant no offense." He bowed and turned abruptly, closing the door behind him with a loud snap.

"Andrew!" Phyllida said. "Was that really necessary?"

"I won't have it," Andrew said. "I won't have anyone discussing your behavior, or mine. It may seem innocent enough, and no doubt it was, this time. It's a natural impulse for servants to take an interest in the doings of their masters. But leave it uncorrected and the entire household will think nothing of parsing every little thing—who visits, who stays the night, who didn't come home, who sleeps where. Our every move, our every thought, will be picked over and hashed out until our lives will be as public as those of the beasts in the Tower of London's menagerie."

"Surely you're exaggerating."

Andrew glared at her. "How do you think I keep my position in society, living as I do? By having a loyal and discreet staff, that's how. Everybody who works here knows what I am, what my nature is. But I pay well, above the average, and I'm a fair and easygoing master. Anyone who doesn't wish to work in this kind of household is free to seek employment elsewhere, with an excellent reference, I might add, and no hard feelings. I've been master here for almost ten years, since my father died. Not one person has chosen to leave, other than a maid or two who married. But it all depends on the one thing I demand: on keeping one's thoughts, good and bad, to oneself."

Phyllida nodded. "I do see, Andrew. I hadn't reasoned it all out so thoroughly. I shouldn't have teased about the lock on the door."

Andrew laughed. "No, I quite enjoyed that. I didn't mean that you must feel inhibited in your conversation—quite the opposite." He sorted through the letters on the tray, fastening onto the battered package. "Good God! At last!" His face was pallid and his hand trembled slightly as he tore it open. Smaller bundles of what looked like individual letters tied with string tumbled out, along with a large folded sheet. "Forgive me, I must attend to this."

Phyllida sat in silence while Andrew perused the sheet of paper, scrawled in a loose hand comprising relatively little text. She expected he wanted to be left alone, but she was not finished eating, and she couldn't suppress her curiosity. The package looked as if it had come a long distance, over both land and water, judging from the stains on the outer wrapping. From overseas . . . from the Peninsula, perhaps?

"Cunt!" Andrew said.

Phyllida looked up in shock.

"Whoring cunt," Andrew said and stood up. "Goddamned wide-arsed, double-dealing, two-faced bitch." He leaned on the table, staring at Phyllida with unfocused eyes, not really seeing her, crumpled the large sheet, strode to the fireplace, and threw it on the flames, as the startled footman moved aside. "Burn in hell, Harry Swain," Andrew said, "you and your sodding prick of a Captain Quincy." He watched the blaze for a minute or two, the flames licking lazily at the heavy paper, the small fire barely turning the edges black. When the outside began to char, he burst into tears and seized the poker, scrabbling in the growing conflagration, apparently trying to bring the letter out again.

"Do you need help, sir?" the footman dared to ask.

"Yes, damn you!" Andrew shouted. "Get that goddamn letter out of the fucking fireplace, for Christ's sake."

The man winced at the language and the tone but took the tongs and the shovel and worked hurriedly, managing to save the bulk of the letter, scraping it forward out of the grate onto the stone hearth. Andrew snatched at it as it emerged, smoking and blackened, burning his fingers on it and dropping it on the floor. "Shit," he muttered as he licked his fingers. "Shit, fuck, piss."

Phyllida and the footman shared a worried glance. "Thank you for acting so promptly," Phyllida said. "Perhaps you should leave us now."

"Will you be all right, madam?" the footman asked.

"Certainly," Phyllida said. "He is my husband."

"Yes, madam," the footman said, bowing and escaping with relief.

Phyllida hoped she had been correct in her brave words. Andrew was at the moment standing on the hearth, staring down at the piece of damaged paper, tears falling unheeded and coursing down the creases in his cheeks on either side of his prominent nose. "Come," Phyllida said, putting a hand on his arm. "Come and sit back down and have some tea."

Andrew had no reaction. He allowed Phyllida to lead him to the table and sat down in his place while she poured him a cup of rather stewed tea. He craned his neck once in the direction of the fireplace. "Harry," he whispered.

"I'll bring the letter," Phyllida said. "Don't worry. Drink your tea."

Andrew nodded and obeyed, taking a large swig of the tea, choking, and spewing it back in the general direction of the cup. Most of it went on the table, some hit the saucer, the rest of it spilled onto his waistcoat. "What are you trying to do, poison me?" he said. "Can't a man get something decent to drink in his own house?"

"Of course," Phyllida said. "Which would you prefer? Arsenic or hemlock?"

The attempt at humor went unacknowledged. "Brandy," Andrew said.

Phyllida rang the bell. A cold and stiff Yardley answered the summons, but when he saw Andrew's state and heard the request, he softened. "Mr. Carrington has had bad news," Phyllida said.

"Yes, madam," Yardley said. "May I be allowed to express my condolences?" After Andrew's scolding, it was a serious question.

"Of course," Phyllida said. "Mr. Carrington will be most appreciative, when he is in a better condition to hear them."

"Thank you, madam," Yardley said and went for the brandy. Obviously the man thought someone had died. Still, Phyllida decided it was more important that this influential member of the staff be back in sympathy with Andrew than to clarify the precise nature of the bad news.

The spirits restored Andrew to a semblance of rationality, if not equanimity. He fingered the scorched edges of the letter, but did not attempt to unfold or smooth it. He sat quietly for a long interval, wiping his face with a napkin, while the flow of tears ebbed to a trickle and dried. Eventually he looked up and around the room, like a baby just waking to consciousness. "Phyllida," he said. "What are you doing here?"

"I was having breakfast when the post came," she said. "I'm sorry, Andrew."

"Oh, God," Andrew moaned and laid his head in his hands. "What an ass you must think me."

Phyllida stood over him and tried to put her arm around his shoulders. "Because you love someone so much you are hurt when he stops loving you? No, Andrew. I think you are very human. I am only sorry you had to suffer such a loss."

Andrew shrugged off her comforting arm and looked up into her face. "Aren't you going to laugh at me and sneer at my pathetic attachment, a man in love with a boy, an unnatural passion for one of His Majesty's troops?"

Phyllida gaped. "I wouldn't think of it! Why would I? Is that how you see yourself?"

"It's what the world thinks," Andrew said.

"Not the whole world, surely," Phyllida protested. "Not your friends in the Brotherhood of Philander. Why don't you go around there when you're feeling better? They should be sympathetic."

"Ha!" Andrew said. "That's all you know. They'll laugh at me, say we told you so. Ever heard the song 'The Girl I Left Behind Me'?"

Phyllida stared at the strange question. "Of course," she said. "Everyone's heard that. It's what the troops play when they—Oh."

"Oh, indeed," Andrew said. "You see? That's me. I'm the stupid bitch Harry left behind. All my friends said I should put him out of my mind. He was gone. Even if he wasn't killed, he'd forget me, find someone else. But I couldn't let him go. I wrote to him every week, every day in the beginning. And he wrote back, for a while."

"And then he stopped," Phyllida said. She remembered her visit from the Swains, Charlotte's nervous question about her brother. "And now he's written that he's in love with someone else, and he's returned all your letters."

"He's been going on and on about this fucking Captain Quincy for months," Andrew said. "I should have read between the lines, but—"

"But no one wants to face that truth before he has to," Phyllida tried to soothe. She was almost ready to start using foul language herself, but somehow she didn't care. Andrew was talking to her like a person, like a fellow human being. If it meant having to hear a few other choice epithets, no great harm done.

"What about your father?" Andrew asked. "Was he faithful to your mother?"

Phyllida fought her initial reaction to say it was none of his business; she understood the reason behind it. "How can I know?" she answered. "I was fifteen when he died, and he'd been overseas for a year by then. But I think he was, in spirit, at least. My mother never complained—about that, at any rate. They were married, after all, with three children."

Andrew laughed in a bitter, vicious tone. "Ah, yes," he said. "Marriage. Don't you think I would have married Harry if I could? All you people think you're so goddamned superior with your marriage and your children. And we poor sodomites are damned for loving and damned for not marrying. Damned for existing, damned for being different, and damned for not hiding ourselves away like lepers. Damn, damn, damn."

"I don't think that," Phyllida said. "You may damn and goddamn and fuck and shit and piss at the world all you please, Andrew. But not at me. I married you knowing what you are and you will not include me in your damnations. It's not fair."

Andrew stared in horror at the unladylike language before breaking into howls of wild laughter that threatened to turn into sobs again. "Come here," he said when he saw how she had shrunk back against the far wall. "I won't hurt you, Phyllida. Please. Come here and let me tell you how grateful I am for you, that you married me."

Phyllida took the chance and went. She let Andrew set her on his lap, let him draw her head against his chest, still wet from the spewed tea, and let him stroke her hair. "Are you grateful, Andrew?" she asked. "Are you glad you married me? Would you rather be alone for a while?"

"Yes, yes, and yes," Andrew said, the words reminding him of a very different conversation, what seemed like a very long time ago. "But not just yet. Stay with me, please, until I'm stronger. Do you mind?"

"No, I don't mind," Phyllida said. "I want to. Are you able to eat any more or would you like to lie down?"

"Actually," Andrew said, "I think I'd like to—" He stopped, his face going as white as the tablecloth. He had the forethought to push Phyllida away before he clutched his head, bent over, and vomited the entire contents of his stomach onto the floor. Then he groaned, rolled gracefully off his chair, and lay on his back in a faint.

ANDREW AWOKE IN THE DARK. It was his room, his bed; he could tell that much. As for the rest *Harry*. He remembered the letter, the anger. And Phyllida. Oh, God. He had ruined that. If ever there had been a chance of making a success of this marriage, he had destroyed it. He rolled from side to side in the bed, plucked at the covers, and moaned.

"There, he's awake," a woman's voice said. "Andrew? Can you hear me?"

"Fldaaa," Andrew said. "Msrreee."

"Don't press him, Mrs. Carrington," a man's voice said. "It always takes him a while to come out of these episodes."

"But he'll be all right?" The woman again.

"He should do," the man said. "A migraine is an uncomfortable thing while it lasts, but it causes no permanent damage so far as I know."

The voices faded out.

"JUST LET HIM SLEEP," MR. Stevens said. "I've left some laudanum, but there's no need to dope him if he sleeps naturally. When he wakes, if he's still in pain, give him a small dose. Otherwise, he should be fine in a day or two."

"Thank you," Phyllida said. "Thank you for being so encouraging."

"I am a physician, you know," Stevens said. "If I thought it were more serious, I would tell you. But Carrington has been a patient of mine for years, since I set up my practice. His migraines and I are old acquaintances."

"I've never seen one," Phyllida said. "I'd heard the word, but I didn't know what it meant. Andrew said nothing to me."

The doctor shrugged. "Men don't like to boast of their frailties, even to their wives. Especially not to their wives."

"But what about—" Phyllida started the question before realizing how improper it was.

"Yes?" Stevens prompted.

"Nothing," Phyllida said. "I just want to be sure that Andrew's not an invalid. That it's safe for him to—" Again she was inhibited with a stranger.

"Ah." The doctor began to see the direction of the questions. "It's all right, Mrs. Carrington. I understand your concern, and your natural delicacy of expression. Very commendable. To answer your question, your husband can resume all his regular activities with no danger, as soon as he feels able. All activities." He stared meaningfully into Phyllida's earnest, upturned face. "Does that put your mind at rest, Mrs. Carrington?"

"Yes, thank you," Phyllida said. "You're very kind."

"Not at all," Stevens said. "Tell me, how long have you been married? I saw the notice in the papers, but—"

"Just a little over two weeks." Phyllida blushed, for some reason.

"I see," Stevens said with a smile of comprehension. "Still on your honeymoon, eh? Don't worry. Your husband will be up and raring to go in a day or two, I promise you." He winked. "Haven't lost our wager yet."

"What? How?" Phyllida gasped. "Is it all over town then?"

Reginald Stevens coughed and bowed slightly. "Forgive me for presuming, Mrs. Carrington. I thought you knew when you sent for me. I could not have treated your husband all these years without being privy to the particulars of his life. A life, may I say, that is different from mine only insofar as the life of a wealthy gentleman of leisure is easier than that of a man who must work for a living, albeit in a profession." He smiled genially at her abashed look. "Nobody expects a doctor to have a human side. But I have seen all the members of the Brotherhood of Philander in my capacity as physician, and most of them in the role of, shall we say, friend."

"Oh." Phyllida had no rational reply she could think of. She tried to study Mr. Stevens covertly, sliding her eyes sideways without appearing to stare. He was younger than he at first appeared, his formal manners making him seem middle-aged when he was probably only a few years older than Andrew. He was well dressed for a doctor, in a clean and relatively new coat, a simple yet tailored shirt, a modest cravat, and plain, neat pantaloons. He was of sturdy, almost portly build, not yet fat but solid, with receding brown hair and undistinguished but pleasant features.

"Yes," Stevens said, noting her poorly concealed inspection. "Even your husband."

"I'm sorry," Phyllida said. "I didn't mean—"

"Perfectly natural," Stevens waved off her apology. "And you needn't let it trouble you. It was years ago." His eyes went unfocused for a brief moment. "Quite a stallion, your Andrew. Last I heard, he had taken up with a young fellow in one of those newfangled regiments. Green jackets."

Phyllida gave up matronly modesty. "Harry Swain, Ninety-fifth Rifles," she said. "That's what brought this attack on. He's been over in the Peninsula for almost three years now and just this morning Andrew got one of those cruel letters, breaking things off."

"Three years?" Stevens exclaimed. "That's extraordinary!"

"How do you mean?"

"Perhaps it's different for women," Stevens said, "although I doubt it. Three years is a ridiculously long time to hold on to the memory of a love affair. Swain did Carrington a favor. Ought to have done it sooner."

"But do you think it will make a difference?" Phyllida asked. "In terms of Andrew's recovery."

"Hard to say," Stevens said. "I've never thought him to be of a melancholy disposition. Do you know—that is, forgive me for asking, but—"

Phyllida laughed, pleased at the turnabout that Stevens was now embarrassed. "Yes," she said. "If you're asking whether Andrew has had lovers, yes. He hasn't been moping about celibate for three years."

"No," Stevens said, not yet ready to meet Phyllida's amused gaze, "I shouldn't think so, an energetic man like him. What I meant was, has he been in love?"

Phyllida shook her head. "How can I answer that? We've only been married two weeks."

"Yes, yes," Stevens said. "But before that. Did he mention anything, anybody?"

"You don't understand," Phyllida said. "I just met Andrew two weeks ago."

"My goodness!" Stevens was thoroughly routed. "What an amazing woman! I congratulate Carrington on his good fortune. If he has the least bit of sense in that handsome brain box of his, he'll have fallen in love with you."

"As a woman," Phyllida said, "I wouldn't bet on it."

"Now, now," Stevens said, bowing over her hand and taking his leave, "false modesty doesn't suit you. Just give Carrington a little time. Bound to fall in love with a beauty like you. Not all men like us are impervious to feminine charms."

"No," Phyllida said, "what I meant was, as a woman, I am unlikely to set high odds on any man's having the least bit of sense."

Stevens threw his head back and roared with laughter. "Just go on as you've been, Mrs. Carrington," he said when he caught his breath. "If your husband's not back in the saddle again in a day or two, you must send for me, but I suspect all should be well."

They had reached the door, and Stevens bowed again to Phyllida as the footman showed him out. "Damme if I don't double my bet at White's," he said to himself as he descended the front steps. "Now, who can I trust to place it without spiking the odds?"

"MADAM." YARDLEY HOVERED AT PHYLLIDA'S side after the doctor had gone. "If you please, can you tell me? How is the master?"

Phyllida smiled at the old retainer's obvious concern. "Apparently it is not so serious as it looked," she said. "Mr. Stevens assured me that he has treated Mr. Carrington for years, and that these migraines do not leave any permanent damage."

"Never seen him took so fierce," Yardley muttered. "I swear I meant no harm by my words. Would you tell him that, madam?"

"Yardley," Phyllida stopped and looked into the old man's eyes. "What happened had nothing to do with you. I told you, Mr. Carrington had bad news in that letter he received. Please don't upset yourself."

"Is he— That is, that there Harry Swain. Begging your pardon, madam, but do you know if he's been wounded or—" Yardley was as tongue-tied as everyone when it came to his master's private life, but apparently just as knowledgeable.

Phyllida felt her eyes misting. It was touching, a whole household devoted to an irascible but generally fair and decent young master, determined to protect his reputation but all of them intimately acquainted with the facts. "Nothing so bad as that, Yardley," she said. "Only the ending of their friendship, you see, and returning Mr. Carrington's letters."

Yardley shook his head. "Thank the Lord for that. Still, they take it hard, the young 'uns. Master Andrew always took it hard."

"I will tell him of your concern when he wakes up," Phyllida said. "Mr. Carrington will be glad of your sympathy, and the rest of the household's."

"Thank you madam," Yardley said. "But you won't let on what I've said on the subject of this Harry Swain, do you hear?" The old man forgot all his deference to his new mistress in his worry that his master should not learn that the staff knew all there was to know of him, and loved him anyway. "He won't like thinking that his private doings are known downstairs. Not that they are, mind you."

"Hush, Yardley," Phyllida said. "I understand. I won't breathe a word. And thank you for your discretion."

Yardley watched until the mistress was safely in the dining room with the door shut before pulling another offending piece of mail from his pocket. It had come several days ago and he had been holding it all this time, waiting for the right moment to ask the master what to do. It seemed he had waited too long. He couldn't bother poor Mr. Andrew with this, not after his distressing news and bad turn of sickness. Yardley had sworn that he was no longer in communication with his nephew and, strictly speaking, he had not broken his word. But this was the third letter that had come within the past year, and he had hoped to consult the master before passing another one on.

Wishing fervently he had had the good sense not to learn his nephew's new place of abode, Yardley went to the master's study, brought out a bottle of ink and a pen from the unlocked cabinet, crossed out the Grosvenor Square address and wrote in the correct one, then placed the letter with the others to be posted. The secretary, Mr. Turner, would see to it. What harm could it do, after all? Surely young Walter had some acquaintances who wished him well, who did not know or did not care about the wretched business of the White Swan, and had no other way to reach him than through his uncle. A shame there was no name or return address on the outside. It never occurred to the trusting old man to open the letter.

PHYLLIDA GATHERED UP THE REMNANTS of the ill-starred letter and the contents of the package from the breakfast room to keep for Andrew when he woke up. The room had been cleaned, the fireplace swept out, the packets of tied letters placed in a neat pile beside the large burned sheet at Andrew's place. The table had been otherwise cleared, the food returned to the kitchen and pantry, the tablecloth crumbed and scraped. The noisome pool of Andrew's stomach contents had been wiped up and the floor mopped. A sour smell lingered, however. Phyllida rang and had the anxious footman open the windows.

"The master won't like that," the man complained. "Lets in soot, he says."

"I suppose it does." The miasma over London was more noticeable in the changeable coal-burning month of March than it had been during the late spring of Phyllida's season four years ago. "But it's better to air the room out, before Mr. Carrington comes down and gets sick again from the stench."

"Yes, madam," the man said. "Will he be all right, do you know?"

"The doctor thinks so." She looked more closely at the footman, realizing he was the man who had been in attendance during breakfast and had witnessed Andrew's attack. "I'm sure Mr. Carrington will wish to apologize for the strong language he used when he wakes up. It was only his emotions overtaking him that made him so forget himself."

"It don't matter," the man said. "I know he didn't mean no harm." He tried to contain his own emotions, and failed. "I remember that Harry Swain. Too young he was, for all his great size. And wild, goin' off with all them other soldiers. You tell the master, madam, would you, that we're all sorry and there's plenty more fish in the sea."

Phyllida picked up the letter after the man had gone. She no longer had qualms about spying, seeing that everyone in the house knew as much, if not more, than she did. She unfolded the paper carefully, trying to keep it intact. The heavy sheet, waterlogged from its journey, was dated a good month earlier and placed the writer merely "on the road from Ciudad Rodrigo." It was scrawled in a loose hand that left wide margins, and was perfectly legible once the worst creases were smoothed out.

The letter began conventionally, if less than truthfully:

My dearest Andrew,

I ought to have written you before, but as you can imagine, on campaign there's not always leisure. I don't know an easy way to say this, so I'll just write it plain. I can no longer swear that you hold the first place in my affections. Robert—Captain Quincy, that is—my commanding officer and my very good friend, says that it is wrong of me to let you go on believing our friendship is the same as it has always been, and that I owe it to you to set you free, as I am freeing myself. To this end I am returning all of your letters I can find. You are welcome to keep mine if you wish, as a remembrance of the love we once shared. Please, Andrew, know that I will forever cherish the memory of our time together, and that you will always hold a place in my heart.

Your ever-loving Harry.

The missive ended, dishonestly as it began.

Phyllida was tempted to crumple it up again and throw it back on the fire. Except there was no fire now, and the letter was not hers to dispose of. She grimaced at it in distaste. It was the letter of a very young man, she realized, little more than a schoolboy. Hadn't Andrew said something about that? *A man in love with a boy.* Still, lots of men of Andrew's age fell in love with women ten years younger, and people expected the girls to be faithful, to treat their lovers with courtesy.

Perhaps she was making too much of it. Andrew was equally at fault. He might sneer at the marriage vows that had kept Phyllida's father faithful to her mother, and many other husbands and wives together over longer separations, but the fact was it did make a difference. Not because of their being of opposite sexes, but because of factors like age and children. Phyllida's father had been forty when he died, the father of three, married for sixteen years, many of them spent at home. Any young girl who fell in love with a soldier knew she'd never see him again if he went away without marrying. That's what that song was all about, what all the jokes and stories about soldiers—and sailors—were about.

It was human nature. Men's nature, at any rate. Just because the one left behind was also a man didn't change anything. Even if Andrew and Harry Swain had been able to marry, Phyllida guessed Harry would have found a way to wriggle out of it somehow. He was, as the indignant footman had mentioned, too young, and wild, and tending to go off with the other soldiers. Not the makings of a good husband—or wife—whichever role he played in the relationship. *Did* Andrew and his lovers see themselves in male and female roles, Phyllida wondered. Or was it all men together?

Phyllida choked down the inappropriate laughter that rose in her throat, gathered up the letters, refolded the charred sheet, and wrapped them all up in the outer package before going upstairs to check on her bereaved husband.

Andrew was sleeping peacefully when Phyllida peeped in on him. She sat for a while beside the bed, pulled the covers up over his shoulders, and stroked a timid hand over his clammy brow, smoothing the dark curls back from his forehead. He flinched at the light touch, becoming agitated and muttering what sounded to Phyllida like more curses and four-letter words. She was not doing him any good here.

Out in the corridor, Phyllida was startled to run into Andrew's secretary. "Mrs. Carrington!" The young man seemed equally surprised to see her. "How is Mr. Carrington? I understand he had an attack of migraine."

"Yes, Mr. Turner," Phyllida said. "He received some bad news. Thank you for your concern, but it's better not to disturb him now. He's sleeping, and the doctor says that's the best thing for him."

"Actually, Mrs. Carrington, it's you I wish to see. I was wondering—did you have a chance yet to look over the kitchen accounts?"

Phyllida, her mind ever on the alert for suspicious behavior and sinister conspiracies, the better to stretch out the chapters of her fiction, was suddenly wary. Why would he be worrying about such a trivial thing now? He had already pestered her earlier this week.

"Why, no, Mr. Turner," she said, watching for his reaction. "Was there something in them you wished to add or change? Just write it down and I'll make the adjustment when I go over them."

The young man smiled and spread his hands in an apologetic manner. "Nothing so simple, I'm afraid. The whole system is antiquated. No one coming to it fresh could be expected to make heads or tails of it. I thought I should go over it with you the first couple of months to explain it to you and answer your questions."

Phyllida stared. Mr. Turner had seemed an innocent young man, unobtrusive and quiet. Since the negotiations over the marriage settlement, Phyllida had barely seen him. Although he lived in the house and worked for Andrew, he was not exactly a servant. He was entitled to take meals with Andrew and Phyllida, but he had generally absented himself from the upstairs table. It must be uncomfortable for him, the idea of joining the intimate dinners and suppers, just her and Andrew and, sometimes, Richard, not to mention the suppers with Rhys—no, he must have decided to eat downstairs, or out, or in his room.

Phyllida was convinced her suspicions were not misplaced. "You forget, Mr. Turner, I am the eldest of three daughters. My family was not so elevated that I was allowed to ignore the rudiments of household economy. I am quite familiar with the keeping of kitchen accounts. If you want the job back, I am more than happy to hand it over, but Mrs. Badger was insistent that the mistress should do it. When Mr. Carrington is better and has time to be troubled with such tedium, I will discuss the matter then." She moved to pass along to the boudoir.

Mr. Turner grabbed her arm. "Please, Mrs. Carrington," he said. "Let me have the book. I'll do the accounts this time, and when Mr. Carrington is well, I'll ask him what he prefers."

Phyllida glared at him and snatched her arm free. "Why are you making such a fuss over kitchen accounts? Is there something going on with them I should know?"

"That's just it," he said. "There may be. It's why I need to look at them. No point in making accusations before I have the facts."

"Well, why didn't you examine them before?"

"I wasn't sure until this month. And when Mrs. Badger gave them to you instead, I became certain. But without seeing them . . ."

Phyllida stared harder. The light in the corridor was dim, and Mr. Turner had the kind of face that gives little away. She had been skeptical from the start of the conversation, but he could be right. The only way to know was to go over the damn accounts book herself. The last thing she wanted. She had Andrew's health to worry about, and the galleys to proof. Mr. Edwards had been incensed over the minor emendations she had made so far, although slightly more amenable when he had seen how meticulously Phyllida had fitted them to the type that had already been set. Still, it would take a great deal of persuasion to get him to accept the idea of a substantial change in the novel's ending, with the probable delay in publishing.

They had reached the door of her boudoir, the door that she and Andrew had teased each other over just a short time ago. "I'll have a look for the accounts book," Phyllida said. "It may take a while. I've had so much work to do on my novel I just put it aside and forgot about it. It's buried somewhere under a pile of galley proofs. When I find it I'll bring it down." She turned the knob, hoping it would stick, and unhappily felt it open smoothly.

There was a bump against her side and she was shoved into the room. The door was kicked shut and the bolt shot home. "Tell me where it is, bitch," Mr. Turner said.

Phyllida pointed to the work on her desk. "In there somewhere, I think." The change from deferential underling to threatening bully was so sudden Phyllida could not immediately adjust.

"Give it here," he said.

Phyllida walked to the desk, trying to think. She was locked in with a man desperate enough to molest her in her own house, her own rooms, with her husband not twenty feet away. She lifted a few sheets, pretending to search. "I told you," she said. "I misplaced it. It'll take me time to find it. Why don't you leave me to look for it and I'll—"

Mr. Turner's arms went around her, and before she fully understood what was happening she was being dragged and pushed into the connecting bedroom. "You've had your chance to give it up easily," he said. "Now I'll take what I want."

Phyllida had no chance to run. In the same moment she considered her next move, she found herself on her back on the bed with this quiet, diffident young man kneeling over her, fumbling under her skirts and undoing the flap of his pantaloons. This time she didn't hesitate. She sucked in a deep breath and let it out in a piercing shriek, kicking at Turner and pummeling with her fists. She tried to sit up but was pushed roughly back down.

"Hellcat," he said. He backhanded her, so hard she tasted blood, and threw himself on her again, pinning her with his weight. "Why are you fighting me? You must be desperate for it, married to that cocksucking sodomite."

Phyllida went limp, waiting her chance. When she felt a vulnerable part of his anatomy coming within range, she lifted her knee sharply, putting as much force into it as she could. The man screamed in pain and rolled away.

Phyllida jumped off the bed, ran to the door, and tugged at the bolt, shouting as loud as she could all the time. God, it was like something in a nightmare. The lock really did seem to stick. She tugged and pried at it, tearing a fingernail, and Turner was on her again, his arm around her neck, his other hand squeezing her breasts in a painful grip.

"Please," Phyllida said. "Don't do this." She screamed again for help.

"Missus?" A voice from the corridor. "You stuck in there, missus?"

Turner let Phyllida go and backed away. "Keep quiet," he hissed, "or I'll tell."

"Tell what?" Phyllida said. "Yes!" she called. "The lock's jammed!"

"Everything," Turner said. "About your sodomite husband and all his friends at the Brotherhood of Philander."

"Stand back," the blessed voice called. "I'll bust down the door."

Phyllida moved to one side. There was a crash and the splintering of wood, and the large man who worked in the square's central garden came stumbling through. "There," he said with satisfaction. "Told the master better do it afore you got stuck."

The broken door sagged on its hinges, the lock wrenched away and dangling from the jamb. Phyllida got a glimpse of one or two other people in the corridor—Pumfry, Andrew's valet, and Joan, the downstairs maid—but once they saw that the cause of the noise had been taken care of, they were gone about their work again in an instant.

"Kevin?" Phyllida said. The man nodded and she grasped his grimy paw and shook it heartily, smiling into his surprised and grinning face. "Thank you! Oh, thank you so much! You can't imagine how frightened I was."

"From being stuck in your room?" he said. "Don't you fret. You woulda been let out soon enough." He stared at her face. "You hurt, missus?"

Phyllida touched her sore cheek where Turner had struck her. She didn't want to raise suspicions now, with the man still in the room. She turned around to look for him but the room appeared empty. "Mr. Carrington had bad news this morning," she said. The words came out without conscious thought. "He was very upset, and he said things he didn't mean."

Kevin's kind, open face clouded over. "That's all right, missus. I understand. The master has a temper, but it don't last long. He'll be right again in the morning." He touched a finger to his forehead and lumbered away down the corridor.

Phyllida ran after him. "Will you get someone to repair the door?" she asked. Her voice sounded high and breathy, like a scared child's.

Kevin glanced around. "O'course, missus," he said. "I'm just after seeing Mr. Yardley about it."

"I'll come with you," Phyllida said. "I don't like being alone in there."

Kevin shook his head in sympathy. "You got a fear of being trapped?" he said. "Lots of folks like that, can't abide a locked door or a shut window."

"That's it," Phyllida said. "Makes me nervous. And then when the door really did stick—"

"That's all right, missus," Kevin said. "We'll rehang the door, and we'll oil the hinges and the lock so it turns easy. Probably all it needed before, but what's done is done."

PHYLLIDA SAT IN THE DRAFTY breakfast room, oblivious to the cold air raising goose bumps on her skin, waiting for her pounding heart to subside, while Kevin went in search of Yardley and a carpenter. *She had as good as accused Andrew of striking her.* She had almost been raped by Mr. Turner, but she had let Kevin, and no doubt the rest of the household by now, think Andrew had abused her. And judging from the look on Kevin's face, the household would blame her for telling, rather than Andrew for doing it. Which was a despicable attitude in general, but correct in this case, and oh, *why* had she done it?

Everything, Turner had said. *I'll tell everything about your sodomite husband and all his friends. . .*

She saw it again, the same vision she had had the morning after her wedding night, when she had talked with Sir Frederick and Andrew, and learned of the dangers they faced. *Andrew locked in the pillory, the mob throwing filth, his face bloodied, eyes blackened, perhaps blinded, nose and teeth broken . . .* She choked back a sob.

The one person who was entitled to leave marks like the bruise on her face was Andrew. A man could beat his wife much worse than a mere slap or a box on the ears, with impunity. If she told the truth, Phyllida would be condemning herself and her husband, both. It was always a losing proposition for a woman to accuse a man of rape if he wasn't caught in the act. And even then. Phyllida had heard stories—women torn and bleeding below, made pregnant, given the pox, and still the men had prevailed, saying the women invited it. Hadn't Turner said the same thing? *She must be desperate, married to a sodomite.* Who would doubt that, except Andrew's friends? And what could they do about it anyway, not being witnesses?

And then there was that horrible wager. If there was the least hint that the child was someone else's—she couldn't bear it. Andrew had said, just this morning, how glad he was she had married him.

They had been teasing, reaching a precious moment of harmony, had been planning to make love tonight. No, she couldn't let Andrew worry over this. And what real harm had come of it, anyway? She hadn't been raped, not even close. The attempt to hearten herself by making light of her trouble failed, as most such efforts do.

"There you are, madam." Yardley came into the room and shut the windows. "You'll catch your death, sitting in this draft." He sucked in his breath as Phyllida looked up and turned her face to his. "I beg your pardon, madam. I did not mean to disturb you." He wouldn't meet her eyes.

She must look terrible if Yardley was so discomposed. "Has the carpenter come yet?" she asked.

"On his way upstairs, madam. Won't take long before your room is good as new. Perhaps you should wait down here."

Yardley didn't want anyone to see her, to see the evidence of Andrew's mistreatment. She was in total agreement, wanted nothing better than to hide in her boudoir, wash her face, perhaps try some of the makeup that Gladys and Rhys had given her as a parting gift. But she remembered that Turner had still been inside when she had followed Kevin downstairs, and she had to be sure that the secretary had taken advantage of her absence to get safely out and away. And she could not possibly be alone when she checked the room.

"I'll just go up and see how things are coming along," Phyllida said, ignoring Yardley's faint protests.

She heard voices on the landing as she headed up the stairs. A gaggle of people—the carpenter, Kevin, Mrs. Featherstone, Nan, Joan, and Mr. Pumfry—stood exclaiming in the doorway of the boudoir. They fell silent as Phyllida appeared, then stood aside to let her through.

The broken door had been removed and the gaping doorway revealed a scene of devastation. Galley proofs were strewn all over, on the furniture and the floor, crumpled and torn and stepped on. The little writing desk was ruined, the drawer broken open in a tiny parody of the door to the room, the hardware of the lock prized away from the delicate veneer.

In the bedroom, as Phyllida walked through in a horrified daze, the spectacle was worse. Chests and drawers were open and ransacked, gowns and undergarments tossed out on top of the papers. A bottle of ink had been smashed, spilling over the mess. Of all the garments, the beautiful pink-and-cream ball gown had borne the brunt of it. That last sight was too much for Phyllida. She sank down on top of the mess, put her head in her hands, and bawled like a child.

THE CONSENSUS WAS THAT A bold and lucky thief, seeing the footmen and carpenter going in and out the back, and sensing confusion, had taken advantage of a unique opportunity to loot a Mayfair town house.

"But how did he get in and out with no one seeing him?" Mr. Pumfry asked.

Mr. Turner appeared in the middle of the discussion, strode into the feminine rooms as if completely at home in them, and pointed to the open casement, the curtains fluttering in the breeze. "We can see how he got out, at any rate," he said, smirking at Phyllida's scowl.

Nan looked up from where she sat beside her mistress on the bed and ran to the window. "Nah," she said, looking down the sheer drop of three stories to the yard in back. "He'da broke his leg—or his neck."

"Perhaps he had a rope," Mr. Turner persisted.

"Then where is it?" Nan said.

"Took it with him, of course," Mr. Turner said, becoming visibly annoyed.

"How?" Mrs. Featherstone pursued the point. "How does someone climb down a rope and then untie it and take it with him? It doesn't make any sense."

"What if he's still here?" Mr. Pumfry whispered. A hush fell over the room.

"Easy to find out," Kevin said. He pushed through the knot of people in the doorway, waded into the muddle, thrust his head into the large wardrobe, and kneeled down to check under the bed, shouting quite unnecessarily loudly, "You in there, thief?" He stood up and smiled at the gawking crowd. "No one to home," he reported.

Yardley and a couple of footmen, attracted by the ongoing and rising commotion, came tramping up the stairs, peered through the press of bodies, and exclaimed. The voices rose and fell, theories were offered and shouted down with derision. "Please," Phyllida said. "You'll wake Mr. Carrington."

"If he ain't awake already, he must sleep like the dead," Mrs. Badger grumbled, having climbed from the depths of the kitchen after hearing that a burglar had been caught in the act of plundering Mrs. Carrington's room. "What was he after, anyhow?" she asked.

The non sequitur was understood by all. "Jewels, of course," Joan said. "They allus go after the lady's jewels."

"Which explains the disarray," Mr. Turner said, smug and arrogant, so certain of his guilt going unsuspected. "Mrs. Carrington seems not to possess anything of value."

It was an infuriating and correct comment. Phyllida recalled that she had been promised jewelry as part of the marriage settlement, and had not been given any, a fact for which she was now both thankful and resentful. Turner would probably not have dared to take them, but if she had had the jewels available, he could not claim the destruction was the work of a thief. Any ordinary burglar would have helped himself and not left all her work and her new clothes in a shambles.

"But why ruin everything?" she wailed.

The household reacted with typical awkwardness in the presence of any victim to whom no real comfort can be given. They coughed and murmured, but said nothing aloud.

"Spite," Mr. Turner said. "It is always safer, Mrs. Carrington, to keep one's valuables in an obvious place, rather than to secrete them and risk the violence of a search. As we see."

It was a veiled threat, but Phyllida, even in her fragile state, was sensitive to the implications. He had not found it. He had torn her two rooms apart, had vandalized her painstaking work with her proofs and rummaged through her intimate garments—and he had not found the accounts book. She felt a reviving surge of energy and smiled despite her misery.

"Thank you for the advice," she said to Turner. "But there are some things so precious that one will rather lose anything else than surrender them."

"Not at the cost of one's virtue, surely," he said, his voice low, insinuating and filled with menace.

"Whatever are you talking about?" Mrs. Featherstone rose surprisingly to Phyllida's defense. "You've no right to say such a thing to the mistress."

"Indeed, Mr. Turner," Yardley said in his most severe manner. "You may be a gentleman in name, but you work for the master same as the rest of us. Mr. Carrington won't take kindly to you saying such things about his good wife, and him lying sick in the next room."

Others weighed in with their opinion, all in support of Phyllida. The marks on her face seemed to help her case for some odd reason. People always wanted to believe what was least frightening: that there had been a common act of wife-beating this morning, not a sexual assault or a disturbance over an unfaithful lover; that an audacious thief had temporarily stormed the bastion of the Carrington fortress and had been balked of his object, not that there was an intruder still in the house, or worse, that a member of the household had perpetrated such a crime; and most important of all, that the natural order of things was soon to be restored. God in His heaven, the master on his feet, the mistress at his side, and all the servants in their appointed places, from lady's maid and gentleman's man down to butler, housekeeper, footmen and maids, and cook below. And no sneaking secretary would be allowed to upset this hierarchy.

"Thank you, everybody." Phyllida stood up and put an end to the discussion. "I appreciate your kindness and understanding, but I think we should all get on with our work now, myself included, and try to keep quiet for Mr. Carrington's sake. I know you will have to make some noise with the door, but the sooner it is started, the sooner it will be done." She got everyone herded downstairs except the carpenter and his helper, smoothed her hair and clothes, and went in to see how Andrew was holding up.

HE LAY AS SHE HAD left him, tucked under too many covers in the darkened, stuffy room. She had a moment of panic, sitting on the bed and putting her hand inside his shirt to feel for a heartbeat. It was strong, although a little too rapid, and his breathing was noticeably loud in the stillness. She felt like a fool, but a happy fool.

He woke at her touch. "What the devil was all that noise?" he asked.

Phyllida shut her eyes briefly, overwhelmed with gratitude that he was lucid. "Nothing much. I am sorry it disturbed you." She tried to smile and put a humorous tone into her voice. "You won't believe it, but I actually was stuck inside my boudoir. I had to have one of those enormous men break down the door after all."

Andrew caught her hand where it still rested on his warm, smooth chest. "Did you really?" he murmured. "I wish I had been in there with you." He pulled her hand out from his shirt and kissed it. His tongue traced a trail of moisture across her sweaty palm.

Her muscles contracted all over, in one sudden movement, so that her body spasmed on the bed. "So do I," she moaned. "Oh, so do I."

"What is it, Phyllida?" he asked. "What is the matter?"

"Nothing, Andrew." She shook her head. "Nothing. I just found it frightening. It's silly, but I don't like being confined like that."

"No sillier than me feeling sick in a closed coach." He brought her head down to rest on his chest and stroked her face. She tried to stay still but the touch was painful and she flinched. Andrew drew her head upright again and looked into her eyes. "What has happened, Phyllida? Tell me the truth."

She shook her head. "Nothing, honestly."

"Don't lie to me," Andrew said, his voice harsh, weary from the pain and raspy from the vomiting. "Pull the curtains so I can see." When she hesitated, he struggled to sit, moaning as his head came upright, but continuing the attempt until he gagged. "Do as I ask, or I'll keep at it until I spew again. Now there's a threat." He laughed despite his obvious distress.

Phyllida was compelled to obey. She opened the curtains, and the window while she was at it, so he could have some relatively fresh air as well as light, and came to stand beside the bed again. The marks on her cheek were a darkening bruise, with a couple of beads of dried blood where the skin had been broken.

Andrew swore. "Who has done this to you? I'll kill the bastard."

"Please, Andrew," Phyllida begged. "Leave it alone."

"Who are you afraid of?" Andrew said. "Because I promise you, I will not be confined to this bed beyond a day or two, and whoever it is will have a long time to repent as I flay his cowardly hide from his back. Or would you prefer I smash his face in with my fists? It's your choice, my dear." He waited, and, getting no response, added, "I would offer to shoot him but it's too quick, and the authorities frown on homicide, even when it's justified."

Phyllida was in torment. It was on the tip of her tongue a dozen times to tell the truth, and each time her mind warned her of the terrible consequences. Andrew arrested, along with all his friends—elegant Pierce and sweet George Witherspoon, and Sir Frederick, who had looked after her family all these years, and the dandified Sylvester Monkton, witty and likable beneath the brittle façade—trials and horrific punishments to follow, or else having to flee the country. So many innocent lives ruined. And beyond that, who would believe that a secretary had ransacked her room and assaulted her, all over a book of household accounts? It was not a credible story. She would not believe it herself if she heard it of somebody else.

"It's— It's not what you think, Andrew," she said. "You were very distraught this morning, with the letter from Lieutenant Swain, and—"

Andrew exclaimed and stared. "Now hold on a minute. Are you saying *I* did that to you?"

Phyllida gulped and shut her eyes, praying to the god of expedient lies and necessary half-truths—Mercury, she thought it was—that she was doing the right thing. "No, Andrew," she said in just the right kind of pathetic, sniveling voice that meant the opposite.

"I don't believe it," Andrew said. He lay with his eyes closed. "I remember getting the letter, and I remember you shouting some very unladylike things at me." He grinned briefly, but frowned again in concentration. "And the next thing I can recall is lying in this bed and that pompous Reggie Stevens prosing on about migraines." He let another few minutes go by. "My God, Phyllida. And you've been tiptoeing around the truth instead of kicking my arse as I deserve."

"You don't deserve that, Andrew," she said, tears flowing. "You were so sick and upset. And it's only a slap on the face. It's not as if— I mean, it's nothing."

"As if what?" Andrew asked. "My God, what else did I do?"

"Nothing," Phyllida repeated. "Please don't upset yourself. Just rest and get well. That's all I ask."

Andrew groaned. "It's all I can do for now," he muttered. "But I promise you, my dear and sweet wife, when I am back on my feet, I will make up to you for what I did. And if I ever, ever, lay a finger on you again, or leave one mark on that flawless skin, I want you to promise me that you'll take one of my pistols and shoot me right between the eyes."

"I promise," Phyllida said. What did one more lie matter?

THE DOOR WAS REHUNG by the time Phyllida emerged from Andrew's room, having left him sleeping peacefully. She found Nan already at work trying to sort out her clothes, tossing the sheets of proofs aside like so much rubbish. Which they were, Phyllida thought. For the first time since she had begun her strange career, Phyllida felt no interest in the product of her labors, but she pulled herself up in horror. If she decided to give up her writing on her own, that was one thing, but she would not let a sneak thief and spying rat and rapist like Mr. Turner make that decision for her.

She bent down and started gathering up the proofs, smoothing them out, then sorting them into piles. Although some of the sheets held the imprints of Turner's boots, most of them were still in one piece. There were only a few loose scraps needing to be fitted together and fastened in place with pins.

"Most of your gowns can be saved, madam," Nan said. "Just need to be steamed and pressed." She shook her head over the ball gown. "Why would anyone want to go and do a thing like that?"

"It's what Mr. Turner said," Phyllida answered. "Spite." She pointed to the proofs on the table. "Can you read, Nan?"

The maid shook her head. "A little, madam. But you don't have to worry. I never looked at your writing. I don't pry. Unlike some people." She glowered at the chaos, as if at the face of the intruder.

"Do you know your numbers?" Phyllida asked.

"Oh, yes, madam. Them's easy."

"Then you can help me with these. I've got to put all these pages back in order. You see how they're numbered on the upper corner?"

"But what about your clothes?"

"They can wait." Phyllida reached a decision. Up to now, she had done all her work with Mr. Edwards by correspondence. When she had lived in Sussex it had been the only possible way, and since coming to town she had not changed the system. It worked well, and she was accustomed to it. But today, if possible, she would gather up her work and pay her publisher a visit. After what Mr. Turner had done, she would be happier with this batch of proofs out of the house. And it might be a good idea to let Mr. Edwards see he was dealing with a married lady now, a woman of substance, not an inexperienced girl he could browbeat into working on his schedule.

She still wanted more than anything to hide behind closed doors until her face healed and people had forgotten the morning's incidents. But that was a luxury few people enjoyed. No, she must go on with things as usual as far as possible, until she could decide how to fight Mr. Turner. And she had to find that blasted accounts book. "If you see a book of kitchen accounts, Nan, let me know."

"Kitchen accounts? What would they be doing here?"

"I told Mrs. Badger I'd look them over, but I seem to have misplaced the book."

Nan laughed. "Wouldn't it be funny if that's all the thief got away with—kitchen accounts?"

"Wouldn't it, though," Phyllida agreed.

WITH NAN'S ENTHUSIASTIC HELP, the proofs were collected and sorted in less time than Phyllida had dared hope. Only one page was missing, and Phyllida was sure she could reconstruct it from her copy of the final draft. Over Nan's and Yardley's well-meaning protests, the carriage was sent for and Phyllida was soon on her way to the City and Mr. Edwards's office, the rescued proofs tied up neatly in brown paper beside her. The address was a narrow, dingy building in a narrow, dingy street, and Phyllida was glad of the waiting vehicle, the driver, and the footmen, as she climbed the stairs. The clerk in the outer room, a ferrety individual who reminded Phyllida of Mr. Turner, did not at first believe that she was an author, and did not wish to let her in, but her stylish clothes and bonnet, and the fact that she had arrived by carriage, did more than any words to convince him of the inadvisability of this course. He knocked on the inner door, announced the visitor, and slithered out again.

Albert Edwards turned out to be a short, plump, middle-aged man in a dirty coat that reeked of stale tobacco smoke. "Miss Lewis!" He stood up from behind a desk piled with proofs, bound copies, manuscripts, empty but unwashed wineglasses, stoppered bottles of spirits, and a half-eaten sandwich. "Or should I say Mrs. Carrington? What a surprise." He blinked at the vision that had entered his drab warren. "A very pleasant surprise."

"How do you do, Mr. Edwards," Phyllida said. "I thought it was time for us to meet, especially as there was an unfortunate incident at my house this morning." She explained about the supposed break-in and unwrapped the soiled proofs.

"Oh dear, oh dear," Edwards muttered while she talked. He stood unpleasantly close, looking over her shoulder, but straightened and brightened when he saw the damage was not as bad as her words had led him to fear. "Now, now, my dear," he said, attempting to pat her face but thwarted by the deep lappets of the bonnet. "Nothing worth upsetting yourself over."

Phyllida flinched and moved away, but not soon enough to prevent the man's catching a glimpse of her darkened cheek, the bruise too livid for total concealment, even with liberal application of Gladys's heavy stage makeup.

Mr. Edwards chuckled at her discomfiture and chucked her under the chin. "Bet I know why your husband boxed your ears." He rummaged in the drawers of his desk and pulled out a stained, greasy book that was startlingly familiar. "Found this bundled up with the last batch of proofs." He held out the missing accounts book.

Phyllida took the book with a mix of gratitude and fear. "I can't thank you enough," she gushed like the idiot he no doubt already thought her.

Mr. Edwards was still relishing his masculine superiority. "I know how it is with you new brides. Think it's all poetry and kisses and dancing till dawn, but it's the domestic arts that count in the end. I suppose your Mr. Carrington said a lot of harsh words about you wasting time on your novel instead of paying attention to your wifely duties."

Phyllida nodded uncertainly. She had brought this on herself, and the repercussions would apparently extend all over London and beyond. "It has made me think perhaps I should give up the idea of publishing this book at all."

Mr. Edwards felt his stomach turn over at the words, but he was used to dealing with fickle authors and their wavering courage. He squared his shoulders and prepared for a bracing lecture. "Aye, well, a young man would say that when he's got a hold of a pretty piece like you, begging your pardon, Mrs. Carrington. But don't you listen to him. Now, you just keep better watch over the kitchen, but don't you let him stop you from writing. We'll do better with this book by far than the last, and we didn't do at all badly then, did we?"

"No," Phyllida said.

"No, indeed. And these emendations you've been sending—I admit I wasn't best pleased when you began making changes after the work was in proofs, but I've been looking them over, and I want to say one thing. I don't know what goes on in marriages these days, but this stuff sells. Oh, yes, Mrs. Carrington, I can see you blushing. You know what I'm talking about. And once word gets out there's the hint of, let's say, immodesty—and written by a female—people will just snatch the book off the shelves. You wait and see."

"I was a little worried," Phyllida said. "But, well, these ideas just came to me, and—"

"That's all right," Mr. Edwards said. "No need to explain. Marriage opened your eyes, did it? Good thing, too. Now, let's see what you have here."

He cleared off a chair, offered Phyllida wine in one of the dirty glasses, which she was almost so far gone as to accept, and settled in for a technical but spicy discussion of the safest way to express unnatural relationships between men, sexual acts not confined to the standard one between men and women, and other interesting topics. "So long as you don't spell it out you're all right," he concluded. "But you have to be careful. And yes, your heroine will have to die at the end. Unless—" He got a faraway look in his eye. "Unless you could write it ambiguously. Don't say anything straight out. End it the way you plan to, but say something like, 'They *thought* she was dead.' Or she left a letter and disappeared, no one knew where. But don't actually leave her, for example, stabbed to death and buried. Do you see where I'm going with this?"

"I think so," Phyllida said. "Leave my options open."

"Exactly," Mr. Edwards said, pleased at the meeting of minds. "If this book sells, and it ought to give those hacks at Minerva Press a real run for their money, you might want to continue the story. Have Millicent come back, perhaps recovering from amnesia, or—"

"Melisande," Phyllida said.

"Whatever. The point is, just make it tragic enough to satisfy the prudes, but nothing final that can't be explained away in the next book."

"If there is one," Phyllida said.

"Mrs. Carrington," Mr. Edwards said, taking a stern tone. "Don't let an overbearing husband govern your life. You're young, in love, and you want to please. But once you're stuck at home with a couple of screaming brats, and he's gallivanting around town with his friends, you'll be glad to escape to Bohemia again."

"The Balkans," Phyllida said.

"Wherever," Mr. Edwards said.

"So you're not upset about the last-minute changes?" Phyllida said.

"Didn't you hear what I've been saying? I'll sell more copies of this one book than I've sold of all the other muck put together. Only natural I don't like redoing work on short notice, but in this case the inconvenience is justified." He gasped at the realization that he had let sympathy for his young and attractive author almost run away with his business sense. He had worked hard to convince her to stay the course with this book, but it would never do to let her think that he was too eager. "And I shall have to take the expense out of your share of the profit."

Phyllida smiled and relaxed. It was going to be all right. "No, Mr. Edwards," she said. "That is not acceptable. If the changes will sell more copies, then it will benefit us both. Perhaps you should pay me more for the rights. After all, it was a different book you bought, in a way. A lesser book."

Mr. Edwards raised his hands and sat back. Not such a dithering female after all. "Now then," he said. "Let it go. Worth a shot. I'm not paying you more for the rights—that's a done deal. But I won't charge you for this work. As you say, it'll benefit us both. Now, when can you have the last proofs back to me?"

Phyllida chewed her broken fingernail. "After Easter," she said. "Two weeks. Once the season starts I expect I won't be able to do any more work for a while. And when do you think the book will appear?"

"Well, now." Mr. Edwards sat back and cogitated in turn. "I did promise to try to get it out before the end of the season. But that was before I knew about these changes." He hadn't devoted much thought to the season before, but seeing the modish look of his mysterious young author rather changed his perspective.

"What about bringing out the first two volumes independently?" Phyllida asked.

"You mean, whet their appetites and make them wait for the conclusion?"

"Why not?" Phyllida said. "Better than missing the season entirely, trying to publish all three volumes together."

"True." Looking at his young author's smart clothes, and listening to all this talk of the season, led Mr. Edwards to wonder: "Just who is your husband? Seems like you've moved up in the world. Carrington. The name is familiar, but there's a lot of Carringtons."

"Andrew Carrington," Phyllida said with blithe abandon, pride in her husband outweighing caution. "Do you know him?"

"Andrew Carrington? Tall, thin man? Dark hair?" His eyes goggled at Phyllida's nervous nod. "But he's— I mean, *the* Andrew Carrington? Heir to Newburn? My God." He sat back again while his heart adjusted to the rush of blood to his head. "Do you have any idea how many books we could sell if you were to put your married name on them?"

"No!" Phyllida was on her feet in a second, leaning over the desk. "Absolutely not. I promised not to use my real name. He'd never forgive me."

"I suppose not." Mr. Edwards was forced to concede the point. "But *Andrew Carrington*. He's— That is— He's"—Mr. Edwards gave up looking for euphemisms—"*rich*! Why do you need to go on writing, married to him? You can't have paid for those clothes just on the income of your last book."

"I enjoy writing," Phyllida explained. "It's not just for money. I mean, I like earning my own income, but that's not the only reason I write."

Mr. Edwards had seen another complication. "I can't," he said. "I can't publish this book if you're his wife. He'll put a bullet through my head, and do a lot worse than box your ears, I imagine, if he finds out."

"Nonsense," Phyllida said. "It's in my marriage contract that I'm allowed to write, so long as I use a pen name." She saw there was no more point in discussing things with the man in his current state, and gathered up her gloves and the fatal accounts book. "I'll deliver the last batch of proofs to you after Easter, and I'll expect to see copies of the first two volumes in the bookstores before the season is out. Good day, Mr. Edwards."

"That's all right, then," Mr. Edwards muttered. He laid his head in his hands as Phyllida swept from the room. "Of course Mr. Andrew sodding Carrington won't guess that a book full of indecent goings on and unnatural friendships between men was written by his wife. Why would he? After all, it's in the marriage contract." He groaned, repeating Phyllida's innocent words aloud.

What choice did he have? This book was the one property that might keep his business solvent. The worse it was from a moral standpoint, the better it was for sales. If only he hadn't asked, he could say he didn't know whose wife she was. He could still say it, but he didn't think he could keep a straight face. And with the notorious Andrew Carrington gunning for him, he might as well give up now. Look what the man had done to his sweet, pretty bride, just for misplacing a dreary book of household accounts. Although, now that Mr. Edwards recalled his quick look through them, the money certainly flowed through Carrington's kitchen like water through a millrace.

He sat up and ran his hand through his thinning hair. This was England, damn it. A man couldn't be snuffed out just for publishing another man's wife's book. Let Carrington do his worst. Bert Edwards knew a thing or two about Andrew Carrington and his friends, if it came to it. If Carrington threatened to sue, he'd come right back with his own accusations. Not that he approved of that. Everyone had some vice or other. It was contemptible to sic the law on someone just because his vice happened to be illegal. Still, it was a relief to know, if he was ever facing the wrong end of one of Carrington's deadly pistols, that he had a weapon of his own.

ANDREW WOKE LATER THAT AFTERNOON. His migraine was gone, but he had a dizzy, light-headed feeling and he felt, unusually for him, like lingering in bed. He would be glad of a wash and shave, but there were still a couple of hours before it was time to dress for dinner.

There was something evil lurking just at the outer edge of memory, something he couldn't quite see and didn't want to face, but knew he must. *Time to end the charade with that so-called secretary. Was that it? Afraid to stand up to Amberson?* No, he had never found that sort of confrontation difficult, although he supposed it would take a great deal of tiresome negotiations to dispose of the man without raising suspicions.

Harry. He remembered the pain of the letter, and Phyllida comforting him. The loss of Harry's love was distressing, certainly, but not evil, not so bad that he hadn't seen it coming for months. This other thing— No, he couldn't pin it down just yet. Wasn't ready.

He picked up the book he had bought a couple of days ago. Just about the worst thing for his head right now was reading, but that was what he wanted. Escape. He had been passing a bookseller's, a decent sort of place, and he had had a sudden inspiration. Asked for anything that had come out recently by an unidentified or unknown writer, the sort of thing a young lady might write who would not wish to have her name known publicly, the shop assistant had suggested this.

Andrew opened the front cover. "By a lady," it said. Just a page or two, he decided. He'd just read the first few pages to see if he was right.

Two hours later he was sure of it. It was perfect. A widowed mother with three daughters, reduced circumstances forcing the family to live in a cottage on the estate of a titled relative. He tried to imagine which one Phyllida saw herself as—sensible Elinor, or Marianne, full of sensibility—and decided she was a mixture. True, the narrative was told through the eyes of Elinor, but that could be merely a device, the best choice to present a supposedly balanced viewpoint. Besides, although Andrew knew Phyllida to be a very sensible female indeed, he was well aware of her deep passion and her sensitivity.

It was clever of her also to have made the necessary minor changes yet kept the situation so similar. She had moved the cottage to Devonshire instead of Sussex and made the mother a lady instead of a whore, but there was no denying the resemblance. He certainly hoped the whole episode with the scoundrel Willoughby was fictional, and decided it must be. Phyllida was far too intelligent to fall for the practiced deceits of so obvious a seducer, no matter how pretty a face and engaging a manner the man might possess. As for that boring stick Edward, Andrew had a fleeting moment of concern that the oily Leighton Coulter, whom Phyllida had professed to be so delighted to see knocked down, might be the original. He dismissed that thought. There had not been a hint in her demeanor before or since their wedding that she was pining for someone else.

The only thing that bothered him was the writing. It was good—excellent, to be honest. And Phyllida had claimed that she didn't write as well as Mme. D'Arblay. She had described her work as gothic romance, and denied it was art. But this prose was elegant, sharp, and conveyed a surprising depth of emotion beneath its sophisticated, cutting wit. Like Phyllida herself, like her conversation, only better—because, he supposed, she had time to refine it.

It must be feminine modesty. A man might boast of his accomplishments and, if they were worthy, the world would join in applause, but let a woman do anything, no matter how admirable, and call attention to herself, and she was condemned.

He laid the book aside as his stomach growled. It wasn't really his cup of tea, this book. The story was all centered around petty, domestic, feminine concerns. It had certainly opened his eyes to the constraints under which even the most passionate and gifted lady was forced to live, but as entertainment it was uncomfortable. He would never have heard of the book, much less cared to read any of it, but for marrying Phyllida. Still, he was glad he had, and he was determined to read it to the end. He was hooked. He wanted to know how it all came out.

"*Sense and Sensibility*," he said the title aloud. How appropriate. He had married an authoress and discovered a writer.

ONCE ALONE IN THE SAFETY of the coach, Phyllida found herself shaking. It was done now. She was committed. She had been on the point of pulling out of the bargain. It would have been easy enough. Just by forgoing a couple of Mme. Argonne's gowns, she could buy the rights back from Mr. Edwards and be done with it. But not because of Mr. Turner, she told herself again. No, she would not throw away all her hard work, and the pleasure she'd had in putting her new experiences down on paper, for the likes of him.

Which brought her back to the accounts book. She still clutched the tattered pages tightly in her hands and, as the coach threaded its way through the narrow streets in a meandering westerly direction, she opened it up. A very short time showed that her initial reaction had been well founded. As she had noticed before, all the prices were high, but they could be within normal range for a large household in the metropolis. It was the sums at the ends of the weekly columns, the ones in a different hand, that were the key to the mystery. The writing was almost deliberately illegible, jotted in a crabbed little script with a smudged pencil. The language might not even have been English, for all Phyllida could make of it. And the sums were huge. Tacked on to the end of a month's groceries and household expenses, they changed the outgoing amounts from a logical if extravagant total, to embezzlement.

Phyllida could not see blunt Mrs. Badger concocting such a scheme, even with help. Nor could she imagine any of the loyal, devoted staff wanting to steal from Andrew, even if they could. No, this examination of the book proved her first suspicions: that Mr. Turner, a secretary trained in bookkeeping, in arithmetic, in letters to banks and other places of business, had been carrying on a methodical monthly theft from Andrew's great wealth.

She could almost, if not quite, sympathize. Like Turner, no doubt, she had grown up in genteel poverty, clinging to the edges of the gentry, just scraping by with enough to avoid sinking that one fatal level to the merchant classes, those who made their living—quite a good one, often—from the despised sphere of trade. It was oh-so-tempting to take from someone like Andrew, who apparently had not missed a penny of this loss.

Still, if Turner had done nothing more than this, she would have gone, book in hand, to Andrew, shown him the evidence, and seen the man punished without a qualm. Stealing was wrong, however rich the victim, however poor and deserving the offender. People were hanged or transported for far less than Turner's crime, and although Phyllida had often cringed at such harsh sentences in the abstract, when the injured party was someone she cared for, she would prefer to see justice done.

But Turner had done far worse. He had attempted to rape her, and he had threatened the legal equivalent, a sort of public defilement and ruin, of Andrew and his friends. Her love for Andrew would have led her to wish to protect his interests merely from a thief. Now that her emotions were aroused on a far more immediate, physical level, she wanted not just exposure and punishment—she wanted revenge. It was an ugly, angry feeling, like war and bloodlust. Phyllida had never known it before, but she knew it now, recognized it for what it was.

She thought uncomfortably of the "rape" she had accused Andrew of committing against her. Now she had experienced the real thing—or almost—and the contrast was illuminating. Whatever else Andrew might have done, it was not rape. Clumsy lovemaking, perhaps, rough and hasty. Rape was another thing entirely. Rape was not exciting, nor did it lead to pleasure. It did not make her blush and think of Mr. Turner and wish to be with him again. In fact, thinking about him at all made her want to be sick and scrub herself raw everywhere he had touched her. And she wanted to kill him. If these were not the sentiments of a proper, refined female, so be it. Her books already proved that such feelings did not naturally occur to her.

Oh, Lord. Her book. All that stuff in her book about rape and depravity and Melisande's growing love for her "rapist"—all based on a character very much like Andrew, his body, the way he talked, and Phyllida's acknowledgment of her own desire. She must hope that her anonymity remained intact, and trust that Andrew and his friends would be unlikely to read such tripe.

But what about this book, the book in her hands? The book that was her one piece of incriminating evidence against Turner. The book he had nearly raped her to get, that he had destroyed her rooms for. She knew she dared not keep it in the house. But where?

She looked out the window of the coach as they approached Mayfair. An address came to mind; Agatha Gatling's invitation to call. The sun was low on the horizon, but still shining. She probably had just enough time to pay a quick "morning" call. She stuck her head out the window to give the coachman the direction, only a street or two out of the way home.

The man at Miss Gatling's door was hesitant, but when he heard the name he invited her to come in and wait. Miss Gatling and Mr. Witherspoon were dressing for dinner, but he would see if they would receive her.

In a couple of minutes, Miss Gatling came bustling into the drawing room. "Mrs. Carrington!" she exclaimed. "I had quite given up hope of seeing you here."

"I beg your pardon for calling so late," Phyllida said. "I did not mean to interrupt your dinner preparations." She twisted the book in her hands and looked worriedly toward the door.

"No, no," Miss Gatling said. "Nothing like that. Just Pierce coming round to eat his mutton with us as usual. In fact, you're welcome to join us if you like and—oh my goodness! What has happened to your face?"

"Nothing," Phyllida said, wishing fervently for the days—a hundred years ago and more—when a respectable lady might venture out wearing a mask. "A misunderstanding."

"A misunderstanding? My dear girl, I understand that mark very well, I assure you. Just get your bonnet off and let me have a look. Has Mr. Stevens been to see you? Yes? Good. I hope he settled Carrington's hash for him." She rang the bell before Phyllida could say anything of substance, called for brandy, and had Phyllida's bonnet off and her face turned to the light when Mr. Witherspoon came in.

"Mrs. Carrington!" he said. "How nice to see you." He came over to the window. "My word! Did Carrington do that? I never thought him capable of striking a female. Just wait until Davey sees this. He'll draw his cork, never mind he's small. Saw him bring down someone every bit as tall as your husband and twice as heavy one time, just for his making an indecent comment to me."

"What?" Phyllida said, in danger of losing her bearings in the conversation.

"Didn't catch it myself," Witherspoon said with regret. "And Davey never would tell me what it was. Just marched up to the fellow, asked him if that remark was intended for me, and when he admitted it was and started to repeat it, Davey popped him one so hard he practically lifted him straight up off his feet. Made an awful crash when he landed."

"George!" Miss Gatling said. "Mrs. Carrington don't want to hear your prattle of fisticuffs, not after what she's been through."

"Please," Phyllida said. "It's not quite what you think. I shouldn't have come here and involved you in this."

"Now see here, Mrs. Carrington," Miss Gatling said. "I imagine you're shaken by what's happened, and very much afraid of your husband. But we'll protect you. Between George and me, and with Pierce and Verney, your brute of a husband won't be able to get at you again. I imagine even that cold fish Monkton won't care to stand by and see you so abused, especially as he and Carrington are never on the best of terms. We can send a message to your abigail, have her bring some things over. Even if your husband finds out you're here, he can't get past Ferguson on the door. Scots, you know. Tough as old boots."

The brandy was brought and offered, but Phyllida declined with thanks. She didn't trust herself to keep up this horrendous lie as it was, and with strong drink in her she would lose all discretion. It had been a long time since she'd eaten, since that truncated breakfast this morning. Miss Gatling took a glass, however, and so did Witherspoon, while Phyllida contented herself with ratafia.

Witherspoon hovered close, apparently fascinated by the vivid colors of the bruise. "Did Carrington really do that?" he asked.

Phyllida took a deep breath. She had to put a stop to this. "No," she said.

Miss Gatling gasped and looked affronted.

"Didn't think so," Witherspoon said, satisfaction in his voice. "I can always tell when someone's fudging the truth. Got a good eye. I paint, you know."

"Well then, Mrs. Carrington," Miss Gatling said. "If not your husband, who?"

"Really, Aggie," Witherspoon said. "None of our business."

"Not in general, no," she replied. "But Mrs. Carrington has made it our business, by coming here to ask for our help. I assume that's why you called?" At Phyllida's embarrassed nod, she fixed her dark brown eyes on the younger woman and said, "Who was it?"

"I think I'd better have some of that brandy," Phyllida said. "Can you promise me that none of this will get back to Andrew?"

The lady and her brother exchanged a look. "No, I'm sorry," Miss Gatling said. "We can't promise any such thing. Carrington has been our friend for years, you see, and if there's something come between you, secrets or a disagreement, we will have to take his side."

"Yes," Phyllida said. "Of course. I'm glad he has such loyal friends." She put down the glass and took up the accounts book. "I was hoping I could leave this with you. It's important that it not fall into the wrong hands, and especially not be returned to our house. I'll— I'll just have to think of something else." She stood up, reached for her bonnet, and fell over in a faint.

Witherspoon caught her before her head hit the edge of a table. "Really, Aggie," he said. "We should have at least heard what she had to say."

"Poor girl," Miss Gatling said, picking up the book that had fluttered out of Phyllida's hands as she fell. "All in a dither over kitchen accounts. You know, George, there are times when I'm actually grateful for this face of mine, because the more I see of married life the less appeal it has."

LORD DAVID PIERCE, WEARING FORMAL dinner attire, bounded up the stairs to Miss Gatling's house and knocked on the door. It was a form of vanity to dress up so for a casual meal with friends, and to put his valet to such trouble for clothes that would be ripped off in a frenzy of lust only a couple of hours later, but he liked the ritual of it. And it showed respect for Agatha, expressed his appreciation better than any words for the way in which she accepted his love for George. In fact, he thought, as Ferguson ushered him in with a bow, he was beginning to think there was more to his feelings for Agatha than respect and appreciation. Much, much more.

"Mrs. Carrington is upstairs, my lord," Ferguson said.

"What?" Pierce's mind was on other things and he didn't make the connection. "Mrs. Carrington?"

"Aye, my lord. Called just when the missus was dressing for dinner, had a glass of that ratafia—" he wrinkled his nose in Scots disdain for so weak and cloying a beverage, "—and fainted dead away."

Pierce shook his head and wandered into the dining room. The table was laid for three, as usual, so she had not been expected.

"Davey," Witherspoon said from the doorway. "I'm glad you're here." He moved into Pierce's embrace like a child to its mother's, although with far more heat. "Aggie's with poor Mrs. Carrington and she won't let me in, and I'm scared."

Pierce stroked the angelic face and golden waves of hair. "Scared, George? Why? Ladies faint all the time." He laid a chaste kiss on the broad, smooth forehead and a rather less chaste one on the bowed lips.

"Oh, that's good," Witherspoon said of the kiss. "No, Davey, but you see, someone hit Mrs. Carrington. Left a terrible bruise all over the side of her face. Broke the skin. We thought it was Carrington of course, but it wasn't."

"My goodness!" Pierce exclaimed. "Who was it, then? And where's Carrington in all this? And— Oh, good Lord! Don't tell me he shot the villain already and is on his way to the continent."

Witherspoon shook his head, nuzzling against his friend's sharp features. "Can't tell you anything, Davey. She fainted before she said any more. And Aggie told her not to say anything, because we would have to take Carrington's side, but oh, I do feel ever so sorry for her. She's so pretty and kind, and it makes me sick just looking at that big purple bruise and thinking of someone doing that to her."

"Me too," Pierce murmured. "Me too." It was what he liked least about these friendships with men, and paradoxically what always drew him back for more—the way it forced him out of the conventional, straitlaced façade he had worked so hard to construct at school, and in order to escape his father's beatings. And then required him to reveal his true feelings.

"Oh, there you are, David," Miss Gatling said. "I suppose George has told you about poor Mrs. Carrington?"

"Hello, Agatha," Pierce said, wondering if she noticed she'd used his Christian name, or done it deliberately. "George has told me what little he knows. What the de— I mean, what is going on?"

"Why don't we sit down to dinner," Miss Gatling said, "and I'll tell you what Mrs. Carrington told me. Yes, George, she's awake now, but she's lying down, and I think it's best if she spends the night here. Mrs. Winslow is taking a tray up to her."

They settled into their places, Miss Gatling at the head of the table, Witherspoon at her right instead of way down at the foot of the table, Pierce opposite him on Miss Gatling's left. It was both frustrating and delicious, being forced to eat while watching his beautiful friend only a few feet away, so close but just out of reach. By the end of most meals he was so hard it was torture having to walk the several blocks to the Brotherhood. How often had he been tempted to request to spend the night here. But he would not compromise Agatha's reputation. He suspected Agatha knew all this very well and was testing him to see if his love was stronger than his lust. Most nights it was, but there were times. . .

Tonight was different. The story Miss Gatling told was succinct, the few facts quickly recounted. It was the solution that had them all arguing and discussing, well into the evening, even George forgetting about the pleasures of bed that he usually demanded the moment the meal was finished and his sister had left them to their port.

"By God!" Pierce exclaimed. "I'd like to tie that little rat to a bed and take turns with everyone in the Brotherhood doing to him what he tried to do to Mrs. Carrington." He made no apology for his coarse sentiment, nor did Agatha appear affronted.

Witherspoon looked sick. "I don't want to do that, Davey," he said. "Please, may I be excused from it?"

Pierce reached across the table and held his friend's hand. "I was not seriously suggesting it. It was my way of expressing my anger.

And, just to be clear, George, I promise I will never require you to do anything you do not wish to do."

Miss Gatling poured herself a glass of port and passed the bottle to Pierce. "On a more practical note," she said, "how can the man be exposed and punished without compromising Mrs. Carrington?"

"I don't understand, Aggie," Witherspoon said. "You said she fought him off. Why can't she just tell Carrington and let him deal with it?"

"Because, George," Miss Gatling said, "most men do not have your trusting nature. With the best will in the world, and even loving his wife very much, Carrington will forever entertain suspicions if he learns the truth."

"Suspicions? About what?" Witherspoon asked.

"That any child she has is not really his," Pierce said. "That it is the bastard of this blackguard Turner."

"But we could tell him," Witherspoon said. "We could write one of those legal documents, an affie— An affir— What are they called?"

"An affidavit?"

"That's it. And we'd all sign it and swear that Mrs. Carrington wasn't violated. That she was very brave and fought the man and got away."

Pierce groaned and laughed. "If you want to be beaten and shot by Carrington," he said, "that sounds like as good a way as any to go about it."

"George, dear," Miss Gatling said, "why don't you look in on Mrs. Carrington and see if she's awake."

Witherspoon rose eagerly, remarking only: "I suppose you want to talk secrets with Davey, but I don't mind."

"Do you, Agatha?" Pierce said once they were alone. "Wish to talk secrets?"

"Yes, David," Miss Gatling said. "Although not the sort you two men find so enthralling."

Pierce reached for her hands. "And what sort would they be, Agatha, dear?"

Miss Gatling withdrew her hands, but slowly, and with a dark red flush coloring her face. "I'm afraid I shall have to inform Amberson about this."

"Amberson?" The name drove all romantic thoughts from Pierce's mind. "Geoffrey Amberson? You think Carrington's involved in that sort of thing? I don't believe it."

"Carrington?" Agatha said. "Of course not. But I had a look in that accounts book, and I'll tell you this, David. Whatever else that supposed secretary is about, he's no bookkeeper."

"Good God," Pierce said. "Don't you think we ought to let Carrington know what's going on in his house?"

"If it were only Carrington to consider," Miss Gatling said. "But Mrs. Carrington is holding something back. I think we should wait and see what Amberson has to say."

"You don't think *Mrs.* Carrington is involved in—" Pierce began. "Oh, Lord. You think she really was forced by that little pig?"

"No," Miss Gatling said. "Not that. I think he threatened her in some way that's made her afraid to confide in anyone—us or her husband."

"I don't like it," Pierce said. "I don't like going behind Carrington's back."

"Just let me write to Amberson," Miss Gatling said. "He'll know how to handle this. In fact, it wouldn't surprise me to learn that he knows about it already."

"And since when have you become so friendly with Amberson?" Pierce said.

"Because of George, of course."

"George? By God, Agatha, do you mean to tell me that Geoffrey Amberson is mistreating George? Because I warn you now, I'll—"

"Be quiet, David, and sit down. He never touched George. I made sure of it. That's how I came to— To do work for him occasionally. A kind of quid pro quo."

Pierce clenched his fists. "Don't tell me he's taking advantage of you."

"Oh, David, honestly." Miss Gatling laughed. "You are very sweet. No, I merely do a little ciphering for him once in a while. Nothing much—there's little one can do on this side of the Channel. There's a government office Amberson oversees near Abchurch Street where a few of us toil away at what is called, with the most fanciful imprecision, 'secret writing.'"

"What a remarkable woman." Pierce took her hands again. This time she did not withdraw. "Agatha," he whispered, seizing the chance to put his arm around her plump shoulders. "May I call you Agatha?"

Miss Gatling snorted. "You have been, David, for some time now."

Pierce read this as a good sign. "And I see you are using my Christian name, Agatha. I am glad we are reaching an understanding."

"Are we, David?" Miss Gatling asked, turning to look the little man square in the eye.

"It is for you to say, Agatha," he whispered.

"I had rather thought it was for the man to say," she said. "But I'll make it easy for you, David. I will be party to nothing that in any way compromises George or hurts his feelings. Is that understood?"

"And what about you, Agatha? What would you prefer?"

"Me?" Miss Gatling slipped out of the embrace with obvious regret. "I would prefer to be having this conversation in daylight, without George and Mrs. Carrington upstairs."

By the time they parted for their separate beds, they had decided no more than that Carrington—and George—must be kept in the dark until they heard from Amberson.

Philip Turner rearranged papers and sharpened pens in Andrew's study, waiting for the ax to fall. *What had come over him, attempting Mrs. Carrington in that way?* He was losing his grip. Not surprising, really, given the provocations he was subjected to on a daily basis in this den of iniquity. Amberson had not properly prepared him for the arduous duty he was undertaking, when he placed Turner here.

Eventually it occurred to him that Carrington, incapacitated by migraine, might still be in the dark, literally and figuratively, about the morning's doings. Mrs. Carrington had gone out—to her publisher, she claimed. He had time to fix things, to get himself out of this scrape, if he acted fast. He had brought the Vere Street house down, and he could bring the Brotherhood of Philander down, too, although it would not be quite so easy. They did not let just anyone in there; he could not come and go at will, as he had at the White Swan, picking up his information and biding his time. But he would find a way, and he would bring it down and everybody in it, starting with his nominal employer.

Andrew Carrington thought himself so far above the rest of the world, with his wealth and his pedigree and his public-school, university breeding, that he seemed to think he was immune to the laws that governed society. But he was wrong. He had one serious vulnerability. Sodomy was a capital offense, even for gentlemen. Even titled men were not above this law, the natural law of God and the Bible, codified into the laws of Great Britain as well.

How to use it, though? It was folly to think an employee could simply stroll into a magistrate's office, make a lot of wild, scandalous accusations about a member of one of the top families in the country, and not end up in the clink or the pillory himself, tarred with his own brush. No, there would have to be hard evidence; if not some sort of farcical raid on Andrew's bedroom (which Philip was sure would be thrown out of court anyway, based on the "a man's house is his castle" defense), then at least a credible witness who could swear to Carrington's depravity.

Like that street boy. Philip had been disgusted to see the filthy and debased creature, not merely brought in to satisfy a wicked man's perverted desires but given breakfast at the master's own table. It was ironic, he thought, that Carrington knew the servants, even his most loyal staff, would be mortally insulted at being asked to share their table with such scum. No, he had instead inflicted the sight and the smell on the footmen who served upstairs. And on Philip, although he had not stayed at that meal for long.

But how to find him again? Philip knew in general where men like Carrington went to troll for their whores, but which of these places did that "Kit" frequent? Philip did not relish spending hours prowling amongst sodomites, madge culls, and other debauched specimens, all to find one particular speck of dirt in an ash heap of human waste.

He sighed. He had no choice. He must wait until dark, of course, and— Oh, God. What if he was assumed to be a customer, subjected to the obscene overtures and corrupt practices of the denizens of these places? He could not object, not if he wished to pretend to be seeking the services of one of them. No, he would just have to grit his teeth and bear it.

When he emerged from his room for dinner, Andrew was informed of what had occurred during his illness. Yardley and some of the senior staff had wanted to keep the worst from him, but they had known too many times in the past when a similar well-meaning tactic had proved disastrous. No, Mr. Carrington had shown himself to be a capable and forceful master, and he did not appreciate the withholding of truth.

Andrew examined the damaged rooms in silence. Nan had put everything away and, with the help of the other maids, had restored such an air of order and cleanliness that the only real evidence that something unusual had occurred was the rehung door, the broken writing desk, and the ruined ball gown. "Madam fair cried her eyes out over this," Nan said, showing it to Andrew.

He ignored it. "And no one saw or heard anything?" he asked.

"Only the mistress screaming," Pumfry said.

"But the rooms were vandalized after she was let out, isn't that what you said?" Andrew persisted. "Kevin, did you see anyone else with Mrs. Carrington when you broke the door down? And how did the room look?"

The large man scratched his chest and thought. "The room looked all right to me. Didn't rightly think about it. And there was nobbut the missus inside. Fair shrieking with terror she was, sir. And she shook my hand and thanked me as if I'd done her some great service, just for busting down the door."

Andrew had to force himself to speak without betraying emotion. Only his years as master, his double life on the fringes of the underworld, gave him the self-possession to do it. "And Kevin. You must tell me the truth now and not be afraid of what I will think. Did you see Mrs. Carrington's face then?"

Kevin looked bravely into his master's forbidding countenance. "I did, sir. All over red on one side. Hit hard, she was. Broke the skin." He wished, as he saw his master's face freeze up into a mask of self-loathing, that he had dared to lie, but all that Mr. Carrington did was thank him and turn to go back downstairs.

The message from Miss Gatling, saying that Mrs. Carrington had been taken faint and would be spending the night, merely put the last nail in the coffin lid. Yardley had never seen the master look so sick as when he heard that. Not even when his mother died. "I've made a mess of things, Yardley," he said. "My own wife afraid to come home."

"Now, Mr. Carrington, sir," Yardley said, his voice cracking, "you know better than that. Young ladies is forever fainting and having spells." He coughed. "And in a certain *condition*, you know, they feel sick at the beginning."

"You can stop pretending, Yardley," Andrew said. "You saw her face."

Yardley nodded, displaying a tremor, a tic of his facial muscles that Andrew had never seen before. "Lots of men done worse, sir. I'm sure she won't hold it against you. Some women respect a strong husband."

"How dare you?" Andrew shouted, making the poor old man flinch. "How dare you repeat such filth to me in my own house?"

"Forgive me sir." Yardley backed away, quivering. "I only said what lots of people believe."

"Lots of people believe in ghosts and witches," Andrew said. "It doesn't make it true."

"No, sir." Yardley backed into the door. "May I have your permission to leave, sir?"

"Of course."

"I'll be packed and out in the morning."

"Oh, for God's sake, Yardley. I thought you meant to leave the room. No, you do not have my permission to turn yourself out onto the street. You will stay here in service with me until you're at death's door, and then if you wish to retire to a cottage with a pension, I'll consider it. Understood?"

"Yes, sir, thank you, sir. And I meant no offense about Mrs. Carrington. Or about her coming to breakfast this morning, neither."

"I know that, Yardley. And Yardley, would you ask Mr. Turner to see me before dinner? I've a few questions for him."

"I'm sorry, sir. He's gone out. Didn't say where."

"No matter. It'll keep. Now, do you think I can have some dinner? I'm so famished I could eat a horse."

PHYLLIDA WAS SURPRISED WHEN, AFTER a knock on the door, George Witherspoon entered. "May I talk to you?" he asked in his sweet voice. "I won't stay long."

"Certainly," Phyllida said. He was an easy companion, just the sort of mild, sympathetic personality she could bear right now.

"Aggie told us what happened," he said. "I'm sorry if it was supposed to be a secret, but she felt she had to, so we could figure out how to help."

"It's all right," Phyllida said. "She warned me she would. I'm glad, in a way."

Witherspoon came to sit by the bed and took her hand. Phyllida noted how strong his fingers were, blunt-tipped and stained with pigment of some sort. Altogether different appendages from what she expected, judging from the rest of his rather effete, androgynous looks. He had said he painted, she remembered, feeling a kinship. Another out-of-place artist.

"I was raped," Witherspoon said. "I never told anybody."

Phyllida looked up. "I— I'm sorry," she stammered. She couldn't think of what else to say.

"I told Aggie, of course," Witherspoon said. "But nobody else. It was horrible. It was like being raped all over again, not being able to do anything about it."

Phyllida fought the urge to gather the young man in her arms and kiss him. Yet however chaste the coupling, it was not appropriate in this setting, in a bedroom in his sister's house. "But you're telling me now," she said. "Is it something I can help you with, George?" It seemed only natural to call him by his Christian name in such an intimate conversation.

"Oh no. It was a long time ago. He was my tutor. I was twelve."

Phyllida gave up trying to find words and just let him talk.

"He used to cane me, you know, because I wasn't a good student. I did try, but I'm not clever at books and sums. And then one day he said he'd had enough, and when he bent me over to cane me he— He raped me instead. It was so painful, I cried and cried, and I bled, too. I told Aggie. She was like a mother to me. I thought she could do anything, fix anything. But Papa didn't believe any of it."

"That's terrible," Phyllida said. She gave in to her feelings and put her arms around him, letting him rest his head on her shoulder. "How did you manage?"

"My father sent me away to school," he said. "No, it wasn't so bad as it sounds. At least I got away from horrible Mr. Rowbotham. And whatever went on at school it was never as bad as with him, because I hadn't been expecting it then, you see. I had been innocent. I didn't know a thing like that was possible."

"And you think I was raped, is that it?" Phyllida asked. "And that I should tell the truth instead of keeping it to myself and letting Andrew take the blame?"

"I used to think it's what made me the way I am," Witherspoon said, not answering her question directly.

"You mean, that you like men?"

He lifted his head from her shoulder in surprise, and stared. "Why would being raped make me love men? No, I mean, that I'm so slow. I still don't read well. All through school I got the clever boys to do my work for me in exchange for— Well, you know. But I decided that it's just the way my mind is. Not very bright. What Mr. Rowbotham did didn't make me that way."

"George," Phyllida said. "Listen to me. I am honored that you would confide in me like this."

"I thought it was only fair, since we know your secrets."

"That's sweet and kind, just like you," Phyllida said. "But you must believe me when I say I wasn't raped."

"But how did you get away? After he hit you like that?"

"I kneed him in the groin," Phyllida said.

Witherspoon winced, despite his lack of sympathy with the man.

"Yes," Phyllida admitted with a smile. "Very painful indeed. That's how I made it to the door and then a manservant broke it down."

"But didn't he see Mr. Turner then?" Witherspoon asked.

"No, he hid in the other room. And when I went downstairs he was very cool, stayed behind and went through all my things, my writing and my clothes, and he vandalized them." She felt the tears starting again.

"But that's not so bad," Witherspoon said. "Better he ruins your things than you."

"I know," Phyllida agreed. "It's just— It was a beautiful ball gown. I've never had anything half so fine, and I had thought of it as special because of Andrew, the way he looked at me in— In a different gown."

Witherspoon laughed. "I do understand that. And your writing must be special, too. Would you like to see my paintings?"

"Very much."

"We shall have to wait for morning, for the light. And you must know, they are all portraits. And all naked. I like to paint people, not their clothes."

"Oh." Phyllida thought about this. "Yes, I think the morning would be better."

"There's one of Andrew," Witherspoon said. "You can tell me if you think I got him right. I won't be offended. I can always see when people are telling the truth."

THE BOY KIT, RECENTLY DUBBED Marlowe, slunk back into the shadows of the park in the center of the grand square in Mayfair. A person could be sent to Newgate just for being caught loitering in a place like this, but Kit had no intention of getting caught. And he had to see what that little prick was up to.

It was a long wait, but Kit didn't care. He no longer had to satisfy the demands of a keeper; Mr. Carr's largesse had allowed him to buy himself out. Not that that had gone altogether smoothly. He stuck the tip of his tongue into the hole where the tooth had been knocked out and ran a finger along the scar over his eye. Not so many customers for damaged goods, but at least he was a free agent now. He could work or not, as he chose, just enough to pay his share of the rent on his squalid lodgings and keep himself fed. It was a luxury he'd never dared dream of as recently as a month ago.

He hadn't lost his sense of self-preservation, though. And when his friend Billy said that someone was asking for him by name, someone offering a huge sum of money for unspecified duties in a fashionable section of town, he didn't immediately present himself like a country bumpkin to the recruiting officer and say, "Ready for action, sir." Not Kit Marlowe.

No, he had waited and watched and seen that little rat who had been at Mr. Carr's breakfast table, the one who had turned up his nose as if smelling something particularly rotten, and made a hasty retreat from the room, all the while looking Kit over in a way that Kit knew very well. The sort of look they all gave when they wanted it but didn't know it—or, more likely, wouldn't admit it—and you had to go up to them and practically put your prick in their hand and wait for them to ask how it got there and play all innocent. Kit had had enough of those games, thank you very much.

He thought of Mr. Carr, always a gentleman, even when he was so foxed he was saying things he ought not, like what he was going to do when they got home, and asking Kit what he liked to do, as if that had ever mattered. Mr. Carr had seemed to think it did.

Kit sniffed and pushed his hair out of his face. He wished it had been Mr. Carr offering the money, but he knew one thing. If Mr. Carr wanted to see him again, he wouldn't send his nasty little weasel of a secretary to sniff around. No, he'd come marching right up to where Kit worked and say something like, "In the mood for some Greek, Marlowe?" And if anyone nearby heard and laughed or took offense, he'd get that look on his face that made people just turn away and hope he didn't notice them again. Wouldn't even have to say anything. Although if he did say something, it would be choice. A real gent. Said he wasn't a lord, but Kit wouldn't be surprised if he turned out to be one after all.

Kit skulked in the deepest darkness near the fence, while carriages pulled up and discharged the inhabitants into their homes, laughing parties and quarreling couples, and once a fat old gentleman so inebriated that three footmen had to come out and carry him inside. It was apparently nothing out of the ordinary, as they were standing by when the carriage arrived and performed their duty without comment.

Finally, when Kit was so cold and tired he was almost ready to abandon his post after all, he saw him. Mr. Nose-in-the-air Ferret, strolling along, his hands in his pockets, but with a twitchy, watchful manner about him. He reached the grand front entrance of Mr. Carr's house but he didn't go up the stairs or knock. He glanced around as if planning a burglary, opened a small side gate, and went down and around the back.

Kit gave Ferret enough time to get inside, then crossed the square, trying to stroll in that same nonchalant way, as if he belonged here too. "Just here to see my friend, Mr. Carr," he imagined himself saying if asked. "Mr. Carr invited me over for a French breakfast."

He reached the little gate, which wasn't even locked, opened it, and followed the path around the side of the house, into a walled yard with a path to the back door—the kitchen entrance, he supposed—and a series of steps leading down to a cellar. What next? He couldn't very well follow the rat into his hole, assuming he had gone in through the kitchen so as to avoid being heard or seen coming in at this hour. Perhaps he could just take a quick look into the cellar, since he'd come this far. It was probably locked, but as the gate had been open, it was worth a try.

He pulled on the heavy door, which lifted easily after a groan and a creak that had Kit trembling. He waited, heard no reaction, and peered inside. Steps leading down, a coal scuttle. Nothing sinister there. He crept backward down the steps, letting the door close over him. It was pitch black, and he stood still, waiting until his eyes adjusted. Moving forward, he saw shelves, bottles, and such. A wine cellar, more bottles than a tavern.

Might as well stay here, since he'd come this far. It was a long way back to his lodgings, and his roommates would hardly miss him. They'd assume he'd gotten lucky and hooked up with a client for the whole night. He could be raped, murdered, and his body thrown in the Thames before anyone even gave him a thought. His eyes teared up and he wondered what was the matter with him. He'd been on his own all his life that he could remember. Why get weepy over it now?

Because, he told himself, he was getting soft. He'd seen how the rich lived, in their fancy town houses with their silver on the table and their carpets on the floor, their breakfasts that could feed a regiment. He wanted his share. And if he could do a good turn to Mr. Carr while getting it, all the better.

He prowled ahead, feeling for sharp edges and turns, wondering if there was any food to be had. Probably all upstairs in the kitchen. He didn't dare go there. Oh, well. He selected a bottle at random, pulled the cork with his teeth, wincing at the pain, and took a long swig. He almost spat it out again. Like bilge water that was, or piss. Not that he had drunk a lot of those liquids, but they were what people said when they tasted something foul. What he wouldn't give for some brandy or gin, or an honest pint of ale.

He tried another mouthful. Not too bad, really. And the warmth of it spread through his guts and into his body just as well as anything else. He found a cozy corner, sat down, the bottle nestled between his legs, and waited for morning.

PHYLLIDA AWOKE EARLY THE NEXT day, filled with more hope than she had expected. George—she knew she should call him Mr. Witherspoon, but they had become so close after sharing their troubles, she couldn't think of him that way—took her up to an attic before breakfast and showed her his work.

It was astonishing. The room faced north—the best light, he said—and the walls were lined with paintings. Portraits, as he had said, all naked and standing for a full-length view of the figure. Her first reaction had been to cover her eyes in maidenly modesty, but she was not a maiden, she had displayed rather little modesty in her recent life, and she did not like to hurt George's feelings. So she looked. At first from under her lashes with downcast eyes, but eventually she forgot all her qualms and stared.

She had never seen paintings like these. Not just the nakedness. After all, many of the masters of earlier centuries had painted nude figures, on classical or historical subjects, but bare-skinned all the same. Sir Frederick had a lovely scene on the ceiling of a formal dining room in his house in Sussex, showing naked gods and goddesses disporting themselves. No, it was the style that was so odd. She wondered if George perhaps was nearsighted and ought to wear spectacles. Instead of the sharp, delineated features and careful details she had expected, the figures were all rough edges, with thick applications of paint and visible brushstrokes, and a wild mélange of colors that blended into one another with no clear demarcations.

Then she stepped back and really looked. "You see?" George

said, noting her different reaction. "I tried to capture each person's essence."

He certainly had, Phyllida thought. Stripped of their clothes, of the way they were accustomed to presenting themselves to the world, without a means to hide imperfections or exaggerate good features, they had been reduced or enlarged accordingly. She pleased George by finding Pierce's portrait first and giving it serious attention. The small, elegant fashion plate she was acquainted with, denuded of his plumage, was harder—pale and scrawny to be sure, but with a scrappy toughness. "Like a jockey," she mused out loud, "or a prizefighter."

George laughed in delight at her perception. "His mother was Irish. Real Irish, not Anglo-Irish. She died young, like my mother. Davey says his father sent him to school to toughen him, but I think it was so he wouldn't have to see Davey and be reminded."

Phyllida went to Andrew's portrait next, noting the long, slender limbs with their ropy muscles, the dark hair, the proud bearing, just as she remembered from their wedding night. And something else. There was the same sneer on his face, the graceful, arrogant posture, standing with bold, outthrust hips and leaning against a table. But the more she looked the softer his expression became.

"He had just met Harry Swain then," George said. "He was so in love, I wanted to catch that moment, before it changed. It always does, you know, no matter how one promises that it won't."

"I wish I could have known him then," Phyllida said without thinking.

"You will," George said. "He'll look at you like that, I'm sure of it. Would you like to see Harry Swain?"

The enormous blond was striking for many reasons, not only his tall, powerful build and sculpted musculature, and the male member that appeared to be in a semi-aroused state, threatening to burst from the canvas in a new, three-dimensional art form. "He looks so young," Phyllida said. "The face, I mean."

"He was seventeen when I painted him," George said. "Bigger than most men, and still growing. We were all in awe of him."

"Yes, there's something about sheer size that inspires respect," Phyllida said.

George came to stand beside her. "No, I don't mean that. Harry was—is, I suppose—entirely honest. He never lied or pretended about anything, even to save his skin. That's how he went into the army. He was caught with another boy at school, but he wouldn't say he was sorry or admit he'd done anything wrong. The headmaster tried beating him into submission, and Harry broke the cane over his head, and there was a terrific scandal."

"Did Andrew know about it?" Phyllida asked, after she and George had stopped laughing.

"Of course," George said. "We all did. But there was nothing he could do. Harry was still a minor. Lord Swain paid a great deal of money to hush it up, and then he said he was finished with Harry and he never wanted to see him again. That's why he bought him a pair of colors, so he'd be sent overseas."

"Oh, how sad," Phyllida said. She looked again at the portrait, as if the expression might reveal foreknowledge, a sign of the impending tragedy. The open, lusty face looked down at her with equanimity, perhaps a hint of a smile in the round blue eyes.

"Well, it was sad for Andrew, of course," George said. "But Harry had been begging for a commission since he was fifteen."

Phyllida's eyes met George's in a moment of tacit understanding. "Andrew heard from him, just yesterday," Phyllida said. "Harry returned his letters, and mentioned his commanding officer, a Captain Quincy. That's why Andrew had an attack of migraine."

George took Phyllida's hands in his. "Perhaps it's for the best. Andrew is free to love you now."

"I don't think it works that way," Phyllida said.

"I don't either," George said. "I just wanted to cheer you up." They strolled in silence to the next familiar face. "I know you're not ready, and I'd want to wait until that bruise is healed, but you will let me paint you, will you not?"

"Surely Andrew wouldn't like it," Phyllida protested.

"Why not?" George said. "I painted Aggie. See how well she turned out."

Phyllida prepared to dutifully admire the portrait of her hostess, and found there was no need to call upon such a tepid emotion. The little pug lady was startlingly improved. What looked ungainly and squat in the light, gauzy fashions of the day had a power in nakedness, like an empress or a goddess surveying her domain and declaring it worthy. "Goodness!" Phyllida exclaimed. "It's a pity you can't show these."

"Isn't it?" George lamented. "But you know, at the same time it's sort of a relief. I don't have to worry what people will say or whether they will like them. I can just please myself, and any of my friends who wish to can visit and see them."

"Yes," Phyllida said, "but art is meant to be public. If people don't like one's work, that's the price one must pay for the privilege of being able to create something unique. Not everyone can do this, George. You are a real artist."

"And what about you, Mrs. Carrington?" George said. "You do the same thing. You publish your books, but under a false name."

Phyllida slid her eyes toward George. He was far more articulate and poised up here showing off his work than downstairs amongst the originals. She wondered if his air of childlike simplicity in company was merely a pose calculated to break down his friends' resistance and lead them to peel off every layer of self-protection along with their clothes. "Why have you not painted a self-portrait?" she said. "You force all your friends to confront essential truths, but not yourself."

George blushed. "I have tried," he said. "Several times. It always comes out looking insipid or—frightening—and I end up painting over it. I sometimes think portraying oneself honestly is impossible."

"You must stop describing yourself as slow, George," Phyllida said. "You're much too astute for comfort. As for my situation, it's complicated. As a lady, and especially now, having married so well, I can't have my name on the sort of stuff I write."

"Would you let me read it?" George asked.

"Willingly," Phyllida said. "But I doubt you'd like it. Men rarely like improbable romances and horrid gothic plots, and all told from the female point of view."

"I think I might, because I would know you wrote it," George said. "And it sounds very exciting. But it will take me a while. I read very slowly."

"If you read any of it at all," Phyllida said, "I will be flattered indeed." She saw him about to repeat an earlier question. "And yes, if Andrew has no objection, I will be delighted to sit for my portrait—or stand. It may turn out better than Romney's studies of Emma Hamilton."

George looked crushed. "I should hope so," he muttered.

"What a relief," Phyllida said, "that you have a human failing after all, Mr. Witherspoon."

IT SEEMED TO PHYLLIDA that she was returning to a house in mourning, as she was let in the door by a sullen footman, greeted by a Yardley who sounded almost suicidal, and welcomed by a husband who appeared to be in some way afraid of her.

"I am glad to see you, Phyllida," Andrew said. "I began to worry that you found Witherspoon and Miss Gatling better company."

She tried to answer lightly: "They were very kind to me. But I missed my home comforts."

"Will you do me the honor of dining with me?" Andrew asked. "I will understand if you prefer to eat in your room."

Phyllida clenched her teeth until she thought she would break a molar. Pierce and Miss Gatling had impressed upon her the necessity of silence while they decided on a plan for dealing with Mr. Turner. Pierce had taken charge of the accounts book and would keep it at the Brotherhood of Philander. "All joking aside," he'd assured Phyllida, forgetting that she had not been in on the original discussion over dinner the day before, "if that snake tries to force his way in there, he'll get more than he bargains for. A lot more. Safest place for it."

"I would like very much to dine with you," Phyllida said. "Just give me time to change."

Only Nan appeared cheerful, for some odd reason. "Good to have you home again, madam," she said. "Have a nice visit with Miss Gatling?"

"Very nice," Phyllida said. "Which is the most becoming of my gowns, do you think? The green? Oh, what a good job you did of restoring it. No one would guess it had been flung on the floor and trodden on." She prattled on while Nan fussed with her hair and helped her into the gown. She would do her best to play the part of an innocent, absentminded young bride even if it killed her, as long as it helped Andrew.

"Are you feeling better today?" Phyllida asked as she was seated in the dining room. "Have you been out?"

"Yes, thank you," Andrew said. "But no, I have spent a dull day going over all the dreary domestic matters I always avoid when I'm well. By the way, I had an interesting interview with Mr. Turner. He claims you have a book of household accounts."

Phyllida felt her heart turn over—or was it her stomach? "Yes, Andrew," she said. "I was very careless. I wrapped it up by mistake with some of my proofs and sent it to my publisher. When I visited him yesterday he teased me mercilessly." She blushed deeper, knowing that her embarrassed expression only added credence to her tale. "Always tell as much of the truth as you can," Pierce had said. "A lie is easier to pass off when it's close to the facts. One's mind begins to accept it as genuine."

"And where is it now?" Andrew asked.

"That's what's so terrible," Phyllida said. "Mr. Edwards thinks he must have sent it to the printer. He promised to send it back as soon as they find it."

Andrew tried to suppress a smile. So, the incriminating evidence was safely out of the house. Excellent. Let the little rat strangle himself in a mare's nest of self-justification while buying time for Amberson to settle things with more finality. "Please don't trouble yourself over it," he said. "The only thing I don't understand is how you came to have it in the first place."

"Cook thought I should check it," Phyllida said. "And I am sorry to have been so lax, but I was in a great rush with the proofs and—"

Andrew held up a staying hand. "Please. Let us say no more about it. Mrs. Badger is a zealous, loyal servant, but she ought not to have bothered you with it, a new bride on your honeymoon."

Phyllida watched Andrew under her lashes. What was he concealing? Did he suspect her of something, after all? "Mrs. Badger must have known ours was not a love match. And it is the wife's job." She could not help sighing.

Andrew swore and threw down his napkin. "Phyllida, let me impress something on you. Ours may not have been a love match in the way one thinks of such things, but I will not have you turn yourself into the sort of upper domestic servant that a wife so often becomes. From now on, I will go back to my former routine, dealing with my household expenses myself—with the help of my secretary, of course. Have to find some way to justify his keep."

Phyllida stopped eating also. She couldn't choke down another bite. "Oh, no, Andrew," she said. "You mustn't. I promise you I'll do better."

"Never tell me you like checking kitchen accounts," Andrew said, lifting an eyebrow. "Next you'll claim you are positively addicted to embroidery and wish to begin rising early in order to supervise the maids."

"Of course not," Phyllida said. "That is, I detest embroidery. But I am quite accustomed to overseeing a household, especially a kitchen. It isn't fair to you to have gone to all the trouble of marriage and then have to do the wife's chores anyway."

"Enough," Andrew said, raising a quelling hand. "You forget I employ a housekeeper for the express purpose of keeping house. I have treated you abominably, and I will not allow you to go on shaming me with your saintly forbearance. Let us talk of something else."

"Gladly," Phyllida said, racking her brains for an absorbing topic. "I greatly enjoyed seeing Mr. Witherspoon's paintings. They are most . . . unusual."

Andrew took the bait. "George had the balls to show you that obscenity? My God, I ought to call him out."

Phyllida laughed. "I am a married woman, Andrew. Although now that I have seen your Harry, I wonder you didn't wish to marry Charlotte Swain. She looks just like her brother. The face, I mean."

Andrew grimaced. "Harry's face on the body of an enormous, voluptuous woman is just about the most disgusting thing I can think of."

"Oh." Phyllida smiled. "Shall you come and watch when George paints me?"

"No. You will not be having your portrait painted by George Witherspoon, at least not unless and until he greatly changes his style of work. And since when have you two begun using first names?"

"You know you can't be jealous of George Witherspoon," Phyllida protested. "And I would very much like to have him paint my portrait. He is possessed of a genius, I think."

"So do I, actually," Andrew admitted. "I suppose it won't matter if you sit for him. After all, no one but us and our friends will see these works in our lifetime."

"Thank you, Andrew," Phyllida said, strangely depressed at her husband's reasonable and acquiescent demeanor.

He waited for her to look up. "Speaking of genius, I read your book."

"What?" Phyllida had never endured so upsetting a meal.

"Now, I can't begin to imagine all the nonsense that a young lady has to put up with when she tries to do something interesting like write a book, but I want to say that I read it all the way through to the end and I am very proud of you. In fact, I'm rather in awe. When you said you wrote horrid female romances, or however you described them, I never imagined anything like this."

Phyllida felt her mind turning to mush. Had she been given laudanum at Miss Gatling's without her knowledge? Or was she still laboring under the weakness of having imbibed brandy on an empty stomach yesterday? "How do you know it was my book?" she asked.

"I inquired in a bookseller's," Andrew said, "for something a young, anonymous lady had written lately. It was just a guess of course, but once I started reading, I could see it was yours."

"But how? And did you really enjoy such a wild story?"

He laughed. "Not so wild. And yes, I did enjoy it. I could tell it was yours by, first, the similarity of the situation with your own, and secondly, by the wit and intelligence of the style."

"You are very kind," Phyllida said. "But it was not similar at all."

He laughed again, a fond little chuckle, indulging a silly wife. "Of course you changed a few details, for propriety's sake, and to maintain your confidentiality. But anyone who knows you would recognize the setting and the family."

Phyllida tried hard to remember her previous book. *Had* her heroine even had a family? She'd been so wrapped up in the work of getting this one into print she could barely recall any details of the earlier one. It was much like this one, a chase over mountains in a foreign country, a beleaguered heroine held captive in a gloomy, forbidding castle, a noble, blond hero and a tall, dark villain. At least in that one the hero and heroine survived to live happily ever after. Perhaps he meant that "family," although there could be nothing similar about them to anyone he knew. To anyone anybody knew. It was fiction, and not the best. "I still don't believe you read *my* book," Phyllida said, "but whatever it was, I'm glad it amused you and that it has reconciled you to my writing. I do enjoy it."

He left his chair to kneel at her side. "Phyllida. From the beginning, I knew that I had been very lucky indeed in my hasty marriage. In every way you have revealed yourself to be a superior and intelligent companion, and a delight as a wife. And now, reading what you have written, I see it all confirmed, what a jewel you are. I am unworthy of you, my dear. I still don't remember hurting you so, but with the evidence in front of me I can only beg your forgiveness." He waved off her words. "Please, let me finish. What I was going to say is, I *am* your husband, for better or worse, and while it is very much the better for me, I see it is the worse for you. When you are ready, and not before, I will ask the favor of coming to your bed."

Phyllida tried to wait until her heartbeat slowed to normal. No, that would take too long. "Andrew," she said. "I don't know what I can say to such generosity except that I am ready tonight, if you wish."

"My love." He pressed a hot kiss into her palm. "You are kind. You will not regret it this time, I promise you."

NAN CREPT DOWN TO THE cellar while the master and mistress were at dinner, well after the servants had finished their own meal. With luck, she'd have at least an hour before Mrs. Carrington needed her. She hugged herself in delight, thinking of the treat in store. She still could hardly believe it, the vision she'd come across last night, the perfect, lithe body sprawled in sleep, and the beautiful face, the scar over the eye and the missing teeth merely proving he was real, not an angel or a ghost as she had first feared. "Kit?" she whispered. "You there?"

He grabbed her from behind, making her shriek, but he covered her mouth with his hand and muffled the worst of it. "Scared ya, did I?"

"Take more than a ragged little rat like you to scare me," she said. "Ain'tcha gonna kiss me?"

"Nah," he said. "Ain't gonna waste my talents on a scrawny little bitch like you."

She pushed him down on the borrowed blankets and pillows. "I brought you supper," she said, holding out the large package wrapped in a napkin. "But you can't have it till you earn it."

He hooked one of her skinny legs with his foot and tumbled her down gently on top of him. "All I do," he grumbled, "is make my livin' wif my prick."

"More than most can say," Nan said. She would not shame him by pointing out that up to now he had earned his living more with his mouth and his bum. He was her man, and she was proud of him, and proud for him. "Most lose their livings because of it."

"Wot if you get caught?" he asked. "You know, a bun in the oven?"

Nan rose to her knees. "Maybe we should do it standing up. I heard if you do it like that, it's safe."

"A lot you know," Kit said, pulling her down again. "Every tuppenny whore I ever knew, the ones who allus did it up against the wall 'cos they had nowhere else—swollen bellies every last one of 'em."

"You pullin' my leg?" Nan asked.

Kit lifted her skirts and ran his hands up her slender, solid thighs. "Only if you want me to, Nan," he said.

"You know I do, Kit," she said into his shoulder.

"Then I got a better idea than standing up," Kit said. He pulled a package from his pocket, unfolding a long, wrinkled object like a sausage casing. "It's a French letter," he explained.

"Does that go where I think it does?" she asked.

"Where else? See, it's how come I didn't get sick all these years, made the customers use these. But it'll keep you safe, too."

"I wouldn't mind, Kit," Nan said, shy for once, hanging her head. "If it was your baby I'd love it."

"Don't be soft," Kit muttered. But when he was locked between her legs, embedded deep inside her, he was so overtaken with gratitude he found himself saying it out loud, what he swore he'd never say of anybody, to anybody. "I love you, Nan. I love you." He tried to hold back the words, but not in time.

"I love you, too, Kit," Nan said. "Oh, it's just like that play. Like *Romeo and Juliet*."

Which just went to show, Kit thought, that you never could get one sensible word from a female without having to hear ten of nonsense. But they were nice all the same.

PHYLLIDA SMOOTHED HER NIGHTGOWN OVER her body and looked at herself in the mirror as Nan brushed out her hair. Was it her imagination or did her breasts seem bigger, fuller than ever? This was one of Mme. Argonne's diaphanous creations, covering but not concealing. Still, she had been eating a lot, and apart from all this fright over the accounts book, her life had been far less strenuous than at home. No brisk walks back and forth to Sir Frederick's, no housework, no errands into town on the old carthorse. She was putting on weight from sheer indolence, but she couldn't complain. She felt well.

"Thank you Nan," she said. "That's enough. Go to bed now. You look dead on your feet."

"I'm all right, madam," Nan said. "Just a touch of toothache. Mrs. Badger gave me something for it. Knocks you out, but you sleep sound. She's got bottles of cures down cellar. Herbs and such. You ever need something like that, you let me know."

Phyllida barely listened. In the candlelight, and with her long hair waving around her face, the bruise, a little less swollen today, was barely noticeable. She reached for the matching robe and put it on.

"Ain't the master coming in, then?" Nan asked.

"He may be," Phyllida said, "but I'm not waiting to find out. I'm going in to him tonight. I hope your tooth is better tomorrow. Good night, Nan."

Nan took the hint and disappeared downstairs, in the direction of Mrs. Badger's interesting collection of remedies in the cellar.

Phyllida took a deep breath, squared her shoulders, and opened the door to the corridor, peeped out and, seeing it empty, flitted across to Andrew's room. She didn't knock.

He was sitting at his desk, his head in his hands. He was wearing that same shimmery gray dressing gown he had worn their first night together. "Andrew."

He looked up and was on his knees in an instant, his arms around her waist. "What are you doing here?" he asked. His voice was deep but soft, a rumble not a purr, and certainly not a drawl. It was beautiful, warm, the voice of a supplicant, not a commander. Phyllida hated it.

"I wanted to know if you were coming in to me," she said. "Are you going to snap your fingers at me and order me out? Or threaten to remove my nightgown yourself?"

He laid his head against her stomach. Phyllida heard it growl—

Lord! she certainly had had enough supper—but he didn't laugh. "I wouldn't dare do any of those things," he said. "Have I really treated you so arrogantly? But I need only look at your poor face to answer that question."

"Then don't look at it," Phyllida said.

"I don't understand," Andrew whispered. "Why are you no longer afraid of me? Before, when I had done nothing to you, you claimed to be terrified. Now that you have every reason to keep your distance, you come in here and challenge me to strip you, bully you—"

"I am not so perverse as you think, Andrew. I am no longer afraid of you, because you have become so afraid of yourself. And even before that, if you remember, I was reconciled to our bargain."

"What was that?" He pressed his lips against her stomach through the thin fabric of the gown. "I don't recall."

"That I would be your wife in every way, now that Rhys had gone. The week was up. And if I did not let you in, the footmen would break the door down. I was ready."

"My poor love. And look how your courage was repaid."

"Please, Andrew. Can't we pretend, just for the night, that it didn't happen? It wasn't as if you did anything deliberately." The lies just went on and on, but Phyllida was determined to lie *to* Andrew as much as she had to in order to lie *with* Andrew this night. It was the only way to prove her love and exorcise the demons that had come between them.

"I don't think I can do that, Phyllida," he said, standing up. "But I can promise you this. I will do nothing tonight to make you cry, except, I hope, with pleasure."

"That will be lovely," Phyllida said. "And please, can we stay here? Do you mind very much? I have taken a dislike to my room after being locked in."

"I never minded seeing you here," Andrew said. "It was only that I was taken by surprise, that first night. Tonight, it will be an honor." He moved to the door. "Do you have a fear of locked doors?"

"Not if I am locked in with you. It was being alone that frightened me."

Andrew led her to the bed and helped her up. "Now," he said. "This is important. Anything that happens, anything I do that you don't like, you must say so."

"I will."

"Promise me. Promise you will tell me to stop if you are afraid or if I hurt you."

"I promise."

He smiled, looking almost like his old self. "Good. Now, I think you should lie on your back and spread your legs wide. I am going to have a look for a little man in a boat."

THE SCREAMING WAS SO LOUD and went on so long, rising to piercing shrieks, trailing off into moans and crescendoing again, that Mr. Pumfry came out of his room and a couple of the maids crept downstairs to stand in the corridor. "It's coming from the master's room," Pumfry said. "It was like that yesterday when the mistress was locked in, but—"

"But not as loud as this," Joan said.

"I don't dare disturb Mr. Carrington," Pumfry said.

"If something bad's happening, oughtn't we to help?" Gert, the new scullery maid, asked.

There were heavy footsteps on the stairs as some of the menservants came down to see what had brought everybody out of bed. Kevin grinned at the impromptu gathering. "She certainly has a good set of lungs, the missus," he said, winking at Mr. Pumfry. "You sure you ought to be gettin' your jollies listenin' to the master and missus like that?"

"But what if there's trouble?" Pumfry said.

"Ain't you never heard a woman enjoying herself?" Kevin asked. He shook his head. "Guess not in this house. Better get used to it." He saw Mrs. Badger emerge from the lower levels in her nightdress, a wooden rolling pin in her hand. "Won't be needin' that," he said, "unless— Eh, is that Mr. Badger? He's a right big fellow, ain't he? Makes you scream like the missus, I'll bet." He ran up the stairs, laughing and ducking as she swung it at him.

Andrew now understood what men meant when they described certain women as being "screamers." He was fairly confident he had turned the lock, and hoped that Pumfry wasn't even now marshalling Jamie and Kevin to break down yet another door. He flicked Phyllida again with his tongue and she thrashed and moaned. Another few flicks, a carefully aimed breath or two, and she was pulsing again, the liquid gushing from her cleft, and screaming at the top of her lungs. What a woman! He could never in a million years have imagined anything remotely like this. No wonder the ancient gods had concluded, after arguing it out, that women had greater pleasure in the act than men did. Must have been a lot of women like Phyllida back then.

He decided it was time for a rest and pulled his face from between her legs.

"Oh," she said, "I think you killed me."

"I hope," Andrew said, "that is meant as a compliment."

"I died and went to heaven." She sighed. "It's as if flames of pleasure burned through my limbs and dissolved my flesh. How did you learn to do such a thing?"

"From the very best of teachers," he said. "Intuition." He kissed her face, careful to stay on the good side, and put his tongue in her mouth.

"I can taste myself," she said. "How peculiar." She sucked on his tongue and ran her hands over his smooth chest. "What shall I do for you? You will have to tell me."

"You don't have to do anything for me," Andrew said. "Just being with me like this is all I want from you."

Phyllida lay in her husband's arms for a few minutes, savoring the sense of molten, liquefied contentment, before the answer occurred to her. It was so obvious. Hadn't her mother told her this very thing on her wedding night? "Lie on your back."

He was so proud of his new accomplishment, and so oblivious, that he obeyed without question before it occurred to him to wonder what she was up to. He didn't have to ponder long. She had knelt between his legs and had taken his cock in her fist before the thought crossed his mind. "No, Phyllida," he said.

"Hush," she said. "Let me please you as you pleased me." She licked her lips in a most provocative way, winked at him, and began a slow, excruciating series of kisses and swipes of her tongue, starting at the base of his member and moving up the shaft. When she reached the tip, she opened her mouth, encircled the head with her lips, and began a tentative ingestion, all the while playing her tongue over the surface.

"Stop that," he said, although his voice was not as forceful as he intended. All his strength had gone to that one place.

"Why?" she teased. "Don't you like it?"

"Too much," he said, gasping. "It's not right for you to do that."

This pronouncement was so startling that she actually stopped in mid-swallow and took her mouth off him, making him groan. "Not right? But don't your lovers do this? Isn't this what you do?"

He pumped his hips in a helpless reflex, which rather destroyed the effect of his next words. "Of course, my love. But what's right for men isn't always right for women. Certainly not for my wife."

Phyllida laughed. Men were the most illogical, inconsistent people, and always accusing women of irrationality. "That is the silliest thing I ever heard, Andrew. Here's what I propose. I will go on as I have begun, and if I do it wrong, or if I do something you don't like, you will tell me. How's that?" She didn't wait for his answer, but resumed the slow kissing, taking more and more of the shaft into her mouth with each attempt. It was most interesting to see how his member swelled with each caress, lengthening and, especially, thickening, in a dramatic demonstration of the efficacy of her technique.

Andrew groaned again and surrendered. It was more than flesh and blood could stand, to stop such incredible pleasure. He knew it was wrong, knew a wife must not be used as a whore. And there she was, her face all purple, sucking him off like a miserable abused street wench in a back alley.

Phyllida choked and gagged as he came into her mouth. She wondered how people learned to do this gracefully, or whether that was possible. Was she supposed to swallow the seed? What else? She couldn't very well lean over the side of the bed and spit into the chamber pot. Well, she could, but that would not be very ladylike.

Andrew grunted in satisfaction and reached for her, bringing her up to lie in the crook of his arm. He kissed her, noting the taste of himself, as with his lovers. "What a degenerate couple we have become," he said.

"You must teach me how to do that properly," Phyllida said. "You made love to me so well with your mouth, but I know I did not do as well."

"No one does it *properly*," Andrew said. "It is a very improper thing for a wife to do. Although I can honestly say that I have had no other woman do it better."

"Yes," Phyllida murmured, "a master of sophistry."

PHILIP TURNER, CREEPING UP THE backstairs hours later, was stopped dead in his tracks by the screeching. It reminded him of—no, it couldn't be—yes, it was. He tiptoed up further, to the level of the bedrooms. No doubt of it. There could not be two women in this house who shrieked like that.

Mrs. Carrington, that cunning little whore, was playing her tricks on her husband. At least, it was coming from Carrington's room, and, for all his easygoing manner, he would not be so careless as to let his wife entertain some other man in there. Unless . . . Philip pondered whether Carrington was the sort who would enjoy seeing his wife pleasured by another man. Possible. Quite likely, he imagined. Perhaps Carrington had found a way to possess both his wife and a man in the same bed.

He yawned and staggered into his own room. It was an exhausting business, this searching for that damned bum-boy. Up till all hours, and in danger of being beaten, robbed, and worse. Much, much worse. Yet it had its enjoyable aspects. Especially while he still had access to the kind of money that allowed him to pay for what even street whores didn't like to give cheap.

He winced at the thought that he must rise early to see if an unfamiliar face was at the breakfast table, or sneaking out at dawn. But such information would be invaluable. He wasn't getting anywhere with the search for Kit, and he didn't like to trust such an important job to an unknown boy. If he had another approach, knowledge of perverse goings-on with the wife, he could save himself trouble.

The screams reached a peak of shuddering reverberations, then died down. Philip pulled his pillow over his head and hoped to snatch a couple hours of sleep.

OVER THE NEXT TWO WEEKS, the household, with one or two exceptions, seemed to revert to its earlier, premarriage harmony. Mr. Turner, looking increasingly haggard and hollow-eyed, took his solitary meals as before and answered Andrew's probing questions with minimal and evasive answers. Nan, still elated at her new position, nevertheless seemed to have trouble coping with its duties. Mrs. Badger twice found her sound asleep on the hard kitchen floor, where she had gone to wash out some of the mistress's delicate undergarments in the large sink. "Worn to a frazzle, she is, poor thing," the cook said. "All skin and bones and dark circles under the eyes. Can't imagine what she has to do as a lady's maid that's harder than scrubbing pots."

The rest of the staff, divided into two camps—those who favored cork earplugs and those who swore by cotton wool—were united in their approval of the detente between husband and wife, and forgiving of the nighttime din. "No worse than cats," Mrs. Badger admitted. "Only problem is, with my ears stopped up, I'll never catch who's pinching the leftovers from the pantry. That was a whole lamb pasty went missing t'other night."

"Mebbe the missus et it," Kevin said. "All that bed sport takes it out of a body. And she don't appear to be shrinking."

"Don't be coarse," Mrs. Featherstone said. "A big young lout like you would be more likely to steal food. Although Lord knows you eat enough at table."

Kevin belched and rubbed his stomach. "I do, and that's a fact. Know one thing. Whoever the thief is, it ain't our Nan."

The rest of the table looked to the girl, who sat, heavy-lidded, her head nodding over her plate.

"Wake up, girl, and eat," Kevin said. "Won't have the men making you scream 'less you put some meat on those bones."

The time went by easily upstairs, as well. Those few callers who had yet to make the acquaintance of the bride were not received, as the mistress was said to be indisposed. Even Richard Carrington and Lizzie Fanshawe were denied the lady's presence. Only Miss Gatling, George Witherspoon, and Lord David Pierce were allowed that privilege. Andrew resumed most of his usual activities—his morning rides in the park, his shooting at Manton's—but avoided the house on Park Lane. Regardless of Pierce's advice, Andrew would not have felt comfortable fielding the probing questions of his friends, who had so much at stake on his marital activities. "*I* know what happened was an aberration," Pierce said, "just as you do. But it's easier to wait until Mrs. Carrington's face heals before going back into society."

For Phyllida, the last weeks of March went as quickly as the previous week had dragged. Andrew spent more time at home, and Mr. Turner, apparently balked of his object, kept his distance. Phyllida stewed with worry at first that he would say something to her or to Andrew, or that he would accost her on the stairs or trespass in her room again; but as a week went by without incident, she put the evil little ferret out of her mind. She had the deadline to meet for the proofs of the third volume, and her days were spent in happy, productive work.

Her nights were even happier, if not as productive. Andrew seemed unwilling, or unable, to make love to her in the standard way. But he welcomed her into his bed and his arms for long, delirious sessions of "kissing," as he called it, although rarely did their two mouths meet.

"You will never father a child that way," she said one night as he lifted his dark head from between her thighs.

"Is that all I am to you," he teased, "a vessel for providing seed?"

"I am not complaining," she said. "I thought it was why you married."

"There is plenty of time for that," he said. "I'm in no hurry to see you with a swollen belly, unable to enjoy the season."

"All the people who are betting on you will be frantic."

"To hell with them," he said. "If they're foolish enough to bet on such things, let them sweat it out to the end." He gave her a quizzical look. "And how are they to know exactly what we're doing in here?"

"Only that they will see no results."

He cupped a breast that felt as if it had grown from the grapefruit of their first encounter to the size of a cantaloupe, and laid a hand on the soft pillow of her stomach. "If you go on eating as you do, we will see some very fine results indeed."

"I know," Phyllida said. "I try to eat less, but—"

"But I like you plump," Andrew said. "Just not so big you can't open Lady Trent's ball with me next week. Has Mme. Argonne delivered your gown?"

"Oh, yes, Andrew. It's every bit as beautiful as the first one. I would model it for you and offer to let you strip it off me, but I couldn't bear to have a second one ruined."

"Hmm," Andrew said. "We should have kept the old one, just for us."

"I know!" Phyllida said, blushing in her delightful way. "I can ask Harriet to bring that old gown. The one I was wearing when we met. Would that do?"

"Excellent," Andrew said. "But you could barely fit into it then."

"It wasn't mine. It's Harriet's. Mama thought I'd look more appealing in a smaller gown than one that fit me properly."

"Do you know," Andrew said, "I think I have maligned your mother. She seems a very wise woman."

RICHARD CARRINGTON WAS WORRIED, and he didn't enjoy the feeling. It wasn't like Andrew to be evasive and polite; it wasn't like Phyllida, what he knew of her, to hide in her boudoir and not receive callers; that weaselly secretary of Andrew's got on his nerves; and he was tired of living on credit. He dressed with unusual attention to fashion, had his man spend a good half hour on his hair and gave him free rein with the cravat. Having prepared as best he could, he walked slowly to Park Lane and presented his card to the suspicious heavyweight on the door. The damn brute made him wait.

"Mr. Richard Carrington," Farnham informed the startled company.

"Andrew," Monkton corrected idly. "About time we had a report from him."

"No, sir," Farnham said. "Says here, 'Mr. Richard Carrington.'" It was a prerequisite for the post, the ability to decipher the calling cards of visitors, as a mistake could have far worse consequences than enduring a few minutes of boredom or confusion.

"What's he look like?" Pierce asked.

"Like Mr. Andrew Carrington," Farnham said, "only younger. And handsomer."

"A matter of opinion," Verney said. "Might as well show him in."

Everybody stood when he entered. "We are honored," Pierce said. "To what do we owe the pleasure? At least, we can always hope it will be pleasure."

"Oh, sit down," Richard said. "I'm sorry to beard you in your den, but I'm worried about Andrew."

"Good God! What's the matter?"

"Taking it badly, the break with Harry Swain?"

"No, he's over that. Something else must've happened."

"How come *we* didn't hear anything?"

"Nothing," Richard said, alarmed at the tidal wave he had caused. "I didn't mean to ruffle your feathers like this. I just— I can't get a straight answer from Andrew as to how things are going, you see, and I thought you might know."

"Come to think of it," Verney said, "we haven't seen him here in days."

"Weeks," Monkton said. "It's been delightfully peaceful."

"We assumed he was, ah, busy with his wife," Pierce said. "Haven't you been around to see?"

"Well of course, but that's why I'm here," Richard said. "Phyllida won't receive me, but Andrew seems very happy."

After a stunned pause, everybody rose to his feet again, pumping Richard's hand and clapping him on the shoulder.

"But that's wonderful!"

"I say, damned good of you to call and tell us."

"When is he planning to announce it, eh?"

"At White's, no doubt."

"No, at Almack's." There was much raucous laughter at that.

Richard shook his head and tried to disengage from the unwelcome attention. "I don't think that's it," he said.

"But what else could it be?" Pierce asked.

Richard shrugged. "*I* don't know. You tell me."

"What the devil is that supposed to mean?" Monkton asked.

"Damn it," Richard said, "you don't have to take me up short on everything I say. I just thought you might have a better idea than I do as to what might make Andrew float around like a lovesick mooncalf."

"God, is that how he's behaving? What a revolting image."

Reginald Stevens, the physician, came downstairs, chatting with a new member who had been voted in the day before. "Monkton," the newcomer said, having caught only the last phrase, "I knew there was something off about you. Here's a most charming image indeed. Aren't you going to introduce me?"

Stevens shook his head. "Not one of us," he said under his breath. He bowed to Richard, who returned the compliment.

"Then what's he doing here?" the new man said. He advanced toward Richard and held out his hand. "Matthew Thornby. Pleased to make your acquaintance."

Richard shook the hand, wincing at the powerful grip. "Richard Carrington. But as Stevens says, I'm not a member of this club."

The man clung to his hand, squeezing until Richard was afraid he'd have to learn how to do everything with his left. "Oh, don't be too sure," he said. "Lots of fellows say that until they have their first taste of cock. Then they can't get enough."

"Thornby has just come up to town from Yorkshire," Verney said, "after years in America. As no doubt you can tell from his manners."

"Full of scandalous stories of savages and slaves," Monkton drawled, "and I can't bring myself even to begin to repeat what he says about America."

Thornby laughed. "All true, every word. Would you like to hear some details, Mr. Carrington?"

Richard extracted the crushed remains of his hand. "Thank you, but no. I have a pressing engagement with a lady. One with a highly developed taste for cock."

"I think she's pregnant." The soft voice cut through the howls of laughter. Everybody turned to where Witherspoon sat on the sofa in the corner, one leg tucked under him, a book in his lap.

"Who?" Thornby asked.

"Phyllida," Witherspoon said. "Mrs. Carrington."

"You are married?" Thornby said. "My apologies."

"No," Richard said. "My brother."

"That's a relief," Thornby said.

"What do you know about Phyllida?" Richard asked Witherspoon.

"I think she's going to have a baby," Witherspoon said. "The last time we saw her, she looked very plump. And very—serene."

"George," Pierce said, going to sit by his friend. "Remember what we said about talking to the others."

"I do, Davey," Witherspoon said, "but you've all been arguing about it, and I just thought it would be easier if I said what I think."

"But she can't be," Pierce said. "If she were, Andrew would have told us."

"Maybe he doesn't know," Witherspoon said.

"Then why does he look so happy?" Richard demanded. God, he'd had enough of this fancy madge club, and now with that big Yorkshireman giving him the eye, he couldn't wait to escape.

"It's what I said before," Verney said. "Carrington's in love."

THE EASTER HOLIDAY MARKED THE end of Phyllida's honeymoon, as she saw it, and the beginning of her real married life. She had worked hard on the proofs, forcing herself to get through them in record time so that she could throw herself into the dissipations and delights of a London season without a backward glance. She had made her deadline, if only just, but she had made it. The season was starting, her face was completely healed, and her sister Harriet, with Jenny Porter in her new capacity as lady's maid, would arrive tomorrow in Andrew's elegant chaise.

"Are you sure you don't regret offering to sponsor her coming out?" Phyllida asked Andrew as he made the traveling arrangements.

He looked up at her worried tone. "We agreed on it," he said. "I don't go back on my promises. And so long as she does not beg to share our bed, I see no reason for her visit to inconvenience either of us."

"Wicked!" Phyllida said. "I suppose if she were my pretty younger brother you would welcome her into our bed."

"Not that wicked," Andrew said. "Into my bed, certainly. But not the two of you together."

"You are not only a master of sophistry," Phyllida whispered into her husband's ear, "but a monster of depravity. I am glad I married you."

Andrew accepted her kiss on his cheek, rang for a footman, and gave him the orders for the horses at the posting stages. "Speaking of marrying me," he said to Phyllida after the man had gone out, "I have something to show you."

Phyllida smiled. "It is very nice," she said. "But I have seen it before. Can't you wait until bedtime?"

"Now who's a monster of depravity?" Andrew said. "What will I do with you in polite society?"

"As you don't know any," Phyllida said, "I can't see that it matters."

Andrew laughed and had her take his place at the table. He unlocked a large strongbox and brought out several leather cases. "I ought to have given you these before," he said, "but the right moment never seemed to present itself. Go ahead. Open them."

Phyllida opened the one closest to her, the biggest, and gasped aloud. There was a set of rubies—a necklace, a bracelet, and earrings. The stones were large, the settings discreet in order to show off the jewels. She looked up, speechless.

"I know," Andrew drawled, "not your color. Never mind. Try the next box."

"No," Phyllida said. "They're too beautiful for words."

"Surely the author of *Sense and Sensibility* is not at a loss for words," Andrew murmured.

"What?" Phyllida was dazed by the rich, flashing reds and did not quite hear.

"They are the Macallister jewels," Andrew said. "From my mother. They are yours now, but you need not wear them except on state occasions, if they don't go with your gowns. There are other things here more suitable."

"Your mother was a Macallister?" Phyllida said. "That's why—"

"Yes, that's the excuse for all this swarthy hairiness," Andrew said. "Descended directly from Charles II, or so the family likes to claim."

"You don't believe it?"

Andrew shrugged. "Who can say, after a hundred and fifty years? And who cares?"

"I didn't know about that," Phyllida said. "I was thinking about the estate in Northumberland."

"Yes, right on the border," Andrew said. "It's changed hands so many times in the past five hundred years it's more of a ruined fortress than a house. But the land is good." In the silence, he voiced aloud his thoughts of the past days. "I can't help thinking that if I had given the jewels to you earlier, your rooms need not have been torn apart by that thief."

"Better a gown or two ruined, and a desk, than to lose these!" Phyllida exclaimed, beginning to believe the lie, so often had she been required to play along with it.

"Yes, I have wondered what the thief could have been searching for in a writing desk," Andrew said. "In the meantime, look at the rest of these."

The rest consisted of an exquisite set of diamonds and an unexceptional set of pearls. Phyllida was ecstatic. "I have only my locket with my father's miniature, and my glass bead eardrops. I was worried about what to wear with all my new gowns."

"You ought to have said something. You know you have only to ask, when it comes to things like this."

"I didn't want to seem mercenary."

Andrew laughed. "But that is the nature of our marriage. A dutiful sodomite and a mercenary female. Never fear to act in character."

"Don't, Andrew," Phyllida said in a low voice. "Please don't make it all sound so ugly. Just when everything was so nice."

"It is more than nice," he said. "Delightful. I only tease you on the subject because you are the least mercenary lady I know. Any other woman in your position would have ruined me. If she didn't bankrupt me with her milliners' bills or lack of restraint or judgment at the card table, she'd eliminate me by flaunting her lovers, whom I would be required to fight, and end up on the gallows."

"But we agreed I was not to have lovers."

"Ah, yes, your one sticking point. I do sympathize."

Phyllida looked up into his face. "You miss Harry, don't you?"

He nodded. "Not Harry, exactly. I knew, in my heart, he was too young to settle down. But I miss having a man."

"Maybe you will meet someone, now that the season has started."

"Perhaps. Will you mind?"

Phyllida smiled and shook her head. "Not as long as you buy me off properly, with a gown for every day of the year and backing at the high-stakes tables."

Andrew kissed her lips. "That's my good mercenary wife," he said.

LADY TRENT'S BALL MARKED THE opening of the season for the leaders of the *ton*. Although it was presented as an informal, friendly gathering, those in the know were careful to wear something new and to arrive neither gauchely early nor too late to hear all the pent-up gossip from a long winter's absence. "Wear your new ball gown," Andrew advised. "At Almack's you will be just another married lady. The attention will go to Harriet and the other fillies. But tonight, all eyes will be on you."

With that admonition ringing in her ears, Phyllida expected to be as nervous as a witch, but it was Harriet who was a little whirlwind of activity, bouncing up and down every couple of minutes, changing her mind about her clothes, fussing with her hair, and being generally so irritating that Phyllida wanted to slap her. Had it always been like this? Or had the relative solitude of married life spoiled her? Harriet had arrived late last night and had taken supper in her room, so it was not until today that Phyllida had felt the full force of the reunion. Whatever it was, it was a pleasure to be dressed and in the carriage for the short drive to the Trent town house a couple of squares over.

"We could walk there, couldn't we?" Harriet asked. "At home we think nothing of walking five miles—and back again—for a visit. And it's not even raining. Is it?" She stuck her hand out the window. "Silly me. It wasn't raining two minutes ago when we stepped out the door. The air does stink, though. And it's full of soot. However do you bear it? In the country it all smells so fresh. Except of course when you're passing the hog barns, or collecting eggs in summer. That fair raises your gorge, I can tell you."

"I can imagine," Andrew said. "Although I'd prefer not to."

"When were you ever forced to visit the hog barns or gather eggs?" Phyllida scolded her sister.

"You were always writing and pretending not to hear," Harriet said, "but some of us had to help with the work."

"Of course we could walk, Miss Lewis," Andrew broke in on the siblings' argument before it escalated into an all-out war, "but you'd be cursing me after two steps when your slippers were ruined by the dirt. And we'd get peculiar stares from the footmen when we tramped up the driveway."

"Does she ever stop?" he whispered to Phyllida under cover of the announcement of their names at the entrance. "Because if you've had to put up with that all day, I will quite understand if you want to marry her off to the first drunken skirt-chaser who comes her way."

"Don't tempt me," Phyllida answered. "But why drunken?"

"Because a sober man would turn sodomite rather than put up with that in bed."

Phyllida was therefore at her best, aglow with laughter, when the *ton* had its first look at her. She was surrounded by admirers from the start, not only her friends from the Brotherhood of Philander, but a great many beaux who seemed not to care that she was married, or preferred things that way. She did her best to introduce them to Harriet, but although the girl was more conventionally attractive, with a small, slender figure and chestnut ringlets, there was something about Phyllida's lush, blooming femininity that put her sister's dainty prettiness in the shade.

When the music started for the first set, Andrew carved a path through the gaggle of followers and held out his hand. "Gentlemen," he said to the groans and complaints all around, "I have an incontrovertible claim to the prize."

"I do not like to leave Harriet unchaperoned," Phyllida protested.

Andrew replied with a word that ought to have been whispered, or better yet not spoken at all in mixed company. "Where is my philandering brother when we need him?"

"Richard is not my idea of a chaperone anyway," Phyllida said.

"Best there is," Andrew said. "He'd dance with her or even sit with her for a set, because of her looks, but he'd have nothing more to do with her, were she as quiet as a nun. He only likes the married ones. Ah, Witherspoon. Good to see you." He snagged the beautiful young man by the shoulder. "Like to introduce you to Mrs. Carrington's sister. Miss Lewis, here is a very good friend of mine, Mr. Witherspoon, who has been pestering me all week with his desire to meet you."

"Oh!" Harriet was rendered temporarily inarticulate by the gorgeous vision that confronted her. "Why?"

Phyllida rolled her eyes. "Because Mr. Witherspoon is a perfect gentleman who naturally wishes to make the acquaintance of his friends' family members." She lowered her voice. "Do you mind, George?"

"Not at all. Delighted. Would you do me the honor, Miss Lewis?"

"Honestly, Andrew," Phyllida said as he walked her out to begin the dance. "That was very cruel."

"Not as cruel as not being allowed to dance with my own wife at the first ball of the season."

PHILIP TURNER PERVERSELY DECIDED TO give himself a night off the evening of Lady Trent's ball. While it might make sense to take advantage of the master and mistress's absence to continue his pursuit of the street boy, it was equally true that he needed a rest. And Mr. Carrington had become more pointed in his work sessions, asking the kinds of questions that tied Philip increasingly in knots to try to answer.

No, it was dangerous to wait any longer. He had sent a letter, not to Amberson but to someone who would have no choice but to investigate. Someone high enough up that Carrington could not dismiss him with his usual sneer of contempt. It was a gamble, but without the accounts book or any other evidence to incriminate him, one that Philip felt justified in accepting.

Just what the devil was that bitch Mrs. Carrington up to? If she had the accounts book, as she must, why had she not produced it? If only Carrington hadn't taken into his head the crazy notion to marry. Or, at least, why couldn't he have married a typical society lady, governed solely by self-interest, who would never have bothered to look at the accounts at all, or who might have agreed to go into the scheme with Philip? She wouldn't even have to do anything other than corroborate the accusations.

Philip would of course do his best to put some blame on her, telling a story of adulterous goings-on that would make Mr. Carrington do a lot worse to her than box her ears—entertainment that Philip, for one, would pay good money to see—but he rather suspected it wouldn't be believed. Infatuated husbands were the worst.

Confronted with every indication of their wives' misbehavior, they were addicted to cunt, and would lap it up to the end rather than suppose themselves betrayed.

Of course, Carrington was different. Or so Philip had thought. But he had turned out just as bad as the rest, spending every night with his screaming, moaning slut of a wife, driving the whole house crazy with her caterwauling. Although nobody else seemed to mind. No, they went about their duties every day with the idiotic smiles on their faces of people so stupid they actually believed all that rubbish about the pleasure of living in a happy house. Only Philip seemed to feel the effects of sleepless nights, driven to toss and turn, losing the few hours of rest he could hope to get after coming home late from his prowling in the worst parts of town, by the feigned wailings of pleasure of a practiced, deceiving whore.

Well, no use complaining about what couldn't be helped. He had insurance, the key to the cipher concealed on his person, and he would enjoy an early night for a change, spend the time before bed on formulating the rest of a sensible plan. And all thinking went better with something to lubricate the brain. He might as well help himself to a bottle of Carrington's excellent claret. He crept down the back stairs, into the cellar, past the pantry, and toward the wine, then stopped, convinced he heard voices. He waited, not daring to breathe, certain of the identity of one of those voices, and listening to the other, growing increasingly excited as he began to believe in Providence after all.

He leaped out to catch them in the act. "Why, Nan," he said. "What—"

Whatever he meant to say was stopped in his throat as hard, wiry hands locked themselves around his neck. He gagged and choked, tearing at the strong fingers. Then a shattering light, and darkness.

"CRIKEY!" KIT SAID. "WOT IF you killed 'im?"

"Serve 'im right," Nan said, tossing the broken-off neck of the bottle on top of the slumped body. "He's the one what bruised the missus' face."

"Wot missus?" Kit asked.

"Mrs. Carrington, idiot. The lady I'm lady's maid to."

"'E's married?" Kit asked. *Carr, Carrington. Married.* Kit wondered what else he didn't know. "I thought 'e was different. Said 'e was gonna call me Marlowe, after some other sod 'e knew."

"He's a good man," Nan said. "And so's Mrs. Carrington. And this little rat here slapped her face, and she's letting everyone think the master did it when he didn't, which ain't right. You ought to have seen his face when he thought he'd done it."

"Why would 'e think it if 'e di'n't do it?"

"'Cos he has some sort of fits, the megrims or something, and he don't remember."

"So wot's she up to, then, if she's so good?"

"I don't know," Nan said. "I think it's her writing. She writes books that ain't proper. Smutty books. And she don't want the master to know. So I guess this little rat here was going to tell the master unless she kept quiet about what he's doing."

Kit sighed. It was getting to be too much to follow. "And wot's *'e* doing?"

Nan shook her head. "Fiddling the kitchen accounts. I can't read so well, but I'm good with numbers. I had a look a couple of times, and they don't add up right at the end of the month after he's been over them."

"So why'n't you tell the master, then, if you know so much?"

"Who'd believe me? A scullery maid?"

Turner groaned and tried to sit up. "Crikey!" Kit said. "'Stead of jawin' we ought to 'ave tied 'im up."

"I'll get some clothesline," Nan said.

"And be quick about it."

Turner opened his eyes, only to be faced with the image of that whore he'd been chasing fruitlessly for two weeks. "Where'm I?" he mumbled. "What're you doing here?"

Kit judged the man was too groggy to go far. "Wot you up to, then, mister?" he asked. "Why're you sneakin' around lookin' for me?"

Philip wasn't sure of the answers to these questions—his brain seemed not to function at its usual speed. "Because you're beautiful," he said. "Like to play rough?"

"No," Kit said. "But I do when I 'ave to." Nan returned with the clothesline and he hogtied the man good and tight. Everyone knew weasels and ferrets could get in and out of the narrowest holes.

MATTHEW THORNBY DIDN'T GO TO society balls, but he decided to make an exception tonight. That beautiful Richard Carrington might be there, and it was a long time since Matthew had seen anything quite as gorgeous as that. Years, in fact.

It was very educational, and for the most part great sport, to have been put in charge of his father's vast overseas business ventures. But he'd had enough of sea voyages and cotton mills, and as for America, with its plantations of African slaves . . . He shuddered. Just as well those crazy former colonists were spoiling for a war, because as far as Matthew was concerned, he wanted nothing more to do with them. The business had already fallen off from the embargoes and blockades of the past five years. A war wouldn't make much difference. And the Thornbys, after three generations of hardheaded Yorkshire horse-trading sense, had the kind of wealth that could weather more than one reversal without serious diminution. Matthew had paid his dues; he could afford to concentrate on pleasure, at least for a season or two.

He made sure the ball was in full swing before putting in an appearance. Didn't want the droves of husband-hunting girls and their shark-toothed mamas chasing him down the minute he walked in the door. It was perfect timing. The company was in the middle of a set, the few wallflowers sitting in chairs pushed well back from the dance floor, most of them having given up by now. Earlier and they'd be all eager, stationed at the edge of the action, just waiting to leap on a fellow and wrestle him to the altar. Matthew didn't like to seem vain or cruel, but it was inevitable, with his rugged blond looks and immense fortune, that he had had some pretty close-run encounters over the years.

The problem was he liked women. Oh, not to make love to. But they were agreeable and entertaining companions for conversation, so long as one remembered not to use the coarse expressions that were standard between men but that invariably turned a delicate female to stony-faced affront. If one were careful, one could enjoy the kind of intimacy and friendship with a woman that was rarely possible with a man. Men kept their feelings to themselves. You could have eight inches of a man's cock up your arse, with him pumping away, and you saying how you wanted it harder, as hard as he could go, and five minutes later he'd be saying things like "Fine hunting weather we're having" and "How much did you pay for that gray hack of yours?"

No, women were different. They'd tell you their life story after two minutes of chitchat, and confess every sexual peccadillo over a glass or two of sherry. And if they hadn't committed any, they'd make some up, just for the pleasure of sharing confidences. But if women enjoyed venial sins, it was men who had the edge when it came to deadly ones. To sodomy, in fact.

Speaking of which, there he was. Tall and dark, and so slender. As if you could snap him in half with one hand, except he was strong, as tough as rawhide, and didn't break, only bent. And that profile. Lord, you knew he must have something in his breeches with a nose like that. Matthew felt himself stiffening just staring at the man across a crowded dance floor, and moved into the crush in hopes he wouldn't expose himself like a schoolboy watching the sixth-form games.

Carrington was dancing—lithe and graceful, how else—with a beautiful, curvaceous woman. But Matthew didn't waste time on her, not with his goal in front of him. The music was ending and he would have his chance to pounce, but only if he got closer.

Halfway there he stopped. It wasn't Richard. The man was darker, if such a thing was possible, and with the creases in the face that come from being closer to thirty than twenty. And what else was different? Matthew wasn't sure, but he certainly wanted to find out. He smiled and took rapid steps forward.

ANDREW WALKED PHYLLIDA BACK TO her place and offered to get her something to drink. She fanned her glowing face. "Thank you, Andrew. Something cold, if they have it." As he moved away, the legions of suitors converged around her.

"I hoped I'd see you here," Richard said. "Will you dance the next set with me?"

"I'm sorry, Richard," Phyllida said. "It's promised to a very nice young man named Peter Finchley. Perhaps you know him. He's a rather reedy, sandy blond."

"You are a minx and a vixen," Richard said. "A beautiful, blooming minx and a lovely, laughing vixen. Please, Phyllida."

"I can't," Phyllida said. "Have you met my sister Harriet?"

Richard resigned himself to the introduction, unprepared for the onslaught that followed.

"How do you do?" Harriet said. "Oh, you do look so like your brother! It's amazing, isn't it, Phyllida? How do you tell them apart? Well, Richard is younger, of course. Are you married, Mr. Carrington? No? I suppose you need time to look around. I can't begin to make up my mind, everyone handsomer than the rest. Do you know George Witherspoon? He was my first partner, and I don't think I've seen anyone quite as handsome as him. Do you like to dance? I haven't sat one out yet, and I'm not tired at all. Although it is warm in here. Oh no, please don't bother. See, Mr. Finchley has brought me a glass."

Richard, looking daggers at Phyllida, did the only thing he could, and asked Harriet to dance. He contented himself with glaring at Phyllida all through the set, grateful at least for the country dance that necessitated periodic separations from his voluble partner and appreciative of the fact that Caroline Finchley's eldest son looked quite outclassed in the presence of the divine Phyllida. He would have something to say to her when he got her alone, which he was determined to do, if only in revenge for inflicting her sister on him. Although he supposed it wasn't her fault. Family. Nothing one could do except keep one's distance whenever possible.

He watched his sister, Lizzie, and her partner going down the reel. Now there was a sparring match. He'd like to set odds on that contest, who could out-chatter the other. Who would be left standing after fifteen rounds of bare-tongued chin-wagging? Lizzie had years of experience in her favor, and the shamelessness of her upper-class hauteur. But this Harriet was a definite up-and-comer, no doubt about it, pluck to the backbone and impervious to snubs. Just as soon as he got this question of pregnancy settled with Phyllida, and once Andrew had made the proper announcements, Richard was going to get his new bet into the book at White's—the light-middleweight jabbering championship.

"MR. CARRINGTON?"

Andrew turned around at the warm, slightly foreign voice, and looked into the face of a million late-night dreams. Blond, blue-eyed, square-jawed . . . Tanned, with little white creases at the outer corners of his eyes . . . Broad-shouldered, solid waist, narrow hips . . . Muscles like . . . Now he knew how people felt when they described themselves as tongue-tied. "Yes," he said. *I want to kiss you, kneel to you, pull you down and do everything to you until you beg for mercy.* "I think you have the advantage of me."

"Matthew Thornby. I met your brother Richard—at the Brotherhood of Philander, appropriately enough."

"Good Lord. What was he doing there?"

"Asking after you."

"He's not one of them, you know."

"One of us," Matthew said. He noticed the direction the man's eyes had traveled, from face to chest to . . . *Please, say you are. Say you want to kiss me, touch me, do everything to me, and make me beg for more.*

"Yes," Andrew said. He put down the glass he had started to fill with punch. "I could use a breath of fresh air. Care to join me? It's always stuffy at these gatherings."

"I'd like that very much," Matthew replied. "But I don't wish to spend the time riding all the way out to the countryside."

"A wit," Andrew said, "as well as a beauty. Where are you from, Mr. Thornby?" He held out his arm and the man put his hand through the angle of the bent elbow.

"Huddersfield," Matthew said. "That's in Yorkshire."

"So I've been led to believe," Andrew drawled. "If I'd known Yorkshire was so scenic, I would have traveled north more often."

"It's not," Matthew said. "At least, not the cities. I've been out of the country most of the past five years, but—"

"No," Andrew agreed. "In that case, not scenic at all."

They had reached the large French windows on the side of the ballroom, which opened onto the balcony running the length of the back wall of the house. The windows were open a crack, allowing those who needed air to slip out without lowering the temperature inside for the women who, in their thin muslin gowns, might catch a chill if the atmosphere cooled below the level of a steam bath. Andrew pried the door open, bowed Matthew through, followed close behind, and pulled it almost shut again.

The air outside was sharp and acrid but refreshing. There was a crescent moon and a smattering of stars faintly visible through the haze. The balcony consisted of a series of deep embrasures, separated from each other and from the views of those inside the room, by dividing buttresses of masonry. Two generations of revelers had christened the formation "Trent's trysting spot," and the current Lady Trent, who had made her first intimate acquaintance of her husband in the place, had apparently no objection to its continued use for the purpose. Several couples, in the same mood as Andrew and Matthew, were already ensconced in the nearest bays. Andrew led Matthew farther back, to a more private and empty space.

As soon as they reached it, Andrew pushed Matthew in and backed the powerful blond against the wall. He didn't ask, just crushed his mouth over the man's and pressed hips to hips. Their erections bumped in a painful, pleasurable bruising. Andrew reached down to unbutton the man's flap, just as Matthew did the same for him.

"A wit, a beauty, and a mind reader," Andrew whispered.

"Don't know about that," Matthew said with a laugh. "But I know what I want, and I think you want it too."

"If it involves your cock in my mouth and my cock in your arse," Andrew said, "then you think right."

"Happen I am a mind reader after all," Matthew said.

There was silence for the next few minutes, broken only by deep, sighing breaths and stifled groans. "Oh God," Andrew said. "This will never do. Come home with me. We live soft lives in the south of England. Featherbeds, mattresses, that sort of thing."

"I could quite get used to that," Matthew said. "But your brother said you were married."

"So I am," Andrew said. "It's a marriage of convenience. She won't mind at all."

PHYLLIDA SAW ANDREW SLIP out to the balcony with the big blond man and their stealthy return a few minutes later. Throughout the rest of the ball, Andrew was nervous, restless, his eyes glittering pale with a barely controlled excitement. It was like the evenings with Rhys, only about ten times more powerful.

"Will you not introduce me to your new friend?" Phyllida said.

"Not yet," he said, his mouth twitching at the corners. "Later, perhaps."

Lady Fanshawe approached and Andrew groaned. "I can't," he said.

"Can't what?" the deep voice said at his shoulder.

"Take my sister right now."

"With pleasure," Matthew said. "Will you introduce me?"

"You'll live to regret it," Andrew warned. "If you're very lucky, she'll talk your ear off in a few minutes and you'll die from a brain seizure. A relatively quick death, though not painless."

"Andrew, Phyllida," Lady Fanshawe said, "is it not a great crush? I always dread these first balls of the season, but I wouldn't dare miss it for the world. Everyone talks about the ones who aren't here, you know. Any news, Phyllida? Hmm? You mustn't look so coy, we all know what that round, plump look signifies, and it's not overeating. Oh, who is this handsome new face? Andrew, will you not make the introductions? Men are so provoking. Not you, Mr.—"

"Thornby," Andrew said. "Matthew Thornby, my sister, Lady Fanshawe. Mr. Thornby is from America by way of Yorkshire. Or vice versa."

"Versa," Matthew said, bowing over Lady Fanshawe's hand. "My lady. I would recognize you as Mr. Carrington's sister without any introduction. Do you know, if one were to try to describe the appearance of a tall, willowy lady with raven locks and a fascinating, expressive face, one would have only the vaguest image of this unique beauty. One must see it in order to describe it, but having seen it, one is at a loss for words. There are insufficient superlatives."

For once Lizzie Fanshawe was struck dumb. "Elizabeth," she managed to enunciate.

"Are you free for the next set?" Matthew asked.

Andrew glared at him. "Mrs. Carrington was just expressing her desire to leave the ball early," he said. "She is fatigued from the heat."

"Oh, no, Andrew," Phyllida said. "You must have misunderstood. I merely said that this room is rather overheated and that those with delicate constitutions might find it fatiguing. I did not claim to be one of them."

"Excellent," Matthew said. "And you are therefore Mrs. Carrington. I say, Andrew, why didn't you mention that you possessed the two loveliest ladies in London? Want to keep all the beauty to yourself, eh?" He winked in the general direction of the entire company—the smiling ladies and the by now darkly glowering man.

"May I introduce you to my sister?" Phyllida would not waste so perfect an opportunity. "Miss Lewis is making her debut this season."

"I am overwhelmed," Matthew said. "I shall dance myself nearly to death tonight and drag myself home at dawn, too tired to lift my feet for a week."

"Not if I have anything to say about it," Andrew muttered.

"But you don't," Matthew said as he swept Lady Fanshawe off to the dance.

"Be patient," Phyllida said, laying a soothing hand on her husband's arm. "I think he just likes to tease."

AFTER MATTHEW HAD DANCED WITH Lady Fanshawe, receiving a perfectly encapsulated history of Andrew's surprising marriage, the bet at White's, the amusing debacle with Mme. Argonne, and the still-awaited news of pregnancy, he felt well satisfied with his efforts. He danced next with Phyllida, basking in the relative peace and admiring her lush beauty, suspecting she would not respond well to the effusive flattery he had employed with her sister-in-law. He contented himself, and her, with a simple expression of appreciation at the way in which her dress and the pearls so excellently suited her complexion. "Do I understand correctly," he ventured when the dance permitted, "that you and Mr. Carrington have a marriage based on honesty? It is a noble endeavor, although I imagine fraught with danger."

"Yes, Mr. Thornby," she replied. "We have negotiated a number of perilous peaks and sharp turns on our journey. But the vistas at the summit are worth the pains."

"You are a poetess?"

"A writer, yes, but of inferior romance."

"You reserve the superior stuff for your true romance with your husband."

They were separated then and Phyllida did not have to come up with another witty reply, for which she was grateful. This Matthew Thornby was dangerous—a bluff, handsome exterior, with a keen, probing intelligence, an easygoing manner with the hint of steel beneath and the resolve to use it. She hoped Andrew would be careful.

Matthew danced next with Harriet and understood Andrew's warning at last, as his remaining ear was more or less chewed off by the time the final measures of music were played. Still, from the three very different perspectives, he had pieced together a complete and informative picture of Andrew Carrington and his life. What he did not quite see was where the beautiful wife fit in. She clearly knew of her husband's preferences and not only did not mind but seemed in some way to participate in or enjoy them; but she was also in love with him—understandable enough—and worse, from Matthew's perspective, Andrew was obviously in love with her—also understandable. The sexual heat between them was fierce. Get in the way and one might be fried to a crisp by the electric current. But there had been no mistaking what had happened on that balcony earlier.

He could not possibly turn down the invitation Andrew had extended, whatever the price might be. He expected he would burn his fingers, or some part of his anatomy, on that hot body with the piercing eyes and the oh-so-cool voice. But life was too short not to risk all for the perfect love. And Matthew knew he had found it. Come what may, he would go home with Andrew this night.

ANDREW SUMMONED HIS CARRIAGE AS the other families were leaving. Phyllida had been right, as always. If they had bolted too early in the proceedings, the rest of the company would have descended into a morass of speculation about Phyllida's condition. And there was no need to subject her to that unwelcome attention, or to put more pressure on himself. Ever since he had seen her with that horrible bruise, and discovered to his shame that he had been the cause of it, he could not make love to her properly. His body just could not respond with that knowledge literally depressing him. Even after her face had healed, the memory was seared into his brain and worked like the worst of anti-aphrodisiacs, if there was such a thing.

Now, tonight, for some reason, he felt capable. More than capable—hard, lusty, up and ready to go. Because of this Matthew Thornby, of course. But it was interesting how the effect spilled over—God, even his thoughts were reduced to lewd images and double entendres!—to Phyllida. It made no sense, but he knew that by finding this new object of desire, he got also the chance to reclaim his damaged love for his wife, which he had been desparate to repair.

The carriage was brought around and he prepared to hand Phyllida in, placing her on the forward-facing seat so that he and Matthew could sit beside each other across from her and—

"Bugger it!" he exclaimed as he saw Harriet. "Fuck, fuck, fuck!"

Phyllida laughed in an attempt to cover the words. Fortunately, the hubbub of the departing guests, the clatter of the horses' hooves, and the carriage wheels and the cries of the footmen drowned the rest, although the nearest man looked around and grinned.

"Oh, we will," Matthew said in his ear. "As many times as you wish, but you must not say it so loud, or everyone will want to join in."

"I had forgotten my sister-in-law."

"I can walk," Matthew said. "Give me the direction." He smiled as he learned the house was a mere two squares over, watched the carriage pull away, and took a cheroot from his breast pocket, lighting it on one of the torches at the end of the driveway. He could use the time to blow a cloud, clear his head, and think things over. And it would give Carrington a chance to get the house settled for the night, the ladies upstairs, and any waiting servants sent to bed.

Matthew had never knowingly had an affair with a married man—at least not a happily cohabitating man hoping to father a child. Surely even in an arrangement one did not bring one's lovers to one's own house. Yet the address was in one of the most fashionable squares in Mayfair, not a hotel or a madge club, and not the Brotherhood, either. He had almost reached the entrance and he finished his cigar and stubbed it out, watching the few lighted windows go dark.

He had nearly drowned once, on a passage from America made too late in hurricane season. His life had been threatened twice: by a slave-owner for interfering and—more sympathetically, to Matthew's mind—by an angry mob of underpaid mill workers. Death lurked around every corner, and each day might be one's last—or each night. If Matthew rejected love when it threw itself in front of him, what had been the point of surviving this far?

He walked the remaining feet to the entrance, climbed the two steps to the door, and raised his hand to knock.

"WHAT IS THE MATTER?" HARRIET asked as they lurched off on their short journey. "Why would you not take Mr. Thornby up in the carriage?"

"Mr. Thornby prefers to walk," Phyllida said. "Just as you were saying on the way here."

The explanation appeared to satisfy Harriet, and she chattered and exclaimed the rest of the way, her delight over her first genuine society ball, the attractive men she had danced with, the beauty of the women and their gowns, and her fear that her own clothes would not prove adequate for a full season.

"I will buy you an entire wardrobe," Andrew said, "but you must do something for me in return: keep silence in my presence for an entire day. Can you do that, Miss Lewis?"

"Andrew!" Phyllida said. "That is very rude."

"Do you mean it, Mr. Carrington?" Harriet said. "Because if you are joking it is indeed very rude, but if you are serious, just name the day. I would do much more than that for a new wardrobe."

Phyllida shook her head at Andrew before he could make the obvious reply.

"Yes, Miss Lewis, I am quite serious. Now, if you do me the favor of being quiet for the rest of this journey, I will count the time against your day."

Once home, Andrew could not resist taking Phyllida in a crushing embrace and kissing her until her lips were bruised. "Do you mind very much, being alone tonight?" he asked.

"You know I never expected to have you all to myself," Phyllida said. "Just— Be careful, Andrew. Mr. Thornby is sharper than he likes to seem."

"And what do you know of him?"

"Only what I learned during our dance."

"What a pity we men can't dance together," Andrew said.

"Thank goodness for that," Phyllida said, kissing him goodnight, "or we poor women would spend our lives as wallflowers and spinsters."

Andrew sent the last servants to bed and waited until Phyllida and her sister had gone to their rooms. He stood in the foyer, listening for the footsteps and opening the door before the man had a chance to knock. They were in each other's arms the minute the door was bolted behind them. Their kisses were fierce, hungry—the men almost biting each other bloody in their urgency. Andrew pushed Matthew's coat off his shoulders, ripped the cravat from his neck, and began to pull the shirttails from his waist.

"You are mad," Matthew said. "Won't your household be disturbed?"

"They know me," Andrew said. "But we should go upstairs."

They only just made it to the second floor in time, having stopped along the way for more kissing and the opening of pantaloon flaps, and a most injudicious session of fondling. They were staggering and panting as they pushed open the door to the master bedroom and fell on the bed. "God, you are a brute," Matthew said.

"And you, I think, are a slut," Andrew said. "A wide-arsed, willing whore who will take my cock any way you can get it."

"How well you know me," Matthew said. "And after such short acquaintance."

"Oh, there's nothing short about it," Andrew said. He knelt reverently over the big blond, freeing the enormous cock from the straining tight drawers. Andrew watched as it swelled even more from his admiration, then put his lips to it, kissing and withdrawing, wishing to give the beautiful man an early reward for the rigors to follow.

Matthew attempted to hold back, groaning at Andrew's expertise. "Oh God," he said, "you could make a corpse rise."

"What a disgusting image," Andrew drawled, taking his mouth off. "Why would I want to?"

"It was a figure of speech," Matthew said, groaning again at the cessation of pleasure and bucking his hips. "Please don't stop."

"What will you do for me?"

"Anything. Whatever you like."

With the words, Andrew's desire increased almost beyond containment. He allowed Matthew his desperately needed release and Matthew, after a moment or two of respite, performed the same kindness for him, and they rested in a loose embrace, getting their breath.

Matthew ran his hand over the smooth flesh of Andrew's pectorals and tongued the hard little nipples. "Why must you shave?" he asked. "I had quite set my heart on a lovely dense mat of black hair."

"You like that?" Andrew asked. "Most men like it smooth." He circled his palm over Matthew's furry blond chest, fingering the crisp curls. "I admit, the hairy chest has its appeal."

"Would you grow yours for me?" Matthew asked.

"I'll offer you a deal," Andrew said. "I'll stop shaving if you stop smoking that filthy shag tobacco."

"It's cigars," Matthew said. "And how do you know I smoke at all?"

"Such innocence," Andrew said. "The stink is all over you, on your clothes, in your hair, in your mouth."

"I'm surprised you even want to kiss me," Matthew said, sitting up.

"Don't talk like an ass," Andrew said, kissing him and pushing him back down on the bed. "Just give me your arse." He opened the jar of grease and scooped out a large glob, working his long fingers over his own once again stiff cock and in Matthew's tight, already spasming hole. Matthew moaned with desire before they'd even started.

"Do you want me, slut?" Andrew asked.

"You know I do." Matthew rolled over and knelt, presenting himself.

"No," Andrew said. "I want to see your face while I take you."

"Such a masterful man," Matthew said, turning onto his back again and lifting his legs. "Fuck me hard."

Andrew obliged, entering gently but pushing through with a fierce thrust and pulling out almost to the tip before ramming home again. He watched with greedy desire as the narrow blue eyes opened wide at the sudden fullness, reminding him of something he couldn't quite place. *Soft brown eyes, not blue, fearful but willing—*God!*—Phyllida on their wedding night.* The memory only increased his excitement.

Matthew sighed, his jaw slackening, eyelids drooping in surrender. "Lord, that's good. Harder, love. Give me all you've got."

Andrew tried to work up slowly to a sustainable rhythm, hoping to hold on at least a few minutes and not disgrace himself. This man had him so fired up he knew he was barely on the edge of control. He shifted his grip from Matthew's calves to his ankles, gathering himself for the intensity of his release.

There was a crash so loud Andrew thought the bed had collapsed. He shriveled all at once from the start, popping out of Matthew's arse, and the big blond let his legs fall to the mattress with another crash that made the bed frame shudder.

"Shit," Andrew said. "Shit fuck."

"I couldn't have said it better," Matthew said.

They lay side by side, chests heaving, staring up at the underside of the bed canopy. Footsteps ran pounding down the stairs, followed by screaming and yelling that assaulted their ears, the words unintelligible, but indisputably from this house.

Andrew sat up and reached for his dressing gown. "Why?" he asked. "Why can't they schedule the end of the world for a night when I'm escorting my sister to a state dinner or visiting my uncle?"

"Because then it wouldn't be the end of the world," Matthew said. "Come on, we'd better go see what's happening."

"I won't drag you into my trouble," Andrew said. "You stay here, and when it's sorted out, with any luck we can take up where we left off."

"You don't mean to go down there by yourself and leave me up here like a deceitful wife afraid of being discovered?" Matthew said, looking unhappily at his drawers and shirt.

"It's poor hospitality to invite you home for pleasure and involve you in whatever this is instead," Andrew said.

"Can't be helped," Matthew said. "I don't imagine you staged this for my benefit."

"Hardly," Andrew said, opening a strongbox and removing a case of dueling pistols. "I prefer murder and mayhem at the end of an affair, not the beginning."

"A warning?" Matthew said as he pulled his shirt over his head and shoved his arms through the sleeves.

Andrew grinned. "Absolutely. I have my own reputation to consider." He wiped his greasy hands on a gun rag before loading the weapons and handing one to Matthew. "I assume you can shoot."

"I've been known to bring down a bird on occasion," Matthew said.

"Good. I'll blow the first one's head off, and if there's more than one you can have the next."

"Fair enough," Matthew said, feeling the pistol's exquisite balance and noting its hair trigger. He thought better of tucking so delicate and lethal a weapon into the waistband of his pantaloons and held it in his sweaty palm. "Lead the way."

THE SIGHT THAT MET MATTHEW'S eyes was like something out of a dark ritual from the depths of antiquity. A young man, his head bloody, writhed hogtied on the cellar floor, his hands behind his back and connected by a length of cord to his bound ankles. Overturned shelves and broken bottles lay scattered, the spilled wine running like the blood of a hundred human sacrifices. A serving maid and a boy—a very pretty boy, Matthew couldn't help noticing, despite the scar over his eye and being badly in need of a wash and a change of clothes—clung together, shrieking in terror, while the beautiful Mrs. Carrington, her face distorted with rage, kicked at the tied young man, aiming for his sensitive male organs and shouting the most unladylike words. The poor man rolled this way and that, straining against the rope and trying to shield himself, while Harriet danced around behind her sister, attempting to pull her back from her raging assault and receiving slaps and more epithets for her pains.

Andrew paused at the edge of the scene, unable to quite take it in. "Phyllida!" he shouted, striding over to his wife. "Stop that! Can't you see he's tied and injured?" He dragged her away; all the while her foot continued to kick.

"Injured?" Phyllida shrieked. "I'll kill him! Just let me go, Andrew. I'll finish him off and he won't trouble us again." She tried to yank her arm free from her husband's strong grip. "Let me go, Andrew."

"Phyllida! What has got into you?" Andrew drew her further away and put both arms around her. "It's only Mr. Turner." He nodded at Matthew. "Would you mind untying him? Don't want the fellow to croak down here, bound like that. Give the household a bad name and make it devilish hard to hire help."

Matthew knelt to the young man, who flinched and tried to roll away. "There, lad," Matthew said. "Hold still and I'll get you out of this."

"Sodomite," the young man snarled. "Don't touch me."

Matthew looked up. "What's the matter with him?" he asked.

The two young people had stopped screaming at the appearance of their master and were observing the action with the demeanor of those who would like nothing better than a large crowd to melt into. "He's a thief," the girl said. "He came sneaking down here to steal the master's wine."

Andrew, his arms still wrapped tightly around his wife, who was now weeping copiously onto his chest, favored the girl with the kind of withering look that usually requires a quizzing glass to achieve its full effect. "And you naturally decided to help him to some," he said, nodding at the wreckage of the shelves and racks of wine and the broken bottles. "Perhaps you misconstrued the expression 'cracking a bottle.'"

"I only hit him once," Nan said. "He must've rolled around when we was asleep and knocked over the rest."

"That's right," Kit said. "I just tied 'im up so 'e wouldn't slither away during the night. We was going to tell you all about it in the morning."

Andrew stared closely at the boy, and his face broke into a most unpleasant grin. "Ah, Marlowe. How nice to see you again. Sorry you were obliged to come through the cellar in order to pay a visit. Or weren't you visiting exactly?"

The boy gulped and swallowed but stepped forward and tried to answer bravely. "I'm sorry, Mr. Carr— I mean, Mr. Carrington. I wasn't up to nothin', honest I wasn't. I was keepin' an eye on that there ferret man. 'E's a bad 'un, Mr. Carrington. You want to watch 'im. 'E'll do ya a bad turn."

"But he works here," Andrew said. "He's my secretary."

Matthew had finished untying Turner despite his protests and tried lifting him to his feet. The man retched and sagged in Matthew's arms. "I'll carry him upstairs and send for Stevens," Matthew said. "You have your hands full."

"No!" Phyllida said, trying to struggle free again from Andrew's hold, as if to do more damage to the wounded man. "Send for a magistrate and take him to gaol." She gave up the fight and resumed her weeping, burrowing her face against Andrew's damp dressing gown.

"Why?" Andrew said. "What has he done to you?"

Phyllida looked up from where her tears had stained the gray silk black. "He's been stealing from you, Andrew. From the household accounts."

"What?" Andrew said, stroking her wild hair. "Oh— Yes, I see. But that's no reason to truss him up like a hog for the butcher and kick him when he can't defend himself."

"Oh no," Phyllida said. "By all means, let Mr. Thornby tuck him into bed like a baby, and we'll coddle him and have the doctor round and feed him egg possets, and all the time he's—" Her voice cracked as she tried to master her emotions, and she gasped for breath. "It's all right for him—"

"Nan, come and help your mistress," Andrew said. "Then I want to hear from you and Kit here just what the hell has been going on. And unless there's some compelling reason, I will expect you both to be out by morning."

Kit, barely taller than Phyllida, his voice truculent and his hands balled into fists, squared up to Andrew. "Don't you sack Nan, sir," Kit said. "It ain't her fault. She was only helping me, and the missus."

"Helping Mrs. Carrington?" Andrew asked.

"Kit, don't," Nan said.

"I got to, love," Kit said, shaking his head at Nan before turning back to Andrew. "This rat is the one wot slapped yer missus' face."

Andrew felt knocked off balance, almost as if he'd been shot point-blank. He held Phyllida away from him and looked down at her. "Is this true?"

Phyllida, faint and dizzy, lifted her head with difficulty to meet his eyes. "Yes, Andrew. I'm sorry."

"Mr. Turner hit you? And you let me think it was me."

"I wanted to protect you."

"Protect me? From what? From Mr. Turner?"

"He said he would tell—everything."

"So you lied to me. You let me think I had done that to you. Every day for weeks I've awakened with the knowledge that I had done the unthinkable and that I must try to find a way to atone. And all this time it was a lie."

"Please, sir," Nan interposed, trembling but resolute. "Don't blame her. She was that frightened, and not knowing what to do."

"I'll thank you not to interfere."

"Come on, Nan," Kit said. "It ain't the right time to talk to him. Try again after they've cooled off. And if he still cuts up rough, I'll marry you."

"But I don't want to get married," Nan wailed. "Look at poor Mrs. Carrington."

MATTHEW KNEW, IMPOSSIBLE AS IT seemed at the moment, that at some point in the future he would look back on this night with fondness. It was the least romantic night he'd ever spent with a man, and yet he knew it was the beginning of a great change, the transition from the free life of a single man to a chosen marriage, becoming one of a couple. He had sensed it from the very first, when his eyes met Andrew's over the punch bowl at Lady Trent's, that this was not just another pickup, not a one-night "bargain," but love—or the possibility. He could not abandon his lover now, when his world seemed to have collapsed around him in a mysterious series of events that would have been humorous but for the way Andrew looked: as if all life had been crushed out of him other than the perfunctory motions of heart and lungs.

And Phyllida, poor lady—Matthew felt as if he knew her too, or wanted to, could not think of her merely as Mrs. Carrington, the inconvenient wife of his lover. There was more to this than thievery and a lie. He wanted to find out what it was that had turned the serene beauty of the ballroom into the kicking, screeching high priestess of a deathly bacchanal. Later, when Andrew was more composed, Matthew must try to convince him to let the lady tell her side of the story.

For now, he focused on practical things. He set the boy Kit to clearing up the mess, with Nan to help, and took it on himself to watch over the by now unconscious Mr. Turner while Andrew helped his wife upstairs. "Don't touch him," Andrew said, his voice sharp, as Matthew started to lift the limp figure. "Don't let him contaminate you as he has the rest of us." Still, letting the man bleed to death on the cellar floor, or in his room, would not be the best thing for Andrew's character and that of his household, especially as the man had obviously insulted Phyllida in some way. There was incentive on every side to do away with the troublesome little man, and should the worst happen, it would not help matters that Andrew and his wife had a strong motive for accomplishing it.

Matthew walked slowly upstairs after ascertaining that Turner was not in immediate danger of expiring, and waited on the second-floor landing, trying to avoid overhearing the still raging fight between Andrew and his wife. As they appeared to have left the bedroom door open, he could not miss it.

"I don't understand," Andrew said. "How could you let him strike you, violate you, and not come to me for protection?"

"I didn't *let* him do anything," Phyllida said. "He locked me in with him and tried to force me, but—"

"Good God," Andrew said. "What a failure I've been as a husband. Am I so weak and ineffectual? Or do you not trust me to punish anyone who mistreats you?"

"No!" Phyllida screamed. "Oh, Andrew, if you only knew. I didn't want you to have any doubts, if there was a child, that you were the father."

"You need not worry about that," Andrew said. "I won't have any. There will not be a child. At least, not ours."

Andrew emerged from the boudoir, leaving Phyllida in the care of her sister and Jenny Porter, and shut the door behind him. His mouth was set in a grim line. "I warned you," he said. "I shouldn't have dragged you into this."

"I want to help if I can," Matthew said, putting his arms briefly around the slender, tightly wound body.

Andrew kissed him softly and withdrew. "I should not have kept him on," he said. "Not once I was married. I never thought he was dangerous—and certainly not to a lady. I forgot all about him."

"Suppose you had other things on your mind," Matthew said. "Just what was he up to, anyway?"

"Leading us all a merry dance," Andrew said. "If I'd known he would hurt Phyllida— Lord! I wish I'd never agreed to Amberson's scheme."

"Amberson?" Matthew asked. "Geoffrey Amberson?"

"Yes," Andrew said. "You know him? Don't tell me he's inveigled you into his web of deceit?"

Matthew laughed. "God, no. It's simply not possible to travel in and out of the country without one's path crossing his, that's all. How did he get over on you?"

"Christ!" Andrew swore. "Is that what you think of me?"

"No, I don't," Matthew said. "Quite the opposite, in fact. Which is why I asked."

"I'm sorry," Andrew said. "He didn't get over on me. That's the joke. I offered. He said he had an odd fish, a questionable character claiming to have information. Amberson thought the man was most likely blowing smoke, but he wanted to let him run, see where he led, just in case he knew something valuable—or someone. That was a year ago. I was single, never thought there'd be a lady here or any reason to worry about anyone's safety in the household. I told Amberson he could place the man with me. Good disguise, secretary for an idle, wealthy young man about town."

"Very altruistic of you," Matthew commented. "Would never have suspected you to be guilty of that sin."

"I actually do have patriotic sentiments, believe it or not," Andrew said. "My brother Tom is a captain in the dragoons, you see, and I have—had—a friend in the rifle corps. Now look where it's got me. Ought to be me lying on the cellar floor. Serve me right for being so careless."

"Don't talk like that," Matthew scolded. "You're not done for yet. And you can pop me one if I'm out of line, but it seems like a God-given opportunity to get that little weasel out of the house."

"Pop you one?" Andrew said. "It's you who ought to— Turner? Where? And how?"

"Well," Matthew said, "seems you've got your houschold so terrified they've none of 'em come out of their rooms for all this racket."

"It is odd," Andrew agreed. "I imagine they think midnight alarums and commotion are the customary nighttime practice for a married man."

"Aren't they?" Matthew said with a grin. "We can get a hackney, I suppose, and no one the wiser, but it might be easiest just to carry him."

THEY ENDED UP WALKING THE distance to the Brotherhood of Philander, Turner suspended between them, his feet dragging and his head hanging. Only his shallow breathing proved he was still alive. A watchman eyed them dubiously on the corner of South Audley Street but said nothing. Just a typical set of nobs, stinking drunk, returning from a long night. 'Struth, he could smell them half a block away, but so long as they weren't doing anything violent or against the law, best to give them a wide berth. The blond was a powerfully built bruiser and the dark-haired one looked like he'd cut your liver out and feed it to you if you said a word to him. The watchman felt a pang of remorse for the poor little fellow between them, but it wasn't worth his life and livelihood to interfere.

Farnham did a creditable job of not staring when Andrew and Matthew carried the limp body in the door and started up the stairs.

"What rooms are free?" Andrew asked. Blessed with a tolerant household staff, he rarely spent the night at the club.

"Most of them, sir," Farnham answered. "Just Lord David Pierce and Mr. Witherspoon in No. 1 and Sir Frederick Verney and a military guest in No. 2. And Mr. Thornby here has No. 4." Never assume, he'd been instructed when he began his work here. Mr. Carrington and Mr. Thornby might or might not be deep in each other's pockets by this time. It was not his place to take things for granted before he was told. He couldn't help watching as they maneuvered the body around the curve of the landing. "Need any help, sir?"

"Thank you, no," Andrew said. "Although you could send a footman up in a few minutes."

"Very good sir," Farnham said. "Any particular one?"

"No," Andrew called back, annoyed. "It's not a game. The man's been hurt."

They pushed open the door to No. 3, the nearest unoccupied room, and laid their burden down. "I suppose we ought to undress him," Andrew said, "but the prospect is singularly unappealing."

"Let Stevens do it," Matthew said.

"Not fair to him," Andrew said. "Besides, he'll need help."

Turner was not badly built, but his soft flesh and somewhat fusty underclothes were suggestive of a man who took no exercise and paid little attention to hygiene. He seemed inclined to fight such intimate attentions, muttering and pushing against Matthew's hands as the latter worked at the buttons of his coat. "Bitch," Turner murmured. "Play rough."

"Wouldn't dare," Matthew said with a sneer. "Won't go to the gallows for a powder puff like you."

Andrew started on the pantaloons. "Cunt," Turner said. "Can't get enough of me."

"That's it," Andrew said, standing up. "We'll let Stevens deal with him. God knows he's had plenty of practice dealing with foulmouthed castaways."

A nervous footman knocked on the open door. "Mr. Farnham said you needed help, sir." He stared at the ghastly spectacle of the unbuttoned, delirious, bloodied man on the bed, the two tall figures standing over him. "I got a wife and kids. I won't do nothin' unlawful."

Andrew raised his eyes to the ceiling. "Why does the world persist in attributing the most unwholesome practices to me? All we ask is that you look after him until the doctor comes. And don't worry about anything he might say. Not altogether rational at the moment."

"Lord, sir," the man exclaimed, looking much happier, "I couldn't work here if I minded what bosky gentlemen said."

They shut the door to No. 3 and moved along the corridor to Matthew's room. "I can't begin to thank you for all your help," Andrew said.

"I won't object to your trying, though," Matthew said. "To thank me."

Andrew laughed, but his voice was hard. "I should imagine you'd prefer never to have met me."

"You forget, I've spent the last five years back and forth to America. Takes more than a little head-bashing and amateur espionage to scare me off."

"Then I may hope to see you again?" Andrew asked.

Matthew drew Andrew inside. No. 4, like all the second-story rooms, was a suite, with an outer parlor and a bedroom. "Just try to avoid me," he said. "You won't be able to shake me off, not until we finish what we started this night." He opened the door to the bedroom. "In fact, we could do it now." He wrapped his muscular arms around Andrew and pulled him into a fierce kiss, relaxing his hold after a few moments when he sensed no response.

Andrew looked down, embarrassed and confused at the flat front of his pantaloons. He was limp, not a hint of life in the part of him that had never failed—until marriage and its complications had intervened.

"Ah, you're tired, love," Matthew said. "Not surprising after the night we spent. I have to be up early anyway, take a look in at the business."

Andrew blinked. "Business? You mean, go to work?"

"Aye," Matthew said, the Yorkshire coming on strong. "Have to provide for my pleasures somehow. All this luxury and dissipation don't come cheap."

"But, my dear man. Surely you don't have to grub for a living? I thought—that is, I'd heard—I thought your father was a baronet." *Sir Jonas Thornby, the lone "cotton baron" amongst the wool merchants of Yorkshire—that's where he'd heard the name.* He massaged the stubbly line of Matthew's strong jaw in helpless sympathy.

"Happen he is," Matthew said. "And reminds me every day I'm at home how he didn't earn it by sitting idle." He took Andrew's long-fingered hand in his hard, square palm, turned it over, and laid a kiss in the center. "Go on, love. Go home and get some rest. You're going to need it, if you wish to thank me properly for all my help."

On the way out, Andrew tossed Farnham a golden guinea. "I never seen him," Farnham said, catching and pocketing the coin and bowing without appearing to notice the impressive denomination.

"Just so," Andrew agreed. "And don't forget, send for Mr. Stevens, but wait until a decent hour of the morning, as if one of the guests woke up feeling under the weather."

Andrew walked slowly home, his mind as devoid of energy as his body, his hand in his pocket as if to preserve the imprint of Matthew's kiss. He had the foolish wish, forgotten since adolescence, that he need never wash that hand again for the rest of his life.

He had thought after the indiscretion with Kit that he could not sink any lower. But he had. He had married a woman and come to care for her, only to endanger her and expose her to violation and injury by bringing her into his house. And despite fervent protestations on both sides of desiring a marriage based on honesty, they were locked into a framework of lies—she out of fear, or perhaps merely poor judgment, he in order to protect her and ease her mind. And now he had met the true love of his life, the man of his dreams, and he was incapable. He ought to go home and use his pistol to blow out his brains, but he wouldn't give that weasel Turner—or Amberson—the satisfaction.

PHYLLIDA HAD BARELY CLOSED her eyes when she heard the loud crash. She had waited a couple of seconds for the rest of the household to take action, surprised when all the other doors remained closed, the inhabitants apparently so sound asleep that nothing but the trumpet of doom at the end of the world would have awakened them, if that.

Sighing with the burden of being the mistress, and knowing Andrew would not wish to be disturbed on his first night with the dazzling Mr. Thornby, Phyllida had put on her dressing gown and run downstairs, to find Turner bound with clothesline, partly buried under shelves and the remains of broken bottles, Nan and an unknown boy standing over him, watching in horror as he rolled and struggled to free himself. Phyllida had not stopped to think; she saw her enemy at her mercy and took her chance at revenge.

Now the whole horrible truth had come out. Seeing the look in Andrew's eyes when he learned how she had lied to him, she would have given anything to undo it. She would even agree to a divorce and never see him again, if only he did not think the worst of her. Yet she dared not retreat, even to save herself. Turner had threatened Andrew and all his associates, and she had to find a way to warn her husband, however much he despised her.

Phyllida wept and wept until she thought her tears would dry up and never flow again, and still she wept as she went over the events of that dreadful night. Harriet held her in her arms and tried to soothe her, but had no idea what the trouble was, or how to fix it. "We'll go home," she decided. "Maybe it's for the best. Mr. Carrington can divorce you and you can come back home and marry Mr. Coulter instead, the way you was supposed to. I was all set to marry him myself, but I won't now."

At this startling revelation, Phyllida's tears dried. "Marry Mr. Coulter? Is that what you want?"

Harriet nodded. "I did think how grand it was, seeing London and having my very own season. Last night I quite thought I'd like to marry a rich sodomite too, and have such a lovely life. But now I'd just as soon stay at home and be comfortable."

IN THE MORNING—THAT IS, A couple of hours later—Andrew's first thought was to retrieve the accounts book and contain the damage. As far as he could determine, Phyllida had not lied about the book being sent inadvertently to her publisher, so he had Yardley fetch a hackney and he set off for the City.

That was another peculiar thing, Andrew thought, as the vehicle moved slowly through the early-morning throng. None of the servants had been awakened by the sort of commotion that would have had a drunken regiment up and to arms in two minutes. They had expressed proper amazement when they arose and were informed of that minor part of the night's interesting occurrences that Andrew thought they should know, but they were unanimous in their declarations of having heard nothing. Andrew could see, from their rested faces and genuine looks of surprise, that they were telling the truth. Yet Phyllida had heard the crash, and of course he and Mathew had been so disturbed they had lost their momentum, even in the midst of the most engrossing activity.

The horse pulled up in front of Mr. Edwards's office and Andrew ran upstairs. Edwards had only just arrived himself, in none too good a condition either, from the looks of him, and when he saw Andrew, disheveled and weary, with the grim look of murder about his thin lips, he looked ready to faint dead away. "Mr. Carrington?" His voice squeaked and went up an octave. "I— That is— I— What can I do for you?"

"The book," Andrew said. "Just hand it over and I won't trouble you."

"I can't, sir," Edwards said with a groan. "It's with the printer. Too late to stop the presses now."

"For God's sake, man," Andrew said. "Mrs. Carrington told me about misplacing the damn thing two weeks ago and more. Surely you've had time to get it back." He inadvertently took several steps toward the man as he spoke, one hand in the pocket of his coat.

Mr. Edwards, facing the nightmare that had troubled him in his sober moments on and off for several weeks, and not yet fully awake to absorb the import of the actual words, panicked. Taking matching steps backward as the tall, menacing figure moved closer, he raised his chin and said, "Before you try anything, Mr. Carrington, let me say I know all about you and your friends at the Brotherhood of Philadelphia— Phyllida— Philistines— Damn it, I know what you fellows get up to, you better believe I do, and if you threaten me, I'll—"

Andrew smiled, wishing he'd brought his pistols, although it really wasn't necessary. "Do you know what happened to the last person who tried to blackmail me?" he asked, his deep voice sweet as honeyed tea. "He ended up hogtied with his head bashed in. And that's only for starters. He's going to Newgate next, and then Botany Bay or the gallows, depending on my testimony. So before you get any heroic ideas about denouncing sodomy, just think about that. Now, where is that book?"

Mr. Edwards, having backed up to the front edge of his desk and feeling it dig into his rump, ducked around the side and scrabbled in the mass of papers on the surface. "Here," he said. He held out a fat volume. "I'm sorry, sir. I don't *want* to blackmail you. Just trying to keep body and soul together."

"I see," Andrew said. "Merely your natural response to people requesting the return of their property. I shudder to contemplate your reaction to a serious dispute." He removed his hand from his pocket and took the proffered volume. "What the devil is this?" he said.

"It's a presentation copy, hot off the press," Edwards said. "Just the first two volumes, mind."

Andrew dropped it with a thud. "The accounts book, you drunken cretin," he said.

Edwards rummaged around in the drawers of his desk, found a bottle with some liquid still in it, and took several deep slugs with shaking hands. "Accounts book?" he repeated. "Kitchen accounts?"

"What else have I been saying for the past five minutes?" Andrew said.

"Now just hold on," Edwards said. "You mean you're not trying to prevent the publication of Mrs. Carrington's novel?"

"Why would I want to do that?"

"Because I assure you, sir, that had I known you were Mrs. Carrington's husband, I never would have agreed to bring out her work."

"Then it's a good thing you didn't know."

"But by the time I found out, sir, I had already paid—" Edwards sat down at his desk and tried to understand the words he had heard. "You're not trying to stop the printing?"

"Why would I?" Andrew said. "If this book's anything like the first one, I'll buy a score of copies myself and give them to all my friends."

"You'll what?" Edwards poked about in the detritus on the shelves behind him and on the floor, found a glass, and came around to the other side of the desk. "Care for a drink, sir?"

Andrew waved him off with a sneer. "Thank you, no. If I wish to poison myself I can do that very well at home in more salubrious surroundings. I must say I'm surprised that such exquisite writing as Mrs. Carrington's has to be published in such a low establishment."

"I assure you, Mr. Carrington, sir," Edwards said, "those fly-by-nights at Minerva Press don't have any better."

Andrew shrugged. Minerva Press, indeed. He knew that name, a byword for producing the worst kind of sensational trash, only a step or two up from obscenity. What it had to do with the kind of work Phyllida produced, he couldn't imagine. "All I want is the blasted accounts book and I'll leave you to your, ah, breakfast," he said.

Edwards gulped the rest of his bottle, fortifying himself with the worst sort of false courage. "Accounts book, is it? Your wife took that back weeks ago. I remember it very clearly, her coming here with her face all bruised. And let me say, sir, you may think you're within your rights to knock about a sweet lady like Mrs. Carrington, all over some damn household accounts, and legally you are, but if you touch her again, I'll—"

"Blackmail again?" Andrew said. "You back on that?"

Edwards slumped into his chair as the air went out of him with a wheeze. "But I gave it to her, I swear I did. I just don't like to see a lady badly used."

"As it happens," Andrew said, "neither do I."

The two men eyed each other from their different perspectives. Edwards had a brief moment of awareness, wondering what it was, exactly, they were fighting about. "Go on, sir," he said, his voice deferential, pointing to the discarded volume, "take this copy of her new book. It's even better than the last."

Andrew took the inky volume, shoved it in his pocket, and headed home. When he got there, he supposed, he would have to strangle Phyllida and then file for divorce. But all he wanted was to hold her in his arms and kiss away her tears and promise her that rat Turner could never hurt her again. Then he would break another bottle over the man's head, kick him in the balls, and throw him in the Thames.

In the meantime, he'd read her new book. He opened it to the title page. "*The Marriages of Melisande, or, A Balkan Tragedy*," it said. "A new romance by the author of *The Loves of Lavinia*. In three volumes, to be published serially by Mr. A. Edwards." There was a crude woodcut depicting a fleeing woman, no doubt this tragic Melisande, while a man on horseback—or at least that's what Andrew assumed what looked like a baboon mounting an elkhound was intended to represent—pursued at a distance.

Andrew slammed the offensive little volume shut, tempted to toss it out the window except that the gutters in this part of town were already overflowing with filth and Andrew did not approve of making conditions even worse for the people who had to live here. The man had given him someone else's work, a piece of cheap romantic rubbish. He wondered if this Edwards even handled Phyllida's work.

Still, the man had seemed familiar with Phyllida and her books. Andrew was quite sure, however, that the publisher of *Sense and Sensibility* was not a Mr. A. Edwards. Perhaps she had decided to change publishers.

Well, it didn't matter. All that mattered was that Phyllida had lied to him again, had got the accounts book back after all. He would have to find it. Where could she have hidden it? Of course—she had visited Witherspoon and his sister the day of the attack. Andrew knocked on the roof of the hackney. "Park Lane," he ordered the driver.

ANDREW ARRIVED AT THE BROTHERHOOD in time to observe Mr. Stevens's professional assessment of the patient. "Concussion," he said. "Caused, judging from the smell and the pieces of broken glass embedded in his skull, by being hit over the head with a wine bottle. Although how he made it all the way here from the tavern afterward is a mystery. And the quality of the claret seems far superior to that served in most places given to brawling."

"Thank you, Reggie," Andrew said. "You don't have to lie for me. The fact is, the fellow let himself in the back of my house after a night out. One of the servants mistook him for a thief and decided to mete out justice herself rather than bothering a magistrate at so late an hour."

"A woman did this?" Stevens asked. "My goodness. And the bruises all over the fellow's sides?" At Andrew's nod, Stevens put his hand on Andrew's arm. "You all right, Carrington? You look as if you've sustained a blow or two yourself."

"Let me ask you something," Andrew said. "When you came to the house the day I had the migraine did you see Mrs. Carrington's face? How did she look?"

Stevens's eyes narrowed at the question. "Very well," he said. "A beautiful woman. She was looking very fine indeed."

"No bruise on her face? Or a mark, as if she'd been struck?"

"Good God, no!" Stevens said. "Why? Was she attacked? By this fellow here? She ought to have kicked him in the balls."

"That's apparently what she was doing," Matthew said, "when unfortunately we intervened." He sidled in at the door to No. 3 and put his arm around Andrew's waist in a gesture of solidarity.

Andrew sighed with gratitude for the comforting presence and put his arm around Matthew. "Thought you had to work," he whispered.

"Wanted to hear the verdict," Matthew replied. "Worth them docking my pay."

"Oh, hullo, Thornby," Stevens said. He took in the situation with a wink. "You didn't waste any time, I see."

Matthew smiled but shook his head. "I think, this time, I was overhasty."

"No, no," Stevens said. "Carrington is a most respectable fellow. Mustn't let a little domestic disturbance bother you."

"Not that," Matthew said. "I think I've done Mrs. Carrington a great disservice."

"That's why you moved him, I take it," Stevens said. "Was wondering about that." He stood in silence, observing the two men. "Have something to show you. Like a second opinion." He had the footman roll Turner on his side. "Pull his shirt up. There. What do you make of those?"

The scars were old, as healed as they would ever be, crisscrossing weals of pink flesh over the man's pale back.

Matthew let out a low whistle. "Seen something like that a few times in America. Slaves on cotton plantations. Never thought to see it on an Englishman."

"You've obviously never served in the military, my dear," Andrew said, turning away.

"And you have?" Matthew replied. "Any road, look at those soft hands. He couldn't have been a ranker."

"What about you, Carrington?" Stevens asked. "Ever noticed these? He was in your employ for almost a year now."

Andrew glowered. "He was my secretary, Reggie, that's all. I don't force myself on every young man who works in my household."

Stevens cleared his throat. "Of course not. Only meant you might have heard something, been privy to a confidence."

"We weren't lovers or friends or even on good terms. He was—Stealing from me. The only reason I kept him on was to have the satisfaction of proving it."

"May never get it, Carrington," Stevens said. "That's quite a crack on the head he suffered, and dragging him through the streets didn't help."

"Do you mean he could die?" Andrew asked, not altogether unhappy.

"Very possibly," Stevens said. "The Brotherhood doesn't really need the scandal right now."

"I won't subject Phyllida to the man's presence at home after what he did," Andrew said. "If there's to be a scandal, better here, where we can band together to protect ourselves."

"He'll need complete rest," Stevens said. "If he's to regain his wits, he must be kept immobilized. And if he can't drink or feed himself—"

"What do you want me to do?" Andrew said. "Watch at his bedside, wipe his fevered brow, hold his hand and feed him egg possets?"

"A reliable and trustworthy nurse would be his best hope," Stevens concluded, ignoring the sacrasm.

"He'd better live," Andrew muttered, "because as soon as he's back on his feet I'm going to put a bullet right between his beady little eyes."

Pierce and Witherspoon emerged from their room as Andrew and Matthew moved into the corridor, discussing with Stevens the arrangements for Turner.

"Hullo, Carrington, Thornby," Pierce said. "Thought I saw you at Lady Trent's. You certainly didn't waste any time."

"Get stuffed," Andrew said.

"Had quite a night, did you?" Pierce said.

"Isn't that your Mr. Turner, Carrington?" Witherspoon said, peering in at the door. "Did you do that to him because of what he did to Phyllida?"

"I wish," Andrew said. "But I'll do something to you, both of you, for coming between me and my wife."

"Look, Carrington," Pierce said. "There's something we'd better tell you."

"Yes, there bloody well is," Andrew said.

"I'm sorry," Pierce said, "but we thought it for the best."

"Don't blame Phyllida," Witherspoon said. "She only did what we told her to do. She didn't like keeping secrets from you."

"Where is the book?" Andrew asked.

"We'll get it," Pierce said. "But I want your promise you won't do anything to Mrs. Carrington."

"Damn it, I'm not a wife beater," Andrew said. "It's you who let me go on thinking I was."

"I know," Pierce said. "I truly am sorry. What are you going to do with him?" He nodded at the prostrate body on the bed.

"Buggered if I know," Andrew said. "I can't do anything without the evidence of the accounts book, and—"

"Poor Mrs. Carrington," Pierce said, "carrying that dangerous book around with her."

"So she did have it," Andrew said.

"Yes, she brought it with her when she came to our house," Witherspoon said. "She was so worried, and she fainted, and Aggie and Davey and I talked it over and we thought we'd keep it for her until we could figure out what to do."

"Really?" Andrew said, closing his eyes against the waves of pity that assailed him. *I was an injured party too*, he protested silently. *I had been lied to for weeks, led to believe I'd struck my wife . . .* "And what did you figure out?"

"We never did," Witherspoon confessed. "Why did you bring him here?"

"Because it's not pleasant for Mrs. Carrington having him in the house," Matthew said.

"If I'd known what he was capable of," Andrew said, his voice as severe as his face, "I would not have brought Phyllida into the same house with him in the first place, nor left him there all this time to torment her with worry."

Pierce sighed. "George, my dear, better get Carrington the book."

Witherspoon ducked back into the vacated room and returned quickly, handing Andrew a book, which he jammed in his pocket on top of the disgusting romance.

"That's quite a bulge," Matthew said. "People will think you're in love."

Andrew cursed and pulled out the romance. "Here, you might enjoy this." He handed it to Witherspoon.

Witherspoon looked at the cover. "Thank you, Carrington. I am enjoying it. But I already have a copy."

"Do you mean you actually read this stuff?"

"Oh, yes. It's very good. I'm not just saying it."

Andrew shrugged and gave up. He had more important things to worry about than Witherspoon's peculiar tastes in reading. "These doors can be locked from the outside?"

"I think so," Pierce said. "A precaution, in case of a raid. Gives the fellows inside a chance to clean up and get dressed while the enemy is searching for the key or breaking down the doors."

"Why not just make sure the residents lock themselves in?"

Pierce raised an eyebrow. "Do you always remember in the heat of the moment?"

"I imagine we will, from now on," Matthew said.

"Assuming we ever have any heated moments again," Andrew said.

"Cheer up," Witherspoon said. "At least Turner can't cause any more trouble."

"I'll believe that," Andrew said, "when I see him shackled on the transport ship, and not before."

It was only after he was home and had pulled the book out of his pocket that he saw the mistake. Instead of the modest little book of household accounts, he opened the equally worn and stained cover only to see, like a recurring nightmare, *The Marriages of Melisande*. Unlike Andrew's copy, this one had an inscription: "To my dear George Witherspoon, an artist of the highest caliber. From one whose greatest talent lies in her choice of friends—Phyllida Carrington."

Andrew groaned and threw the book in the grate. As there was no fire, little damage was done when he retrieved it a few minutes later. Witherspoon would probably want the damned thing back.

Why did Phyllida have to give Witherspoon this tripe? Why couldn't she give him something worthwhile, like her own book?

Andrew noticed the dog-eared and crumpled pages that showed the laborious traversing of the turgid prose. Because the poor man could barely read, of course. *Sense and Sensibility* would only be wasted on someone with no sense and far too much sensibility.

AGATHA GATLING CLOSED THE BOOK, laid down her pencil, and rubbed her tired eyes. The soft knock at the door seemed perfectly timed. "You may come in, George," she said. "I'm about to stop work for the night."

Her brother sat next to her at the table and examined the sheets of paper covered in matrices of letters and numbers, some crossed out, and stretches of words with blank spaces, Xs, and question marks interspersed. "Did you figure it out, Aggie?" he asked.

"I think so," she said. "It's not easy working with such a small fragment. Fortunately he appears to have been using one of the ciphers we've already broken."

George picked up one of the scraps. "D, E, P, H, I, L," he read aloud. "That looks like Delphi. Don't see what Greece has to do with anything." He picked up another scrap. "A, N, D, R, E. That's easy. French for Andrew. Oh! You don't think it's Carrington?"

"No, dear," Miss Gatling said. "You may rest easy on that account. Put them together, why don't you, like this, and now tell me what you see."

"Delphi-André," Witherspoon read. "That makes no sense at all."

"It's not Delphi," Miss Gatling explained with maternal patience. "Not everybody spells backward and inside-out the way you do. I think it's the name of your club in French. *De Philandre.* The Brotherhood of Philander."

"The Brotherhood? Are you sure?"

Miss Gatling shook her head. "No, I'm not sure, George. The thing about these numerical ciphers is, once they start using three- and four-digit combinations, there are enough of them to code a word all in one group, or by syllable, or letter by letter. So one can't simply count the most common combination and assume it's the letter E, for example."

"You know I don't follow a word you're saying," George said.

"Yes, dear." Miss Gatling smiled up at her brother. "That's why I feel safe in telling you all this. And looking at the ridiculous sums in this accounts book, it's the only meaningful interpretation. I mean, honestly! Five pounds, eight shillings and sixpence for one month's worth of tea? Even in a large establishment like Carrington's, it's preposterous. And see here—four pounds, ten shillings for milk. Unless it's from the mare of a unicorn, that simply isn't credible. Whereas, using the key to this diplomatic cipher, we begin to find recognizable words and phrases." Miss Gatling pointed to boxes on the grid at her elbow. "The number 586 can stand for the syllable 'phil,' and 410 can be the name 'André,' and so forth."

"But why would a French agent be writing secret messages about the Brotherhood?"

"We don't know yet that I'm right." Miss Gatling had learned long ago not to frighten her brother with grisly reality unless and until it was absolutely necessary. "I ought to have done this when we first got the book, instead of letting Pierce take it, but at the time we thought it more important to safeguard it from Turner and his ilk. You were very clever not to give it back to Carrington yesterday. Tomorrow, when he comes after you in one of his towering rages, you must simply do as we discussed, apologize for making a muddle."

"I hate lying," Witherspoon complained. "He's already furious with us for interfering between him and Phyllida. Can't we tell him the truth?"

"Not yet," Miss Gatling said. "I heard from Amberson yesterday. He wants us to keep this quiet until he can take over."

Witherspoon's face went a whiter shade of pale. "Geoffrey Amberson? I wish you didn't have to be so friendly with him."

"Look at me, George," Miss Gatling said, putting an arm around his sagging shoulders. "Geoffrey Amberson cannot hurt you. However he may have threatened you in the past, he can't touch you now."

"But what about you, Aggie?"

"Now, George, we've been all over this. He has no interest of that nature in me—in any woman. My relationship with Amberson is strictly professional."

"That's what Davey said. But I can't help worrying. He's very . . . slimy. He pretends to ignore you, lets you think you're safe, and when you're not paying attention, he . . . pounces." Witherspoon shuddered.

Miss Gatling almost shuddered herself at the graphic and entirely credible description. She could imagine it all very clearly. It was Amberson's method, how he recruited so many of his unwilling agents—the pounce, the defeat, and the endless blackmail. She forced herself to show none of her thoughts. It was, she told herself in bracing, if silent, tones, another benefit of her lack of looks, that Amberson would never be tempted to sample the other side of the fence for a jade like her. "Pierce was right," she said. "In fact, where is he? Shouldn't he have called for you by now?"

"I'm going to meet him at the Brotherhood. I wanted to wait up and see what you got."

Miss Gatling sighed. "And you'll have to tell him, I dare say."

"I can't keep anything secret from Davey," Witherspoon said. "We love each other. It's wrong to have secrets when you love someone."

THE MAN WOKE TWO DAYS after his unhappy meeting with the wine bottle. His thoughts were hazy, vague, a morass of misty recollections and frustrating bits of unconnected images. Blinding sun, enervating heat, pain and humiliation, followed by sea and rain, pervasive chill and damp, and a bland-looking man . . . *No, not that. Not that shame.* He tried to trace back from his most recent memories: narrow streets, an elusive boy, and a woman. He remembered a staircase leading down to a cellar, and hearing—and seeing . . . He sighed and let it go.

The sheets were clean and soft against his skin; his body felt warm, fresh, renewed. Faint sounds aroused his curiosity. He opened his eyes. The room was luxurious, with dark paneling surmounted by flocked paper that glowed red and gold in the flickering light from a small fire in a grate. A screen was placed in front to shield him from the heat. He lay in an enormous canopied bed with a firm mattress and rich hangings that complemented the wallpaper.

A picture on the facing wall caught his attention. Two young men dressed in the elaborate costume of the previous century, their long hair curled but left unpowdered, one tall and dark, the other small and blond and with a thin line of scar lifting the corner of his mouth, stood with their arms around each other, the hint of smiles on their handsome faces. There was something disturbing about the picture, despite its agreeable subjects and symmetrical composition. The man blinked his eyes several times then squeezed them tight shut and opened them again. Yes, that was it. Look at where the black-haired one had his hand. Not the one around his partner's waist, but the other. And the blond was gazing, not straight out at the viewer but slightly up and to the side, the better to simper at his tall friend with the roving hand. Meanwhile his own free hand was. . .

"Cunts," Philip muttered and closed his eyes.

"Oy!" a familiar voice remarked in his ear. "You're awake, Mr. Weasel. Thought you was a goner."

Philip opened his eyes and looked into the face that had haunted his dreams. "You!" he said. "How did you find me?"

"Wasn't 'ard," Kit scoffed. "You flashin' yer blunt all over Covent Garden. Ought to be more careful."

"Where am I?" Philip asked.

"Where d'ya think?" Kit answered. "The Brotherhood of Philander."

Worse and worse. The name had a sinister connotation. "Who are those two shameless cunts in that picture?" Philip asked.

Kit moved to the painting and pointed, happy to show off his excellent memory and recently acquired knowledge. "This one 'ere, the little blond gent wif the scar, is Marcus Lambert, Lord Melford, the founder of this institution. And this bloke, the tall drink o' water wif the dark 'air and long nose, is Lord Rupert Archbold, third son of the Duke of Freyne, 'is what they call companion." He grinned. "Suppose you know all about that, companions and suchlike."

Philip focused on an earlier part of the recitation. "Melford?" he repeated in agitated tones. "Did you say Lord Melford?"

"That's right," Kit said. "Says 'ere, 'now the Sixth Earl of Ish—Isham.'"

Philip groaned. "Oh God, I've got to get out of here."

"Wait'll I tell Mr. Carrington you're alive. Dunno if he'll thank me or give me the sack."

"Mr. Carrington?" Philip repeated the name, his heart racing with an indeterminate but violent anxiety. "Does he know I'm here?"

"'Oo d'ya think brung ya?" Kit said. "You'd best be workin' out whatcher gonna tell 'im."

"Tell him? About what?"

Kit shook his head. "Oh, man, you're for it now. Mr. Carrington don't like liars and sneak-thieves. Better off admittin' what you done straight out and askin' for mercy. 'Ow d'ya think I got this job? Not that I'd choose playin' nursemaid to a weasel if I 'ad me druthers, but it beats Newgate. Plus I got a wife to think of."

"You're . . . married?" Somehow this was the most unlikely fact of all.

"As good as," Kit said. "Tell you somefink you might not know, Mr. Ferret. A bit o' pussy now and then, regular-like, ain't 'alf bad."

Philip closed his eyes. The more he thought about what he'd learned, the less he liked it. Carrington, Melford, the Brotherhood of Philander—he tried again to place the names, knew only that they should not go together in this way. And his dirty angel *married*? And what was he to do about retrieving his cipher? No, he was better off where he'd been, dreaming, lost, safely out of time and place. His head fell back on the pillows, and he relapsed into a coma.

THE NEXT DAY ANDREW received an unexpected visitor. Anthony Lambert, Lord Melford, was a distinguished widower of forty-nine, whose elongated emerald-green eyes, slanting slightly up at the outer corners, gave him the look of an intelligent, curious cat. He was the son and heir of the Earl of Isham and held an important if obscure position in the government, somewhere between the Foreign Office and the Horse Guards. "Received a damned peculiar letter last week," Melford said, apologizing for his unannounced call. "Fellow who works for you making some very unpleasant accusations. Was going to throw it on the fire, but thought I ought to let you know what's going on in your own household."

Andrew took the letter and held it unopened, making polite conversation. "How is your father? And Lord Rupert?"

"Isham's spry as ever," Melford said with a sigh. "Although sometimes I think his wits are more often in the last century than this one. Uncle Rupert had an attack of apoplexy over the winter, fortunately a mild one. He's up and about now, almost back to his usual style. Uses a walking stick to great effect, like an old French grandee."

"I thought we hadn't seen them as often as we might," Andrew said.

"Yes," Melford agreed. "Rupert's taken to saying the Brotherhood is a young man's club and the rest of you fellows don't care to see a pair of wrinkled old arseholes. His words."

"They mustn't feel unwelcome. Founders' Day coming up in a few weeks," Andrew said. "I do hope they'll be able to attend. Guests of honor, you know."

Melford sighed again. "Papa says they'll both be there with bells on. Better warn you, I wouldn't put it past him to mean that literally. Bells and nothing else."

Andrew laughed. "And how is Lady Isham? And your brood?"

"Young Marc is still safely up at Cambridge, thank goodness. Bella's having her coming out next week at Almack's. Whole house is in an uproar—gowns, jewels, ribbons and lace. Don't suppose you have to worry about tripe like that." He paused, seeing no response in Andrew's drawn, closed countenance, and cleared his throat. "As for Mama, she is impatient to meet your wife, Carrington. Says she suspects she's a kindred spirit, whatever that's supposed to mean."

"I'll tell Phyllida to call on her," Andrew said. He took advantage of the awkward pause in the conversation to unfold the letter. His face darkened as he scanned it. "My God! How did you get this?"

"That's the funny thing," Melford said. "It was addressed to me. My first thought was that it was meant for Amberson. More in his line, this sort of muck, except I doubt even he'd have the balls to try it on with you." Melford clenched his fist. "I was tempted to hunt down this self-styled 'loyal subject and concerned patriot' to thank him in person for dumping such a load of rubbish on me, but the more I read it over the odder it looked."

Andrew held the offensive missive between two fingers. "The only thing that's odd is that the man had the gall to put this stuff in writing. If I'd known he was sneaking around, spying on Mrs.

Carrington, I'd have cut his liver out and fed it to him, piece by piece." He looked up at Melford's sympathetic face. "Not literally, of course."

"Of course, of course," Melford said in the soothing tones a government minister learned to employ early in his career. "Very understandable sentiment." He waited until Andrew looked less likely to reach for the carving knife. "I do beg your pardon, but now that it's been brought to my attention, however unsought, I have to ask. This, ah, 'suspicious correspondence with a member of His Majesty's forces overseas.' Anybody I know?"

"Honestly, Melford," Andrew said, "those were love letters, pure and simple. Harry Swain—you must have heard that story."

Melford shook his head, then snapped his fingers. "Wait. I have it. Scandal at Eton? Young reprobate hustled off to the Peninsula?"

"That's right," Andrew said. "Father bought him a commission in the Ninety-fifth Rifles. Harry gave me the push just last month."

"Takes after his father?" Melford said. "Big blond buck, no sense of discretion."

"So you did know him," Andrew said.

"Only by reputation. Last person I'd suspect of anything underhanded."

"Oh, for God's sake, Melford," Andrew said. "Harry Swain couldn't lie even to escape a caning at school. He had nothing to do with this."

"And just what does 'this' refer to? And how did you come to employ such a person as this Turner?"

Andrew shrugged. "I ought to have told you at the start. One of Amberson's nasty little schemes. In fact, I wonder he doesn't keep you apprised of his intrigues."

"That's the one good thing you can say for Amberson," Melford said. "Keeps his dirty work strictly to himself. If it blows up in his face the rest of us are in the clear, and if he learns something useful he takes all the credit. Only fair, really. I suppose this is going to be one of the blowups."

Andrew nodded. "I'm sorry I ever agreed to be a party to it. Turned my whole household upside down for nothing, and the worst of it is I subjected Mrs. Carrington to the man's insults."

Melford shook his head. "You young fellows. That's what I can't fathom, how you were able to sleep at night with an enemy agent in the house. I know you've a reputation for sangfroid, a crack shot with the pistols and all that, but in the dead of night, taken unawares . . ."

"Enemy?" Andrew repeated. "Oh, no. Nothing like that. You give me too much credit. According to Amberson, Turner approached us. Claimed to be of French extraction, a generation or two back, but harbored an extreme sense of mistreatment and injustice, so much so that he wished to help us against his own people. Amberson decided to set him up in a situation where he could communicate clandestinely with émigrés and others of uncertain loyalties, without their knowing we were on to them."

"But why all this nonsense with kitchen accounts?" Melford asked.

Andrew explained how Turner altered the numbers in the weekly totals of the accounts book to transmit encoded messages through another agent at the bank. "If you think about it, an accounts book is ideal for ciphers. I mean, a letter that consists of nothing but numerals is bound to raise suspicion, but unless you examine the arithmetic closely, what's to cause alarm in a humble book of accounts?"

"True, true. Very ingenious," Melford mused aloud. "I don't suppose you know which cipher they were using? There are disturbing rumors just now coming out of Abchurch Street."

"The cabal of secret-writing specialists and cipher-breakers?" Andrew asked with a smirk. "Isn't that their stock in trade, disturbing rumors?"

Melford frowned and pursed his lips. "I shouldn't be telling you this, but since we've got this far—" He paused, waiting to see if Carrington betrayed avid curiosity or nervous agitation, but saw only polite attention. "There's a man over in the Peninsula, Major Scovell, a cavalry officer on the quartermaster-general's staff, who's this close—" Melford held his thumb and forefinger a fraction of an inch apart, "—to cracking the most difficult cipher we've ever seen, the *grand chiffre*, or Great Paris Cipher. He's far ahead of our rather puny efforts over here. But if it turns out that the cipher has already been broken and your secretary has the key, well, it rather puts a different interpretation on this whole scheme."

Andrew forced himself not to show how sick he felt. By God, he'd have a score to settle with Amberson if the man had perpetrated something close to treason under Andrew's very roof. "I'm sure there's no danger of that," he said. "I have the accounts book, if you care to see it."

"I certainly would," Melford said. "And any other information you may have on this Turner's origins." He sat rigid during Andrew's brief absence, wondering what on earth had possessed him to go into government service during what must be the longest period of continuous conflict since the fifteenth century.

Andrew returned with the accounts book and a slim folder and handed them to Melford. "That's the lot—what Amberson supplied as a cover. I doubt any of it's legitimate. Just the two letters of reference, from a Sir Ralph Underdown in Manchester and a Mr. Samuel Chase in Liverpool. Don't even know if they're real."

"Hmmm," Melford said. "Lot of traffic to and from America

through Liverpool. Or used to be. Could be at war with those hotheads any day now."

"Now that you mention it," Andrew said, "there is one interesting thing. Little rat has a set of perfectly ghastly stripes on his back, not recent. Never seen anything like it, although Matthew—Matthew Thornby, that is—claims to have seen something similar in America."

"Damned savages," Melford muttered. "My father goes off on a tirade every time the subject comes up." He glanced at the accounts book. "Well, that's a relief, at any rate. One of the old three-digit diplomatic ciphers, broken last year." After studying the page for a few more minutes, however, he frowned and cleared his throat. "I don't like to upset you any further, Carrington, but I have sufficient familiarity with this cipher to see that it contains a mention of the Brotherhood."

Andrew exhaled slowly, thankful the news was no worse. "Whatever Bonaparte and his generals may be planning, I doubt very much it concerns what they would most likely call the 'English disease.'"

"Always thought that referred to suicide," Melford murmured, smiling.

"So it does," Andrew replied, grinning back. "Every Englishman knows sodomy is the Italian vice."

"Doesn't it worry you, though?" Melford asked. "A spy sending coded messages about the Brotherhood?"

"Not really," Andrew said. "It was all conducted under Amberson's supervision—or so he assured me at the beginning. You know his methods. When I thought about it at all, I actually felt sorry for the little bugger, until—"

"Andrew," Melford said. "Please. Listen to me. You know I'm on your side. But I need to understand what was really going on if I'm to help."

Andrew's face looked like that of a man backed to the wall. In two seconds he went from a joking, slightly world-weary comrade to a man facing burning at the stake. "I'm sorry, Melford. It becomes instinctual to keep the secrets of the Brotherhood from outsiders, even someone as sympathetic as you, and with such a close connection."

"I don't know whether to feel insulted or flattered," Melford said, his facial expression remaining neutral while his mind turned over the possibilities. Growing up the son of the most notorious sodomite in the country, Melford had learned early the unfortunate necessity of evasions and half-truths. It had, in fact, been excellent preparation for his career in politics. He only wished it did not have to blight so many potential friendships.

"A man with a probing intellect like yours surely recognizes a compliment when he hears it," Andrew said, attempting his usual confident drawl. "And the arrangement with Turner was established under the terms I described. Only as the weeks passed with no results, Amberson became convinced, as did I, that this Turner had obtained little if any worthwhile information on the war or the French. What he does have is an obsession with wealthy sodomites, with the Vere Street coterie, and now with us. With me and my friends. And the best way to protect ourselves was to allow him to continue with his intrigues until he exposed himself—and his confederates, if any."

"Yardley," Melford said. "He names him right there in the letter."

Andrew closed his eyes and waited until he could speak without showing his fury. "Yardley is my butler. His nephew, the man Turner refers to, was one of the two owners of the White Swan. The Vere Street house."

"And just how long do you intend to let that situation fester?" Melford inquired.

"Yardley, my Yardley," Andrew said, "has been with my family close on forty years. He is no more responsible for his nephew's activities or choice of business than my Uncle Francis is for mine."

"Quite," Melford said. "Seems an invitation to disaster, though."

"It's a bluff, that's all," Andrew said. "When the White Swan was brought down, Cook, one of the owners, was caught and pilloried, but the other—young Yardley—disappeared. Turner no doubt hoped to discover his whereabouts and use him against his uncle and me and my friends at the Brotherhood, but he overlooked one fact: Yardley, the nephew, never betrayed his friends or his clients. He was a businessman, nothing more or less. And my Yardley, the uncle, has steadfastly refused all correspondence with him, on the principle that it protects both him and us. And it is only right that I continue to give a home and employment to an old retainer who has done nothing wrong. Nor, as I see it, has his nephew. So Turner was running into a dead end there."

"What do you suppose caused Turner to write this letter, though?" Melford asked, returning to the original problem.

"Insurance," Andrew said. "He knew he had made a mess of things, losing the last accounts book, attacking Mrs. Carrington."

"Attacking Mrs. Carrington? You mean, physically?" Melford lowered his voice. "Frankly, I'm surprised the blackguard's still alive after what he's been doing."

"Well, damn it all!" Andrew exclaimed. "I didn't know about that until a couple of days ago."

"All I mean is," Melford persisted, his voice little more than a whisper, although the two men were alone in the room, "if you find yourself in a difficult spot, I'd be more than willing to use the government's resources to help you out, you see?"

"That's very generous," Andrew said. "Fortunately for your better instincts, the little rat met with an accident."

Melford raised an eyebrow. "Did he, by Jove?"

"Not what you think," Andrew said. "One of the servants caught him helping himself to wine out of my cellar and, ah, gave him a bit more than he'd bargained for. Concussion."

"How's the man now? Is he conscious?"

"Apparently not," Andrew said. "Had a brief moment of lucidity yesterday, but by the time I got there I couldn't get any sense out of him."

"I suppose I'll have to question him," Melford said, his voice unenthusiastic.

"You're welcome to try," Andrew said. "I must warn you, he's at the Brotherhood. After his vicious nature came to light, I couldn't continue to subject Mrs. Carrington to his presence in this house."

"But the Brotherhood!" Melford said. "The very place he wants to bring down?"

"What choice did I have?" Andrew asked. "And, besides, now that he's established there, even assuming he recovers enough to cause trouble, he can no longer claim to be untouched by whatever activities he tries to accuse us of."

"Quite so," Melford said in a weary tone. "I'm beginning to wish I'd waited for Amberson after all."

"I suppose he has a lot on his plate right now," Andrew said. "Badajoz, I mean."

Melford's mouth tightened, the lips thinning to bloodless lines. "What do you know about that?" he said.

"Take it easy, Melford," Andrew said. "Only what anyone with a relative in the military knows. You remember my brother Tom. Captain in the dragoons. I wouldn't call him a model correspondent, but he does write occasionally and he's got a good eye for tactics. It was pretty clear what the objective was after Ciudad Rodrigo."

"Sorry, Carrington." Melford's mouth relaxed into an attempt at a smile. "I'm afraid this whole business has me on edge. We're at a critical juncture right now. The next captured letter may very well give us not merely the key to the *grand chiffre* but the whole purpose behind discovering it—knowledge of the French marshals' plans. A chance to turn a miserable, ongoing strategic retreat into a war of attack."

"I do apologize for dragging you into this, however unintentionally," Andrew said.

"And an interrogation at the Brotherhood isn't my idea of a social evening," Melford continued, as if he hadn't heard.

"There's no requirement of participation, you know, especially for the son of our esteemed founder," Andrew replied. "If you condescend to set foot in our den of iniquity we'll consider ourselves honored."

Melford chuckled, relaxing into acceptance of the absurdity of it all. "I've been a sorry disappointment to my father all my life, at least in that respect. Suppose it wouldn't kill me to gladden his heart in his golden years. Send a note round when the rat wakes up, will you?" He shook Andrew's hand on leaving, his face growing grave. "I hope you won't take offense, but I was expressly charged with delivering a message from my father; to wit, he and Uncle Rupert have a lot riding on you and they expect you not to let them down." At Andrew's blank look, he added, "Stud duty. Don't like to put the pressure on, but you've become the cause célèbre of the sodomites."

Andrew could only give a sick smile and nod. There was no point blaming Melford, especially as the man was going out on a limb to quash the Turner mess. "Doing my best," he said.

"All anyone can ask," Melford said. "We'll look forward to the announcement of a happy event before too long, I hope."

KIT MARLOWE CROUCHED BESIDE A chamber pot in the Brotherhood's garden and gently swirled the contents with a stick. A passing serving-boy sniffed. "Lost a ha'penny?" he asked. "Or just thirsty?"

Kit wanted to kick himself for being so eager that he had not gone far enough off the path. "You can 'ave a drink if you want," he said. "But it'll cost you a tanner." He stood up and jabbed the stick at the boy.

"Bet you'd drink it for a tanner," the boy said, stepping back but not giving up. "Bet you drink buckets of piss from all the sods after they've—"

Kit poked him in the eye with the stick and turned his back as the nasty little bugger howled and ran off. Checking to make sure no one else was in sight, Kit moved to a secluded patch of bare earth and emptied the pot. There it was, the skin still miraculously intact. Kit nudged it gently back and forth with his shoe until the worst of the pot's filth had been rubbed off on the earth, then lifted it between the tips of two fingers and hurried to a safer place behind the shrubbery that bordered Hyde Park. It took the merest nick with a ragged fingernail to slit the delicate membrane, and the condom's mysterious filling was revealed.

Kit wanted to cry for the second time in recent days. What had he hoped for? Bank notes, of course. A roll of Bank of England notes was just about the only thing Kit could imagine worth anyone's secreting in this bizarre way. He'd never seen something like this come out of someone's arse without seeing it go in first. No wonder Mr. Ferret had cried and moaned and clamped his sphincter shut as if about to be buggered by the devil himself. But nature calls, and no one can hold it in forever.

And what was the object of such fiendish ingenuity? A bunch of meaningless papers, numbers and letters and the occasional word aligned in a sort of table. Kit could almost swear ordinary writing wasn't like this. It usually went in long, unbroken lines across a page, sometimes crisscrossing vertically if the writer needed to save paper. Accounts and ledgers had columns with totals at the bottom. But this—this was neither one, just a grid of squares, most filled in, a few empty. What a bleeding waste.

Still, it must be worth something to somebody, or why go through the misery of sticking it up your bum and holding it in for so long? Kit furled the papers tightly and folded them over to make a rounded tip, as they had been inside their sheath, then slid them carefully in his front pocket. You never knew when something might be useful.

He wished he could read, so as to have a better idea of what he was dealing with. Perhaps Nan might know. But he didn't want to share this discovery with anyone, not even her. Not that he didn't trust her. She had risked her position and livelihood for him, and given him her maidenhood; her love was too new and too precious for him to discount it. But the instincts of self-preservation, built up over seventeen years of adversity, did not atrophy from a week or two of good fortune.

No, Kit would hold on to his disappointing find, take his time, and figure out what was to his best advantage. Hadn't he done well so far? And all from meeting Mr. Carrington. He wondered if he ought to show him what he had found. Then he remembered that terrible night, Mrs. Carrington trying to kill the ferret-man, and Mr. Carrington's face when he learned the truth. It was too complicated and too dangerous for Kit to wish to be drawn in any further there. Best to keep his mouth shut, as always.

A WEEK WENT BY—AT LEAST, Phyllida assumed it did. Morning followed night, evening succeeded day, and she went through the motions, answering when spoken to, dancing if asked, eating and drinking what was set before her, although she did a poor job of that. Anything she did manage to choke down tended to come right back up again. Her new dresses, whose seams had been in danger of bursting, hung loose on her smaller form and would have to be taken in.

Andrew escorted Phyllida to those events at which their absence would be remarked on and lead to more rumors, but his coldness and lack of attention were proof to all of the failure of the marriage. The speculation on the bet at White's, which had reached a fever pitch in Andrew's favor after the appearance of the glowingly happy couple at Lady Trent's, plunged into an abyss against him a few days later, as the fashionable world saw yet another commonplace example of the wreck of affection on the rocks of marital discord.

In Grosvenor Square, it was no better, despite the disappearance of Mr. Turner. Andrew rarely dined at home and made no conversation when he did. Even the servants kept their distance. Although Andrew, in interrogating Nan and Kit, had abjured them strictly from talking, word had flowed out through the mysterious channels of household news. The others learned something of the deception and, protective of their good master and his feelings, let Phyllida know where she stood in their esteem—somewhere below the level of the coal scuttle.

"What did I tell you?" Mrs. Featherstone said at the downstairs table a couple of days after the interrupted night, savoring her moment of triumph. "Up to no good with all that writing. Hand in glove with that sneaking rat Turner, I'll be bound."

"Now, Mrs. Featherstone," Yardley said. "We don't know all the facts."

"We know enough," Mrs. Badger said. "A lady don't accuse her husband of hitting her, whether he done it or not. And if he ain't—why, that's worse'n lying straight out."

"I'll tell you this," Kevin said. "She weren't shamming when I broke the door down. Frighted out o' her wits she was. Wouldn't be surprised if that little weasel had his way with her and she too scared to tell the truth."

"Unused to it, more likely," Mrs. Featherstone said, the only member of the staff who did not appear more sorry than smug at the recent developments.

Only Nan was loyal—and cheerful. "I see I'm in your debt, Nan," the master had told her the day after the trouble, when he'd had the chance to consider things with a cool head. "It was your quick action that brought Kevin upstairs so promptly to free Mrs. Carrington, wasn't it?" He had not sacked her for hiding Kit in the cellar, only remarking that while he could not condone such underhanded dealings in general, the results in this case had so justified the irregularity as to be overlooked.

What's more, he had offered Kit a real position, with wages: looking after the wounded man. "I imagine playing nursemaid to a spy and a blackmailer is not much to your taste, Marlowe, but consider the alternatives. And if you do well, there will be more appealing, and lucrative, opportunities."

"You oughta hear yourselves," Nan said to her judgmental fellow servants. "See what the mistress is up against? You none of you believe her. What was she supposed to do? And the whole world watching her middle to see if she's breeding."

"You'd defend her against adultery, even murder," Mrs. Featherstone said. "We all know why. Birds of a feather. Any other master would've turned you out in your shift after what you done."

"I know the master done me a kindness," Nan said. "But that don't make the mistress a liar and a whore, for all your snooty superiority."

"Lud!" Mrs. Badger exclaimed. "Hark at her! Talkin' like a bloomin' actress. I do beg your pardon, milady, for offending against your delicate sensibilities."

Nan laughed. "I might just be an actress one of these days. Or married and with a lady's maid of my own. Once I learn to read and write—"

"You'll be able to read the words of your sentence when you're brought to Bridewell," Mrs. Featherstone said with a sniff. "And write your own confession."

"Don't you mind those old harpies," Kevin said. "I'd pay a hard-earned shilling to see you on the stage in breeches."

"And I'd let you in for free," Nan said, glad of the friendly young man's championing, and blushing vividly when the hoots and jeers of the others recalled her to the double meaning of her words.

"I'll hold you to that," Kevin whispered as she fled upstairs.

"The master found Kit a position," Nan confided to her mistress. "At a gentlemen's club. Said if Kit works hard and learns to read, he can move up. Then we can get married."

"That's nice," Phyllida said.

"Will you miss me?" Nan asked.

"Why? Where are you going?"

"When we're married." Nan was beginning to be worried by her formerly vivacious mistress's lackluster appearance and sporadic attention. "Might stop working once I'm married."

"You can live on Kit's wages?"

Nan sighed. "Not hardly. But if I have a baby. Can't be a lady's maid with a baby. The master was right kind to let me stay, after what I done. Think it was for your sake, madam, but I can't work with a swollen belly, nor a babe."

Phyllida blinked and woke from her torpor. "You're pregnant, Nan? Are you happy?"

"Nah, I got more sense than that. All I mean is, I could be, in time. Things happen."

"They certainly do," Phyllida agreed. Her life was as strictly segregated, it seemed, as a Muslim lady's in a harem, relegated to her sister's company, and her maid's, and shown in public only on the arm of a silent and uninterested husband merely for the purpose of proving his continued possession.

And of course the possession did not extend to the realm of marital intimacy. Phyllida was grateful for her sister's presence, if only as a warm body in the empty boudoir and bedroom. Although Harriet had been given a guest room, she rarely used it other than as a dressing room, preferring to relieve her sister's enforced solitude. They would lie awake at night in the bed, where Andrew had once, weeks ago, stretched out full-length, his boots resting on the footboard, and they would talk.

"I suppose he only wanted a wife for show," Harriet said.

"You don't understand," Phyllida said over and over, as if she could make herself, and him, understand by repetition. "He wanted a child, an heir. He didn't care about appearance."

"Did he ever . . . you know?" Harriet was endlessly curious and hopelessly childish in her ability to express herself on this topic.

"Of course," Phyllida said. "On our wedding night, and after. And then he used to— Oh, it was lovely." She turned her face away and swallowed hard. Comparing her miserable situation with what had been a brief moment of paradise always brought her close to tears.

"I still don't see what all the fuss is about," Harriet said. "That Mr. Turner didn't actually force you—did he?"

"No," Phyllida explained for the thousandth time. "Andrew is hurt because I lied to him. I let him think he was the one who hit me." Torn between hoping Turner was rotting in gaol and that he was dead, she could not hear a mention of the little rat's name without feeling a twinge of nausea—and anger. In gaol he might talk as he had threatened, but death was too kind a fate for him.

"Most men wouldn't mind," Harriet said, "so long as your virtue wasn't compromised."

"Most men are pigs," Phyllida said. "So long as their wicks are dipped regularly, they don't care tuppence for their wife's feelings."

Harriet giggled. "Mama would smack you for talking like that."

"Mama was the one who told me that," Phyllida said. "And in those exact words."

"Anyway," Harriet continued, unperturbed, "I suppose Mr. Carrington and that Matthew Thornby are dipping each other's wicks regular." She nudged her sister in the ribs.

Phyllida didn't rise to the bait other than to say, "I should hope so."

"Doesn't it bother you at all?" Harriet asked. "I know it was an arrangement, but you seem to care for him."

"Of course I care for him," Phyllida wailed. "That's the whole problem. Oh, I wish I'd never set eyes on that filthy accounts book."

ANDREW RESIGNED HIMSELF TO Almack's Assembly Rooms. It was bad enough when things had been going well, but now that his marriage was exposed for the travesty it was doomed to be, the thought of dragging his poor automaton of a wife and her chatterbox of a sister through an evening of enforced gaiety, in environs of strict decorum, was as perfect a definition of purgatory as he could imagine. Not hell, for the evening would have an ending. He must bear that comforting thought in mind as he shepherded his charges through the throngs of husband-hunters and young men on the lookout for easy prey. No trips to the balcony tonight. There were no balconies.

He had considered telling Phyllida and Harriet that he had been unable to obtain vouchers, but had quickly rejected such an obvious lie. Lady Jersey was always friendly to an attractive and socially prominent man and could talk the other patronesses into allowing a poor relation a chance at finding a husband. He had arranged for vouchers a month ago, as part of the wedding agreement to give Harriet her coming out, and her dance partners had been chosen. Andrew scowled as he recalled the list—doubtless Lady Jersey's little joke—all of them members of the Brotherhood.

At least Matthew would be there. Andrew didn't think he could have got through the last week without the solid presence of the sturdy Yorkshireman. Matthew was dependable. You could count on him to be there, to keep a level head, and, when the worst had been safely negotiated, to be always hard and ready for it. Unlike Andrew. He would have been close to eating his gun if it hadn't been for Matthew soothing and stroking and kissing and assuring him that it was just melancholy. That once he sorted things out with the weaselly Turner, and with Phyllida, he'd be his old self in no time. Andrew doubted that things could ever be that good again, but it was kind of Matthew to say it.

They were announced at the entrance and pushed their way into the crowd. It was fortunate that the only marriageable member of their party was Harriet, with no portion other than what Andrew might be inclined to give her out of family obligation. The heiresses were besieged almost on the doorstep by shady characters, even here. At least Phyllida, as a married lady, was relatively safe for the purposes of an Almack's assembly.

Andrew led the two women to a space with some chairs. "Will you be all right? I think I'll check the card room."

"Of course, Andrew," Phyllida said in a lackluster voice. She did not turn her head, and as for her smile, he had not seen that in a week. A long, miserable week, brightened only by Matthew.

"My dear," Andrew said under his breath as the big blond appeared at his shoulder. "I was just thinking about you."

Matthew's eyes darted below the waistband of Andrew's black satin knee breeches, the required dress at Almack's. "Not too forcefully, I hope," he whispered. "Can't ask a lady to dance with your heart so blatantly on your sleeve, so to speak."

"I won't be dancing," Andrew said. He ignored the coarse humor, having no taste for it now that he was more likely to be the butt of jokes than the instigator. "Shall we see who's in the card room?"

"Cards?" Matthew recoiled as if Andrew had pronounced a curse. "At Almack's? But my dear, Almack's is for dancing."

"Almack's is for forcing all the free young ladies and gentlemen of one's acquaintance into the same slavery the rest of us married couples endure," Andrew said. "The least one can do is allow us poor leg-shackled prisoners a rubber of whist."

"Whist." Matthew shook his head at Phyllida. "Not a practice I intend to take up before I reach eighty, if then. Mrs. Carrington, will you do me the honor of holding the second set free for me? I am fortunate indeed in having the incomparable Miss Lewis bestowed on me for the first set."

Phyllida shook her head. "I'm sorry, Mr. Thornby. I don't feel quite the thing tonight. I doubt I'll be dancing at all."

Matthew sighed and led the eager Harriet out. Phyllida had not willingly danced, or laughed, or so much as cracked a smile in a week that he could see. He had thought that she would come about after a day or two; then he had thought perhaps she was playacting, in the way of some coquettish females who liked to manipulate their husbands; now he was genuinely worried, especially as she was becoming as rail-thin as her sister-in-law. For Lady Fanshawe, it was natural, and perversely enticing; for Phyllida, it was ruinous, aging her by ten years, sucking the bloom from her cheeks and the sparkle from her eyes.

Phyllida ignored the dancing couples and made a slow circle of the perimeter of the room. She had no goal in mind other than to keep moving, to not stand still long enough to call attention to herself. Harriet would be safe, protected by her very lack of portion from fortune hunters, and by her mother's teachings from seducers of innocents. Phyllida could trust her to Matthew's care and her other partners, all men whom Andrew knew and Phyllida had met, few with an inclination for women and none with the need or desire to marry.

"Mrs. Carrington?"

Phyllida decided to act as if she had not heard. She was not in the mood to indulge yet another old biddy pretending friendship only to be attempting to winkle out answers to give her husband or her son some useful inside knowledge for the bet at White's.

Her path was blocked by a wizened old gentleman, only a few inches taller than herself, grinning at her with a simian face that Phyllida, even in her depressed state, was forced to acknowledge must once have been quite beautiful. He had a faded scar on his cheek, which pulled up the corner of his mouth in a permanent sneer, changing what would otherwise have been bland prettiness into something slightly menacing. Phyllida caught the knowing look in the man's eyes, dropped a slight curtsy, and attempted to move around him.

The man sidestepped neatly and intercepted her. Phyllida stepped to the other side and he followed, hopping with nimble, quick-footed movements and grinning more widely than ever. "Mrs. Carrington? I ain't going to ask you to dance no matter how you try to lead me on. Lady Isham wishes to speak to you. Perhaps you did not hear her over the music."

Phyllida looked around. The person who had first called to her was an equally short and elderly lady, as plump as the man was lean. "I beg your pardon, sir," Phyllida said. "I have not made the acquaintance of Lady Isham."

"Which is precisely why she wishes to speak to you," the man said. "As do I." He held out his hand and bowed. "Marcus Lambert, Lord

Isham, at your service. Come. The world will be so confounded by seeing me with so young and beautiful a lady on my arm, they will forget all about you and your husband for the rest of the season. Or a month, at least, which should give you some respite."

Phyllida took the man's arm. He appeared to be the sort of person who always went directly for what he wanted, secure after a lifetime's experience of being certain to get it. But he was old enough to be her grandfather; his manner, while roguish, seemed benign, and his eyes possessed a humorous twinkle behind the cloudy rheum of age. Phyllida felt no fear, only curiosity.

Lord Isham led her to a chair beside his lady, made the necessary introductions, but did not sit. "There, Bella," he said. "You two have a nice chin-wag while I pry Rup loose from his latest victim." He sauntered off in the direction of the card room, lifting his quizzing glass to ogle every passably handsome young man who crossed his path, but making steady progress.

"Now," Lady Isham said, "I do apologize for the strong-arm tactics, but I simply must to talk to you." Her voice was clear, with a hint of cockney—refreshing and incongruous in this setting. "You are the girl who married Andrew Carrington?" At Phyllida's nod, she said, "Good. How much did he pay for you, by the way?"

"What?" Phyllida could only stare. She started to rise, but Lady Isham put a hand on her arm, the fingers surprisingly strong, the nails, even through gloves, digging into her flesh like claws.

Lady Isham's laugh was like the cackling of a witch. "Don't be such a little Quaker," she said, her voice losing all pretense of gentility. "It don't suit you. Now, I will tell you straight out that I bought my husband, just as your husband bought you. Over a hundred thousand my dad paid for Melford, as he was then, and we never had cause to think we got the worst of that bargain. I am not trying to embarrass you; I merely want to have a business discussion."

Phyllida coughed to regain her voice. "The wager again," she said. She felt ready to cry from disappointment. She didn't know what she had been expecting from this odd meeting, but not that.

Lady Isham patted her hand. "Now, now dear. It's not the wager, precisely. More a question of honor."

"I have done nothing," Phyllida protested, furious that this old harridan could be accusing her in public. "I have never betrayed my husband."

"Oh, la!" Lady Isham said, unfurling her fan with a snap and flourishing it in the manner of a belle from a Hogarth painting. Phyllida wondered the woman didn't wear a patch or two of black satin on her face in the fashion of fifty years ago. "Such modesty. More than I can claim. Marc—Isham, that is—and I would roll the dice many an evening. Winner to enjoy the favors of our mutual friend, Rupert. Loser to wait his turn, or hers, although I tried very hard not to lose." She let out another of her dreadful cackles and nodded across the floor, where Lord Isham was leading another elderly gentleman from the card room. "Ought to have seen our Rup when he was young. Make your knees turn to jelly, he would."

Phyllida tried but failed to pretend not to understand. She stared at her lap, her knuckles whitening as she clutched her fan until the sticks snapped and she sat up with a start, letting out a whoop of laughter that turned heads as far away as three rows of chairs over. "Oh!" she cried, gasping for breath. "You didn't!"

"That's better," Lady Isham said. "You looked as if you haven't had a good laugh in a month of Sundays. And yes, we did precisely what I said. Although come to think of it, sometimes we cut cards instead." She glanced over at Phyllida's red face, the tears streaming down. "You get it all out, dear, and when you're ready, you must tell me what's at the root of this estrangement from your Mr. Carrington."

"I can't," Phyllida said, looking nervously over her shoulder. Any listening audience had already had the discretion to turn away in semi-profile.

"When you're ready," Lady Isham repeated in the placid tones of a cat waiting by a mouse hole with no other exit.

They watched the dancing couples for a few minutes, and Lady Isham indicated a young lady with chestnut hair and narrow green eyes that slanted up at the outer corners, partnered by an unusually tall and handsome man with dark red hair. "My granddaughter and namesake, Isabella Lambert, making her entrance into society. That vision of loveliness beside her is Lord Bellingham. Has Mr. Carrington mentioned him?"

Gervaise Alexander Warburton, Marquess of Bellingham, elder son of the Duke of Coverdale, known to his friends as Alex, was probably the most eligible bachelor in the kingdom, and the most elusive. He was young, just down from Oxford last year, interested in pursuing a career in politics, and was, by all accounts, sociable and down-to-earth—and the heir to one of the wealthiest and most eminent peers of the realm. A catch, in fact. And not, to Phyllida's certain knowledge, a member or even an occasional guest at the Brotherhood of Philander.

"Yes, my lady," Phyllida answered Lady Isham's question. "That is, he pointed him out to me once and—" She was forced to bite back the rest of that recollection. *A rather more interesting wager than the unimaginative one of which we have been made the object,* Andrew had said at one gathering, during that idyllic time when their marriage had been going so well. *Man who can seduce the beautiful Bellingham and provide incontrovertible proof has his membership in the Brotherhood paid for a year.*

"And?" Lady Isham prompted. "Marc was rhapsodizing about him all the way here in the coach when he learned he was to be Bella's first partner, until Rup and I were ready to throttle him."

"Now, what d'ye say, Rup?" Lord Isham had returned with a tall gentleman in tow. This second man looked to be Isham's contemporary, but was not as agile; while he held his back straight, he listed slightly to the left, wielding a walking stick in the manner of one who carries it merely for its usefulness in whacking stray dogs and importunate urchins out of the way. "Regular stunner, I should think, but you're the better judge."

"She'll have to be, Marc," Rup said. "Dash it all, I was just about to give old Wilmot the coup de grâce. Luck running very hot tonight."

"As if there's anything worth raising one's temperature for in the penny stakes of Almack's," Isham said. "And wait'll you see Mrs. Carrington before you talk about hot."

The newcomer was introduced as Lord Rupert Archbold. Upon hearing the name, Phyllida, forcibly reminded of her recent conversation with Lady Isham, was obliged to hold up her broken fan in an attempt to hide her deep blush and broad grin, which happily compensated for her recent emaciation.

Lord Rupert studied her in grave silence for a couple of minutes before settling into a chair beside her. When he smiled, his entire face changed, taking on a sympathetic warmth with only a hint of friendly mockery behind the emerald-cool eyes—an erotic hazard rather than a tangible threat. "Good Lord," he said in a voice that had once purred like Andrew's, Phyllida imagined, although now it had a slight rasp, not unpleasant, like the susurrus of silk on wool. "Ought to have been introduced to the lady before listening to Carrington's tedious recitation. It's perfectly obvious. Carrington's in love for, shall we say, every apparent and understandable reason, but he takes you for granted because he purchased you." He looked over at his friends. "Bella did the same with you, Marc."

"I never," Lady Isham said.

"Ha!" Isham said. "Rup found you out, Bella. I never blamed you for it, my dear. In the nature of all commercial transactions. But what shall Mrs. Carrington do about it?"

"I can speak, you know," Phyllida said. "And just because Mr. Carrington has been regaling his friends with the intimate details of our marriage doesn't mean I am willing to discuss it all with strangers."

"But now we have been introduced," Lord Isham said, "we are no longer strangers."

"Besides," Lady Isham said, "who better to advise you two through the perils of a sodomite's marriage than the founders of the Brotherhood of Philander?"

"Now then, my dear Mrs. Carrington," Lord Rupert said, "you must show your husband you are worth the no doubt extortionate fee he paid for you. You must laugh and flirt, whisper and ply your fan. Does he have a lover?"

"Of course he does," Isham said. "Matthew Thornby. Must have pointed him out to you half a dozen times. Big blond buck. Could raise a blue-vein throbber in a one-balled parson." He made a growling noise in his throat.

"Marc!" Lady Isham said, her voice sharp but smiling. "Behave yourself."

"Excellent," Lord Rupert said as if there had been no interruption. "Mrs. Carrington, you must become very friendly with Mr. Thornby."

"But I am," Phyllida said. "He's very agreeable. It isn't anything improper."

Lord and Lady Isham shared an expressive look at such naïveté. "The point is to make Mr. Carrington think it is," Lady Isham said.

"That's despicable," Phyllida said. "And it wouldn't work anyway. Mr. Thornby is not romantically inclined to women. I refuse to jeopardize my marriage any further just so that you can win a bet."

This time it was the two men who exchanged worried glances. "It's not the money, you know," Lord Isham said. "It's a matter of honor."

"That's what Lady Isham said," Phyllida said. "And nobody seems to believe me when I say I have not betrayed my husband. I did something worse—at least I think he could forgive infidelity more easily. I— I— Lied to him, about something very serious."

"Dear me," Lord Rupert said. "Life is filled with such drama when one is young. But it is not your honor we are talking about. It is Mr. Carrington's and, by extension, the honor of all men who are not, as you so delicately put it, romantically inclined to women. A chance to prove their manhood, so to speak."

Phyllida, still watching the dancers, realized where she had seen distinctive green eyes like Lord Rupert's—long, narrow, slanting upward to the outer corners. On Lord Isham's granddaughter, Isabella Lambert. "Oh!" She raised her fan again as the realization hit.

"There, now," Lady Isham said. "We have given you a lot to think about. Marc, my dear, would you and Rupert excuse us please?" The men, looking distinctly unhappy but recognizing the impenetrable authority of female solidarity, bowed and took their leave.

Lady Isham nodded at the retreating backs of her husband and his—their—friend. "Marc was always independent, a law unto himself," she said. "Never minded what the world thought—or said. I think that's what I admire most about him. But most men don't have his stomach for a fight. He was in the army five years before we married. So handsome he looked in his red coat. A major at twenty-five, all earned. Didn't have the money to buy his promotions. North America—that's where the worst of it was then. Dreadful scars he has on his body, not just that rather fascinating one on his face. But he liked the life. Only sold out because his father died and he had to settle down and marry." The floodgate once opened, the reminiscences looked as if they might gush all night.

Phyllida saw Andrew emerge from the card room just as Lord Isham and Lord Rupert reached the doorway. The three men bowed to each other and stopped to chat, looking vaguely in her direction.

"Marc never minded that our son had a look of Rupert." Lady Isham was still living in the glorious past. "I think he loved him all the more. But I made very sure the next one was his—Marc's, I mean. You can expect a man to be generous once, but you oughtn't to make a habit of it."

Andrew approached the two women, bowed to Lady Isham, and kissed her hand. The set ended and Matthew, surrendering Harriet to Lord David Pierce, her next partner, looked around for his friends and sauntered over. Andrew maintained his recent characteristic silence, but Matthew repeated his earlier request. "Now that you have had a good long sit-down, Mrs. Carrington, perhaps you will reconsider your rash decision to maintain the attitude for the entire night?"

Phyllida, grateful for the rescue, assented readily and stood up, before realizing that she was now following the distasteful instructions of Isham and Archbold to the letter, and with an alacrity that bordered on the indecent.

Lady Isham, seeing her hesitation, said, "Go on, dear. It's only a dance."

"Just what were those two old buzzards saying to Phyllida?" Andrew asked Lady Isham as Matthew led Phyllida into position in the lines of couples.

Lady Isham fanned herself vigorously and winked. "Now, Carrington," she said, "you can't expect me to divulge a lady's confidences."

"Dash it all," Andrew said, "she's my wife."

"Then you'd better start treating her like your wife, hadn't you?" Lady Isham said.

"GOD, I'M SORRY." ANDREW ROLLED away from Matthew and stared up at his reflection. Funny how familiar it looked. Like himself. No indication, apart from the one treacherous piece of anatomy, that he was useless, worthless, no longer a man.

Matthew reached a hand over and patted his lover's shoulder. "Don't keep saying that, love. It'll come back, if I have to spend the next year on my knees." He chuckled. "Can't say I find that thought insupportable."

Andrew shook off the hand and turned his back. "Don't know why you bother with me."

"Oh, so that's it," Matthew teased. "Want me to take you from the rear." He palmed the firm buttocks and slid a finger into the crease, enjoying the sensation as the muscles clenched tightly around the probing digit. "Tempting, but you know that's not my style."

"Nor mine, anymore," Andrew said.

"Look, love," Matthew said. "What we have is nothing to complain about. A lot of men, it's all there is to their love, and both content."

"But not you," Andrew said. "When we first—that first night—you knew what you wanted. What I wanted."

"You," Matthew said. "I wanted you, however I could have you. That's still what I want."

"I've been thinking," Andrew said.

"Oh," Matthew said with a groan, "no wonder you're feeling a strain."

"Bitch," Andrew said, but turning onto his back again and smiling. "I think you should move into Grosvenor Square."

"You mean with you and Phyllida? No, Andrew. Can't say it doesn't sound intriguing, but it's not a good idea."

"Why? Phyllida won't mind. You don't have to worry about her."

Matthew frowned. "Maybe I don't. But you should. Worry about her, that is. She's your wife, Andrew. And she's damned unhappy. The last thing she needs is another man in the house, all the gossip and rumors."

"What do you know about it? You ever been married?"

"No, but I've been on friendly terms with many women, spent time in intimate conversation with them. Probably a lot more than you have. I think I understand Phyllida's situation."

"Oh yes?"

Matthew had learned to be wary of that supercilious tone. "Before you get on your high horse, Andrew, hear me out."

"Don't worry," Andrew said, his voice bitter. "We both know there's no riding going on here."

"If you could stop feeling sorry for yourself for five seconds," Matthew said, "you might spare a thought for Phyllida. How do you think it is for her, knowing she's lost not only your love, but your trust and your esteem? Everywhere she goes in society, and even at home, people blame her for the failure of your marriage."

"That's absurd," Andrew said.

"Is it?" Matthew said. "Forgive me, love, but I heard you, you know, telling her there wouldn't be a child."

"It's no more than the truth."

"My God," Matthew said. "I didn't think you could be so cruel."

"Cruel? Do you think I'm withholding myself from her on purpose? That I prefer being little better than a eunuch? You're very kind to me, Matthew, but—"

"Oh, sneck up," Matthew said. "It's not kindness, you stupid git. I can't keep my hands off you. Or my mouth." He stroked Andrew's chest, like soothing a restless animal, tugging at the wiry new hairs. "Your mane is coming in nice and full. I know the difference between a stallion and a gelding."

Andrew's heart thudded at the arousing touch. "Which makes me—what?" he said, but with the hint of a smile at the corners of his mouth that Matthew had come to recognize and welcome, a harbinger of interesting developments on the horizon. "A Shetland pony?"

"No," Matthew said, "more like an Arab steed with a clumsy rider, that's bruised its shins on a wall and is shy of jumps. One of these days, with the right jockey, you're going to clear that hurdle with inches to spare and never look back."

"Seems you have your metaphor reversed," Andrew said, but still with the quirk of a smile. "Arse-backward, one might say."

"I guess I do," Matthew agreed. "But you see the sense of it. And Phyllida is too compassionate a lady to hold a case of nerves against you."

"You speak from direct experience?" Andrew said, his eyes narrowing.

"Nay," Matthew said, broad Yorkshire infusing his voice. "What would a simple fellow like me know of nerves?"

"Oh, you north-country louts," Andrew said. "An answer to everything." He nuzzled the square jaw, and the two men kissed and played with each other until Andrew broke away in frustration. "I need a good secretary."

Matthew exploded with helpless laughter. "I never heard it put like that," he said when he could form words. He pushed his voice up several octaves, attempting to imitate a coy female. "Oh, sir, what an extraordinary secretary you do have. What a great many *letters* you must write, to be sure. No wonder they say the *pen* is mightier than the sword. And your *inkbottle*! So full of *manly spirit*!"

"That's enough," Andrew said, provoked to smile in spite of his ill humor. "That's not exactly what I meant. What I was trying to say is, there's a vacant position in my household, and I am offering it to you. If nothing else, it could save you the expense of lodging here."

"You're serious?" Matthew said. "Happen I don't fancy being kept."

"Oh, hell," Andrew said. "Go ahead, take everything the wrong way. It's a genuine position, with duties and responsibilities, not a sinecure. And it pays well, probably better than what you're getting now. Two hundred pounds a year."

Matthew whistled. "For writing a few letters and handling your banking?" he said, the mischievous smile returning to his face despite his best efforts. "Nay, I don't believe it. You're trying to cozen me into an irregular situation."

"I just don't like to see you living as a wage slave, grubbing in that wretched warehouse in the City or wherever you go," Andrew said, suspicious of the man's tone, but unsure where the implausibility lay. "And then having to throw it all away on these overpriced rooms."

Matthew cocked an eyebrow. "Membership's expensive, even

without room and board. A lot more than your two hundred a year."

"How do you manage, then?" Andrew asked.

"Oh, hand to mouth and day to day, a little support from the family," Matthew said. He raised his voice again. "Good sir, if I please you, perhaps you could help me out?"

"Now who's being mercenary?" Andrew said, but laughing.

"You are," Matthew said. He sat up and wrestled Andrew down, pinning his arms above his head and straddling his hips. "You think money can solve any problem, but all it's good for is buying the things it can, and leaving you free to pursue the things it can't." He bent his head and kissed the sardonic mouth before it could utter the drawling jeer.

"And this?" Andrew said when he was allowed to breathe. "You think I'm buying this?"

"You may try," Matthew said, "but I'm not selling." He lowered himself in the bed until his mouth was close to the enlarged cock. *Not so limp after all*, he thought. *We'll be flying over that fence sooner rather than later, and Andrew will be the one doing the riding.* "No, our only bargains must be bartered in fair trade. Love for love's sake and nothing more." He scraped his tongue across the quivering, drooling head.

"Oh God, that's good," Andrew said. "I don't deserve you."

"And whenever did love have anything to do with deserving?" Matthew inquired, before opening his mouth wide and swallowing.

MARCUS LAMBERT, SIXTH EARL OF Isham, and Lord Rupert Archbold climbed the broad stairs of the Brotherhood of Philander. Archbold leaned heavily on his walking stick and favored his right leg; Isham maneuvered easily but continually looked around him as if unsure they were in the right house. "Used to be red," he said. "The wallpaper. And there was a very fetching portrait of—What was the fellow's name?—Singer. You know, Rup."

"Farinelli," Archbold said. "That was taken down years ago, Marc. Went out of fashion, thank goodness, castrating boys for their voices."

"Farinelli," Isham repeated as they reached the first landing and Archbold paused for breath. "But he was beautiful. Not fat like some." He poked his lover in the ribs. "Almost as beautiful as you, Rup."

The tall man leveled his cane at his lover like a rifle. "Now, Marc, you old goat. I know you're in a hurry. But you'll have to wait for me to get my wind."

Isham pressed himself against Archbold's body. "Don't have to wait. Not here. That's why we started this place. No hiding, no pretending, no women to offend—and no spying rats to worry about. Do anything we like, whenever we like, wherever we like."

"You always were a shameless hussy," Archbold said. He pushed Isham away, but gently, like loosening a baby's fingers from antique lace. "I, for one, like a bed and a room with a door that locks. I'm too old for those molly wedding chambers with open doors and a sharp-eyed audience in the corridor."

"Never too old, Rup," Isham protested. "Once you're too old for that, you're dead, or should be. Besides, you could always win their applause."

They climbed to the second floor and made their way with steady purpose to their room. The door was locked. "Damn it!" Isham said. "What's the matter with servants these days? They know No. 3 is our room. Just because we don't come here as often as we used to—"

Archbold fished a key out of his coat pocket. "Never let it be said I was caught unprepared. Always carry a spare."

"You," Isham declared, "are the noblest of God's creation, a man with a head on his shoulders and a yard in his breeches."

Inside the suite, Archbold moved to stand before the portrait, staring morosely at the two beautiful figures from half a century ago. "That was once a man," he murmured.

Isham stood beside him and put his arm around his friend's waist, looking up to his face, recreating the pose in the painting. "That is both unoriginal and maudlin, Rup. Even a fine figure like Marlborough couldn't hold a candle to you, and you know it. You're as much a man as ever, which at our age is no small thing." He winked and cackled. "Get it, Rup? No *small* thing, eh?"

Archbold stooped to kiss Isham's lips. "Your sophisticated wit always did go over my head. Kind of you to elucidate. Come on, Marc. Might as well enjoy it while we still can."

They sauntered arm in arm into the bedroom. Philip Turner, his head recently unwrapped from its bandages, slept peacefully, a candle on the table providing a soft light. The bedclothes had drifted down in the warm room, the top edge of the sheet barely covering his hips. He was all too obviously naked underneath.

"Oh," Isham sighed. "They gave us a present. How thoughtful."

"Must be a mistake," Archbold said. "Explains why the door was locked, though. Too dangerous."

"Dangerous?" Isham said. "He looks a perfect lamb. Do you want to go first, or shall I?"

"I don't think we should touch him," Archbold said.

"That is very rude," Isham said. "The least we can do is unwrap him after the fellows went to all this trouble. If you don't wish to share, you can watch." He sat on the bed and peeled back the sheet. "Oh, very nice. Look, Rup. He likes me."

Turner awoke to a delightful and rare sensation. He deliberately kept his eyes shut, the better to savor his imaginings. Was it his dirty angel pleasuring him so expertly, or the woman? The picture in his mind was a combination, the round, pretty face of the woman with the hard, flat chest and narrow hips of the boy. He groaned as the skillful mouth brought him to climax, and opened his eyes.

The screams had the footmen running on the instant, yet when they reached the second-floor corridor, all seemed quiet.

OLIVER, THE FOOTMAN WHO HAD witnessed Turner's arrival, stood very still, listening for a repeat of any suspicious noise. It was strictly against club rules to disturb the gentlemen in their rooms. A man would be sacked on the spot for interrupting the members at their pleasures. But if murder or assault were committed on his watch, it would be Oliver's head on the block, too.

It was mid-afternoon, a dead time in the upstairs bedrooms. Most boarders brought a guest in late at night and stayed until mid-morning. Even Pierce and Witherspoon rarely spent time in their room during the day. Only Isham and Archbold, the club's founders, had wanted to enjoy an afternoon tumble, as they called it, the old dears.

A whimpering, moaning sound came from No. 3. Too late, Oliver remembered that they had left that injured man in there, forgetting that the two gaffers considered it theirs. His heart sinking, Oliver knocked on the door. There was no answer and the door was locked. The sound continued. Praying that he was doing the right thing, Oliver took the master key from his pocket.

The sight that met his eyes was shocking, even after five years of seeing men at their most vulnerable. The wounded man, naked and flabby, was keening and wailing, oblivious to the two old men who tended him with vastly differing degrees of concern. Lord Isham, his clothes disheveled and with a disgusting stain on his waistcoat, rocked the man in his wiry arms, crooning to him like a mother to a sick child. Archbold, his back to the revolting spectacle, was holding the decanter, pouring a glass of brandy with shaking hands.

Archbold turned at Oliver's entrance. "Damn it," he said. "Thought the door was locked."

Oliver bowed and tried to back out. "It was, my lord. I heard screams. I thought there was trouble. Please forgive me for disturbing you." *That's it,* he thought. *Done for. Sacked. Have to tell Mary the bad news.*

"Who is it, Rup?" Isham called.

"A footman," Archbold replied. "Apparently they give a master key to anybody who asks."

"Well, bring him in, Rup. Maybe he can tell us."

Oliver, wishing that, five years ago, he had had the sense to take the other job, the one that paid a tenth the wages of this one, but in a private establishment, came slowly forward at Archbold's urging. "I'm sorry, my lord," he said in answer to the questions. "I don't know anything about the man. Mr. Carrington and Mr. Thornby brought him in, and they have a boy to look after him." He peered around the room as if Kit might be hiding in a corner. "And where has that little rogue got to?"

Isham pointed to the welts on Turner's back. "Look at this," he said, his voice quavering in indignation. "Worse than anything my grandfather did to me. Thought I'd seen it all, in the army. North America, you know," he explained to Oliver. "Unimaginable savagery. Colonists had the nerve to call themselves Englishmen in those days. At least they don't pretend that anymore. But this!" He directed his attention to the weeping man in his lap. "There, there, young man. We'll find out who did this to you, never fear." He lowered his head to plant kisses on Turner's moist face, stroking the soft hair back from his forehead.

"Honestly, Marc," Archbold said. "Use some discretion. For all you know, the man's a criminal."

"Rupert!" The old officer's voice rang out in a reprimand.

Archbold jumped as if he'd been goosed. He hadn't heard that tone in years. Oliver found himself straightening up, sucking in his gut, and standing to attention.

"*We* are criminals," Isham said in his army voice, the major passing on the colonel's less than complimentary opinion of his troops. "You and I and everybody in this house—we're all criminals. It doesn't excuse this. Nothing warrants this. Next you'll be defending the mob that nearly killed those poor fellows from the White Swan when they were put in the pillory."

"Now listen here, Marc," Archbold found his voice at last. "Just because we live in a benighted society that lumps us in with murderers and thieves doesn't mean we have to make common cause with them. And it's my belief that Carrington and Thornby brought this man here to keep him under guard. Not to give you some sort of anniversary gift."

"Not doing a very good job of it, are they?" Isham muttered. "I think I'll have some of that brandy. And bring some for this pretty young fellow, too. Can you tell me your name, sweetheart?"

Turner caught his breath, gulping back the tears. It had been a wonderful release to cry, an indulgence he hadn't enjoyed in twenty years, even through the worst of it. And it was lovely to be rocked and held, crooned over and kissed. But he must not let it sway him from the path of righteousness. "Philippe," Turner said, as it came back to him all at once. "My name is Philippe."

21

TIME PASSED, BUT PHYLLIDA couldn't say if it was two weeks or ten. It was not an entire season, she knew that, because then they would have moved somewhere else—Brighton, probably—then someone's country house for a shooting party, or Leicestershire for the hunting.

The war news occupied only a few people's thoughts and conversation—those, like Phyllida, uninterested in gossip, newspaper accounts of adultery and divorce, and fashions—the bloody and costly assault on Badajoz, followed by the shocking aftermath, the days of unchecked looting and rape. Phyllida thought of what her father would have said, how men who had suffered through the carnage of the spiked walls and point-blank musket fire, seeing the wounded trampled beneath their comrades' boots and buried alive under their friends' corpses, relieved their terror by visiting atrocities on the inhabitants who had forced the siege rather than surrender.

Phyllida wished she could run riot, at least smash a few windows or tear down a fence. She did not want to hurt anybody, other than Mr. Turner, but it was eating away at her to have no outlet for her fears and shame. Instead there were balls and routs, dinners and suppers, card parties, theater parties, masquerades at Vauxhall Gardens, and excursions to the countryside. And always, on set days of the week, morning calls to receive and to return.

If it weren't for Mr. Thornby, Phyllida didn't think she could have faced so many forbidding countenances, the array of disapproving people lined up like a firing squad, waiting for her first misstep to give the signal for annihilation. But Matthew, as she had come to call him at his insistence, supported her, where Andrew was inclined to abandon her to her fate. Entering a room, beginning a dance, at the theater and at parties, Matthew would appear at her side, take her arm, and guide her through the maze like a faithful suitor, giving her all the steadfast devotion of a lover with the undemanding friendship of a woman. And with his broad shoulders and muscular build, the way his urbane, boarding-school affability could change to rustic northern belligerence at a moment's notice, no one dared challenge him or say a word.

She could almost wish to have married him instead, but for the inconvenience of memory, the torture of her body's response to the tall, dark man who looked through her with his piercing gray eyes and made her heart flutter and her thighs sticky with desire. And would as often turn his back or say something cutting if she dared to appeal to him.

"Pardon me," a female voice said. "Is this chair occupied?"

Phyllida looked up from the corner seat where she had taken refuge at this latest ball—whose was it? Oh yes, Lady Finchley's—to see the enormous Miss Swain bearing down on her like a royal yacht in full sail. She smiled and shook her head. "Please, sit. Although I should think a young lady of looks and fortune would have little chance of becoming a wallflower. And where is your chaperone?"

"Mama is indisposed tonight, and Lydia—Mrs. Swain—is an easy mistress. And now that I am in my third season I may please myself. I only like to dance with men who are taller than me. Which limits it to two, and that's on a good night."

"Yes, it must be difficult," Phyllida murmured as she scanned the room. It might be useful to have a project, an interest beyond Harriet, who was in many ways a hopeless case. Portionless, more or less resigned—perhaps looking forward—to Mr. Coulter, Harriet provided little scope for anyone wishing to further her interests. Miss Swain, now. She was the daughter of a wealthy peer, and her buxom blond looks, there were few men who would profess to find her an antidote, no matter how unmanned some of them felt in her shadow. The embodiment of masculine pulchritude from Almack's swam into view. "What about Bellingham?" Phyllida said, pointing discreetly.

Miss Swain blushed and looked away. "Alex? He's on my dance card for the next set."

"I'm glad," Phyllida said.

"Mrs. Carrington?" Miss Swain said. "Forgive me if I intrude, but you do not appear to be well."

"Just a trifle under the weather. So many late nights." Phyllida's voice was cool.

"I worried— I mean, I wasn't sure if what I said about my brother Harry might have caused a misunderstanding."

Harry Swain. Phyllida had almost forgotten. She smiled with more warmth. "I take it he has come safe through the recent action?"

"Yes, he wrote a real letter this time," Miss Swain said with a broad smile of relief. "Two entire pages. But I fear he has not done so well by Mr. Carrington. And if any of it is my doing—"

"Miss Swain, it is kind of you to concern yourself." Phyllida saw the girl was genuinely worried, as if her private conversation in a drawing room in London had any power over the affections of a young man engaged in a bloody and horrific war hundreds of miles away, across an ocean and in another country. Better to shade the truth ever so slightly. "Mr. Carrington and your brother reached the end of their friendship in an amicable parting. Nothing you said has had any ill effects."

"But you and Mr. Carrington are not— That is— I am afraid that you are unhappy."

Phyllida took the girl's large gloved hand in hers. The fingers were long and strong, the hand of a horsewoman. "You are kind. I assure you, Miss Swain, if there is any discord between Mr. Carrington and me, it is not because of your brother, and certainly not because of you."

"Charlotte," Miss Swain said. "I wish we may be friends and that you would call me Charlotte."

"Words I have dreamed of hearing." The tall figure of Lord Bellingham loomed over the women where they sat. "I think this set is promised to me, Miss Swain." His hazel eyes, heavy-lidded and beckoning, took in Charlotte's companion. "How do you do, Miss—"

Charlotte made the introductions. "So you are the fair Mrs. Carrington," Bellingham said, bowing. "I see London society has more to offer than I suspected. May I inquire if you are free for the set after this?"

Phyllida found herself agreeing. It was not as if she were stealing anything from her friend. No respectable young people who were not engaged could dance two sets in a row at these formal, public gatherings. For the first time in weeks, she was looking forward to a dance.

She watched them as they took their places. Bellingham was an excellent dancer, managing his height and long limbs with grace. Despite his dark red hair, his complexion was free of freckles, pale but smooth, without blotches or ruddiness. He had a classic profile and the lithe build of an Apollo, rather than the robustness of Jupiter or brawn of Mars. Phyllida sighed. She enjoyed looking at him, but in the end all it did was point up the contrast with Andrew, almost as tall, so dark and swarthy, his ropy muscles, his pale eyes and sneering mouth. . .

"I begin to think," Matthew said in her ear, "I have a right to feel jealous."

Phyllida startled. "Jealous? Of Bellingham? I did not think he was one of your set."

"All the more reason," Matthew said.

"Andrew told me about the wager on Bellingham at the Brotherhood. He didn't mention that he was in the competition. I *am* sorry, Matthew. I imagine he's so accustomed to freedom, he doesn't realize how hurtful it is to you."

Matthew almost blushed. He had never known a lady to speak so freely. It was the one thing, in all his reasons for hoping to save the marriage he saw crumbling before his eyes, that made him most wish to champion the lady's cause. She was an original. "Andrew? No. I meant that *you* do not find him displeasing."

"How could I?" Phyllida said. "How could anyone who is not blind?"

"Exactly," Matthew said with an exaggerated sigh.

"You are teasing," Phyllida said. "I think, perhaps, you are right. I think *you* are the one making *Andrew* jealous." She laughed impulsively—more of a giggle or a gurgle—the first time Matthew had heard it in weeks. The lighthearted sound nearly broke his heart, and the playful exchange gave him an idea.

"May I sit?" he asked, taking her assent as given, moving the vacated chair slightly further back and closer to Phyllida's. "You are wise to select this secluded corner."

Phyllida scowled. "You make it sound as if I'm conducting an intrigue. Everybody thinks I've betrayed Andrew, and—"

"The world always thinks the worst—and usually gets things wrong, no matter how one tries to set them straight," Matthew said, bending his head close, almost touching his shoulder to hers. "We might as well give them what they expect."

Phyllida jerked her head away. "No! You, of all people. I thought you were safe." She looked ready to cry.

Matthew took her hand. "Don't be foolish, sweet lady. I'm the safest there is. All I meant is, better they think it's you and me than you and someone else." He held her hand closer to his chest and lowered his head again. "Andrew invited me to live with him—with you." He saw her eyes widen, the flush in her cheeks. "Don't worry, I told him no."

"I'm sorry," Phyllida said. "I thought— I mean, I don't like to presume, but it seemed as if you love him."

"It's not presumption to use your eyes," Matthew said, looking away. "Doesn't mean I need ruin other people's love."

"But how could you do that?" Phyllida said. "Our marriage was an arrangement. Surely Andrew explained it to you."

"Many times," Matthew said. "Every time the subject comes up, in fact. Never knew a clever man to be so dense."

"Even if he did care for me a little once," Phyllida said, her voice sounding strangled and low, "he'll never forgive me for what I did." She looked up, her eyes pleading. "I wish you would come and stay with us. It would be nice to have a friend in the house, besides my sister, of course. And I think it would help things—with me and Andrew."

"I still don't understand," Matthew said, momentarily putting aside the thought-provoking implications of that last statement. "What terrible crime did you commit that Andrew, that soul of rectitude, can't forgive?"

Phyllida was forced to smile briefly. "You were there. You heard. I lied. I let him think he hit me."

"Because you were afraid of Turner," Matthew said. "What could that little rat have said or done that made you more afraid of him than of Andrew?"

Phyllida shook her head. "I can't talk about it. Please don't try to get it out of me. If only I could be sure he was somewhere where he can't make any more mischief, but Andrew won't tell me what he did with him."

"Ah. I begin to understand. Please, say no more. I ought not to have teased you." His voice had gone from soft and warm to distant and formal.

The music ended for the first dance of the set. The dancers stood in place, the ladies fanning themselves, chatting with their neighbors or surveying the room for a partner for the next set. "Come," Matthew said in a lighter tone, standing and tugging on Phyllida's still-captured hand, forcing her to rise. "See, there's other latecomers looking to form a quadrille. Dance with me. Let me try to make you forget the beautiful Bellingham."

"Easily done," Phyllida said, trying to match his mood, not realizing until too late how the words would sound. "I prefer an experienced man to a boy, no matter how beautiful."

Matthew coughed to cover his surprise. "Just when I thought my tanned countenance and muscular form would carry all before me, I find it is age before beauty after all that wins the day." He was rewarded by her laughter as he led her to the end of the row of dancers, fitting in neatly to the formation already begun. It would work, he was sure of it. He smiled into her eyes as they made the turn and gripped her hand more tightly.

Andrew, strolling at the edge of the room, heard the laughter through the music and conversation as if all other sounds had been cut off. How long had it been, he wondered, since Phyllida had laughed, or shown any pleasure at all? Why did it pierce his heart so to imagine that she could be cheerful again, but only when she was not with him? He saw Matthew, his head thrown back and his chest out, strutting in the dance, smiling into the eyes of— Damn it, it was. His deceitful, feigning meek wife was flirting. Flirting with his lover.

"DRAT," PHYLLIDA SAID UNDER HER breath, attempting for the tenth time to force a tiny button into a minuscule hole while holding together two edges of cloth that were cut too tight to reach across her middle, no matter how she had shrunk recently. The one social event she enjoyed these days was the reading lessons, especially as she seemed to have lost all desire to write. Only this teaching gave her some substitute of pleasure. George was a dear to have come up with the idea and made all the arrangements, and she ought not to mind so much about wearing the disguise.

She had thought, when she started her writing, that it was a way to fill a void, that facing life as a poor spinster, stuck in the country, had led her to escape her constrained existence by creating fictional romances to enjoy, a more fulfilling life for her to inhabit through her characters. But marriage had only intensified her desire to explore her new feelings in prose; it was the ruin of her happiness that had left her imagination barren.

"Here, madam, let me help," Nan said. She was already neatly, and apparently comfortably, attired in a laundered and mended set of Kit's old clothes. But then the girl was small and thin as a child. "Hold your breath while I pin it."

"I'm not built for men's clothes," Phyllida complained. "I don't see why I have to go through this. It's not as though we're spying." *That's exactly what it is*, she thought to herself, at least in her case. Making sure that little weasel hadn't carried out his threats against the Brotherhood. Andrew didn't seem the least bit worried. And when Phyllida remembered the stern lectures on discretion she had been given the morning after her wedding, she was ready to scream.

"It's just to get us in the door," Nan said, rehearsing the same argument each time. "It's a gentlemen's club, see. No petticoats allowed, not even maids or laundresses. So if we want to look like we work there, we got to put on the breeches. As soon as Mr. T— That is, as soon as his probation is over, Kit'll ask the master if he can go out, and we can have the lessons here."

They crammed caps over their pinned-up hair and put on heavy jackets, uncomfortable on a warm spring day, but necessary, especially in Phyllida's case, to cover their thin shirts. They went down the back stairs and out, heads lowered, looking at the pavement, clumping in their boots, scurrying along to Park Lane and around to another back entrance and up the narrow back stairs, to wait breathlessly in the corridor for Witherspoon to signal the all-clear.

Once safely ensconced in room No. 6, Phyllida flung off the jacket and cap and shook out her hair, unbuttoning the flap of the breeches so she could sit without damaging her anatomy. Kit crept in silently as ever, shutting the door and locking it. "Lord, Mrs. C.," he exclaimed, seeing the long hair tumble down and noting the expanse of bosom beneath the shirt, "it's a wonder you wasn't nobbled today. Even a cross-eyed cock bawd at midnight could tell you wasn't the genuine article."

"I will assume," Phyllida said, raising her chin and affecting a haughty demeanor, "that that was intended as a compliment."

"Oh yes," George said, attempting to translate. "He means you look very pretty and— Ah— Womanly."

"Thank you very much," Nan turned on her Romeo. "And what about me?"

"Didn't say I liked it," Kit protested. "Like 'em straight up and down and full o' ginger." His speech was rewarded, appropriately, with a none-too-gentle cuff on the back of the head that nonetheless left Kit with a satisfied smile.

"Now that the social niceties have been observed," Phyllida said, "perhaps we can get down to business. Take out your books, please, and open them to chapter thirty. Mr. Witherspoon, will you begin?" At Phyllida's insistence, they were all called by their surnames, equals for the purposes of education. Phyllida, as teacher, was the only hierarchy.

George, nervous as always, cleared his throat and began reading aloud, the others following along in their own books, obtained from Phyllida's stock of presentation copies. With a great deal of prompting, he managed to produce:

> "You have a visitor, my dear," Lord Iskander said, ushering Melisande into the large stone hall of the castle keep. "I regret I cannot leave you two alone to enjoy your touching reunion, but honor, you know . . ." His voice trailed off.
>
> Melisande stared at the prostrate figure dumped unceremoniously before her. The large form, the blond hair, was

curiously familiar. She bent down. "Ludovic!" she gasped out.

The man lifted his head. "Melisande? Is it really you, or am I dreaming?"

"Oh, Ludovic." Melisande fell on her knees and cradled his bloodied face in her lap. "What has he done to you?"

Ludovic groaned. "Nothing to worry yourself over, my love. But you? He has not mistreated you?"

Melisande lowered her gaze. "No, Ludovic. You must not concern yourself with my well-being."

The young man struggled to stand, but was too weak. He sank back with a groan. "My lord," he addressed his captor. "I must request that you allow me to redeem your prisoner, my betrothed."

Lord Iskander stepped forward, coming out of the shadows between the wall sconces like a wraith from the atmosphere. "Indeed?" he said, his deep voice purring with sarcasm. "And how do you intend to recompense me for my generosity?"

"Surely you would not hold a lady against her will?" Ludovic said. "Regardless of whether her intended husband can meet your terms for ransom."

"No," Iskander agreed. "I do not hold a lady against her will."

"Then I may take her away with me as soon as I am able?"

"As to that," Iskander said softly, "we shall see. We shall see what her choice is, and yours, when the time comes."

"I will never choose anything but my beloved," Ludovic said, eyes open very wide and jaw outthrust.

"You must wait," Iskander said, "until you know all the choices. And until you have heard the entire history of Melisande's sojourn in my domain. But tonight, and until you are recovered, you are my guest." He snapped his fingers, and his eunuchs came at a run. "Convey our honored guest to my chamber."

"Yours?" Ludovic said. "That is too great an honor."

"Yes," Iskander said with a humorous look, "I rather think it is. But I find, now that I have had a glimpse of your perfect form and have gazed on your manly features, I am unable to resist. I must discover precisely what it is that has kept Melisande so enamored of your memory all these months." His pale eyes gleamed red in the torchlight, and his voice had sunk to a whisper by the end of this speech. He bent down, and with one extended finger traced the line of Ludovic's cheek and jaw, until the young man flinched and turned his face away.

"No!" Melisande cried, looking up into her captor's—and lover's—hawk-like face. "No, Iskander, you must not!"

"Must?" Iskander repeated. "My dear, that is not a word you may use with me, as you are well aware. And surely you would not deny dear Ludovic the opportunity to experience his own—awakening? Indeed, I suspect he will thank me on the morrow, as you did, and deplore your attempt to shield him from his destiny."

"I say! Does that mean what it sounds like?"

"Cor!" Kit exclaimed. "You can't get away with selling that! They'll put you in Bridewell."

Phyllida looked both smug and nervous. "I think I can. Mr. Edwards went over it very carefully."

"However did you think it all up?" Nan asked.

"Perhaps," George said, "it was being married?"

Phyllida blushed. "Some of it. At the end. It's strange, but I just imagined the three main characters out of the blue. And then when I met Andrew—Mr. Carrington—it was as if he were one of the originals."

"Lord Iskander, to the life. Won't 'e be fit to be tied when 'e reads it!" Kit said, eyes glowing at the imagined row. "Betcha 'e pulls out his— What d'ja call it—scimitar—and—"

"No, no," Phyllida said. "Mr. Carrington won't read stuff like this, I'm sure of it."

"But he has a copy," George said. "He offered it to me a month ago, and I told him how good it is."

Phyllida moaned and shook her head. "He couldn't have. It's only just going on sale now."

They had worked at *The Marriages of Melisande* for weeks, at George's suggestion, backed by Kit and Nan's enthusiastic seconding once they had sampled the story and become engrossed in its gothic plot. All of Phyllida's advocacy of primers or a simple alphabet or, worst of all, the Bible, had been rejected in no uncertain terms.

"It's so Kit can get a better job," Nan had explained. "He ain't big enough yet to work the door, but if he can read the names of the guests and such, he can do more than just maid's work."

"See, it's better if it's somefink we want to read," Kit had seconded his girlfriend's argument. "'Cos we'll pay attention then. I'm a quick study, Mrs. C. I'll get the 'ang of it faster'n a dry bob—"

"Mr. Marlowe." George's voice, unusually stern, had cut him off. "Mrs. Carrington doesn't want to hear about that."

"Can we go on?" Nan asked now. "I want to know what happens with Lord Iskander and poor Ludovic."

"Please," Phyllida agreed, eager to return to the safety of fantasy. "Miss Crowder, why don't you continue from where Mr. Witherspoon stopped?"

Nan, her voice faltering at first, but nudged by her beau, soon picked up the narrative with enthusiasm.

Melisande was allowed in to see Ludovic late the following morning. Her betrothed lay recumbent amongst the heaps of cushions and throws scattered across the Oriental splendor of Lord Iskander's couch. A couple of eunuch guards stood impassive in the corners, watching in silence to ensure their master's honor was not sullied. Even in sleep, Ludovic's open, manly countenance had a petulant, almost dark expression, which Melisande had never seen before.

She touched his cheek gently, watching in growing dismay as the firm young flesh twitched and the young man awoke, scrabbling against the soft bedclothes as if to free himself from nonexistent bonds. His eyes opened and he stared unseeing. "No," he muttered. "No, my lord. It is wrong, a sin."

"Ludovic," Melisande whispered. "It is all right now. It is I, Melisande."

"Melisande?" Only now did Ludovic's eyes fasten onto her face. "It is really you?" He reached for her hands, but before they could enjoy the blessed, chaste touch of yore, he flushed in shame and drew his hands away. "I am no longer worthy of you."

Melisande fought back tears. "Nor I of you, my love," she whispered, so low Ludovic had to strain to catch the words. "Yet I love you still."

"You?" Ludovic said. "He has forced you against your will? And still you live?"

Melisande felt the blood freeze in her veins. Lord Iskander had won, as he always did, as he had foretold. "Yes, Ludovic," she said. "I had no weapons to hand at first. Later I found, to my everlasting shame, I had neither the will nor the desire to end my existence, even to restore my honor."

Ludovic sat up, his smooth, muscular arms and chest as naked as an innocent babe's, forcing Melisande to turn her head away, although she could not resist the occasional peek from under her lashes. "Find me a weapon, Melisande," he said, "and I will free us both from further degradation."

"No!" Melisande cried, throwing herself on his neck. "I am not worth it! But you! You have no need for such sacrifice, I am sure."

Ludovic pried her arms loose and flung her away. "Is this the pure maiden I once loved?" he asked, his lip curling in distaste. "Could I have pledged my life and my sacred honor to defend this polluted vessel?"

"Such tragic sentiments on what should be a festive occasion," the familiar deep voice drawled as Lord Iskander entered his chamber on silent feet. "Surely we have much to celebrate." He approached the bed and stared from the naked man sprawled in grief on the cushions to the weeping woman kneeling on the stone floor. "Rise, Melisande," he commanded, holding out his hand to help her to her feet. "There is no reason to mourn the defection of an inconstant lover. The loss is his, not yours."

"I am not her lover," Ludovic said, his voice sounding boyish and sulky. "We kept ourselves pure, saving our virtue for our nuptial bed. And now—now, all is ruined."

Lord Iskander smiled down at the impassioned words. "You are new to love, my dear, and unaccustomed to the way in which purity of thoughts can meld with corporeal acts to create a higher, one might even say, nobler, condition." He tugged on Melisande's hand, still caught tightly in his, and led her forward to the side of the bed. "Sweet Melisande, like you, resisted this eternal truth at first, but she has learned. Learned the lesson well, I may add. You would do well to attend to her teachings."

The clock on the landing chimed the hour, and Kit exclaimed: "Bloody 'ell. I got to go. Don't you be sneakin' a look at the end wifout me."

"Don't worry," Phyllida said. "I know it is difficult for you and Miss Crowder to study on your own, due to the demands of your jobs. Perhaps, Mr. Witherspoon, you could read ahead for our next lesson, and prepare a summary? That way we shall have a chance of finishing the story by the end of the season."

George looked both flattered and alarmed. "Surely, Mrs. Carrington, you could summarize your own work far better than I could."

"But I am not the one learning to read," Phyllida said. Relenting at his mute appeals, she added, "I will help you, if you like."

"On one condition," George said. "That you begin your sittings for your portrait."

"Oh no." Phyllida sat back in dismay. "Besides, I'm too thin."

Witherspoon cocked his head and considered. "You were. But I think you're filling out again."

AGATHA GATLING STUDIED HER REFLECTION in the cheval glass in her brother's room. It would do. Not well, but enough for her purpose. Nobody looked twice at an under groom, or whatever she would be taken for. Not a gentleman, that was certain. No, she looked like some middling sort of servant, or a shop assistant. Nothing so smart even as a liveried footman.

Actually, she decided, the clothes rather suited her, the high-collared jacket and cravat disguising her lack of neck and less than imposing chin, the pantaloons and boots suiting her stocky build far better than flowing skirts and deep décolletage. Too bad she couldn't make a practice of it, although why it should matter . . .

Agatha turned away from the glass and put her self-pitying thoughts aside. Amberson had written that he would be returning to England at the next opportunity and intended to question Mr. Turner. A packet boat had docked last night, and Amberson was not the sort to waste time. She could not allow him to be in the same house with George without her protection.

She knew Pierce was assiduous in looking out for his beloved, but there was something about Amberson that delighted in separating couples and afflicting the gullible and trusting. Agatha was not trusting. Nobody, ever since her dear papa's death, had succeeded in convincing her that trusting him was a sensible idea, nobody except George. And it was he who needed protection now.

"Och, madam, yer nivir goin' oot like that," Ferguson said as she tramped down the stairs.

"Just going over to Park Lane," Agatha said. "Safer like this."

"Safer to stay at home like a decent lass," Ferguson muttered, but only after she was halfway down the street. Ferguson knew his mistress better than to contradict her to her face. Would have made a good Scotswoman, Miss Gatling. He hoped he wouldn't have to see her shackled to that Irish-looking git, Lord David Pierce, but he rather suspected it was too late. Not really a bad sort, Pierce. Just not man enough for Miss Gatling.

MELFORD AND GEOFFREY AMBERSON gave up on finding Lord Isham or a hackney in the chaos outside the Houses of Parliament and decided to walk. "My father probably didn't attend today," Melford said. "Says he's not going to waste his few remaining years nodding off to a lot of long-winded speeches and warming a hard bench when he can put his bum to better use. Sorry, but you know how Isham always tries to shock."

Amberson merely shrugged and looked amused.

"As for our other business, we can put it off. One day more or less won't make a difference."

"Sorry, Melford," Amberson said. "Can't agree with you. We have been given a rare gift, a perfect opportunity, with all the attention focused elsewhere. You're welcome to leave me to it, however, if it's not to your taste."

"I suppose you know that's the sure and certain way of keeping me involved," Melford said, and acknowledged Amberson's satisfied smirk in glum silence.

Once out of the milling throngs of Westminster, they were able to hire a hackney for the rest of the drive to Park Lane. The man on the door at the Brotherhood, never having set eyes on Melford and uncertain of Amberson's membership status, took their cards and made them wait in the vestibule, although not for long. "Forgive the delay, my lord, sir," he apologized as he bowed them in. "Can't be too careful."

"Absolutely right," Amberson said. "And the next time you receive unknown visitors, no matter how exalted they appear, do not, I repeat, do not let them inside the door until you are sure of them. Understand?"

The man nodded, a sick expression on his face. He remembered Amberson now, from several months back. Sort of man who looked perfectly harmless from a distance but close-up had the cold eyes and flat demeanor of a murderer—or worse. "Yes, sir," he said. "Won't happen again, sir."

"Quite a handsome piece of property you have here," Melford said as they ascended the stairs to the first floor. "Would fetch quite a sum on the market."

"Yes," Amberson said. "One must agree your father and Archbold were most perspicacious."

"My mother, really," Melford said. "She's the one with the head for business."

Ensconced in comfortable leather chairs and offered a friendly drink, the two men were welcomed with surprise and caution by those few members who chose to while away a sleepy afternoon in a clubroom parlor instead of partaking of more active exercise outdoors—or upstairs. Monkton gave Melford a challenging look from his seat at the card table. "Decided to follow in your father's footsteps at last?" he said. "Oughtn't to reject it without trying it once."

Melford felt himself blushing, a humiliating experience for a man almost fifty, but told himself it was a hazard of being Isham's son. "Actually, Monkton," he said, keeping his voice level, "I did try it once. Thirty years ago, my eighteenth birthday. My father arranged a night of celebration for me and a friend—a private room and a select company for us to choose from if we wished."

"Oh, how divine," Monkton said. "And you were not tempted to make a practice of it after so enticing an introduction?"

"Not really," Melford said. "As Voltaire remarked in a similar situation, once is a philosopher, twice is a sodomite. I was content to remain a philosopher."

The others clapped and laughed, pleased at the diplomatic phrasing of the rejection. Melford was a gentleman, their founder's true son, even if he could not share their disposition in all ways.

Pierce strolled into the parlor and stopped in the doorway. "Melford! We are honored indeed. And Amberson. Haven't seen you in ages. What brings you here?" He coughed and reddened. "Sorry, old man. Wasn't thinking."

"Hullo, Pierce," Amberson answered, a hint of mirth in his bland voice that matched his look of a quiet, ineffectual man of indeterminate age, with a soft body and receding blond hair. "As a matter of fact, your question is not at all misplaced. It is, alas, duty rather than pleasure that brings me here. Although, in this case, there is the slight possibility that the two pursuits may be related."

Melford shuddered inwardly. Amberson, although closer in age to Carrington and most of the others here, held an even more shadowy government position than Melford's and with greater latitude of operation. At any given moment he might be engaged on either side of the Channel, and it was often noted by some of the more alert ministers that when one thought him in England, that was when he was most likely to be sitting in on one of Wellington's staff meetings, and when one was certain he was in the Peninsula he would just as often show up at Almack's, or riding in Hyde Park, or ruining some incautious young hothead at faro or dice at White's or Brooks'. He had few acknowledged friends; those who worked with him knew that his tastes ran to the questionable and disreputable, and that he enjoyed interrogations of recalcitrant subjects, the bigger and tougher the greater his pleasure in breaking them, and all without any overt use of force. It was rare for Amberson to show himself so openly, and Melford could only conclude that this Turner was a bigger fish than his talk with Carrington had led him to suspect.

"I suppose you haven't yet heard the news," Melford said, giving one last try at putting off the inevitable. "Perhaps you'd like us to come back tomorrow."

"What news?" Verney said. "Your play, Monkton."

"About Perceval," Melford said.

"Who?" Monkton said. "Piquet." He laid down his hand. "That's it, Verney. Nothing left but your drawers. Not that we haven't seen it all before, but rules are rules."

"Spencer Perceval," Amberson said. "The prime minister."

Verney stood up and began a slow peel of his tight underwear. Few of the men lounging recumbent in the capacious chairs and sofas even bothered to sit up; Melford flushed and averted his gaze, but Amberson stared, a furtive smile changing his smooth, carefully maintained features from insipid to distinctly sinister.

"What about the prime minister?" Monkton asked.

"I say," Verney said. "Least you can do is not talk politics when a fellow's baring his soul."

"That what the fashionable world's calling it now?" Pierce said. "Might want to do some serious soul-searching myself," he added, to perfunctory laughter. "And since when do you care about politics, Monkton?"

"Since the so very discreet and mysterious Mr. Amberson

deigned to visit," Monkton said, sidling over to the man. "Been so long since we've seen you, we were beginning to wonder if you'd had a change of heart—or do I mean soul?"

"In your case, Monkton," Amberson said, "neither one." He put one finger under Monkton's chin, like a customer examining the goods at a fancy brothel. "No, definitely heartless and soulless."

"In that case, exactly up your street, I should think," Monkton said, knocking the hand away. "One of these days I might surprise you, Geoffrey."

"And Prinny might lose two stone this year," Amberson said. "But I wouldn't wager on it. Which reminds me, how's our friend Carrington?"

"Don't remind us," Pierce said.

"What about the prime minister?" Verney said, since no one seemed to be looking at him anymore.

"Assassinated," Melford said. "Thought you might have heard."

"When? How?" This news made the others sit up and take notice.

"An hour or so ago," Amberson said. "Shot. One bullet, apparently straight to the heart, speaking of hearts."

"But who?"

"Man named Bellingham," Melford said, and was startled by the chorus of groans and outright sobs all around. "You know him?"

"We know *of* him, of course," Verney said. "Wanted to get to know him rather better."

"But why?" Pierce said. "Why would a beautiful young man, with his whole life ahead of him, throw it all away?"

"Heard he wanted to get into politics," Verney said.

"Not the best way to go about it, though, is it?" Monkton said. "Still, Perceval won't be missed. One of those damned evangelicals," Verney said. "Ought to give Bellingham a medal."

"Can't, you know," Pierce said. "Sets a bad precedent, rewarding someone for murder of a public figure. Besides, won't get anyone but duelists and desperadoes to stand for Parliament if we let assassination go unpunished."

"As opposed to the selfless public servants we have now?"

"Oh, you know what I mean."

"Will they hang him?"

"Suppose they'll have to."

"Ain't he exempt from corporal punishment? Benefit of peerage."

"Not for murder. Just means they'll behead him instead."

"Not a peer, you fool. It's a courtesy title. Last time I looked, his father, Coverdale, was very much alive. Fine-looking man for one of his years."

"Are they absolutely certain he did it?"

Amberson winked at Melford. "Suppose we ought to tell them?"

"Seems cruel not to," Melford said. "And yet—"

"Yes, it's such delicious sport, watching the uninformed wallowing in their delusions." Amberson cleared his throat. "Gentlemen, you will be relieved to hear that the man who shot Perceval is not, in fact, the young Lord Bellingham, but a businessman with a grievance, a Mr. John Bellingham. No relation."

"You sure?"

"I say, that is good news. Ought to have said at the start."

"Didn't give us a chance," Amberson said, rising from his seat and setting down his glass. "Well, my fellow philanderers, I suppose I'd better get to it." He did not look unhappy. "Which room is he in? Melford, would you mind? Ought to have a witness."

Melford, looking distinctly unhappy, rose and followed his colleague.

PHILIPPE KNEW HE HAD TO get out of here. It had been too long a respite, lying between sleep and waking, dreaming of his angel. Then those two old devils had brought him to life with a shock. He wished he'd killed them both instead of letting them uncover his shame, but it was too late to be worrying about that. Besides, they were old, near death. What would it matter in a month or so?

The situation wasn't really so bad. Philippe knew a few things now. He knew where his clothes were kept, when mealtimes were, and when his angel, with the prosaic name of Kit, left him alone for a mysterious appointment in a nearby room. And Philippe had obtained two great assets, one of which was going to come in handy very soon—the spare key he had lifted from the pocket of the taller of the devils, the one the goatish little pervert called "Rup." All Philippe had to do was wait and choose his moment.

Down the corridor, in room No. 6, a reading lesson had come to an end. Witherspoon opened the door cautiously, checked the passageway, and sounded the all-clear. Nan and Phyllida tiptoed out, followed by a nonchalant Kit, who worked here and had no need to explain his presence. The two women ran toward the back stairs while Kit stayed behind to lock the empty room.

Just as the women reached the stairway, a slight figure barreled out of room No. 3, one hand concealing something in his pocket, and made a dash for the stairs. All three, looking the other way over their shoulders, collided and recoiled in surprise. Phyllida and Turner eyed each other, faces inches apart. "You!" was expressed in accents of equal loathing from both parties. "What are you doing here?"

Turner, in whose dreams the image of this very face had frequently appeared, sometimes as a shameful but enjoyable visitation, other times as a mocking torment, recovered first. Putting one arm around Phyllida's neck and bringing his other hand out of his pocket, he pressed the barrel of a pistol to her temple. "Do as I say," he said, "and I won't hurt you. Make a noise, any noise at all, and I'll blow your head off."

Phyllida couldn't help it—she sucked in a lungful of air and started to scream.

Turner cocked the pistol's hammer with an unmistakable and ominous click. "I mean it, bitch. Shut up for once in your life." *Unbelievable. Mrs. Carrington, showing her true sluttish nature, wearing indecent attire and infiltrating a men's bawdyhouse. And falling literally right into his arms.*

Witherspoon, Nan, and Kit stood still in their various positions in the corridor, not daring even to breathe. Phyllida gulped and smothered her scream. She was cursed, no doubt about it. Her nemesis, the nightmare that had ruined her marriage, her very life, was not, as she had hoped, dead, or in Newgate, or on his way to New South Wales, but right here, in the club he had threatened to ruin, terrorizing her as before. She tried to twist out of Turner's grasp.

"Stop that," he ordered, jabbing her face with the pistol's barrel.

"Easy, Mr. Ferret," Kit said. "You don't want to shoot nobody."

Turner looked around at the voice of his angel. The desires warred within him—murder and vengeance for the corrupt, deceitful harlot who had almost destroyed him, affection and gratitude for the good angel who had saved him. "No," he agreed. "Don't want to waste a bullet on a whore, a stinking sewer overflowing with men's lustful emissions."

Witherspoon crept closer. "How dare you speak so of a lady?" he said. His voice squeaked; to his fury, he was reminded of that terrified, abused twelve-year-old boy he had once been. He forced himself to breathe, and lowered his voice. "If you must have a captive, take someone of your own sex."

"That lets you out, you simpering little girl," Turner said. "Better a genuine Fanny Laycock than something neither fish nor fowl."

"He's more of a man than you are," Phyllida said. Her right hand, the one Turner couldn't see, inched along the seam of her breeches, feeling for what she hoped and prayed was where she remembered it. "You're nothing but a sneaking, spying rat, a coward who attacks women—"

"Shut. Up." Turner tightened his grip on the gun and the others held their breath. He looked from one to the other, the demon and the seraph, the serpent and the savior. *An easy choice. Who would want to spend eternity with this shrew?* "Kit," he whispered. "Kit, come with me."

"Don't you touch him," Nan said. "You filthy, cocksucking—"

Turner prodded Phyllida's face again with the pistol. "Tell your tommy girlfriend to be quiet," he said, "or I'll put this between your legs and let loose, just the way you want it."

Kit put his hand on Nan's arm, silencing her. "If I come wif you," he said, "you'll let Mrs. Carrington go?"

"If that is your pleasure, *mon ange*," Turner said. *His angel was calling to him. It was his destiny to be saved, after all. He could free himself from the woman's hellish dominion, and he and his angel could fly away to paradise. All he had to do was . . . but the pistol had only the one shot* . . . He battled the strange fog in his mind that made every minor decision arduous.

Phyllida felt the man's tension through the arm around her neck, the deep-seated vibrations like a heavy pot on the verge of boiling. He was mad, about to lose all control. "Don't, Kit," she said. "You can't trust him." She found the pin that held the breeches closed, pulled it out, and jabbed it into Turner's hand. He screamed and jerked his hand away.

Phyllida fell to the floor, scrambling on hands and knees. Witherspoon lifted her up and held her, feeling an almost guilty pleasure as she trembled in his arms.

Turner stalked toward the terrified, huddled group, holding the gun in outstretched arms. "I ought to shoot one of you now," he said, hating the way his voice wobbled in his rage. "But I must not lose sight of my purpose. Kit, my angel, will you come with me?"

Kit squared his shoulders and approached, never taking his eyes off Turner, but murmuring to Nan. "Don'tcha worry, love. 'E won't 'urt me. 'Im 'n' me's old friends, ain't we, Mr. Weasel?"

"Philippe," Turner said. "My name is Philippe."

"Right then, Philip," Kit said. He submitted to Turner's arm around his neck and the gun barrel at his cheek, all the while making subtle motions with his hand behind his back to indicate the others should move away. "Where we off to, Philip Ferret?"

"Where does this stairway lead, Kit?"

"Park Lane."

"Excellent," Turner said. "Let us enjoy a stroll in Hyde Park, my angel."

MELFORD AND AMBERSON HAD JUST reached the stairs when two ragamuffin boys came pounding down, screaming in high-pitched voices, followed by a miserable George Witherspoon.

"He's scarpered!" "He has a pistol!" "He's got Kit!" "You got to help him!"

Nan, louder even than her mistress, ran to Pierce, the one she recognized from seeing him as a visitor at Grosvenor Square. "Please, sir. You got to help him."

Pierce raised his quizzing glass at the shrill tones while Melford looked taken aback and Amberson seized the hand of the bigger boy, who twisted and fought and tried to get loose. "Hold still, boy," Amberson said in his sibilant voice.

Phyllida knew when it was hopeless to struggle and stood motionless, hanging her head, trying not to breathe. Amberson reached down and forced her head up with his other hand. "Most interesting," he said. "I have the feeling I've seen you somewhere before."

"You leave her be, mister," Nan said, recognized her misplaced pronoun too late, and covered her mouth.

Amberson laughed, plucked off the cap, and watched with the air of one proving a complicated mathematical formula as the long brown curls came tumbling down. He snapped his fingers. "Drury Lane," he said, his voice plummy with satisfaction. "*Romeo and Juliet.* That was quite an entrance you made then, but I think this one has upstaged it."

Pierce, doubting his eyes but unable to deny the evidence, said in outraged tones, "Mrs. Carrington?" He turned to his lover. "George. What is the meaning of this?"

Witherspoon looked as if he was going to cry. "I'm sorry, Davey. I wanted to learn to read better. I wanted you to be proud of me."

"And dressing Mrs. Carrington in that revolting and inappropriate costume and sneaking her in here where she does not belong and has no right to be was to make me proud?"

Phyllida took a deep breath to steady herself, wrenched herself out of the sinister man's hold, and said, "Please, everybody. Pay attention. Mr. Turner has escaped. He has a pistol. I assume it's loaded. He has taken Kit hostage and is heading for the park by way of the back entrance."

"Well, well," Amberson said. "A woman with a man's head on her shoulders. Unfortunately the clothes don't suit you in the least." He looked up. "You heard Mrs. Carrington. We'd better snap to it." He rang for footmen, directing them to the rear of the building and to scout the park. He ran up to Turner's room, ascertained the facts of his recent occupation and more recent escape, ran downstairs again, light on his feet for so sedentary a figure, and pulled a far more modern pistol from the deep inner pocket of his coat. From the worn look of the grip, it appeared the pistol had seen regular and frequent use.

"Pierce, you stay here in case there's news and to coordinate our actions." Amberson looked at Nan. "A rather better impersonation," he remarked. "But not impenetrable to the trained eye." He pocketed the pistol, took out a small pad and a pencil, scribbled a note, tore off the sheet, and handed it to Nan. "You, wench. Find Mr. Carrington and give him this. And make sure he brings his pistols. Loaded. Melford, if you please, and Witherspoon, come with me." He grabbed Witherspoon by the hand and towed him along to the back entrance.

"Amberson," an authoritative voice called from the direction he was heading. "Let George go."

Amberson peered ahead to the shadowed gloom of the rear passage. All he could see was a nondescript sort of figure—a groom or a post boy—yet the voice sounded almost feminine. "Who the devil are you?" he asked.

"Aggie?" Witherspoon said. "Oh, Aggie, I'm so glad you came. Mr. Turner has escaped, and he has a gun and—"

"Miss Gatling?" Amberson had placed the voice, if not the figure. "I suppose, as it made so little impression on Mrs. Carrington, it would be useless to point out that this is no place for a lady." He dropped Witherspoon's hand and moved a prudent distance away.

"As you have a more serious situation here than organizing a dinner party or a country dance," Miss Gatling said, "yes, it would seem rather a waste of time."

Amberson turned to Melford. "Is it my imagination, or was this once a gentlemen's establishment? Nothing but tommies, flats, and masqueraders these days."

Melford rolled his eyes. "Just be grateful Isham isn't here to see it. His language would blister our ears, not to mention those of the ladies."

"Ladies?" Amberson said. "I don't see any ladies in the vicinity. Do you, Melford?"

Pierce ran down the corridor. "Amberson," he called. "Mr. Witherspoon can be of no assistance."

"It's all right, David," Miss Gatling said. "Mr. Amberson has reconsidered."

"Agatha?" Pierce said, coming closer and staring. "My God, Agatha! What is going on? First Mrs. Carrington, now you." His heart pounded; the blood rushed from his head, then back up again. He felt an embarrassing situation coming on and turned away to hide it. "You really ought not to wear an outfit like that in company, Agatha. People will get the wrong idea."

"And what idea would that be, David?" Miss Gatling said.

"You know, Aggie," Witherspoon said, "those clothes look very becoming. Don't you think so, Davey?"

"Much as I hate to interrupt love's delicate awakening," Amberson murmured, "I'm afraid I must concentrate on more urgent business."

"Your compassion astonishes me," Melford said with rare sarcasm. He looked over to Witherspoon. "You can recognize the man, I take it?"

"Oh yes," Witherspoon said. "Not a distinctive face at all."

"Really, Witherspoon," Melford chided, "try to collect your thoughts. This is important."

"No, no," Amberson said. "It's an excellent point. Little rat has the sort of face that blends in. Very hard to spot if you don't know what you're looking for. Of course, he has a hostage now. Don't know what Carrington was thinking, putting him in the way of so much temptation."

"He wanted to protect Phyllida—Mrs. Carrington," Witherspoon said.

Amberson directed a basilisk stare in Witherspoon's direction. "I see. Meanwhile allowing her to prowl the upstairs bedrooms looking like an overstuffed sausage."

"Let it go, Geoffrey," Melford said. "Carrington's been under quite a strain."

"So it would appear," Amberson said. "I shall have to have a word with him when all this is sorted out." He brushed past Miss Gatling and Pierce as if they weren't there and stalked furiously toward the back entrance.

ISHAM AND ARCHBOLD, IN A shocking state of undress, emerged blinking from their temporary room, No. 5. "What the devil is all that noise?" Archbold said.

"A raid," Isham said with cheerful certainty. "Been saying for fifty years we ought to quarter a troop of musketeers here."

"That's sedition," Archbold said.

Isham shrugged. "Rather go down fighting, take some of the bastards with me. Better than sitting in a locked room, wringing my hands like a woman, waiting to be captured. Although might be exciting to be ravished by a grenadier. Always liked the look of the grenadiers."

"If only you'd shared that aspiration with me before," Archbold said, "I would have had an incentive to serve my country more actively."

They listened to the growing commotion that seemed to be divided between downstairs and outside, with some faint noises from upstairs. "The enemy has infiltrated our defenses," Isham decided. "This is it, Rup. Give me a last kiss for love's sake. Who knows when we'll meet again, in this world or the next?"

Archbold obeyed automatically, too accustomed to Isham's odd moods to make much of it. He almost fell over when the little man, after bestowing a lusty smack on his lips, along with a generous serving of tongue, bellowed in his good ear, "Stand to arms! Enemy inside! Stand to arms! Form in rows of three!"

A footman came running along the corridor. Isham snagged the man's arm. "How many men on the muster rolls?"

The man stood still, thinking. "About twenty, twenty-five, my lord, counting all shifts. Thirty if you count the kitchen staff."

"Enough for seven or eight across," Isham said, nodding dismissal. "Might be able to hold out until relief comes. Hop to it, man." He reached for his pistol, discovered he wasn't wearing a coat, nor a shirt, shoes, or drawers. "Ha! Caught us with our breeches down. But we'll show 'em. Show 'em a well-drilled force of mollies, naked as the day we were born, can defeat a bunch of tight-arsed, sneaking spies any day of the week. STAND TO ARMS!"

He went back inside his room and dressed hurriedly, urging Archbold to follow and fretting that the enemy would be on them at any minute. Archbold had a serious moment of fright when he saw his partner foaming at the mouth, inarticulate sounds sputtering from between rigid lips, his limbs jittering in all directions, until Isham regained the capacity for speech and explained that the left-hand pocket of his coat was missing its pistol.

"Think, Marc," Archbold said, attempting a soothing tone. "When do you last remember having it? This morning? Last night?"

"I don't know. How the hell should I know?"

"Don't you empty your pockets at night?"

"It's the coat I keep here. Told the servants not to touch it."

"Well then," Archbold said. "Not to spoil the perfect love affair, but that little felon of yours, Philippe, probably took it a couple of days ago."

"After I sucked his prick? Damned ungrateful."

"That's what I was trying to tell you," Archbold said. "He's not to be trusted."

"Poor little fellow," Isham said. "Might have needed it for protection. Ought to have asked, that's all. Be glad to lend it to him. Ought to have asked. At least he left me one."

He pulled the pistol from his right pocket, ran out to the corridor again, eyes sparkling, rejuvenated by the return to military life. "The troops are assembling in the drill yard," he said, peering out a window on the landing that overlooked the garden. "Damme but they're a ragtag bunch! Where the devil are their uniforms? And that fellow there don't appear to have a stitch on. But we'll whip 'em into shape, eh, Rup?"

ANDREW READ THE SCRAWL FROM Amberson and swore. "It's fortunate you found me at home."

"Please, sir," Nan said. "You got to help him. He's got Kit."

"Kit?" Andrew said. "Marlowe?" He smiled at Nan's frantic look. "Don't worry. Your Kit has handled worse than that little ferret."

"He's got a gun," Nan said. "Please, sir."

"All right, I'm coming." Andrew sighed, dated the last page—11th May, 1812—and headed upstairs to his strongbox, Nan close on his heels. If it wasn't for being short a secretary, he wouldn't have been at home on such a pleasant afternoon, going over his accounts and his correspondence, when he could have been out riding or at the Brotherhood, with Matthew. Except Matthew was probably busy at his own paperwork. How had having money and position led to this? He shook his head. "If Mrs. Carrington asks, tell her I've gone out, but don't say where or imply that it's anything urgent."

"She knows," Nan muttered.

"What's that?"

"Just hurry, sir. Please."

"Don't see there's much I can do," Andrew said. "Little rat could be halfway to the docks by now, stowed away on the next ship to the continent."

"Said he was going to the park."

"The park?" Andrew said. "Bastard's mad. Stark, staring, raving mad." This was what he got for trying to do a good turn for his friends and for his country. He jogged at a measured pace to save time, not wanting to get winded, mulling over Amberson's instructions. It was never a good idea to obey a man like that blindly. Sort of man who would send you on a forlorn hope with an unloaded musket or lead you over a cliff, all the while making sure to pull up well short of the edge himself. Still, Turner had to be stopped. But even if Amberson wanted Turner dead, Kit should not have to pay with his life.

Nan followed, matching his pace with ease, her breeches and shirt suiting her childlike build and not impeding her movements like the cumbersome skirts. The man on the door, bewildered by the unconventional comings and goings, barely gave her a second glance as she tagged along on Andrew's heels, and let her in without comment. "They're all in the back, sir."

Andrew ran through the entrance and along the passage. He was distracted by a blowsy, sulky boy holding up unbuttoned breeches in one hand, who emerged from a side door and took his arm.

"Thank goodness you came so quickly," Phyllida said. "He didn't go to the park. He must have heard people coming after him. He's gone upstairs instead. To the roof."

"Phyllida?" Andrew said. He stared wildly around, searching for the source of the familiar voice, not believing that the scruffy figure before him could possibly be his feminine little wife. He looked down at the tangled brown curls, noting the swell of bosom beneath the shirt and the luxurious curving hips and rounded belly forced into tight breeches that didn't completely close. He fought the disgust that rose in him like nausea, swallowed several times, trying to master it, and lost the battle. "How dare you?" he shouted. "How dare you prance around in those clothes, showing yourself off like a third-rate actress in an obscene farce?"

"Clothes?" Phyllida screamed at him. "How can you even think about that now?"

Andrew compelled himself to breathe. "You're right. Now is not the time. But later, Phyllida, I will want a thorough explanation for this impropriety. My God, what must everybody think?"

"That you would rather waste time arguing about your wife's clothes than catching a fugitive who may be guilty of treason," Phyllida answered. She tried to keep her voice level and low, but it rose higher and louder with each word. "You brought that weasel in here, the very place he threatened to destroy. You lectured me on discretion, on being careful of your reputation, and then you brought in an informer. Even if you don't care about yourself, what about all your friends? What is the matter with you?"

Andrew felt the shrill words boring into his skull and was unable to catch the meaning beyond the first sentence. "Treason?" he said. "Oh Lord. Melford said he wanted to wait for Amberson. Where are they?"

"On the roof, Andrew. As I said."

"There you are, Carrington." Amberson sauntered in from the back, as calm as if he were at a garden party. "You have something for me, I believe?" He accepted a lumpy parcel from Andrew, pocketed it, and turned to thc rear again, saying over his shoulder, "After you've dealt with this tiresome matter, I'd appreciate it if you could make clear to your wife the nature and practices of a gentlemen's club, especially as regarding the entrance of females, whatever their attire."

ANDREW STARED THROUGH the last rays of the setting sun, sighting on the figures that stood out like haloed angels in a religious tableau. "Ought to shoot now," Pierce said, "while the light has him dazzled."

"Damn it, Pierce," Andrew said. "For once can you allow someone to manage his own business?" He studied the situation for a long minute while the sun crept down over Hyde Park until it was below the level of the opposite rooftops. Turner had his arm around Kit's neck, the barrel of the pistol pressed against the boy's cheek. He was saying things, but too softly for anyone to hear five stories below.

Isham, convinced by the concerted efforts of his son and the members of the club to hold off on his plans for close-order musket drill, watched Andrew with a critical eye. "Don't approve of these sniper johnnies. War ain't a duel. No use pretending it's an affair of honor, but oughtn't to skulk about behind trees picking off the epaulet-men like a pigeon shoot. Should just line up the troops, let the enemy advance within range and then—bam!—open fire, three shots a minute. Blast 'em to kingdom come. Any left alive, run 'em through with the bayonet. Worked in France. Worked in America."

"As a matter of fact, Marc," Archbold said, "didn't work so well over there last time."

"Don't believe it," Isham said. "Must've been the cavalry's fault."

"Hush, Papa," Melford said. "Let Carrington do his job."

"Not your father," Isham said. "Fine boy, but not your father."

Andrew turned his head in exasperation. "My lord," he said. "Do you want this informer and blackmailer to get away and send us all to the pillory or the gallows? Or can you be quiet and let me bring him down?"

"A rat?" Isham said, unable to make out the identity of the sun-skewered, red-lit figure five stories up. "Can't abide a rat." He waved a hand. "Fire when ready, man."

Andrew aimed again, just as Turner jabbed the pistol into Kit's face. "'E says don't shoot," Kit called. "Says if you try anything 'e'll shoot me." He paused for effect. "'E's bluffin'."

Turner jabbed him again, hard enough to make the boy cry out and to struggle, precariously close to the edge.

Andrew adjusted his aim a fraction of an inch and squinted. Behind him, Isham held up his left hand, flourishing a white handkerchief in an elaborate series of moves.

"What the devil are you doing, Marc?" Archbold said.

"Dear me," Amberson murmured. "Haven't seen that since my school days."

"Papa," Melford said, "you mustn't distract Carrington. Very difficult, shooting at that angle, and the sun setting so rapidly."

"Stop scolding, Tony," Isham said. "Thought that little ganymede up there might need encouragement."

"Waving the white flag?" Archbold said. "Don't see how that helps."

"No, it's a different kind of signaling," Amberson said. "Everybody used to know the handkerchief language. Greek, French, top, bottom, manly or girly. Lost now. Only ganymedes, streetwalkers know it—if them."

"I can't believe you don't know it, Rup," Isham said, aghast.

"I was never a dedicated molly like you, my dear," Archbold said. "You were my one and only interest in that direction. Never had to learn that jiggery-pokery."

"Just the pokery, eh?" Isham said. "And damn good at it, too."

"Will you all shut up?" Andrew said without turning his head.

MATTHEW, FAIR BURSTING WITH HIS news, bade the hackney stop and walked the rest of the way. The streets were becoming impassable as the report spread from block to block and people came pouring out to gossip and speculate and hear the latest rumors. He pushed through the crowds—even Piccadilly was coming to resemble a Bartholomew Fair—and lit his evening cigar from the twist of an obliging lamplighter. He had promised Andrew to give up the vice and he had kept his vow, all except this one treasured moment, the reward after a day's work, the invigorating rush of nicotine that left him primed for the greater pleasures ahead. He was always careful to gargle and brush his teeth with mint before meeting Andrew; there was little danger of being detected.

He reached Park Lane and walked up the steps. "Have you heard?" he asked the man on the door.

"They're in the garden, sir," the man said. He looked worried, distracted, as did everybody.

"Out in back?" Matthew asked, surprised. "Think they'd be in the street."

"Can't see the roof from there," the man said.

Matthew decided not to pursue it further. Strange events made people act strange, and England hadn't seen something like this—well, since the Civil Wars, more than a hundred and fifty years ago. And even that had had a whitewash of legality laid over it. He walked through the house and into the garden, surprised by the large group, Melford and the sinister Amberson, Isham and Archbold, Pierce and Witherspoon, Monkton and Verney—naked, of course—and most of the servants, including two shabby-looking boys and a seedy groom, all staring up.

"Guess you heard—" Matthew said.

"Careful, man." "Quiet." He was shushed on all sides.

Matthew held back what he had been about to say, and followed everybody's pointing fingers. There was Andrew, his dueling pistol in his hand, arm outstretched, aiming, not straight ahead but angled up, toward the roof. The setting sun had just gone down behind him and the stark figures were outlined now in gray and black. The tail end of glorious rainbow colors, fading fast, spread out behind Andrew in a contrast of light and dark, like one of those talked-about new paintings of storms at sea and hurricanes.

Matthew looked more closely at the figures on the roof. Damn it, it was Turner and the pretty boy that Andrew had pressured into looking after him. Matthew had known from the start that wasn't a good idea, but it wasn't his call to make. He took a final puff on his cigar, preparing to throw away the butt, just as a gust of wind picked up the smoke and hurled it all in one compact clump directly at Andrew's elegant head, tilted slightly to the side, one eye nearly closed as he prepared to squeeze the trigger.

The smoke dealt Andrew a blow like a roundhouse punch. He blinked, staggered, coughed, steadied himself, realigned his arm, aimed, and fired.

Turner jerked and dropped his weapon. The gun fell clattering down the slope of the roof, firing its one round as it went, luckily pointing up and out in the direction of the park. Kit clung to the eaves as the wounded man, screaming in a thin voice, cartwheeling like a tumbler, arms outstretched, toppled over the edge and landed in the balcony of the large second-story bedroom known as the honeymoon suite.

Andrew, his face pasty gray, leaned over, vomited into a flower bed, and fainted.

THE VOICES CAME THROUGH THE haze, distant at first, then sharper. "Bellingham? The beautiful Bellingham? I don't believe it. I haven't had a chance to paint him yet."

"No, no, my dear. Someone else."

"Better forget it, Pierce. Take too long to straighten it out." *Verney's voice.*

"Try not to upset yourself, George, dear. David will explain it to you later." *Agatha Gatling. How odd. Andrew could have sworn he was at the Brotherhood.*

"But they said Bellingham. I heard it distinctly. And no one's even won the wager."

"Why don't you try?" *Monkton, his voice rich with malice.* "You could visit him in gaol, give him some comfort before he swings."

"I warn you, Monkton." *Pierce, spoiling for a fight as usual.* "Stop teasing George or I'll land you in gaol where you'll be able to give as much comfort as a French whore in a Russian barrack." He almost choked as he remembered Miss Gatling's presence, while Monkton laughed at his discomfiture.

Andrew opened his eyes as the futile conversations roiled above him. It was dusk, the twilit sky a velvety shade of blue. The earth was soft under his back, still warm from the mild spring day. "Did I kill him?" he asked. "I couldn't see. What happened?"

"You fainted," Phyllida said. She knelt beside him, her hair tumbling over her shoulders, her breasts straining against the thin cloth of her strange costume. She undid Andrew's cravat and opened his shirt, gasping in surprise at the profusion of black hair that was revealed and entwining her fingers in it, making him shiver with pleasure. "That was very heroic, but you ought to have warned me that Mr. Turner was here."

"I'm sorry, my love," Andrew whispered. "I didn't want to worry you."

"But why didn't you send him to gaol?"

Andrew glanced up, moving only his eyes, attempting to make out faces in the gloom. "Didn't have much choice in the matter." He winked and squeezed her hand. "And I never thought you'd be so hungry for cock that you'd sneak in here."

Phyllida squinted, trying to read his expression. "What did you say?"

Andrew ignored the stabbing pain in order to turn his head a fraction of an inch. "I ought to have guessed that an eager little slut like you would go to any lengths to satisfy the itch between her legs."

Phyllida felt tears of joy forming in her eyes. "Foulmouthed beast," she said, stroking his cheek. "Let Mr. Stevens help you into the house."

"Where's Matthew?"

"Here I am, love," Matthew said. "I'm that sorry for everything. You ought to have told me."

"I did tell you," Andrew said, pointing to the open neck of

his shirt and the tuft of hair. "I kept my end of the bargain."

"Carrington awake?" Stevens came bustling over. "Good. Somebody help me get him into bed."

Matthew stepped forward and bent down.

"Not you," Stevens said. "Sorry, Thornby, but you reek of cigars, which is probably what set Carrington off in the first place."

"I say, Carrington," Witherspoon said. "Heard the news? The beautiful Bellingham shot the prime minister."

"Don't worry," Pierce said. "Not our Bellingham. A different man."

"Funny his being named Bellingham, though," Witherspoon said. "Think someone should call on him just to make sure?"

"This is all very interesting," Phyllida said, "but are you going to let Mr. Carrington lie here all night?"

"I can walk," Andrew said, trying to sit up, feeling his gorge rise, and falling back with a groan.

"So I see," Phyllida murmured.

"I'll be all right," he said. "Just so long as you don't take up cigars to go with the breeches. When we get inside, wench, you will remove those repellent garments or I will do it myself." He tried to snap his fingers but found the effort too great and let his hand fall to his side.

Phyllida laughed to disguise her real emotion—the first, liberating ripples of the cessation of constant low-level pain. "Brute," she whispered. "Fiend."

"Mrs. Carrington!" Stevens was shocked by the words he heard as he and a footman hoisted Carrington to his feet. "Now is not the time for reproaches. Your husband needs gentle, wifely attention."

"Mrs. Carrington," Andrew said, "was merely expressing her love in our own subtle idiom."

"What an ugly boy," Isham said, peering through the gloom at the odd figure clutching its drooping breeches and scurrying after Andrew. "Fat arse, tits like a woman. Know it's hard to hire decent help in a place like this, but still, ought to be able to do better than that."

"I rather fancy," Archbold said, "that it is a woman. Carrington's wife, you know."

"What? Can't have that, can't have that," Isham said. "Respectable club. Don't like to chew a man out when he's wounded in the course of duty, but once he's on his feet again something will have to be said."

"Yes, my love," Archbold said. "Why don't we go inside?"

"Coming in?" Pierce said to Matthew as the others filed through the French windows.

"Not yet," Matthew said. "Might as well enjoy a last cigar."

THEY FOUND TURNER, A HUDDLED shape of bent limbs, lying in a pool of blood on the balcony of the honeymoon suite. Amberson, always the first to arrive at any scene of accident or mayhem, stood staring down, his face impassive. Kit, only slightly the worse for wear, with no more than a few cuts and scrapes, watched from a corner. Nan, so small and unobtrusive she had crept in through the crowd unnoticed, stood protectively by Kit's side. The others, shooed from Andrew's room by a suddenly fierce Phyllida, looked on from the suite's windows, Isham and Archbold in the forefront.

Amberson bent over the body, extended his hand, and pulled a long rope of gleaming red stones from Turner's inside pocket. "Just as I suspected," he said. "The Carrington rubies. Defense of property. Justifiable homicide."

"Can't fool me with that conjuring trick," Isham said. "Next you'll have me believe you've found a shilling in my ear. Humbug."

Melford went to Isham, nodded significantly to Archbold, and tried to lead the little old man from the room. "Come on, Papa," he said. "I think it's time you two went home."

"Ain't really your father, you know," Isham said. "Rup got in ahead of me with your mother." He smiled mistily up at the tall old man, companion of fifty years.

Melford rolled his eyes. "Yes, yes," he said in his ministerial voice, repeating the lines of a recurring conversation. "I know. But you gave me your name, treated me like your own. You're my father in every sense that matters."

"Don't feed me that pap," Isham said, pulling his arm free. "I may be old but I'm not senile. If you were my flesh and blood I'd have drowned you in the baptismal font. Tainted lineage, back three generations. Won't pass that on."

"And what about Anne?" Melford asked, despite his better instincts.

"Oh, she's a girl," Isham said of his middle-aged daughter, happily awaiting the birth of her second grandchild. "Don't affect girls."

A faint groan emerged from the body. "Crikey! 'E's alive," Kit informed the startled group.

Stevens, summoned from Andrew's bedside, knelt for a long time over Turner, calling for light to be brought rather than taking the risk of moving him. "Head wound's just a graze. Bleeds like a pig but looks worse than it is." He stood up with a grunt and pressed his palms against his tired back. "As for the rest—broken collarbone, broken ankle. And, of course, another concussion, just when he was recovering from the first one. The body will mend, but I doubt he'll ever regain his full faculties."

Amberson swore under his breath. "Thought Carrington could manage better than that."

"Carrington? What do you— Oh, the shot," Stevens said. "Neatest bit of shooting I ever saw. Bullet just parted his hair. An inch either way and he'd be dead or . . . untouched. And when you consider how close Turner was to the boy—"

"Poor little Philippe," Isham said. "Just because Carrington decides to get married, oughtn't to end his *amours* like an Oriental despot."

"Now listen to me, Papa," Melford said. "I know, I know, not my father. But listen. 'Poor little Philippe' was not what you think, and certainly no innocent. He was an agent, a spy for the French—"

"Don't believe it," Isham said. "Besides, what could he possibly learn over here?"

"He claimed to have obtained the key to the *grand chiffre*, or Great Paris Cipher—Napoleon's military code."

Isham stared, uncomprehending. "What about those lash marks, then? Ask your nasty boyfriend Amberson about that."

Melford shrugged, grimacing an apology at Amberson.

"I'm flattered," Amberson said, glad of the distraction. "And that's an excellent question, my lord. The man's an American of French ancestry, Philippe Tournière. And, apparently, a former slave. Thornby was the one who put me on to that."

"A slave?" Isham said. "You mean a black? Are you blind? Fellow's lighter than Rup here—at least, before he went gray. Makes Carrington look positively Ethiopian."

"But you see," Melford said, "in America—"

"America?" Isham said. "Thought you said he was French. Anyway, sounded like he was from the Midlands."

"There is a similarity in accent," Amberson said. "But Turner is from New Orleans or thereabouts. Louisiana, you know. Large French population."

"As I was saying," Melford continued, "in parts of America, if a man has but one African great-grandparent on the maternal side, and if it can be proven, he's a black by law and can be treated as a slave."

"Ridiculous," Stevens muttered. "No basis for that in science."

"In other words," Archbold remarked, "if his coloring were darker it would be acceptable to flay him like a beast? And just where would you draw the line? At me? At Carrington?"

"Not what I meant at all," Stevens said, flushing. "Look far enough back in anybody's family tree and you'll find a black sheep."

"Pun intended?" Melford asked.

"All I mean is," Stevens said, "making distinctions between people based on fourth-generation heredity is absurd."

"That's it, then," Melford said. "The entire nobility of England, and most of the gentry, had better give up its titles and its lands and hand the government over to Kit here and his ilk."

Kit, hearing his name, looked up in alarm. "I tried to keep an eye on 'im, sir. Only took an hour off for a reading lesson now an' then."

"He should not have been left alone, even for an hour," Stevens said. "And the entire burden of his care should not have been put on a boy."

"Don't worry, boy," Amberson said. "It's not your fault. Little rat had to be disposed of somehow, but the best planning in the world can't anticipate everything. Wish I could claim he was the one who shot the PM and see him safely hanged, but since they already caught the real criminal . . . Remind me to have a word with Thornby before I leave, would you, Melford?"

"That'll be the day," Melford said, "when you need reminding."

"I take it you, ah, obtained the information you were seeking?" Archbold said.

"That's the worst of it," Amberson said. "He never did produce the key to the cipher, nor did he betray any accomplices, assuming he had either. If we can't force or trick the truth out of him, best to kill him and have done with it, but instead we're left with the worst of all possibilities—alive but useless." He saw the others eyeing him like mice mesmerized by a cobra, and cleared his throat. Amberson was discovering a strange new desire to talk and unburden himself, and did his best to strangle the monster at birth. "Getting back to the matter at hand, we think this Turner, or Tournière, was passing for white until his ancestry was discovered and he was subjected to the rough justice of the plantation, thus leading to his desire to emigrate and betray his former countrymen. Not the French, but the Americans."

"North America," Isham said, shaking his head and looking solemn. "Most savage place on earth. What do you say to that?"

"I say," Archbold said, "that we're in no position to throw stones, living as we do with the glass houses of our own plantations in the West Indies."

"But how does giving us the cipher hurt the Americans?" Pierce was emboldened to ask from the front of the until now silent crowd.

"Only on the principle that the enemy of my enemy is my friend," Melford said. "If he helps us in our war against the French, and if we're soon to be at war with America too, then he has helped America's enemy."

"Not to mention the rather significant fact that France and America have been allies over the past forty years," Amberson said, "although sometimes disguised under the name of 'neutrality.'"

Isham turned to Amberson and appeared to recognize him for the first time. "I know you. Sort of man that does the government's dirty work. Because you enjoy it, eh? I'm not leaving Philippe to these torturers and spies. Yes, Tony, that means you, too. Taking him home with us."

"My lord," Stevens said, "the man is in no condition to be moved, other than to a bed in this house."

"Then we'll stay here," Isham said. "You, boy." He waved Kit over. "Fine-looking young rascal. You the one looking after Philippe? Good, good. Mind staying on the job a little longer?"

Kit considered carefully before answering. "I'll be 'appy to go on looking after Mr. Philip, my lord. I've grown that fond of 'im, an' 'e can't do me no 'arm now. *And* I'll need a rise in pay. Gettin' married." He held Nan's hand, drawing her forward.

"Married?" Isham said. "A pretty young fellow like you? Nonsense."

"Why not?" Kit said. "You did, my lord. An' I'd stake my left nut you was as pretty as me."

"Ha!" Isham said, more pleased than affronted. "Cheeky little devil. All the beauties are. Know they can get away with it." He studied Nan briefly and frowned, looking up to Archbold and speaking in the loud whisper of the partly deaf. "Don't like to say anything to the boy, but his friend don't appear to have any equipment. Flat as a girl."

"Yes, Marc," Archbold said. "That appeared to be the substance of the conversation. Marrying a woman, you see."

"A woman? What the bloody hell is wrong with young fellows these days? First Mrs. Carrington, now this— What d'ye say your name is, girl?" Nan wisely declined to answer, stepping back behind Kit while Isham continued to rage. "Didn't start this club just to have it turned into another damned brothel. Need a place for men's men. Men like us. Man wants to take up with women, none of my business. Lots of decent fellows seem to go in for that, even Rup here. Not for me to judge. Difference is, we had standards in my day. Knew not to bring women into a molly house. Don't want to wake up, find yourself sharing a bed with somebody's wife—or your own."

"Perish the thought," Archbold said. "It's been an unusual day, Marc. I don't imagine we'll have to worry about seeing females in here after tonight."

Isham calmed at the familiar voice and touch. His color lightened from the dangerous dark red as he appeared to become reconciled to the immorality of modern society. "Very well, boy," he said to Kit. "Suit yourself." He looked up at his lover. "Well, Rup, how about it? Never did have a proper honeymoon. Didn't go in for such folderol when we were married."

"And what will I tell Mama?" Melford asked, a reluctant grin spreading despite his efforts to contain it.

"Tell Bella Rup and I are tying the knot tonight, but she's welcome to join us tomorrow for a romp. If everybody else is bringing his wife here, might as well bring mine."

"The worst of it is," Melford confided to Amberson as they strolled back to Westminster, "if I were to mention so improper a suggestion to my mother, she'd probably thank me for the message and be packed and moving into the Brotherhood first thing in the morning."

"A different generation," Amberson said. "My parents were much the same."

"I STILL DON'T UNDERSTAND," WITHERSPOON complained as they trooped downstairs. "Mr. Turner is African? He doesn't look it. I would like to paint a black! Wonderful change of palette."

"French, mostly, from what I could gather," Pierce said. "Hard to tell with these Americans. All mongrels."

"As if we're so pure," Miss Gatling said. "Most of us are a mix."

"Speak for yourself," Monkton said, passing them on the stairs. "I'll have you know my family is unadulterated blue-blooded rotter, back twelve generations."

"What's that?" Witherspoon said. "German?"

"A joke," Miss Gatling said. "And very well put, Monkton."

"You're too kind," Monkton murmured. "What worries me is this unidentified accomplice. Could be one of us, for all anyone knows."

"That's absurd," Pierce said. "We've known each other for years."

"Except this Thornby," Monkton said. "Nobody even heard of him before a month or two ago. Then he suddenly appears—from America, I might add—makes his move on Carrington, no less, and *voilà*—all this trouble starts."

"I don't believe it," Witherspoon said. "Thornby is one of the nicest fellows I've ever met."

"I agree," Verney said. "And we all know the sort of man Carrington goes for. Look at Harry Swain. Doesn't mean there's anything sinister in their getting together."

"I don't like to speak ill of a fellow behind his back," Pierce said, "but we were here, George and I, when Carrington brought Turner into the club, after he was injured the first time. I had the distinct impression it was at Thornby's suggestion."

"What I don't follow," Monkton said, "is why, if Turner, or

Tournière, or whatever his name is, was a French agent, Carrington brought him here at all."

"Because he attacked Mrs. Carrington," Pierce said in a low voice.

"Attacked?" Verney said, pushing forward, oblivious to Miss Gatling's blushes and stares. "You mean forced? But that's dreadful. No wonder Carrington wanted to kill him. Surprised he didn't do it earlier."

Pierce shook his head in Miss Gatling's direction. "Not the time and place. But not that bad."

"I'm relieved to hear it." Verney studied the unknown figure. "I say, Pierce. Who's your handsome friend? Aren't you going to introduce us? Although I do feel we've met somewhere before." He smiled into Miss Gatling's mortified countenance, unconsciously flexing his muscles and showing off his physique. "Rather shy, isn't he?"

Witherspoon, unable to contain himself, broke into whoops of laughter. "It's Aggie! My sister. Told you you looked good in those clothes!"

Verney, thoroughly routed, covered himself with his hands and fled to the safety of his room, too distraught to notice Matthew standing in the shadows.

"Miss Gatling," Monkton said, "you deserve some sort of reward. You have accomplished what nobody else has been able to do in over a dozen years—convince Sir Frederick Verney to keep his clothes on."

MATTHEW, HAVING METICULOUSLY WASHED, INCLUDING his hair, and chewing mint leaves, found Andrew asleep in room No. 6. Phyllida, still dressed in shirt and breeches, sat nodding in a chair beside the bed.

"May I come in?" Matthew whispered. "Stevens explained about the migraines. I'm quite clean."

"Of course." Phyllida looked up and smiled. "I'll leave you two alone."

"No need." Matthew pulled up another chair. "Just wanted to see he was safe. Lot of strange doings today, and stranger talk." He could have bitten his tongue as he saw her eyes widen and her complexion blanch. "Nothing for you to worry about. Somebody shot the prime minister."

"I heard," Phyllida said. "They can't think anybody in the Brotherhood had anything to do with it. Is that why that sinister man with the dead eyes was here?"

"Amberson," Matthew said. "What an excellent description. In a way, yes. He was hoping to conduct his foul business quietly and unnoticed, under cover of darkness, while all the attention was focused elsewhere."

"You're laughing at me."

"Not really. Geoffrey Amberson works for the government. But he's also a member of the Brotherhood. I think he took advantage of a timely concurrence of events, but that's all it was—coincidence."

"The government? You mean—an agent? A spy?"

"In plain English, yes."

"I know he came specifically to see Mr. Turner. And he wanted Andrew to kill him." She looked to the door and shuddered. "It's probably silly, but I can't help feeling that that Mr. Amberson could creep in here and— And— Do something to Andrew. Mr. Stevens said he was terribly angry when they discovered Mr. Turner wasn't dead after all."

"Mrs. Carrington. Phyllida," Matthew said. "You're tired and upset. Nothing can happen to Andrew here. He's perfectly safe."

"But you were worried, too. You said so when you came in."

Nothing like a woman for fastening onto an inconvenient truth and refusing to let go. Worse than a terrier with a rat. "I love him, as you do," he said. "It's only natural to be concerned, after seeing him faint like that. Doesn't mean there's anything real to be afraid of."

"Please, Matthew. You must tell me. What was Andrew involved in?"

"Andrew? Very little. It was Turner who was—"

"Just tell me, Matthew. Please."

"Ciphers, apparently. French military ciphers, coded messages using numbers."

Phyllida sat back with an odd sense of relief. "That's what was wrong with the accounts books. I should have known Andrew wouldn't have been fooled by simple embezzlement. Still, I wish he had killed Mr. Turner. It would be one worry off my mind."

"Nay, lass." Matthew was shocked, as so often, by the outspoken Mrs. Carrington. "You wouldn't wish that on your husband, having to flee the country."

"But if it was justified," she said. "If Mr. Turner was spying and betraying military secrets . . ."

"From what I understand," Matthew said, "Turner had very little to betray. I think he was all bark and no bite."

"No," Phyllida said. "He could bite—and wound. I just— I wish— If I'd known he was here I would have taken one of Andrew's pistols and shot him myself." She spoke louder than she intended, gasped, lowered her head, and watched as two large tears dripped onto the coarse fabric of her breeches, one on each knee, leaving two large stains.

Matthew had a moment of revelation, understanding, as he

should have long before, just what crime Turner had committed that could make a lady like Phyllida want to kill him. Not just striking her, but worse. Matthew did the only thing he could. He put his arm around her shoulders and drew her close until her head was resting on his broad chest.

Phyllida knew she should resist the impropriety, but the feel of the warm, fresh-smelling masculine flesh, the strong arms holding her so gently, and the way he stroked her hair, was too great a solace to reject. She sniffed, tried to hold back, and let loose with all the tears she had thought long since spent in a month and more of estrangement and hurt.

"There, there," Matthew said. "There, there, love."

"I'm sorry," she said, gulping and hiccupping. "I don't usually cry like this. I've cried more this past month than in the previous twenty years. And I'm ruining your nice clean shirt."

"There's a tragedy worth weeping over, indeed," he said. "And a sad commentary on marriage." He lifted her face and kissed her wet cheeks, first one, then, after a turn of the head with finger to chin, the other. He kissed the tip of her nose and her damp, fluttering eyelids. After that there was nothing to do but kiss her mouth. *Sweet. Warm and wet and soft. So sweet, and so innocent. No wonder Andrew loved her, and wanted her, and felt unmanned at the thought that he had failed her. . .*

Andrew chose the moment to wake up. He opened his eyes, saw Matthew betraying him with a fat, slovenly boy, knew he was dreaming, and closed his eyes again. Had he seen the boy somewhere before—desired him? No, impossible. Rounded, soft curves like a woman. He must remember the dream for later. He and Matthew would enjoy a laugh.

Matthew ended the kiss with regret. "Let me escort you home, sweet lady," he said.

"No, I don't dare leave him alone. One of us should watch through the night with him."

"He'll be all right for a half an hour. And it really isn't proper for you to be here."

"I know." Phyllida explained about the reading lessons. "I knew it was wrong, coming here dressed like this, but I told myself I was keeping an eye on things."

"What an enterprising lady," Matthew said, filled with admiration despite his better instincts. "And the doorman and the footmen, I take it, were fooled by that getup that would be hooted off the stage at a Vauxhall masquerade?"

Phyllida was able to laugh now. It was so good and perceptive of Matthew not to have commented on the kiss. Just an expression of chaste comfort, from one friend to another. "No, of course not. Nan and I had to sneak in the back. But you see, Mr. Turner threatened to tell about the Brotherhood. About Andrew and everyone here."

"Did he, now? And what would he know about it?"

"Nothing," Phyllida said. "Until you and Andrew brought him here."

MATTHEW, HAVING ENSCONCED THE footman Oliver in Andrew's room with strict instructions to open the door to no one but himself, and having seen the lady safely home, returned to the Brotherhood and walked upstairs to the room with the rat in it. He considered knocking, thought better of it, and pulled out the master key, moving so quietly that the boy saw and heard nothing until the door was locked again from the inside. Kit, sitting beside the bed and watching Philippe's shallow breathing, startled when the large man appeared at the door of the bedroom.

"'Ere, wot you want, mister? This is a private room, it is." He slipped past Matthew into the outer room, shutting the bedroom door.

Matthew smiled, looking wolfish. "What do you think I want? The usual." He unbuttoned his flap as he spoke.

"Now you wait a minute," Kit said. "I'm tending Mr. Philip. I don't have time for that, even if I wanted it. Which I don't."

"I suppose you have no use for five guineas, then," Matthew said. He pulled the gleaming gold coins from his pocket, tossed them in the air, and caught them again.

Kit swallowed at the sound and the flash of bright color. "Suppose a bit o' French would be all right."

"Five guineas for a French kiss?" Matthew said with a laugh. "Sorry, lad. I may be plump in the pockets but I don't throw my brass away that easy. No, it's the other I want."

Kit shook his head, looking uneasy. "I'm done wif that, sir. Gone respectable. Thought you didn't go in for that, anyway, goin' up the back alley. Thought you took it from Mr. Carrington."

Matthew's smile was less wolfish. "Plain speaking," he said. "I suppose all the beauties know they can get away with it. But that's just it, you see. Mr. Carrington is incapacitated at the moment. And he and Mrs. Carrington seem to be reconciled. So I must seek my pleasure in other ways." He snapped his fingers, making Kit jump. "Come on, you little whore. What's the fuss? Five minutes, five guineas. You'll never make that kind of money again, no matter how well you tend to 'poor little Philippe.'"

Kit stared. "You 'eard? I didn't see you there."

"No, I made sure of that. Well, what'll it be? Will you take me and my five guineas, or will you take me without them?"

Kit knew when he was cornered. "Tell you what, mister. Just let me use the privy, make myself all nice an' clean for ya, an' then you can 'ave wot you came for."

"How fastidious," Matthew said. "But you will not leave this room. You'll use the pot."

Kit sighed and tried to move back into the inner room, but found his arm held in an implacable grip. "You're 'urtin' me," he said.

"I will hurt you," Matthew said, "if you try to put anything over on me. You'll use the pot here, where I can see you."

"That's disgusting!"

"I imagine you've done a lot worse for a lot less than five guineas. I imagine at one time you'd have done just about anything for five guineas. Now, it's your choice, boy. You can go on playing innocent, until I force what I want from you, or you can give me the key to the cipher and I won't trouble you again. And I'll pay you the five guineas either way. I admit, I'm impressed at your integrity. Perhaps Andrew knew what he was about, trusting you."

Kit sat down in another chair, defeated. He felt oddly safe for the first time in weeks since discovering the strange papers and their method of concealment. "'Ow'd you guess?"

"Because Philippe talks to you," Matthew said. "I saw him, up on the roof, before I saved his life. He wasn't threatening you. He was whispering endearments."

"'E was wot?" Kit said. "Wot's them when they're at 'ome?"

"You can stop playing the ignorant waif. I know about the reading lessons."

"Mrs. C. spilled the beans?"

"Yes. So you'd better tell me everything. I don't want Andrew—Mr. Carrington—to have any more trouble from your little friend. Or from you."

"I'd never do Mr. Carrington a bad turn," Kit protested. "*He* was the first one to talk to me like a human being. *He* was the one got me this job."

"Exactly," Matthew said. "Which makes it all the more damning to see you conspiring with this madman against Mr. Carrington and everybody else in this club."

"Mr. Philip ain't mad," Kit said. "Just a little dicked in the nob. Can't hardly blame him, after what they done to him."

"And what, precisely," Matthew asked, "did they do?"

"Buggered him till he couldn't . . . do his business, if you know what I mean. All tore up and bleeding." Kit's voice was tight with fury, eyes cast down, reliving it as if it had happened to him, as it very well could have if he'd been less careful, got in with the wrong crowd, or accepted the wrong pickup on a slow night. "Then they whipped him raw. Used a whip with knots on it, till there wasn't a strip of skin left on his back. Then they poured salt water on him and left him for dead."

Despite his familiarity with men at their worst, Matthew felt himself moved. He'd seen some of it, but not all. Not what went on at night, out back, when the wealthy cotton merchant had gone home to England and the drink and the excesses took over, the maddening power that comes with owning men, body and soul. "My God," he said. "Why?"

"Dunno for sure," Kit said. "Says 'cause he had his way with his friend's sister. Says she wanted it. They was in love."

Matthew groaned. "He ought to have known."

"That don't make it right," Kit said.

"No. But it isn't right to ruin the Brotherhood, either, no matter what was done to him in America."

"He wouldn't," Kit said, unable to look Matthew in the eye.

"What did you think he was doing?" Matthew asked, not expecting an answer. "And just how did he get a copy of something like the cipher, anyway?"

"Said he got it from a man that worked at— At— Some place in . . . Upchurch Street."

"Are you sure? That's a very serious accusation."

"That why those Whitehall toffs was here?"

"Yes. It's time to give it up, boy. It's too big a secret for you to be carrying around. And you wouldn't want to help Boney defeat our fellows, would you? Now, here's what I want you to do—"

"—Right you are, guv'nor," Kit said after the instructions had been followed to Matthew's eagle-eyed observations. "Just how'd you know, anyway, about where we hid it?"

"Old sailors' trick," Matthew said. "And I've spent a lot of time on ships."

AMBERSON STOOD LISTENING IN THE silent corridor. It was late; all was still, even the last "bargain hunters" having made their choices or given up and gone to bed. He moved along to the spy's room and let himself in. The boy Kit was awake, sitting in a chair near the bed. He turned his head as the door opened but did not seem surprised at Amberson's silent entrance.

"How's our patient doing?" Amberson asked. "Awake yet?"

"No, sir."

Amberson fished for a coin. "But you'll tell me when he is?"

"Yes, sir," Kit said. "Soon's 'e opens 'is eyes." He grabbed for the coin, but Amberson was too quick, holding his wrist in a grip that made Kit bite his lips not to whimper.

"We'll have a look now," Amberson said. "While poor little Philippe can't play his usual tricks."

"You can't kill him," Kit protested. "Not in cold blood."

Amberson fastened his expressionless eyes on the boy. "What a vivid imagination. I have no intention of killing anyone. I am merely going to oversee a physical examination. You will be my hands, and witness."

The operation was quick and gentle with Kit's deft touch. Philippe, deep in a coma, barely sighed as the slim fingers probed his body and pulled the smooth package from his cavity.

Amberson smiled. "Open it, please. I prefer not to soil myself with the waste of an American spy." He examined the pages, his eyes growing round and hard as two copper coins. He took Kit's throat in his hand, squeezing just enough until the boy's eyes began to bulge.

"Where is it? I'm tempted to cut it out of you. Such a very pretty little fellow, to be sure."

"I don't have it," Kit rasped through his bruised vocal cords. "It's Mr. Thornby, like the note says."

"And since when do you read?" Amberson hissed.

"Since last month," Kit said. "And I can write. It was me wrote the note."

"Was it, now?" Amberson studied the boy caught in his grasp, staring with his head cocked slightly to one side like a praying mantis preparing to dismember a butterfly. The eyes were round and pleading, the small bowed mouth mewling up at him like a kitten about to be drowned in a bucket. When had he ever hesitated to hold the feeble, struggling body beneath the surface? Until now. Here was the perfect remedy for the long day's frustrations and missteps, a quick bout of the familiar sordid brutality. *And he didn't want it.* Lord knows he was tired, but it was the spirit, not the flesh, that was unwilling. He loosened his grip, grimacing as the boy scuttled backward. "Another time, perhaps, I will see you again. Once all this foolishness is behind us."

"Not if I see you first," Kit muttered, scowling as the door closed and the lock was turned from outside.

Nan emerged from behind the bedroom door, the fireplace poker held in one hand. "He gone?"

"For now," Kit said. He coughed and hacked, unable to clear his injured throat, and took several swigs from the decanter.

"If he comes back," Nan said, swinging the poker like a baseball bat, "I'll be ready for him."

"Crikey, it's good to have you on my side," Kit said. "But you hadn't oughter crack any more blokes on the noggin. Could get in trouble."

"Would you have done it?" Nan asked. "With Mr. Thornby, I mean?"

"Nah," Kit said. "He didn't want that. He was just testing me, like."

"But five guineas!" Nan swallowed and looked at the floor. "We can get married on that. Supposing he'd only give it to you if you done it?"

"I told ya," Kit said, staring with narrowed eyes at his intended. "I'm done wif that. Honest."

"Well, I'd do it," Nan said. "Just once, for five guineas."

Kit slapped her, hard enough to knock her down. She didn't cry, just lay there looking up at him, her eyes unreadable and her mouth agape. "Don't you never say that," Kit said. He felt the prickle of tears forming and turned away.

"I'm sorry," Nan said. She stood up and put her arms around him from behind. "It's only 'cause I love you."

"I know," Kit said. "It's only 'cause I love you, too. You don't know what you're sayin'."

"Was it horrible?" Nan whispered.

Kit shrugged. The tears were gone, only sorrow at the end of the idyll. "Depends on the bloke. Most of 'em was beasts; some of 'em was real gents. Like Mr. Carrington. I'd a done him for five pence and a good breakfast. Did, once. 'Cept he paid me better 'n that."

"Oh." Nan picked up the poker and put it back on the hearth. "I should go home. Mrs. Carrington will wonder what's become of me."

"I'm sorry if I hurt you." Kit said, unlocking the door for her with the master key he had found in Tournière's coat pocket.

"You didn't," Nan said. "But don't let that Mr. Amberson in again." She kissed him, a quick peck on the cheek, and flitted down the corridor, light and quiet and inconspicuous as a moth.

Kit locked himself in again and sat down on the chair by the bed to feel Tournière's forehead. Hot as a chophouse kitchen in August. He dipped a cloth in the basin of water, wrung it out, and wiped it gently over the man's flushed face. "It's just you an' me, Phil," he said. "Just us ganymedes together."

AMBERSON, HIS PISTOL AT THE ready, strode along to No. 6, rammed the master key into the lock, and turned it roughly. He no longer cared about stealth, and his eyes were already adjusted to the dark. This should not take long.

"You always let yourself in without knocking?" Matthew asked from a chair in the outer room.

"Didn't want to disturb Carrington," Amberson said.

"And a pistol shot at close range is so wonderfully soothing," Matthew said.

Amberson stared at the gun in his hand as if just now noticing it. "Sorry. I've spent so much time in the Peninsula it's become a necessary evil." He released the catch and pocketed the weapon. "All I want is the cipher."

"Not here," Matthew said.

"But your charming note— My God, Thornby. What are you playing at?"

"Calm down, man. I have it. I simply prefer to make the transfer elsewhere, and keep Andrew out of this." He stood up, moving out of the shadows. He was completely naked, the candlelight flickering over his sculptured flesh, blond hairs glinting copper in the reddish glow.

Amberson caught his breath. He was suddenly aware of being almost forty, and of the toll his work was taking—the trips back and forth on packet boats and troopships, the sleepless nights and long days in the saddle. He ran his hand over his face. "Where, then?"

"My room." Matthew led him down the corridor and opened the door to No. 4, using a key concealed in his palm. As soon as they were inside, the door safely locked again, Matthew bent over, his head almost touching the floor, leering upside-down at Amberson between his legs. "Help yourself, Amberson. If you dare."

The man was laughing at him, even now. Amberson sank down on the bed, frightened by his own weariness. He was tiring of the game, just when it was reaching its climax. "How much do you know?"

"No more than you," Matthew said, straightening up. "Just couldn't resist giving you a scare."

"That boy gave me a scare," Amberson said. "Didn't seem the least bit worried that I knew he could read and write."

"Well, well," Matthew said. "Our Kit's too sharp by half. He knows if you get rid of him you'll have no other guide into the dark recesses of poor little Philippe's mind."

"What a mess," Amberson said. "How did things get to this point?"

Matthew shrugged and sat beside Amberson on the bed. "It's always messy, dealing with spies and traitors. More so when you factor in all us madge culls."

"They go hand in hand," Amberson said. "I remember, years ago, thinking I'd do anything rather than betray . . . someone I cared about. And the very next week I was spilling my guts to the headmaster."

"Oh, school," Matthew said. "We all do things we're ashamed of at school."

"Harry Swain didn't. I suspect you didn't, either."

"I wasn't caught, that's all."

"Well, I was caught. And I ratted on everybody I knew, everybody who had trusted me. Afterward I wanted to hang myself. Not for what I'd done, but for the knowledge that I'd do the same again. That's what determined me to be the one doing the catching, once I was out of school. Ninety-nine men out of a hundred will betray their wives, their children, and their dearest friends rather than face public humiliation. If I wanted to live my life on my terms, I had to make damned sure to be the headmaster wherever I ended up, not the guilty boy."

Matthew accepted the confession in silence. He didn't like knowing Amberson had a human side. Spoiled the pure contempt he had enjoyed up to now. "Once you have the cipher, Andrew will be free?" he asked.

"Carrington?" Amberson asked in surprise. "He was always free."

"Then why order him to kill Tournière?"

"Order? Nobody orders Carrington to do anything, at least not so as I've noticed. We agreed it was the best solution."

"For you," Matthew said. "If he'd committed murder at your bidding, you'd have him right where you want him."

"You spoiled that game, though. Very clever, the smoke. How did you arrange it so neatly?"

"Sheer luck," Matthew admitted. "Seems any business, yours and mine and any other, depends on chance and good timing more than we care to think."

"Mmm. And now you have Carrington right where you want him."

"Do I? He might hate me after tonight."

"Not once he thinks it over. A word of advice, man. Carrington has his prejudices, but he's no fool."

"I never thought he was."

Amberson watched as Matthew pulled the folded papers from the inner pocket of his pantaloons hanging over a chair. "How do I know this is the only copy?"

"You don't," Matthew said.

"Ought to make sure," Amberson said.

"How? If you kill Tournière, you'll never know."

"I know, I know." Amberson pulled the candle close and held the papers to the flame. He waited until they were burning thoroughly before dropping the blazing packet in the grate.

"All this trouble for a handful of ashes," Matthew said.

"The value of breaking the enemy's cipher is nil once he knows it's broken," Amberson said. "The more copies of this key floating around, the greater the chance our advantage will be lost."

"But if you already have it, why did Tournière think it was unique?"

"Because I let him think so, of course."

"*You* gave it to him."

"How else? Every month, as we learned more from our man on the quartermaster-general's staff—an excellent man, by the way. Sorry he's not one of us; I would have liked to let him in on what I was doing—I fed Tournière a little more of it, through the ruse with the accounts book and the bank courier. Helped him fill in the grid."

"So there's no traitor in Abchurch Street."

"There'd better not be," Amberson said. "Of course, Tournière thought there was."

"But why?"

"Surely Carrington told you? Or is he too much the gentleman to talk with his mouth full?" He slid his eyes sideways to see how Thornby took the reversion to madge humor.

"Careful, Amberson," Matthew said, holding up his middle finger. "I might have to throw you out."

"You can try," Amberson said, grateful for the relaxation in the atmosphere. He let himself fall back, stretching out across the width of the bed, and sighed as his muscles lost some of their tension. "Tournière's real game was betraying us. He brought down the White Swan, even boasted about it, but I couldn't prove it, and what good would it do if I could? The law's on his side, and he was after bigger game now—the Brotherhood. The real problem, paradoxically, was that our strong defenses—the men on the door, the strict prohibition on bringing in outsiders—worked against us as we were trying to catch him at it. He couldn't get in, and he couldn't inform on anybody, but I couldn't learn any more about him or his methods. So setting him up as Carrington's secretary and going along with his little cipher ploy was a last chance to trick him into revealing himself and any collaborators."

"Must have been quite a shock, then, seeing Mrs. Carrington and her abigail." Matthew could not help smiling, for all his sympathy with the lady.

Amberson groaned and clutched his head. "Appalling," he said. "Absolutely appalling. Actually, the worst, in a way, was Agatha Gatling. Too damned convincing. Although it did have one merit—it pointed up our weak spot—the servants' entrance, and the servants themselves. How carefully are they vetted, do you know?"

Matthew shook his head and lay down beside Amberson. "No idea. I'm relatively new here." After a brief silence, he said, "By the way, were you planning to return the rubies? Or did Andrew promise them as payment for avoiding prosecution?"

Amberson pulled the glittering string from his pocket. "Just an oversight, Thornby. Carrington owed me nothing. I like to make my cover stories as credible as I can." His fingers brushed Thornby's as he transferred the jewels. "I don't suppose you need any extra income?"

Matthew laughed. "Another indecent proposal? Nay, man, I've had better offers."

"Bite me," Amberson said, grinning for the first time in what felt like months. "What did you mean about avoiding prosecution?"

"Tournière attacked Mrs. Carrington. Did you not know?"

"No!" Amberson sat up. "Are you sure?" Seeing Matthew's face, he lay down again. "I can't say I'm surprised. The way she behaves, she's asking for it."

Matthew jumped up, looming over the prostrate man on the bed. "Now I really will have to throw you out."

"Oh, calm down," Amberson said. "You saw her. Hell, imagine living in the same house with that, day in and day out. Even as staunch an opponent of bestiality as I am would be tempted to cover that high-spirited little filly once in a while."

"You might care to remember," Matthew said, "that you're speaking of the wife of my friend. And that women are human beings too."

"Are they?" Amberson said. "I should require far more substantial proof than your word before accepting such a dubious hypothesis."

ANDREW AWOKE, MOMENTARILY DISORIENTED. HE had such a sense of mingled joy and disappointment, betrayal and newfound happiness, he could not at first piece it all together. The stomach-turning smell of cigars, a soft, rounded body wearing unsuitable clothes, and the culmination of the plan to set up and dispose of the informer and spy Turner—what a coil! His lover had made an empty promise—over something trivial, but how many more of his words might turn out to be hollow? And his wife—she had done nothing but lie to him and deceive him, yet she had proved truer to him than anyone else. And she had uncovered his own duplicity. What was he to do?

He remembered his last attack of migraine, the loss of consciousness that had allowed so many misdeeds and their repercussions to spiral out of control. It was reading Phyllida's novel that had given him an escape into pleasure, and he wished he had something like that to take him away from his troubles, for however brief an interval. He felt around in the drawer of the bedside table, a most unlikely source of reading material, pulling out several wadded handkerchiefs, which he dropped with a grimace of disgust, a jar of grease with the top left off, and, wonder of wonders, a book. *The Marriages of Melisande.*

It was fate, he decided. He was, for some reason, destined to read this monstrous piece of filth. When he thought of some of the more appropriate punishments he might deserve, this was getting off lightly. He opened it up and started to read, skimming rapidly through the first, expository sections.

Only after he was well into the third chapter did he allow himself to acknowledge what was obvious from the first. This lurid adventure, with its gothic style and murky undertones of unnatural passions, had Phyllida's stamp all over it, in every way but the name on the title page. Worse, it was his own story—his and Phyllida's and Matthew's. The tall, dark, "sinister" Lord Iskander; the captive, ravished virgin; and an honorable, unpretentious man, a potential lover to both. Andrew was unfamiliar with the mechanics of printing and publishing, but he knew enough to be certain that there had not been time for Phyllida to write this after her marriage. In fact, he remembered quite clearly his new bride working on the large printed sheets called "galley proofs," not manuscript.

What had become of the elegant, disciplined author of *Sense and Sensibility*? That was all too easy to answer. No doubt elated by her first, modest success, Phyllida had been seduced into changing her style to ensure an *éclat* for her next work. How she must have thrilled when a living, breathing version of Lord Iskander walked into her mother's parlor! Andrew grimaced, recalling that bizarre courtship and proposal. No wonder she had been so surprisingly easy to talk into an arrangement that any decent girl would have balked at. *Slut. Bitch. It's a wonder her belly wasn't swollen even now with God knows whose leavings. Mr.— What was his name? Coulter?* Too bad Andrew had only knocked him down.

Andrew wanted to toss the book aside, but he couldn't. He would die rather than admit it to another soul, but he was aroused by the suggestive, sensational plot. He was unsure if his desire was stimulated by the scenes between the blond hero, Ludovic, and the dark Lord Iskander; between Iskander and the heroine, Melisande, who reminded him so forcibly of Phyllida; or by an image of Phyllida herself in the guise of author—the ink-stained fingers, the abashed but defiant look on her face when he caught her at her work; or when he, months ago, had first covered her body with his.

Ignoring his pounding head, he read on, a no doubt sinister smile spreading over his hawk-nosed face as he devoured the pages. Apart from what it said about his taste in literature, Andrew could only be grateful that he was no longer married to the author of *Sense and Sensibility*. That lady had been too sharp, too knowing. She would be a delight to gossip with, to discuss anything from politics to fashions—but to make love, to open his heart to her—no. She could eviscerate him with a well-chosen phrase, demolish him with a sentence. His manhood would never withstand that cold scrutiny. Whatever return of courage Matthew had predicted, Andrew's marriage to her was doomed to be forever barren.

Whereas now that she had metamorphosed into the author of *Melisande*, she was the perfect match for him. She could not turn herself into a dolt however she tried to conceal her intellect; her writing was almost as clever and incisive as it had been in the earlier, chaste novel. But underneath there was something red and throbbing, something low and basic. A quality that, if it existed at all in a lady, was usually buried too deep, rarely discovered by the incurious man who preferred to skim the surface, although sometimes revealed in women of another sort. This daring authoress combined the best of mind and carnality in a mixture that Andrew had thought, up to now, could only be found in men—and few enough of them. Another picture of her came to him, the soft smile and bright-eyed animation she had displayed in the theater dressing room when she had watched him kiss Rhys, and he groaned aloud with the pain of his sudden hardness.

That was her gift. Rhys had seen it before he had. She responded to men together, to men like Andrew and Rhys—and Matthew. Oh, he was a very lucky sod indeed.

THE FOLLOWING EVENING, MATTHEW RETURNED to the Brotherhood after a long day of accounts, of bills of lading, factory plans, and cotton futures, took the last puff of his cigar, and threw it away a few yards before the entrance.

"Good evening, Thornby," Pierce said, passing him on the stairs. "Would you care to join me and the others for a drink?"

"Why do I have the feeling I'm being summoned to the headmaster's office?" Matthew said.

"Nothing like that," Pierce said. "Just a friendly discussion."

"The thing is," Verney said, after they had all settled into their customary places in the back parlor, the only difference Matthew could see being that Verney was completely and impeccably dressed, "the thing is, don't quite know how to say it, Thornby, but—"

"But you think I should clear off, isn't that it?"

"Nothing so bald as that, Thornby," Pierce tried to soften the blow. "Just keep your distance for a while, give Carrington a little time."

"Time to reconcile with Phyllida," Witherspoon said.

"What we mean is," Verney said, "they seem closer to resolving their differences after recent events. The fewer distractions, you see—"

"What everybody else is too polite to say," Monkton interrupted Verney's halting speech, "is that your behavior outside this club has become damned obvious. Everywhere one goes in society, there you are, escorting Mrs. Carrington in to dinner, dancing with her, flirting with her, partnering her at cards."

Matthew swirled the brandy in the glass and watched the flicker of light in its rich depths. "I think you're making too much of it," he said. "Nobody seriously believes there's anything improper between Mrs. Carrington and me. It's just a little harmless dalliance. Seems the lady needed someone in her corner."

"Don't play off those disingenuous north-country airs on me," Monkton said. "I wasn't born yesterday, nor did I recently roll into town on a turnip wagon. And neither did anyone else in the *ton*. The only way you could make the situation any plainer would be to go down on your knees to Andrew in the ballroom of Almack's and swallow him whole. And I suspect even you might balk at that. Wouldn't be good for trade. People don't want to buy their linen—or cotton—already soiled." He raised his hands, palms out. "And don't go planting a facer on me for speaking frankly. This is a very select madge club, not a young ladies' seminary—we tend to draw the line at brawling."

The others held their breath.

Matthew stared at Monkton until the smaller man blinked and lowered his hands. "Perhaps you're right," Matthew said. "I've been thinking much the same thing. Might go down to the country for a while, look over some property."

"You don't have to go immediately," Witherspoon said in his kind voice. "You'll come to the Founders Day celebration tomorrow, won't you?"

"The Odds and Sods dinner, you know," Pierce said. "Of course you're welcome at that."

"You'll have to bring a lady," Verney reminded him.

"And not the blameless Mrs. Carrington," Monkton said. "Carrington's hosting it this year, so you'll have to find someone else."

"I will," Matthew said. "I'll make arrangements to be out of my room the day after."

"Well," Monkton said, standing up. "That's settled then. Sorry to put a spoke in your wheel like this, but the wager, you know."

"I know," Matthew said.

"It doesn't have to be forever," Witherspoon said.

"That's right," Verney said. "Once Carrington and his wife are on good terms again, and there's news of Mrs. Carrington being in a delicate condition, there's no reason you can't come back."

"No," Matthew agreed. "Simple, really. Reminds me of what Dr. Johnson said about a patron. The sort of man who abandons his drowning protégé to his fate, then takes the credit for saving him after he's struggled to shore on his own. Andrew ought to welcome me with open arms."

"Damn it," Pierce said. "That's not what we're asking."

"But that's what it is," Verney said. "Might as well admit it."

"I admit it," Monkton said. "Still, don't lose hope, Thornby. Might be returning sooner than you expect, and to a clear field. Knew from the start this marriage scheme was knackered before it left the gate."

"Don't you *ever* have an optimistic or a cheerful thought?" Pierce said, rounding on Monkton.

Monkton stared down his nose while he pulled his snuffbox from his pocket, opened it one-handed, and helped himself to a pinch. After the moment of gratification, a delicate sneeze, and a brush of his handkerchief, he said, "No, my dear. I was cured of such solecisms long before I left the nursery."

CHARLOTTE SWAIN?" ANDREW SAID. "Surely her mama will not allow it."

"Pierce is escorting Lydia Swain," Matthew said, "and he assures me that the sister-in-law will provide an adequate chaperone."

"Have you met Lydia?" Andrew asked. "Didn't think so. But why the blond giantess?"

"According to my understanding of the proceedings," Matthew said, "every man chooses a lady to escort. You're naturally partnered with Phyllida, so I must select a second choice."

"Is that an admission of guilt, Matthew?" Andrew asked in ominous tones.

"Guilt? About what?"

"Nothing," Andrew said. "Forget it. Explain to me why you want to force a genteel, carefully brought up young lady to endure a night of lewd conversation with a bunch of sodomites and demi-reps."

"Is that what it's going to be? And you're planning to subject Phyllida to that?"

"Awfully protective of my wife these days, aren't you?"

"You know, Andrew, I'm wondering if you didn't do yourself an injury yesterday, maybe gave yourself a concussion. Talking as if you have a screw loose."

"I see. Now I'm a loose screw. Don't know why you put up with me."

"Well, as to that," Matthew said, "I was thinking of going up north for a while, to the country, look over some property I acquired."

"When?" Andrew asked.

"The day after tomorrow," Matthew said, staring at his feet. "Not for long. Just for the summer, a month or two." He looked up in time to see Andrew's haggard face turn a sickly, sallow hue.

Andrew opened his mouth, shut it, took a deep breath, and said, "*Down* to the country, Matthew. One goes *down* to the country and *up* to town."

"It's up on the map," Matthew said, unable to keep the roguish smile off his face. "When you hold it the right way round, that is. North is up."

"Goad me as you will," Andrew said, his eyes half closing in the frozen look Matthew had come to dread, "I will not give you the satisfaction of making the obvious retort to such childishness. And bring whomever you like tonight. Only don't expect the rest of us to turn a traditional festival dinner into a church service for her sake."

ANDREW HAD VOLUNTEERED TO HOST this year's celebration long before he had contemplated marriage, and he had fretted over the arrangements since. Harriet was to spend the night in unexceptionable boredom with Lizzie and Fanshawe, so there was no debutante sister-in-law to worry about. Witherspoon was to bring his sister; that was one other proper spinster for Miss Swain to associate with. Who else? There was Lady Finchley, Archbold's partner for the evening. She was notorious, but eminently respectable, a paradox she continued to resolve in some mysterious way that Andrew could only admire and attempt to emulate.

The evening began well enough. The women were curious about the assassination of the prime minister and the connection, if any, with the mysterious events at the Brotherhood. The narration of the whole, and receiving the women's congratulations on his heroism, kept Andrew comfortably busy for a good half hour. Amberson had assured him and the other members that there was no reason not to talk freely. With society's taste for gossip it was far more practical to circulate the story and quickly dissipate its novelty than to attempt to suppress it, thereby only increasing its appeal; after several removes of narrator, the few sensitive facts of the story would be garbled so beyond recognition as to pose no threat to the truth.

"But who was the man you shot at the Brotherhood?" Lydia Swain asked.

"An American of French descent, Philippe Tournière. One of Amberson's victims," Andrew said.

"Amberson? Geoffrey Amberson?" Lady Finchley said. "Goodness! You are in deep!"

"I was," Andrew said. "The whole business is now thankfully out of my hands."

"All a misunderstanding," Isham said. "Poor little fellow was enslaved and mistreated. Lost his wits."

"A slave?" Cynthia Smiley said. Monkton's escort, she was an improbable strawberry blonde, proudly wearing the sort of dress that had caused Phyllida so much trouble in the early days of her marriage. "How romantic!"

"You wouldn't say so if you'd seen the stripes on his back," Archbold said.

"What I don't understand," Lady Isham said, "is why you were harboring a spy and a blackmailer at the club in the first place."

"Yes," Phyllida said. "That is the part of the whole affair I find most puzzling."

"Amberson, of course," Monkton said. "Man has us all by the short hairs. I'm just thankful he's on our side."

"Our side? England, you mean?" Verney said.

"No, I mean us. Sodomites," Monkton said. "Don't suppose the man really has a side when it comes to politics. Doubt even Whitehall knows for sure. Fellow just likes playing the game, the rougher the better."

"Don't let his character in private matters mislead you," Andrew said. "The man's patriotism is beyond question."

"I don't question that he's a scoundrel," Monkton replied.

"At least he was thwarted of his prey this time," Matthew said.

"Yes, I've never seen him so discomposed," Pierce said. "When that boy announced Tournière wasn't dead, the look on Amberson's face could have stopped a clock."

Andrew laughed. "Wish I could have seen it. Would almost make up for his foisting the fellow on me in the first place."

"You knew," Phyllida said in a low voice that nevertheless carried the length of the table in a piercing note of accusation. "You knew what he was, and you brought me into the same house with him."

"Honestly, Phyllida," Andrew said, "I didn't know the extent of his activities. When I first agreed to Amberson's proposal I thought he was only a French agent. By the time I was contemplating marriage I had completely forgotten about him."

"*Only* a French agent," Phyllida said, looking around the table in exasperation. "Only a man would say that, or fail to see how provoking it is."

"It is unfair," Lydia Swain murmured. "To think of all the excitement you have had in your short marriage, while most of us have to make do for years with stale gossip and tiresome flirtations."

"I think you were very brave," Charlotte Swain said.

"Yes, indeed," Miss Gatling said. "Mrs. Carrington got hold of the man's code book, you know."

Pierce laid a hand on her arm. "Agatha, my dear," he said, "it was only kitchen accounts after all."

"No, David," she began, "I know ciphers when I see them and—Oh, yes, I see." She stared around the table with her protuberant eyes. "Fellow had a dreadful scrawl. Illegible. Looked like code. Turned out to be French in atrocious handwriting. Ha!"

The others followed her laughter but kept their opinions to themselves.

"I understand you are to be congratulated on a new conquest." Andrew, desperate for a change of subject, turned to Verney's companion, Mrs. Sally Green, a sleek brunette of thirty-five, who passed easily for ten years younger. Andrew had escorted her to last year's dinner; they were old friends.

"Yes, my dear," she replied, poking him in the ribs. "Got there ahead of all of you for once. And I don't have to tell you about such tall men. It's not the six feet but the six inches that matter. With him it's easily eight or nine."

"Now don't be boasting of such things in front of me," Matthew teased. "You'll have me all in a pother over where I rank in this cruel hierarchy."

Mrs. Green trilled a note of studiedly genteel laughter. "Oh, Mr. Thornby. I'm sure a big man like you has nothing to worry about."

Miss Gatling cleared her throat. "Don't suppose I've had the pleasure of meeting this gentleman."

"Of course you have, Agatha," Lady Finchley said. She was another young-looking lady, on the wrong side of forty but with brilliant blond hair and displaying a formidable décolletage. "We were speaking of him earlier. Alex, you know. Lord Bellingham."

Phyllida was the only lady, perhaps because she was looking, to catch Charlotte's gasp and flush, the stricken look that passed as the girl admirably controlled her first reaction. Matthew also noticed her discomfort and was reminded of Andrew's warning about mixing the respectable ladies with the others.

"Don't worry, Miss Swain," he whispered. "Mrs. Green is not the sort of woman a man in Bellingham's position can marry. Just sowing his wild oats."

Charlotte looked into the kindly blue eyes. "I know," she said. "I expect it was the shock of hearing the name in that context."

Witherspoon, sensitive to others' reactions, perceived something of the girl's unhappiness. "It's all right, Miss Swain," he said. "It's not the same one." Noticing an air of confusion, he tried to clarify. "It was a different man that shot the prime minister. Our beautiful Bellingham won't be hanged. Davey spent all last night explaining it to me, when he wasn't—doing other things—and he wouldn't lie about something so serious, even to make me happy. Because I'd find out eventually, you know."

"Bellingham, did you say?" Isham said, perking up. "Damn fine figure of a man. If I was twenty years younger, Mrs. Whatever-your-name-is, I'd give you a run for your money. Ow! Damn it, Bella!" He glared at his wife, who had lobbed, with her sure aim, a hard roll across the table.

"Green," Sally Green said, twinkling at the old rogue. "Sally Green. If you were twenty years younger, my lord, I'd expect to be paying my forfeit."

Archbold raised his quizzing glass. "Wouldn't be too cocksure, Marc. Mrs. Green is a damn fine figure of a woman. Ow!"

Lady Isham, having beaned both her husband and her lover, said, "That's enough, you two. Marc, you're too old to be stealing men from the younger ones. And as for you, Rupert, if I catch you ogling any more females in my presence, I'll have you thrown out of the house."

"Never too old, Bella," Isham said. "And if you throw Rup out, I'll go too. We can live at the Brotherhood."

"Suit yourselves," Lady Isham said with a shrug. "Just remember who holds the deed on the building. I can have the entire place emptied in twenty-four hours."

" . . . at Coverdale's place in Surrey. Held quite a celebration for his son and heir's twenty-first birthday last year," Lady Finchley was saying, before lowering her head to whisper, "Anytime you feel a blush coming on, Agatha dear, just remind yourself that you have mixed with these young men in their own milieu, and seen them clothed and on their best behavior. When next you're in their company, think of this conversation and you will have the advantage."

"Don't know if that's an advantage or not," Lydia Swain drawled, her sharp ears having picked up most of the not-so-sotto voce. "Some of them feel up to anything when they're turned out as smart as Beau Brummell, but remove the lacquered shell and all you'll find are shabby, meager little worms."

"Goodness, Lydia! Marriage has made you bitter," Mrs. Smiley exclaimed. "One would almost think your young lord has not lived up to expectations."

"As he's neither a lord nor especially young," Lydia replied, "only a green goose would have had any expectations of that sort."

"And no one would accuse you of being green," Mrs. Green said.

"Nor you, despite that less than original name you chose for yourself," Lady Finchley said. "I remember when you were plain Sarah Cramm. Thought it suited you rather better."

"Ladies, ladies," Andrew intervened. "This is meant to be

a friendly party, not the preliminary bouts for the heavy—ah—featherweight championship. Speaking of which, Pierce, what do you think of Cribb's chances against this latest challenger?"

"After the way he rolled up Molyneux last year," Pierce said, "excellent, I would say. Although one can never be positive until one sees them sparring in the ring."

"If you're going to talk boxing," Witherspoon said, getting up and leaving his place, "I will sit with the ladies."

"What about you, Verney?" Monkton asked, raising his quizzing glass. "Care to give us a demonstration? You strip to advantage."

Verney shook his head. "Dash it all, Monkton. Not here in front of the ladies."

Monkton affected astonishment. "Chivalry, Verney? Not a sodomite's virtue, I would have thought."

"My life is not entirely governed by the pursuit of unnatural vice," Verney protested. "I am as capable of the finer feelings as any other man."

"My apologies," Monkton said. "I did not realize you had gone so long without a good fuck."

"If you can't keep the filth out of your conversation in front of ladies"—Matthew was on top of Monkton before the man had a chance to turn around—"then you can damned well take it out to the gutter where it belongs. Do you understand?"

Monkton yawned. "God, another knight in shining armor. Carrington, will you call off your lapdog or must I kick him?"

Eventually, the ladies discovered a common topic in the appreciation of a new novel that was making the rounds. "It's the most scandalous thing ever," Mrs. Green declared. "And well written."

"Yes," Lady Finchley agreed. "Usually when a book contains so much material of a questionable nature it's almost unreadable, but this *Melisande* keeps one turning the pages."

"You know what I like about it?" Mrs. Smiley said. "The author doesn't waste time on a lot of boring descriptions. She just keeps telling the story. And she doesn't preach at you, either. To my mind, that's a good writer."

A few coarse remarks from the men greeted that comment. "Good bawdry, you mean," Pierce said.

"No, I'm serious," Mrs. Smiley persisted. "If I want a sermon I'll go to church. And if I want scenery I'll go on a picnic. When I read a romance, that's what I want. The story. Yes, I like all the hot stuff. Why else would I read a romance? But that doesn't mean it can't be written well."

Phyllida smiled and ducked her head. "I think that's an excellent point," she said in a shy voice that Andrew barely recognized. "The content need not dictate the style. And a meticulous but dynamic manner of writing can redeem at least some of the disreputable aspects of the story."

"Have you read it, Mrs. Carrington?" Mrs. Green asked, her dark eyes moving up and down over Phyllida's face and body in a speculative way that was most unnerving until one realized she did it with everybody, man or woman.

"I have, yes," Phyllida said, still with that secretive smile turning up the corners of her mouth. "And I confess, I enjoyed it very much, as much as anybody here, I think."

"Rubbish," Miss Gatling interrupted. "I looked at the first chapters and I was disgusted."

"But you looked at it," Lady Finchley teased. "How did you come to have it if it's so disgusting?"

"Oh, George, you know. My brother. Low taste in reading. I suppose I ought to be grateful that he reads at all."

"Aggie," Witherspoon said in a constricted voice, "you should be careful what you say. You don't know who might be listening."

Miss Gatling stared at her brother. "How much champagne have you had, George? We know exactly who is listening. Everyone here at table. The day I can't express an honest opinion amongst friends is the day I give up society altogether."

Phyllida shook her head at Witherspoon and winked. "I thought it was quite good," she said. "Much better than the author's previous one."

"Now there we disagree," Andrew said, surprising the women by his sudden entrance into the discussion. "I read both books recently—*Melisande* and the author's first. That is an outstanding work. Perhaps some of you have read it too. *Sense and Sensibility*."

He was met by a round of blank stares. "I thought it was *The Loves of Lavinia*," Witherspoon said, addressing his lap so that no one heard.

"I read it, Andrew," Phyllida said. "It is indeed an excellent book." She did not appear pleased.

"It sounds dull," Mrs. Smiley said.

"It is," Andrew said, "in the sense that it does not rely on a patently imaginary foreign setting, sensational plot, or gothic horrors. It is a believable and engrossing story, situated in modern-day England, with characters that could be our acquaintances. The events and emotions are as mundane, and as real, as life."

"High praise indeed," Lady Finchley said.

"Well, all I know is, I like a foreign country and a romantic story. I don't want to read about my acquaintances," Mrs. Smiley said.

"Yes," Mrs. Green backed up her colleague. "It's like going to a play. Who wants to spend hours watching the next-door neighbors?"

Andrew shrugged. "Well, my dear," he addressed Phyllida down the length of the table, "it appears you have correctly estimated the level of public taste and adjusted your art accordingly. But I promise you I appreciate finer stuff. You ought to have confided in me before so compromising your talents." He paused. "Ah, yes. I forgot. Confiding in your husband is not your habit."

Most of the ladies, mystified by the exact meaning of the words but alert to the signs of a domestic fight brewing, made innocuous conversation to cover any unpleasantness. Lady Isham, secure in her position as elder stateswoman, entered the fray. "Now, Carrington," she said, "there's no reason to come the ugly because we ladies enjoy reading about the sort of things you men enjoy doing. Damn fine book, I thought. About time an enterprising female put down in black and white what we all think. Can't keep it all to yourselves, you know. Have to share the pleasure a little. Most of us like a pair of manly lovers or we wouldn't be sitting at this table, eh? No shame in that." She laughed in her witch's cackle, looking around at the other women, who followed suit with deliberate heartiness.

"So that's it," Andrew said, his drawling voice cutting through the babble of boxing talk at one end of the table and gothic fiction at the other. "Let a female write it and obscenity becomes literature. And I know just the sort of slut to do it. A pink, plump bitch with ink-stained fingers and a penchant for displaying herself in unsuitable attire." He paused, only dimly aware of the horrified looks of his stricken guests.

Phyllida stood up. "Whatever I have done," she said, her voice shaking with reproach, "I do not deserve this punishment. If you regret this marriage, Andrew, you have only to say so."

Andrew could neither identify nor free himself from the demon that had him in its grip. "You mistake, my dear," he said. "It takes far more than an indecent novel to prove grounds for divorce." The silence was like the stillness between the lightning flash and the thunderclap. "By the way, I do hope you are not still pining for your Edward, because for all our differences I have no intention of freeing you to marry him. Nor, to quote from the more recent drivel, do I care to draw my scimitar at the table."

"If you will excuse me." Phyllida bobbed a quick curtsy to her guests and ran from the room, brushing the hot tears from her eyes.

Matthew stood to go after her, but Charlotte Swain held him back. "You'd better not," she whispered. "Whenever my parents have a row like that they always retire early."

"I say, Carrington," Pierce said. "That was uncalled for."

"What the devil was all that about?" Isham asked.

"Never knew a man to threaten to divorce his wife over a novel," Monkton said.

PHYLLIDA SHUT HER BOUDOIR DOOR, locked it, and leaned her back against it. She ought not give in to such weakness but she wanted to stay here for the rest of the evening. She had enjoyed the earlier conversation, the way the women talked as boldly as the men, each side trying to outdo the other in outrageous repartee. But when Andrew started jeering at her writing, when he claimed to have read her new book and that other recent masterpiece and made the odious comparison, she had to get away.

Strange, but after so humiliating a scene, when one would think she would never wish to write anything more sensational than a thank-you note, Phyllida was ready to start another novel. There was a new work forming in the back of her mind and tonight, despite her husband's cruel mockery, it had moved to the front, beginning the process of emergence. She knew the exact moment and place of its conception—the night before last, in the Brotherhood's garden, when Andrew had fainted and had joked with her like his old self.

She dug her ratty robe out of the bottom of the clothes chest, grateful that Nan had never followed through on her threats to throw it away, and sat down at the writing desk. She brought out ink and pens, found a stack of paper, dipped the pen in the ink, and forced herself to forget everything in the present, letting the thoughts flow.

Another romance, of course. This time, though, Phyllida was determined to give her characters a happy ending. Perhaps she could bring Melisande back, as Mr. Edwards had suggested. Thank goodness she had taken his advice, concluding the story with Melisande's disappearance, Lord Iskander and Ludovic distraught but consoling each other after reading her ambiguous note. "Pursuit will be futile," it read, in part. "I have gone whence no traveler returns." Everybody thought that meant death, but it didn't have to. It could just as well mean Albania or Turkey, especially in these unsettled times.

ANDREW SEIZED THE FIRST CHANCE, when the elderly guests announced their early departure. In the confusion of leave-taking, he slipped away upstairs and knocked on the boudoir door. "You will let me in, Phyllida. I will not have a repeat of all our conflicts. It is tedious and macabre."

Phyllida opened the door. He was struck at the change in her, as if he had not really looked at her in weeks. Her face that had become thin and blotchy over the previous month, and her figure that had not filled out the gowns so recently made for her, had revived. He had begun to wonder how he could have imagined himself lucky to be married to a pretty, voluptuous woman when she was, in fact, a poor, hagridden thing. Now she bloomed and swelled, as he remembered her from their first meeting and from their nights together. In fact, she was fuller, plumper, rosier than ever.

"Why macabre?" she asked.

"Forced to enact the same sequence of events over and over," Andrew said, "like some torment out of Dante. May I come in?"

Phyllida did not answer, merely stood aside.

Andrew took in the tattered, stained robe. "What the devil are you wearing?" he said. "I have never seen anything so wretched, even in a Whitechapel gin mill."

"As I doubt you have ever set foot in Whitechapel, much less a gin mill," Phyllida said, "that statement is not terribly meaningful."

Andrew smiled. "It means this, Phyllida. Take it off, or I will." He snapped his fingers.

Phyllida went very still, almost ceasing to breathe, and her face flushed bright red. "No, Andrew," she said. "After the way you spoke to me at dinner, I couldn't possibly—"

Andrew scowled and opened his fingers as if releasing a captive bird into flight. "Phyllida, surely by now you know that when I say such things it is our own language of love. The other day, at the Brotherhood—"

Phyllida shook her head. "Not this time. And not downstairs, in front of other people. It sounded as though you despise me."

"Never," Andrew said. "I could never despise you. If I despise anyone, it is myself, for enjoying your disgraceful book so much."

"Oh, that's much better," Phyllida said.

Andrew groaned.

"Did you really enjoy *Melisande*?" Phyllida asked, unable to disguise her wistful look.

"I can honestly say I found it both engrossing and moving."

"Truly, Andrew? It moved you?"

This time, for some reason, he felt confidence returning. "It certainly moved one part of me very much." He cupped his hand over the bulge in the front of his pantaloons.

Phyllida flushed again, biting her lower lip and trying not to smile. "You are making fun of me."

"Not at all," Andrew said. "I am merely attempting to explain what led me to such unforgivable behavior at the dinner table, and now to an equally inappropriate and ill-timed desire for intimacy. I perfectly understand if you do not wish to receive me for a while."

"That's fine, then," Phyllida said. "I might like to play our game another time. Tonight I am writing. You have made it quite plain what you think of my work, but it is mine, and I can sell it and other people enjoy it and I will not be shamed into giving up a harmless occupation." She sat down, dipped her pen in the ink, and stared into space, making a valiant effort to ignore her husband.

"Harmless? I don't know as I would go that far." Andrew pulled up another chair and sat facing Phyllida at an oblique angle. "Do you mind if I watch?"

Phyllida waited several seconds before answering, turning her head slowly, as if being pulled from a fascinating reverie into an unwelcome wakening. "Please yourself. It cannot be very interesting to watch someone write. Not like painting." It would be impossible to work with an audience under the most innocent of circumstances. With him there, so close she could hear his every rapid, shallow breath, could feel the heat radiating from his high-strung body, it was torture. But she would not give him the satisfaction of showing it. She stared down at the blank page, dipped the pen again, and put the nib between her red lips, sucking in a ruminative way.

Andrew had never been so hard in his life. He stood up, although the movement was agony, and laid his hand on Phyllida's shoulder. "Please, my love," he said. His voice was low, hoarse, and breathy.

Phyllida looked around, from the hand on her shoulder up to the face, scrunched in a strange kind of suffering. "What is it, Andrew?"

"I had no right to barge in here and expect you to submit to me."

"No." She smiled. "I won't submit to you anymore, Andrew."

He paled until she was afraid he was going to faint again.

An inkling of his problem came through to her. "All I meant, Andrew, is that I will lie with you by choice, but never as submission."

A great explosion seemed to be building inside Andrew's head, like the prelude to a migraine—not painful, not frightening or dangerous, but extremely urgent. He slid his hand on Phyllida's shoulder down and forward, allowing his fingers to enter the V-shaped opening of the robe and descend into the close, sultry valley between her velvety-soft breasts. "Is there a chance you might choose to, now? I have been a brute and you have said you wish to work, but—"

Phyllida stared in suspicion. "But all our guests are downstairs."

Andrew raised his eyebrows. "Would you like them to participate? Very well, but I refuse to make love to Lydia Swain or Lady Finchley. I won't poach my brother's territory."

"You are disgusting."

"And you are a gothic, romantic slut." He took her hand and kissed it. "I know it is rude and unconventional, but I want you very much right this minute. It has been so long."

"Oh, Andrew." She stood up, passing through the welcoming circle of his arms and colliding forcefully with his chest.

His lips met hers in a crushing kiss and he lifted her up easily, despite her recent substantial gain in weight, carried her into the bedroom, and deposited her on the bed. He pushed the ragged gown off her shoulders with rough, hasty hands and opened his flap with such impatience that several buttons popped off and shot across the room.

Phyllida heard the frail fabric tear but she could no longer care for such trifles, not when his kisses were so hot and fierce and when his fingers were producing such wonderful sensations, starting with her nipples and extending out and down along her entire body. . .

"I swore the next time we made love," he said, "I would be as slow and gentle as you could wish. But I don't think that will be possible."

"It's all right. Just tell me you want me."

"Want you? It's all I've been able to think about for weeks." He knelt between her legs, which opened for him so readily, and nibbled at the quivering breasts. His hand stroked along a smooth thigh, down and up again, moving inexorably into the cleft.

"Oh," Phyllida said. "Oh, I dreamed of this, but I thought I had ruined it."

"It was I who almost ruined it. Now don't talk. Just let me make you scream."

"Scream? Why would I—"

His finger between her legs found the little man in the boat. The screams stopped the downstairs conversation dead.

"Perhaps I should see you and Mrs. Swain home," Matthew said. "May I call on you tomorrow, Miss Swain?"

Charlotte ducked her head so that her eyes were level with Matthew's. "Yes, Mr. Thornby. Mama and I will be at home in the morning."

"What was the name of that book?" Monkton drawled. "*Sense and Sensibility*? Might not be so dull after all."

YOU DON'T HAVE TO work so hard at losing, Verney," Amberson said. "I'm perfectly capable of winning the shirt off your back through my own skill."

"Sorry, Amberson," Verney said. "Force of habit. Can't say the same for most of the members."

"No, I shouldn't think so. Thought there was some sort of dinner tonight."

"It ended early. Mrs. Carrington was, ah, suddenly indisposed."

"By which you mean Carrington was in a hurry to make up for lost time."

"How did you know?"

"Oh, one could see that coming the minute he set eyes on her in that odious manifestation as a boy. Is it too late to get in on that wager, do you think?"

"Not at all. Most of us will be increasing our stake."

"Quite a bunch of sharps," Amberson said. "Who do they believe is the phantom accomplice, by the way? Do you know?"

"They mentioned Thornby," Verney said. "As I'm sure you meant them to. I have to say I dislike extremely being put in this position."

"Do you? I'd have thought compromising positions were precisely what you relish most." Amberson noticed Verney's flinch, the tightening of the muscles of mouth and jaw, with a mixture of satisfaction and something else he could not quite place. The game proceeded in silence to its inevitable conclusion. "Well, that's it. Care for some backgammon?"

"Tell you the truth, Amberson. Never thought I'd say such a thing, but I'm tired of games."

"Figure of speech, Frederick. *Backgammon*, you know. And call me Geoffrey."

"Oh, I see. Yes, Geoffrey, that sounds lovely."

"No, Frederick. No, it does not. You must not confuse what we are about to do with love or beauty." He paused to watch the effect on his partner. Interesting. It seemed only to increase the man's eagerness. "Still game?"

"More than ever."

"Good man. Come here." Amberson touched his lips very lightly to Verney's and slid a fingertip slowly down his skin from the pulse under the ear, along the lightly furred chest, the nipple, the abdomen, to fasten onto the large member jutting out as if to reach for him. "Which is your room, Frederick?"

"No. 2. But I don't think I can—"

"Don't think. Don't talk. Just follow me."

"I don't really have a choice, do I? Not when you're holding on to me like that."

"You always have a choice, Frederick. The so very hard Frederick Verney. You can choose to let me lead you upstairs to your room. Or you can choose to put your clothes back on and find yourself another partner for backgammon."

"Take me, then, Geoffrey."

"Are you sure? Excellent. Shh, no noise, until we're inside. I do hope this will be a very long night."

AMBERSON OPENED HIS EYES, GRATEFUL for his good night vision and the comforting darkness. A light would force him to acknowledge the unwelcome burgeoning of a new emotion inside him. He had felt it there on the balcony the other night, the desire to confess, to throw himself at the feet of his fellow men and beg to be taken up as one of them. Now he knew its corollary—tenderness. How revolting. It was that drowning kitten again.

Verney snored beside him, his head thrown back, mouth open wide as if in the grip of strong passion, looking much as he had when awake, a couple of hours ago. Amberson slipped quietly from between the sheets, pulling the covers back up to prevent Verney from catching cold, and fumbled around in the pockets of his breeches for his notebook and pencil.

"It seems I was mistaken," he wrote. "This night was filled with both love and beauty. If the duties of war permitted, every night would be so. As it is, I will say *au revoir*."

He left the scrap of paper on top of Verney's heaped clothing. No, that would never do. The valet would probably scoop it all up in the morning. He crumpled the note, could not bring himself to throw it away, unfolded it, and placed it on the pillow, checking to see that Verney's heavy breathing barely shifted the paper's balance with each exhale, before dressing and heading back to the docks. High time he was in Spain again, where any display of softness was the short road to death.

"I CAN'T BELIEVE," ANDREW SAID, "that we wasted so much time when we could have been so delightfully employed." He lay on his back, comfortably naked now, Phyllida's head resting on his chest, his arm holding her loosely in place.

"I never should have lied to you. Can you ever forgive me?"

"I forgave you long ago, my love. I think I forgave you the very next day. No, it was myself I could not forgive, for being so inadequate a husband and putting you in such danger. To think that you had been so abused and frightened and could not rely on me for protection or even justice."

"It wasn't that," Phyllida said. "I did not dare tell the truth. Turner, or whatever his name is, threatened the Brotherhood. And you and Sir Frederick gave me such a stern lecture the day after our wedding, about discretion and—"

"Oh, God. You really should have confided in me. That's why we were using him in the first place."

"But you said tonight you thought he was just a French agent."

"That is for public consumption. The one fact we could not let slip, Amberson and I, was that his real aim was to bring down the Brotherhood."

"What about all that code?"

"Amberson supplied that to him, from his office of cipherers and secret writing experts in Abchurch Street. That way, if we could catch him at his real game, we'd have something else to hang him for."

"My goodness! Then why take him to the Brotherhood after he was injured?"

"No alternative," Andrew said. "Gaol was obviously out of the question, and I couldn't very well ask Miss Gatling to take him in."

"Miss Gatling! Why would she?"

"One of the cipherers. Or perhaps de-cipherers is a better term. But you mustn't let on I've told you."

"So many secrets. It's enough for at least two more novels." She lifted her head to see how he took that.

"I'm immune to threats of all kind by now," Andrew said. "And I deserve any fiendish punishment you dream up. It is true, however, I never thought he would be a danger to a lady. That is the worst of all, to think of you suffering such an ordeal and with no one to turn to."

"Most men would not care about that. Only their wife's virtue."

"I am not most men. Did he hurt you very much? I should think you might have taken an aversion to the entire male sex."

"No, Andrew. I can't think of him as a man. Not like you." Phyllida kissed his cheek. "I thought of you—afterward. I had not appreciated the difference between rape and making love until I learned what force really is."

"Hell and damnation!" Andrew sat up. "I should have killed him." He slammed his fist into his palm with a loud thwack that made Phyllida jump. "I congratulated myself on being so clever, not putting a bullet through his spiteful little brain, not giving Amberson the ultimate hold over me. I forgot all about your feelings."

"No, Andrew, you were right. That's what Matthew thought, too. It's lucky he came along in time to blow that smoke at you and make you miss."

"Miss?" He lifted one eyebrow. "My dear, the sun was behind me, and in Turner's eyes. If I had wanted to kill him he would have been dead long before Matthew appeared with his loathsome cheroot. A much easier shot."

"Oh. You mean—"

"Yes, I very nearly did kill him after Matthew put me off like that. Are you saying he did it deliberately?"

"He was trying to help you."

Andrew groaned. "Spare me from all good intentions." He studied Phyllida's sprawled body, noticing the rounded curves, fuller than ever. "The boy at the club. The boy Matthew was kissing. That was you."

"Matthew was only comforting me, Andrew. We thought you were asleep."

"I'm sure you hoped I was." He grinned. "It didn't look like his usual style. I trust you don't intend to continue the masquerade, because I will be forced to exercise some belated husbandly authority."

"No, Andrew. I hated it. Besides, I won't fit into the breeches much longer."

"You don't fit now." He let his hand roam, following a logical progression from the pouting lips to the swell of breast to the inviting mound of belly. "What I don't see is why you were doing it in the first place."

The explanation caused a great deal of unseemly mirth and a few less than refined expressions. "Poor Witherspoon, plowing through that scandalous book," Andrew said. "The damn thing kept turning up everywhere, at the Brotherhood and—"

"So that's how you came to read it," Phyllida said. "Although you didn't have to be quite so horrid about it."

"I did not mean to hurt your feelings," he said. "I couldn't help coming to your defense."

"Coming to my defense? No one else was attacking me. Only you."

"Let us say I was defending your old self, your first, pure incarnation. The poor virgin sacrificed on the bloody altar of notoriety and filthy lucre."

"You're beginning to talk like my books," Phyllida said.

Light dawned. "You didn't write *Sense and Sensibility*, did you?"

"No, Andrew. You made an assumption there. I never lied about that."

"I know. I suppose I was taken in at first because it started out so much like your family. Frankly, I'm delighted to have been mistaken."

Phyllida stared into Andrew's face, the better to catch him in the act of duplicity. "Are you? Why?"

"The author of *Sense and Sensibility* is no doubt an excellent woman," Andrew said, laughing at her mistrustful glare, "but I should not feel nearly so easy with her in the exercise of my spousal duties as with the luscious little baggage who wrote about that dreadful flirt Melisande and those two queer culls charitably described as her husbands." He tugged on a stray curl and pulled her head down to his chest again.

Phyllida accepted this questionable encomium without a direct reply. "Why did you quit shaving?"

"What? Oh, an agreement with Matthew. Do you mind?"

"No. So long as I can be with you, I don't care about anything else. Does he prefer it? The hair?"

"We men are peculiar, are we not?"

"Very. But most of you are very agreeable, despite your little idiosyncrasies."

"My love," Andrew murmured. "That reminds me. Please tell me you did not wish to marry that fellow. Because I would hate to think I ruined an affair of the heart for you."

"What fellow? I have never loved anybody before you."

"You gratify me extremely. That tiresome man I had to knock down twice at our wedding."

"Mr. Coulter? You think I was in love with Leighton Coulter? Oh, Andrew, how can you believe such a nonsensical thing?"

"He certainly seemed to think I robbed him of a bride."

"Men. Well, to be fair, it was mostly Mama's fault. She was so worried I would end up an old maid, because of having no money, you see, and Mr. Coulter is an attorney, so he was the best prospect in the village. Mama insisted I try to get him to ruin me, which would have been easy of course. But she never could understand I didn't want him, that I'd much rather be an old maid than marry him. It's not that he was so bad. I just could not care for him in that way."

"What way?" Andrew asked, kissing her. "This way? Or maybe this way? Or perhaps this way?"

Phyllida sighed with happiness. "All of those ways. Oh, Andrew, I am glad you came along when you did. I was that close to surrendering."

"To Coulter? But you said—"

"Mama would lock us in the parlor every evening after supper. She said I should let nature take its course and after that I wouldn't mind so much. But I never could bring myself to go through with it."

"Lock you in? Alone? My God, I have a mind to pay her a visit and lock myself in with her."

"Better not, Andrew, unless you have a secret passion for Mama. She'd merely lift her skirts and ask did you prefer the couch or the floor."

"Wench. Slut. Like mother like daughter."

"Only with you, Andrew. You always call me a slut when you're about to do the loveliest things."

"In that case, slut, I feel another urge coming on to do lovely things. Would you like that?"

"Yes, please, Andrew."

He leaned on one elbow and smiled down at her in a most superior, masculine way, moving the palm of his other hand in slow circles over a nipple, so lightly it was as if he barely touched her. "Now, my dear, this is going to take a while. I have been unconscionably negligent, but from now on I hope you will have no reason to complain."

"Oooohhh," Phyllida moaned. The effect of that feathery touch was like the prelude to possession, coursing along every nerve from her breast, through her middle and down every limb, pooling in that place between her thighs. She twitched and flexed, pressing herself up against his hand in hopes that he would be forced to touch her more firmly.

"No, no," he said, laughing and drawing away. "Not yet, little cat."

"Please," she said. "Please don't wait too long. I can't bear it." Every little movement of his fingertips imprinted itself, burning into her flesh and radiating out in waves of heat that somehow turned to ice as they reached her extremities and back again to flame in her center, erupting inside that secret place. She felt the walls opening and closing in spasms of longing for his forceful entrance. "Please, Andrew."

"We have all night and most of the morning," he said. "There is no need to rush." He sat all the way up, swung a leg over her and grabbed her hands, pinning them out to her sides. He leaned down and took the nipple in his mouth, sucking and running his tongue around its stiff peak.

Phyllida strained against his imprisoning hands, writhing and moaning, feeling her moisture spurting between her legs. "Please, Andrew," she begged. "Please." She broke his hold with one hand, shouting in triumph and reaching for him below, but he caught her hand and held it as before, gloating down at her features distorted with desire.

"Such an eager little bitch," he said. "Quite put me off my rhythm. Now, let me see, where was I?" He bent down and took the other nipple, subjecting it to similar treatment, but released it after she bucked so hard she almost threw him.

"What is it?" Andrew asked, all innocence. "Do you want me to stop? Shall we rest for a while?"

"You are a brute," Phyllida said. "If you stop I will beat you."

"I don't wish to push you or go too fast," Andrew said. "I don't want to frighten you."

"You are impossible," Phyllida said. "*Please* will you go on."

He quivered with his own desire as she thrust her hips up against him, but he was determined to do as he had been instructed, as he could see might eventually repay with interest any effort of self-restraint. He loosed one wrist so he could use his hand, but was immediately assaulted again as she tried to bring him into position. "No, no," he said, swatting her away. "Mustn't touch."

He took both wrists in one hand and held her hands above her head, forcing her to arch her back and expose her breasts to further attentions while freeing his other hand to find the little man in the boat. "That's better," he said. He was becoming accomplished at this, able to gauge the level of her arousal, gently sliding his fingers across the little morsel of flesh, making her wriggle and cry, but without enough pressure to release her too soon. Far from being in danger of losing his hardness, the drawn-out sport seemed only to strengthen his desire. He played back and forth between breasts and cleft until she was rocking in a rhythm that was nakedly sexual and making the most extraordinary high-pitched noise, something between a howl and a whine.

"Now, if you are very good, slut, and if you beg me sufficiently, I may grant you the final favor."

"Oh, oh!" Phyllida was lost now, floating in the ether between body and space. Or perhaps she was drowning in an ocean of icy flame. She knew nothing except this agony that was also joy, this sweet torment that must never end, that had to end, that would kill her if she didn't let it pull her to the peak and push her over the edge. She tossed her head from side to side and continued to thrust with her hips, hearing Andrew's drawling, deep voice from somewhere above her. He was telling her the secret, giving her the code that would free her, if she could only follow the instructions. "Pluh, pluh," she tried to comply. "Unh. Unh." She had lost all ability to enunciate.

He gave a last swipe of his finger to her sensitive, throbbing place and kissed her, thrusting his tongue deep into her mouth as he at last let himself push into her below. He released her hands, and her arms came up to lock around his neck. She wrapped her legs around his waist as their bodies moved in a synchronized dance, bringing them together in a vigorous climax, a miraculous moment that Andrew had never expected to know with a woman.

The footman who locked the house up for the night, the last of the servants to go to bed, smiled to himself as he dug out his earplugs. Always better to work in a happy household, whatever some folks might say.

IT WAS THE MIDDLE OF the night when Phyllida awoke. Strong, wiry arms held her against a chest that was much too hairy for comfort, but she wouldn't change places, even for a string of rubies.

Andrew stirred as she shifted position. "Am I forgiven for that wretched wedding night?"

"You have nothing to apologize for there," Phyllida said. "You did your best."

"Ah," Andrew said. "Damned with faint praise."

"I see one thing hasn't changed," Phyllida murmured. "You have a very high opinion of your abilities in this area."

"Hmm," he said. "I seem to recall, only a short time ago, this same severe critic quite literally in raptures over my abilities in this area."

Phyllida blushed; although it was too dark to see, Andrew could feel the heat. "That is not a gentlemanly thing to say," she said.

"But I do not have to be a gentleman in this bed, just as you do not have to be a lady. So long as we treat each other with kindness, that is all that is required." He laid a possessive hand on her hip. "Would you be kind enough to receive me again, my love?"

"It is not kindness," Phyllida said. "But I think I should tell you the truth."

"Not another secret! Is it dreadful?"

"Not to me. Only you probably won't want to lie with me anymore."

Andrew felt himself growing cold with fear. "I don't believe it. I don't believe you are capable of doing anything so terrible. What could possibly make me not want to lie with you? And it isn't *lying with you* when I'm with you. It's *making love*. Do you understand, you lying little bitch? So you'd better tell me."

Phyllida buried her face in Andrew's shoulder. "'M'ving abub," she said.

Andrew flinched and put his hand under her chin, lifting her face to meet his eyes. "I didn't quite catch that."

"I'm going to have a baby," Phyllida said. "So you don't have to make love to me or lie with me or do anything you don't want to do."

"Please," he said. "Please tell me it's Matthew's."

"No, it's not Matthew's. You ought to know he'd never do that to you."

"Oh, God. It's— I ought to have killed him. Damn it to hell. I knew I ought to have killed him. My poor love. I promise you I'll help you dispose of it as soon as it's born. You'll never have to set eyes on it."

"Andrew! Don't say such a thing."

"We can keep it if you really want it. I don't know how women feel about these things."

"Andrew. Listen to me. It's not Turner's child."

"But you said he forced you."

Phyllida burst into tears. As he had no idea what else to do, Andrew held her and let her cry. After several minutes, Phyllida lifted her head. "Oh, Andrew. You really are the most wonderful husband. You still wanted me, and you made love to me so beautifully, even though you thought another man had—"

Andrew sighed and shrugged. "Well, why the devil shouldn't I? What kind of husband would I be if I stopped loving you because of what some monster did to you? My God!"

"Most men—"

"We have already established," Andrew said in his most supercilious drawl, "that I am not most men. Now what, exactly, did happen? I ask only so that we need never have this conversation again."

"A fighter," Andrew said with approval, after hearing the account of the locked door, the attempted rape, the backhand slap, and the knee to the groin. "Almost makes up for my not killing him."

"And I stuck him with a pin."

"Excellent! Transforms one's entire view of defenseless females."

"But that was only because he held a pistol to my head."

The agitation produced by this elaboration of the recent events at the Brotherhood was such that at least one occupant feared the bed frame to be in imminent danger of collapse. "My God! You could have been killed," Andrew said, when he had been persuaded to lie still. "Most of those dueling pistols have hair triggers."

"Luckily I didn't know about that," Phyllida said. "But you see why I wish you hadn't taken him to the Brotherhood. Finding him there almost made my heart stop."

"At least you're not carrying his child. Thank goodness for that."

"You said you'd let me keep it."

"It's your child, your choice. But I could never care for it. And it would not inherit." He knew he was missing something important. "Wait a minute. Are you saying it's mine? Why didn't you tell me before?"

"I didn't believe it either. And I didn't tell you at first because after only a month one can't really be certain. Then after the second month, we'd been . . . we were . . . estranged. And I lost weight, instead of gaining. I thought it was only nerves that my courses didn't come. So I still couldn't be sure."

"But when could it have happened?"

"When do you think, idiot? We made love three times when we married. It had to be then. And I've missed three courses. I'd be bleeding right now if I wasn't—"

Andrew lay back, waiting for the pounding of his head and heart to subside. "My love," he said. "But why would you think I wouldn't want to make love to you?"

"Because I'm already with child. There's no need to."

"What a drearily Biblical idea of matrimony you have, my dear.

I'm terribly sorry, but I don't share your puritanical notions. In fact, I expect to be very active during the next few months. Once you get too big it won't be comfortable. So I'll be keeping you quite busy until then. What do you say to that?"

"Yes, please. Can we start now? Although I will understand if you need to rest. It will be the third time this night."

"Oh ho," Andrew said. "Now we see your true opinion. You must never underestimate me, my dear."

"I don't want you to overexert yourself," Phyllida said.

"Very kind," Andrew said. "Perhaps, then, instead of my doing all the work, you might like to try riding me."

"That does not sound at all ladylike."

"It's not," Andrew said, throwing the covers aside to show his readiness. "It is, however, just the thing for an insatiable slut who complains that I go too fast and that I go too slow. It has the incomparable advantage of allowing you to control the pace."

"HAVE I TOLD YOU HOW much I love you, wife?" Andrew whispered after Phyllida finished a gratifyingly long and bruising session in the saddle and collapsed on top of him in a warm bundle of sticky, fragrant flesh.

"I always like to hear you say it, husband."

"I love you, my wife, mother of my child." He sat up all of a sudden, excited by his thought, tumbling her unceremoniously onto the mattress. "Wait until I tell Matthew! Won't he be pleased!"

27

MATTHEW LOOKED AROUND THE luxurious suite with regret. It had felt like a homecoming, a dream of contentment. Settling down in commodious lodgings, working at his family's business, finding a lover for the long haul, living amongst men like himself. No more pretending.

He sighed and started to pack. It would be a lonely couple of months, with no guarantee of the renewal of happiness when he returned. On his travels and at home in Yorkshire he had made do: sailors and laborers, the occasional half-pay officer or displaced gentleman. He had never really loved, or looked for a lasting passion. Here in town, with his wealth and his father's purchased title, he had been able to force his way into the *ton* without completely remaking himself to their mold. That he was well built and good looking and could have any handsome buck he fancied had given him the upper hand in so dangerous a game.

But a man must be careful in the country. Never mind that it was his own estate he was going to; if he frightened the horses, as they said, he would be ostracized, reviled, never accepted by his tenants and the local squires. Money meant nothing to them if it had been worked for and did not come with land, handed down for generations. As for the businessmen, the mill and factory owners, the merchants and industrialists—they were as conventional in their morality as the nobs. More, because they had worked for all they had, and had a greater fear of losing it. Well, it was but for a few weeks. Whatever his welcome on his return, Matthew resolved not to become an exile again.

The knock at the door startled him out of his self-pity. "Come in," he called from the inner room. "I'm not packed yet."

"How very fortunate," that drawling voice said, "since there is no longer any need for you to travel."

Matthew rubbed his hand over his face, feeling suddenly as if he had forgotten to shave or put on clean underclothes, and came into the front room to receive his guest. "Time I was going," he said. "No point in my staying on here."

"No point," Andrew repeated. He looked tired, with dark circles under his eyes, and he was not dressed with his usual impeccable elegance; his clothes appeared to have been thrown on in a hurry with no recourse to the services of a valet or the looking glass. But he was strangely animated, his eyes glittering with excitement, suffused with an inner joy that was in danger of bursting out at any moment. "At least I can't fault your honesty."

Matthew was drawn, despite his best instincts, to take Andrew's hand in his. "You must not think me so low as to desert you because of that."

"Low?" Andrew snorted with harsh laughter. "You would be no different from any other man. Certainly I cannot claim a higher standard. I only wish you would allow me a chance to redeem myself before disappearing from my life forever."

"It's not forever," Matthew said. "I hope you will want to see me again when I return. But surely you'll need some time alone, now that you and Phyllida are reconciled."

"So you heard."

"Yes, love. We all heard—downstairs." Matthew chuckled and poked Andrew in the ribs.

Surprisingly, Andrew did not take offense at this obvious attempt to rile him. "She is a bit of a screamer," he said with a hint of misplaced pride in his voice. "No, but it's more than that."

"She sings, does she?"

Andrew raised a fist.

"Nay, love. I can guess your good news. I congratulate you." He kissed Andrew's unshaven cheek and then his mouth.

Their kiss was heartfelt, deep. "I shall be spending more time with her while I can," Andrew said. "But I will still have plenty left for you, I can promise that now. Do you understand?"

"No," Matthew said, smiling. "I think I'll need a fuller explanation, maybe a demonstration."

"Excellent," Andrew said, "because it just so happens that is pre cisely what I had in mind."

Matthew groaned. "God, love, there's nothing I'd like more. But I do have to go, if only for a week or so. I have property to see to."

"What is it?" Andrew said. "A mill? A factory? Can't somebody else handle it, an agent or a man of business?"

"No, it's an estate. A personal holding. I want to take possession, establish myself as landlord and start putting it in order. You see, I'm getting married, too. Charlotte, Miss Swain, that is, has given me a favorable answer and—"

"You're what?" Andrew roared. "Are you out of your mind?"

"No more than you."

"Oh, for God's sake," Andrew said. "I only made my own arrangement because I have a substantial fortune and am heir to a title. Surely there's no need for you to worry about such things."

"Perhaps I care for her."

"That's nonsense. How could you? I mean, if you're looking for a mount up to your weight you can get Tolliver's bay gelding for a lot less than the cost of a marriage settlement to a peer's daughter. And you're free to dispose of him once you've worn him out."

"Careful, Andrew. That's my future wife you're talking about."

"You can't marry Charlotte Swain. Any other woman, but not her."

"Why? Because of you and Harry?"

"What do you know about me and Harry?"

"What is there to know? Seems you still harbor an unrequited passion."

"Before tossing around accusations, you should consider the beam in your own eye. You're jealous of Phyllida. I do love her, very much, but it doesn't stop me loving you."

"Then why should my marrying Charlotte stop me loving you?"

"I don't know, damn it. I just— I wasn't expecting this." Andrew laughed and leaned in, resting hips to hips, arms linked loosely around the broad back. "Where is this phantom estate anyway? Yorkshire? Lancashire? Don't tell me Northumberland, because I know the property up there and—"

"Hertfordshire," Matthew said. "It's in Hertfordshire."

"You said north," Andrew said. "You lying, cheating, teasing—"

"Watch your mouth," Matthew said. "Last time I looked at the map, Hertfordshire's north of London. And Bentwood Grange is in Hertfordshire, last time I checked."

"Bentwood Grange? What does Bentwood Grange have to do with the price of corn?"

"Price of cotton, you should say," Matthew said. "Bentwood Grange is the estate we're talking about."

"But that's— That was the estate of the Gowertons. Some damn mushroom of a cloth merchant bought it up cheap when the line died out."

"The mushroom's son, actually."

Andrew's face went rigid and his eyes hooded over. "I'm sorry, Matthew. You know I didn't mean— But an estate like that, even undervalued, costs thousands of pounds. And you've been going to work— Just what the hell have you been playing at?"

"Not working at three or four shillings a week, no. But keeping my hand in at the business, yes. Why not?"

"The question is rather, why?" Andrew said. "What sort of gentleman works when he doesn't have to? Makes you look like a cit or a tradesman."

"That's what bothers you, isn't it? I am a tradesman—a tradesman's son, at any rate. I know were my money comes from and I'm not ashamed to work at it. But when Bentwood Grange came on the market it seemed a good chance for me. Brings in a decent income, makes me an elector. There's a vicarage I control the living for. So I'm a gentleman now, Andrew, whether you like it or not."

Andrew stood gaping for several seconds. "You damned impostor," he said.

"Not so pleasant, is it," Matthew said, "finding that the brawny laborer you've been buggering is one of your own kind?"

"Don't be ridiculous," Andrew said. "I just— Here you've been letting me feel sorry for you, thinking you were dependent on wages, worried that these lodgings were too dear for you."

"Yes, it has been a laugh, seeing you play the Lady Bountiful—"

"When all the time you could probably buy and sell me ten times over."

"No, no, my love. Once or twice, that's all." Matthew dug a hand into his pocket. "Here, I almost forgot."

Andrew took the package and opened it, blinking at the bright red stones glinting up at him. "My rubies. How the devil did you get them?"

"Oh, Amberson didn't have a chance to return them before he went back to Spain, especially as Phyllida and I weren't letting him into your room. So he gave them to me."

"Amberson," Andrew said. "I ought to have guessed. No wonder you tried to spoil my shot. And to think I offered you the same position as that rat Tournière. How very appropriate. Tell me, did you bend over as eagerly for Amberson as for me? Or did you pretend to be unwilling, to give him his money's worth?"

"You son of a whore."

It was fortunate Andrew was watching Matthew's face. The blow was so sudden he was alerted only by the narrowing of the blue eyes, the shadow of dark emotion that crossed the open, friendly countenance. He barely had time to raise his arm and turn sideways, taking the brunt of it on his shoulder. If that heavy fist had connected where it was aimed he would have been knocked unconscious, or worse. The force and the pain took his breath away as it was.

"You bastard." Andrew staggered and held his fists at the ready.

"I'm sorry," Matthew said. "I don't know what—"

Andrew strode forward, swinging with the momentum of his steps, getting in a body blow and a cross to the face that smashed into Matthew's eye.

Matthew let out a bellow of rage, lowered his head, and charged across the room.

Andrew sidestepped, letting Matthew overrun his target, then drove his right fist once, twice into the big man's midsection when he turned around.

Matthew doubled over, gagging.

"Had enough?" the drawling voice taunted.

Matthew straightened up. "From you?" he said. "I've just got started, you scrawny, conceited fribble." He swung his left in a wild arc, taking Andrew by surprise and catching his face a glancing blow.

Andrew worked his jaw, making sure it wasn't broken. "You insolent, uncouth barbarian." He feinted left, then right, landing several hits on Matthew's ribs.

Matthew backed away, then rushed at Andrew again, aiming a flurry of punches beneath and over Andrew's guard, yet finding them all curiously deflected. He had never deigned to study the gentlemanly art of boxing, thinking it a dilettante's way of fighting. Nowhere in his travels had angry, usually drunken men shown any more skill in their use of fists than a bear mauling a dog. Always Matthew's size and strength had counted for more in a fight than any silly business of footwork and stance.

Andrew shifted his posture, turning his body ninety degrees, and stepped into a jab, slamming his fist into the side of Matthew's head and following through with his shoulders and torso. "Boxing," he said, "is a science, as opposed to head-butting and country brawling." He was curiously loath to work on Matthew the final set of moves that would drop him and put a quick end to the stupid altercation. How often had Gentleman Jackson shown him the way to deal with an unschooled opponent, especially one who outweighed him and who should not be allowed to get in any damaging blows that could be avoided. "Use the uppercut or the hook as soon as you can," Jackson always said, "and put the full force of your body behind it. Dragging out a match is only for amateurs."

Matthew shook his head to clear the fog, watched the graceful figure swaying before him, and popped a satisfying blow over Andrew's left hand into the prominent nose, making Andrew yelp.

"Fighting," Matthew said, "is a man's game. As opposed to high-stepping, caper-merchant ballet dancing."

By now a crowd had gathered in the corridor just outside the open door, maintaining a prudent distance from the large, violent men but attracted to a fistfight like hounds to a wounded stag.

"Drawn his cork," Pierce said. "Now the claret's flowing."

"Ten to one on Thornby," Monkton said.

"Done," Pierce said. "Always a pleasure taking money from the ignorant."

"Ever seen Carrington in action?" Verney asked.

"Yes, of course," Monkton said, "but the thing is, don't know this Thornby. Could be a dark horse."

"These northerners are tough," Verney said, considering. "And look at the size of those shoulders. Double or nothing on the Yorkshireman."

"Easy pickings, man," Pierce said. "This isn't an American Donnybrook Fair, you know. Here's another hundred says Carrington brings him down in five rounds."

While this discussion was taking place, a series of jabs, punches, and roundhouse blows had been exchanged and parried, inflicting relatively little damage. Andrew bore a bruise on his cheekbone in addition to the bloody nose, and Matthew's right ear had gone bright red, a counterpart to the left eye that was closed tight, the flesh swelling around it. Otherwise the two men seemed as game and fresh for the fight as ever. There was a brief intermission while coats and waistcoats were removed and shirtsleeves rolled up, then the sparring resumed.

Kit came out of the honeymoon suite and watched transfixed, mimicking Andrew's stance and following every nimble piece of footwork with his own movements. "That's it, that's it," he muttered.

"Darken 'is daylights and box 'is ears. Left, right, set 'im up, then mill 'im down. We'll show 'im. Show 'im 'ow we fights in London."

Lord Isham was hopping up and down in excitement. "Haven't seen a real mill like this in donkey's years," he exclaimed. "What d'ye think, Rup? The Yorkshireman is heavier but Carrington's got style."

"I'll tell you what I think, my love," Archbold said, stifling a yawn. "I think boxing is just about the most overrated spectacle since they stopped throwing lions to Christians." He looked down to see the angelic face of Witherspoon turning away, his features eloquent with disgust. "What do you say, young man, we take a turn in the garden while these bloodthirsty friends of ours indulge their perverted tastes?"

"Thank you," Witherspoon said, grateful for the sympathy. "That would be very nice. But are you sure they didn't throw the Christians to the lions?"

Archbold shook his head. "No, there might have been some sport in that. At least it would have given the poor beasts a fighting chance."

A roar went up from the crowd as Andrew unleashed a combination of body blows and jabs on Matthew, pushing him back toward the inner room. "That's the way." "Drive him out of the ring." "One, two," the count began.

Pierce looked around to see his friend being spirited away by the tall old man.

"Don't worry," Isham put his hand on the other little man's arm. "Rup's a flirt, that's all. Your friend is perfectly safe."

Pierce, torn between running after George and staying to see the fight, accepted Isham's reassurance. "Some men don't appreciate the science of it," he complained.

"Science?" Isham said. "Don't know about that. Just like to see the muscles and the blood. Ought to take off their shirts." He put two fingers into the corners of his mouth and let loose with a piercing whistle. "Take 'em off, boys!"

"Now there's an idea," Monkton said, pushing forward into the vacated places. "I'm sure Verney here agrees."

"What's that you say?" Verney said. "Quite an exhibition of form, isn't it?"

Matthew barreled back from his disadvantage, swinging his arms and clipping Andrew, striking the prominent, already bloodied nose. The spectators shouted oaths and advice as Andrew clutched his face.

Andrew drew himself up, danced, and feinted, his movements even more tightly controlled with rage. The crowd watched intently, almost silently, sensing a denouement. Matthew held his arms up, guarding his face and his chest. Andrew slid one foot forward, sideways, back and forward again, thumping Matthew's side below the ribcage with his right fist to distract his attention, following with a left uppercut to the jaw.

The big man was knocked straight up, seeming to hang in the air for a second or two, before falling back down with a crashing thud, overturning the little table and throwing a vase of flowers across the room where it shattered against the wall. Whistles and cheers from Carrington's backers mixed with groans from Matthew's supporters and exhortations to get up.

The Yorkshireman lay sprawled, making no attempt to rise. Although he did not appear to be unconscious or even unduly winded, he seemed disinclined to continue the fight.

Verney shook Pierce's hand and gave him his vowel. Monkton followed suit. "Down for the count," he said. "You'll have my bank draft first thing tomorrow, Pierce."

"Think I misjudged Thornby," Pierce said.

"How do you mean?" Verney asked. "No match for Carrington's skill, just as you predicted."

"No," Pierce said, "shouldn't have suspected him of collaborating with Amberson. A man who fights so ineptly can't be anything but honest."

Monkton rolled his eyes. "Such naiveté," he said. "Still, you have a point. Thornby does appear to lack the necessary killer instinct."

Pierce and Verney headed for the stairs. "Coming, Monkton? Isham?"

"Think I'll stay awhile," Isham said. "Might be even more interesting now."

The scene certainly had changed. In the aftermath of the fight, Andrew had thrown himself full-length on top of his defeated opponent. Having planted several deep kisses on his lover's open mouth, he sat up, straddled Matthew's hips, and pinned his hands over his head on the floor. As the remaining crowd watched, he ground his hips into his recumbent adversary's. "Well, bitch?" he whispered. "Am I hard enough for you now?"

"Don't know," Matthew answered, his battered face creased in a broad grin. "You'd better try that again."

Andrew complied, releasing his lover's hands in order to open his shirt and pantaloons.

Matthew reached up to run his finger along the curve of the nose. "I'm sorry if I hurt you, love, but you've a way of saying things that can push a man to his limit—and beyond."

"Me?" Andrew said. "You're the one threatening to leave. But you'll have to do much better than that wretched performance to get away from me."

"Don't I know it," Matthew said. "What are you going to do?"

"Make you sorry you ever thought of leaving. Make you beg for my cock. Make you—"

"Shut up, then," Matthew said. "Stop promising and start doing."

"Come on, my dear," Archbold said, dragging Isham away. "Give them some privacy."

Isham struggled to stay in place but was no match for his friend's commanding height and long reach. "Damn it, Rup, I'm an old man. Might not get another chance to see something choice like those two hunks going at it. Least you could do is let me enjoy it. Anyway, thought you was out in the garden with that little blond slut."

"George Witherspoon," Archbold said in quelling tones, "is a very sensitive and correct young man."

"Ha!" Isham said. "Told you to bugger off, did he?"

"Not in so many words," Archbold said. "Thought I might have more luck with someone who ain't so particular. Sort of fellow who'll bend over for any man with a stiff prick. Someone like you."

"Why, Rup," Isham said, batting his eyes and leaning against his friend. "You say the sweetest things."

THE TWO NAKED MEN LAY panting on the soft Turkey carpet, their clothes strewn haphazardly around the floor. Matthew sported a crushed daisy behind his ear, and a few loose petals were sprinkled over his chest, held in place by the gummy mess of smeared blood from Andrew's nose. Andrew nestled in the crook of Matthew's arm. He was a mass of bruises, not all inflicted during the fistfight, and there was a jagged shard of vase digging into his left buttock. The knuckles of both hands were swollen, and he suspected his nose was, if not exactly broken, at least somewhat bent out of shape. He had never felt so good in his life.

"Have I redeemed myself?" Andrew asked, stroking the curly blond hairs on the broad, muscular chest. "Or are you still pining for Amberson's rough treatment?"

"That's too stupid to answer," Matthew said.

"Not as stupid as you trying to put me off my shot at Tournière. What did you imagine you were doing?"

"I *saved* you from living out the rest of your life under Amberson's thumb. When you think about it, you pompous, condescending, public-school ass, you'll thank me."

"Thank you? Do you have any idea how close I came to killing him because of your meddling? My God! I ought to put a bullet right between your big deceitful blue eyes. Just to show you."

Matthew laughed. "Yes, love. That would show me alright. God, Andrew. I've been worried sick about you ever since I learned you were mixed up with Amberson."

"You've been worried about me. Well, that does say a lot. And before you go around calling people public-school asses you should arrange to have your records from Harrow expunged. Makes you look a bit of a hypocrite."

"Ah. The voting-in to the Brotherhood."

"Suppose you thought I wouldn't look at your credentials," Andrew said.

"I never thought about it one way or the other," Matthew said. "I'm not hiding anything."

"Then why all the broad Yorkshire?" Andrew demanded. "Why all the pretend gaucherie, the country-gawk manner?"

Matthew smiled so wide he seemed in danger of splitting his face in half. "Because you were so easy to fool. One broad 'O' or provincial turn of phrase and you'd be looking down that hook nose of yours, correcting me with a curl of the lip in that insolent, drawling voice, just like the head boy in my fifth form, the one I—"

The speech was cut off as Andrew lifted himself up, just far enough to mash his mouth against Matthew's, pressing hard until the big man could barely breathe. "Hook nose?" Andrew murmured, pulling his lips away a fraction of an inch.

"Aquiline," Matthew said. "Does that suit you better?"

"Much better," Andrew said. He ran his hand along Matthew's beefy flank, down and up and down again, stopping at the top of the thighs. "What did you do to him? The head boy."

"Beat the stuffing out of him one day. Then I . . . stuffed him full again."

"Oh, what a brute." Andrew let out his breath in a sigh, smiling down into the blond-lashed eyes. "You are as big a liar as Phyllida and almost as pretty. But you see I love you both."

"Show me," Matthew said. "Show me how much you love me."

The two men on the floor were fortunately too engrossed in their own urgent business to hear the well-oiled lock turn and the heavy wooden door swing open, nor did they notice the small, stealthy figure that sidled in and scuttled into concealment behind the sideboard. "Yes," Lord Isham whispered, clutching himself in ecstasy and settling into a chair, "show me what I missed."

"MY LOVE," ANDREW SAID A while later, lifting his head from where it rested on Matthew's solid thigh. His tongue traced the line of invisible hairs leading from the massive cock up the sculpted abdomen to the navel.

"That tickles," Matthew said. "Do it again."

"My love?" Andrew asked, having gone back down the trail, fascinated by the way the muscles rippled as he passed.

"Yes," Matthew said. "What?"

"Nothing," Andrew said. "I just like to call you that and hear you answer to it."

"God, you're a romantic fool. My love."

"Yes."

JUNE 1812.

Philippe Tournière awoke, able to move for the first time in weeks. He stretched tentatively and tried to sit up. No, that was a mistake. But his message must be sent, the one he had captured from the cunning, spying bitch months ago. He had lost the accounts book, a lapse for which he could never forgive himself, nor could he expect mercy from his employer. But he had at least salvaged something when he went through the slut's room and discovered her trove of revealing dispatches. He could only hope it was not already too late. "Kit," he whispered. "Are you with me?"

"I'm here, Phil," Kit said, looking up from the pages of the novel he was working his way through. "Glad to see ya feeling better."

"The message. Do you still have it?"

"'Course I do. You told me to keep it for you."

"You are very good, *mon ange*. Now, what about the cipher? Do you know how to use it?"

"I think so. Nan's better."

"I do not like your wife, *mon ange*. I am sorry, but—"

"She don't like you, neither. But you don't have to worry about her. She knows where the money comes from."

"Ah, so mercenary, you English." Philippe lay back with a contented sigh. "Very well, then. If you and Mme. Marlowe would be so kind as to encode the message and send it to the usual address. But you must promise me. Tell *personne*—no one. Not even the so very sympathetic Lord Isham. Promise?"

"I promise, Phil. You want to send your message out, we won't betray you."

Kit brought out the concealed message and sat by Tournière until he fell asleep. The sheet was very large, wider and longer than any books or letter paper Kit had ever seen, and had been folded over many times, leaving it a mass of creases and difficult to read. Luckily, Kit knew the passage well. He had studied it in school.

NAN CLICKED HER TONGUE IN disapproval as she worked, matching up the words on the galley proof with their equivalents on the cipher key and writing the numbers on a piece of letter paper. "He's off his nut."

"He's harmless, Nan."

"Harmless as a snake."

"Don't start that again, please."

"All I know is, you oughtn't to send this."

"Why not?"

"We could get in trouble. What if Mr. Amberson reads it?"

"He won't. And even if he does, so what?"

"He'll know, that's what. He always knows—everything."

"Well, he won't know about this, until it's too late. Crikey! I'd give five guineas to see their faces when they read this."

YARDLEY CHECKED THE POST TO see if there was anything that could not wait for the master's return. It was lonely in the big town house, with the master and the mistress away for the summer. He wondered if that pleasant Mr. Thornby might need an experienced butler for his estate or if it was perhaps time to retire to the cottage Mr. Andrew had promised him. He saw the letter addressed to "Mr. W. Yardley" and sighed.

He had thought this business over and done with. Nothing more had come for his nephew for months, not since the last one, around the time of the problem with Harry Swain. This one was different—hand-delivered, already franked by some peer with an illegible scrawl, with the words "to be forwarded" in pencil in the place where the direction should be. *The absolutely last time*, Yardley said to himself as he wrote Walter's address, a small village on the south coast. Still, blood was thicker than water, when it came down to it. And his nephew had done nothing so very wrong. Only tried to run a profitable business, the sort of place where Mr. Andrew and his friends could enjoy themselves in their own way.

JULY 1812: ALLIED HQ OUTSIDE SALAMANCA, SPAIN

Having set Major Scovell to transcribe the two encoded messages his scouts had intercepted, Lord Wellington poured himself a glass of claret and settled down to ponder the results. The first was most satisfactory, a confirmation of the breakdown in communications between King Joseph and Marshals Marmont and Jourdan, in charge of Napoleon's armies of Portugal and Spain; further proof, if such were needed, of the advantage he could gain by seizing the moment. For the first time since this campaign began, he had the opportunity, perhaps the obligation, to take the offensive in this wretched war of retreat and defense.

He picked up the second message. It began with the letters GOA, the initials of Geoffrey Osborne Amberson, the head of the home intelligence service—a sign of progress in the uncovering of double agents.

"Please, sir," Melisande said. "On my knees I beg you. Do not force what should be given in love."

The tall, elegant man smiled in a way that reminded Melisande of nothing so much as a wolf at the kill. "What are you afraid of, my dear?" Lord Iskander asked. "Afraid that I will ravish you? Or afraid that you will like it?"

His wiry arms caught her and imprisoned her like steel bands. She twisted and writhed, unable to free herself, aware only of the unusual hardness of his flesh, the heavy breathing from his chest—and hers. When his mouth closed over hers she was powerless to fight. She sank down under his weight, falling onto the narrow bed with a sense of inevitability, trying to cry for help but breathless, unable to form coherent sounds. "You may cry out," Iskander whispered. "No one will hear you but I. You will cry out. You will cry again and again, begging for my attentions."

Then the darkness descended, and she knew nothing more.

"De Lancey!" Wellington roared.

The young deputy quartermaster-general appeared in the doorway. Wellington waved the offending message in the air. "What the devil is this rubbish? If this is your idea of a joke, you'll find my idea of a joke is leading the forlorn hope at the siege of Burgos."

Having expected no less than this reaction, William De Lancey bowed and gave a hasty salute. "My lord, I swear that's what the message reads. Scovell went over it a dozen times and I double-checked his work. We decided we ought to show it to you anyway, in case it might have a deeper meaning of which we were unaware."

"It does," Wellington said. "It means Amberson has lost his wits. Here, take a letter."

"Shall I send in an adjutant, my lord?"

"Oh, never mind. I'll write it myself."

Amberson:

On my knees I beg you, no more of this humbug. If you can't stay away from the brandy, have the kindness not to send me your drunken effusions in the guise of intelligence.

Wellington.

Bentwood Grange, January 5, 1813.

"Sophia," Phyllida said. "Andrew wanted me to name her Matilda, if you can believe it."

"It was our mother's name," Lizzie Fanshawe said. "And Andrew may claim he doesn't care, but he really did love her very much. He was the eldest, so it hit him very hard when she died, and he was just at the most vulnerable time of his life, seventeen and going off to Oxford, so you see it really doesn't seem like such a terrible thing to want to name his daughter Matilda."

"No, it doesn't," Phyllida agreed. "It's her middle name. Sophia Matilda."

"A pity you had to have a girl," Lizzie said. "At least she looks like her father."

"Yes, I've never seen an infant with so much hair," Phyllida said, smoothing the cap over Sophia's head and tucking one little black wisp under the lace trim.

"So all the unbelievers who wouldn't pay up last spring are confounded now," Lizzie continued. "I do hope their creditors make them pay interest, I really do, because it's insulting enough to have been wagering against Andrew at all, when everybody knows he has a reputation for manliness, but to imply that he would permit his wife to be unfaithful, why it's just adding insult to—"

"Insult to insult?" Richard Carrington interrupted. "But that's the *ton* for you. Why stop at one insult when several can be heaped on one's head at once?"

"Sound rather bitter, old man," Wilt Fanshawe said. "For someone who must have done quite well from the dear child's existence."

"Yes," Richard said. "I made a very tidy sum on that wager. The thing is, I, ah, let the proceeds ride on another wager that didn't turn out so happily. Bet it was going to be a boy."

"Well, of all the cork-brained things to do!" Phyllida exclaimed.

"You're beginning to talk like my brother," Richard said. "But I suppose it was rather foolish."

"Rather foolish?" Lizzie weighed in. "To throw away your winnings from a sure thing on a fifty-fifty chance? Really, I don't have words for such stupidity."

"You at a loss for words?" Richard said. "Almost worth the price to see that. Won't happen again this century."

"When are you due?" Phyllida asked Lizzie, attempting to head off another argument between siblings. There'd been far too many of those in the past week. And it was incongruous to see the woman pregnant. She looked like a constipated snake that had ingested an uncut watermelon.

"Not until March," Lizzie said. "It's all so tedious, but what can one do? At least I have easy deliveries."

"I still find it difficult to believe that you have children at all," Phyllida said.

"Thank you," Lizzie said with a satisfied smirk. "Everybody says so. Wilt says I look just the same as before my marriage, and that was eight years ago. Once I drop this foal, my figure will go right back."

"Very true, my love," Fanshawe confirmed. "I expect to have my graceful sylph again in time for the season."

Sophia Matilda let out a wail of distress.

"Poor thing," Lizzie said. "Ring for the nursemaid."

"Oh, I think she's just hungry," Phyllida said. She opened her dress and put the mewling child to her enormous breast as Lizzie shrieked in horror and Richard, torn between avid curiosity and, for a refreshing change in his life, embarrassment, contented himself with standing sideways to the display and sneaking glances out of the corner of his eye. Fanshawe harrumphed and made a show of turning his back, all the time looking over his shoulder until it seemed his neck would twist completely off.

"Phyllida! You mustn't!" Lizzie said. "You'll completely ruin whatever is left of your figure if you do that."

"As there's nothing left of my figure, it seems silly to worry about ruining it," Phyllida said, laughing up at the distraught woman. "And of course I want to nurse my own child. I love her so, I can't imagine giving her over to someone else."

"Yes, we have to pry the little wench out of her mother's arms just to let the nursemaid give her a bath or change her swaddling," Andrew said, entering the room. "Phyllida, my love, when you've quite finished shocking my family, may I have a word with you in private?"

"No, Andrew," Phyllida said. "You just don't want me to feed our child in front of other people, as if it were something unnatural. But you will simply have to get used to it, because I have no intention of hiding away and missing all the conversation whenever Sophia is hungry."

"Well said," Matthew said, following Andrew into the room. "We lower orders must stick together against the repressions of a decadent nobility."

"My father was a gentleman," Phyllida protested. She winked at Matthew. "But my mother was a—"

"Your mother," Andrew said, "was, and is, an amiable and charming lady, and will continue to be so as long as she is my mother-in-law. And, like all relatives, best kept at a distance. How did this reprehensible subject get started?"

"Only because I was telling your wife that if she insists on behaving in this irresponsible and lowborn way, she'll lose her figure and make you a laughingstock," Lizzie said. "Can't you make her stop? Don't you have any authority as a husband in your own home?"

"No," Andrew said, "none at all. And it's not my home. It's Matthew's. And as you see, he always takes Phyllida's side. It's two against one, and there's no relief in sight, especially now that his betrothal to the sizable Miss Swain of the almost as sizable fortune has come to such an abrupt end."

"That is cruel, Andrew," Phyllida said. "Are you very unhappy, Matthew?"

"Devastated," Matthew said with his broad smile. "Crushed, heart-stricken and dwindling into a decline."

"I know the feeling," Richard said with an answering grin. "Nothing for it but a restorative application of brandy and loose women—or men."

"There will be no application of loose members of either sex," Andrew said. "The whole thing was a mistake that Miss Swain had the consideration to put right."

"If it was a mistake," Lizzie said, "why did you propose in the first place?"

Matthew shrugged. "I like Miss Swain. She's intelligent and unaffected, and I suppose I felt sorry for her. She was understandably upset when she learned about the beautiful Bellingham installing Sally Green in that house in Soho."

"Never a good idea, proposing to a woman who's pining for someone else," Fanshawe said. "She's bound to say yes, just to spite the other fellow."

Richard nodded. "It was decent of her to recognize the truth and set you free."

"She's playing a dangerous game," Lizzie said, "if she thinks she can hold out for Bellingham. Ten to one he marries that Mrs. Green in the end."

"Oh, I hope not," Phyllida said. "That would be dreadful. Anyway, I think he does care for Charlotte. He's just too young to want to settle down yet."

"But by the time he's old enough," Lizzie said, "she'll be an old maid."

"Even if he waits two more years," Phyllida said, eyes kindling for a fight, large bosom heaving with wrath, "Miss Swain will still only be twenty-two, the age I was when I married Andrew."

"Precisely," Lizzie said. "An old maid."

The contortions and eruptions which this statement generated in Sophia Matilda's food supply caused that sensible female to howl with rage. "Now see what you've done," Phyllida said. "Honestly, Lizzie, I don't know how you managed to produce three children without learning the slightest thing about them."

"Now see here," Fanshawe said.

"Two," Lizzie said. "This lump isn't a child yet. And I don't have to know about them. Why should I? That's what the nursemaid is for. You ought to be ashamed of knowing anything at all, married to a man in Andrew's position."

"What does Andrew's position have to do with being a good mother?" Phyllida said.

"Nothing whatsoever," Lizzie said. "That's what I'm trying to tell you. He doesn't need a good mother. He needs a good wife. And a good wife and a good mother are never the same person."

"And sometimes the same person is neither one," Phyllida said.

"What did you say?" Lizzie screamed.

"I say," Fanshawe tried again to defend his wife.

Fortunately, the entrance of the nursemaid to take Sophia to be changed prevented the escalation into an all-out war.

"Where are you holding the ceremonies tomorrow?" Richard inquired once peace, in the form of a smoldering standoff, had been restored between the ladies. "The chapel?"

"Where else?" Matthew said. "Nice to have a use for it."

Fanshawe harrumphed again. "Pardon me for interfering, but it don't seem right. A chapel, you know, without a minister."

Andrew raised his eyebrows and Phyllida leaned forward eagerly, waiting for the fireworks. "The Reverend John Church, you will be happy to know, has agreed to preside."

"The Reverend Church?" Fanshawe repeated. "That's rum. Sounds too smoky by half. Surely he's not Church of England."

"The man was a foundling," Matthew said. "Left on the steps of a church. The charitable group that took him in gave him his name."

"He's a dissenting minister," Andrew said. "And as true a Christian as any man here, including you, Fanshawe, I imagine. If you don't wish to witness the marriages tomorrow, you and Lizzie are free to leave."

"But we have to stay!" Lizzie wailed. "It's why we came."

ANDREW AND MATTHEW STAYED BEHIND as the company went to change for dinner and the nursemaid brought Sophia back, clean and sleepy, for Phyllida to finish nursing. Andrew laid his hand on Phyllida's shoulder, admiring his daughter and her hearty appetite with a fond smile. *Like mother, like daughter.*

"Are you terribly disappointed that she is a girl?" Phyllida asked.

"Disappointed? I am delighted."

"But you do not yet have an heir."

"Precisely. And you have not yet earned your estate in Northumberland. Which means," Andrew said, as he raised his hand to stroke his wife's soft cheek and she leaned into the touch like a cosseted cat, "that as soon as you are able, we will have to go to work."

"That does not sound very tempting," Phyllida complained. "Matthew, I appeal to you. Would you care for such a cold invitation?"

"Indeed I would not," Matthew said. "Work is not at all what I look forward to with your husband, despite the fact that he once promised me a very interesting secretarial position. As I recall, I would have been required to write a *prodigious* number of letters. And there was an absolutely *enormous* inkbottle—"

"That's enough," Andrew said, glaring at his lover. "You two are the most shameless, provoking pair a man ever had the misfortune to marry."

"Then we are well suited," Phyllida said. "Andrew, confess it, you would be very unhappy with a prim and proper wife and a lover who held himself apart from the rest of your family."

"I confess," Andrew said. "And it gives me an idea. Instead of threatening my wife with responsibilities, I think we must remind her of the pleasures ahead when she returns to health."

"Oh, no," Phyllida said. "That is most unfair."

"Merely an incentive," Andrew murmured, sitting on the sofa and patting the place beside him. "Everybody makes a greater effort when there's a reward in sight. Now, Matthew, my love, come here and give us a kiss."

Matthew complied with a proper peck on the cheek and a show of reluctance for Phyllida's sake. "Don't you think we should wait until later?"

"No, no," Andrew said. "It's been an entire month since the birth. Phyllida will like to see that there is something to look forward to besides midnight feedings and changing dirty swaddling. Come on, man, don't be shy."

Matthew, seeing Phyllida's avid stare, eyes opened very wide, and the way her breath was already coming in short gasps, gave up all pretense of embarrassment and leaned into another, deeper kiss.

Andrew held his lover close for a long session of fondling and kissing until the men were breathing heavily and had begun to work up a sweat. "Now, wife," Andrew said, breaking away, Matthew panting in his arms, "what do you say?"

"Oh," Phyllida sighed. "That is lovely. I think there is time for me to add something like it to my new novel before it goes to the printer. I am calling it *The Memories of Melisande*, because it is a continuation of my last book, which sold so well. The heroine disappeared at the end, and now she returns, although she has lost her memory. So you see, I have a great deal of latitude to try some exciting scenes, because even if they are terribly improper they can always be explained away as the products of poor Melisande's confused imagination. Can you and Matthew show me that again? I want to be able to describe it all correctly. I especially like the part where you put your leg over his."

"I think," Matthew said under the barrage of curses that issued from Andrew's lips, "that your weapon has just exploded in your face."

LORD AND LADY DAVID PIERCE, riding in a closed carriage, only discovered that the perch phaeton they had been following for some time belonged to Sir Frederick Verney when they all bowled up together on the curved driveway of Bentwood Grange and Sylvester Monkton, straightening the folds of his caped driving coat and smoothing his windblown hair, climbed down from the phaeton's passenger seat. There were handshakes and congratulations all around as the footman let them in and they were engulfed in chatter.

Phyllida embraced Lady David and led her upstairs to rest—a desire repudiated by that robust lady—and to change out of her traveling clothes, an offer accepted with thanks.

"You do look well," Phyllida said. "Marriage certainly agrees with you."

"Yes," Agatha replied, eyeing her blooming hostess. "Almost as well as motherhood appears to suit you." She threw off her bonnet and pelisse, revealing a figure much altered in the middle. "As you see, I'm in the way to following your example. No more wearing breeches for the next few months."

"Wear breeches? Why would you want to?"

Agatha raised an eyebrow. "More comfortable, don't you think?" To Phyllida's emphatic shake of the head, she said, "No? Well, they suit me. And David likes 'em on me—or more precisely, likes *me* in them." She was surprised and gratified to see she had made the other intrepid lady blush. "Truth is, had to allow Pierce to make an honest woman out of me before I became the latest *on dit*." The sharp burst of staccato laughter took any last vestige of modesty out of the statement.

"George has been very unhappy," Phyllida said.

"I can imagine," Agatha said. "Frankly, never thought I'd get in whelp. Won't see thirty again."

"Lady Wellington was almost thirty-five, you know," Phyllida said. "She had the two sons, one after the other, just like that, and she hasn't half your vigor."

Agatha nodded as if Phyllida had said something profound. "You're right, of course. Ought to have known we couldn't keep it under wraps. Only gave in to David when I saw it couldn't be helped."

"Didn't you want to be married?" Phyllida asked. "Don't you care for Lord David?"

"Love him more than anybody, except George," Agatha admitted. "That's the problem. Didn't want to hurt his feelings."

"But don't you see?" Phyllida said. "That *is* what hurt him—that Lord David had . . . had . . . oh . . . any way one says it sounds so coarse."

"As if I mind," Agatha said. "Had his way with me, you mean."

"Not that," Phyllida said. "It looked as though he was refusing to do right by you. George never imagined he'd have to defend his sister's virtue, you see, and certainly not against the man he loves most in all the world."

"Oh, dear." Agatha sighed heavily and sat down. "I hadn't thought of it that way."

"No. I imagine you're so used to seeing George as a boy who needs your protection in place of a mother's, you forget he's a man now, with a man's feelings."

THE REVEREND JOHN CHURCH, A handsome and effusive man in his early thirties, his dark hair brushed up into a puffy version of the Brutus style, greeted his hosts with a flood of praise that managed to combine enthusiasm and flattery without falling into the error of obsequiousness. He shook hands with Matthew, exclaiming at the flourishing appearance of the vast estate, even in winter, and thanked Andrew repeatedly for the use of his luxurious chaise, declaring himself not at all fatigued from his easy journey and quite ready to meet his latest parishioners.

"No, no," he said with his winning smile, as he was ushered into the roomful of family and visitors, and the introductions began, "don't tell me. Let me see if I can recognize the other couple myself."

"Don't look at me," Monkton said with a sneer, putting his glass up to discourage familiarity. "The day I take on a partner until death does us part, man or woman, is the day you can lock me up in Bedlam."

There was a quick flurry of wagering as the men recalculated the odds on Church's perspicacity with the reduced pool of contestants.

Church turned back to the waiting gentlemen, paced the line, and began with Fanshawe, taking his hand, stroking the palm lightly, and staring earnestly into his face, until that gentleman was moved to pull away, exclaiming, "Now see here, I'm all for peace in the family, but I'm damned if I'll be subjected to any more of this indignity."

Lizzie laughed and held her husband's hands, drawing him a little apart. "There, there, Wilt. You've been very gallant, and I promise to make it up to you." She kissed his cheek, smoothing his frown with a long, slender finger, adding in her penetrating whisper, "*Tonight*, after the weddings. Now, what do you say to that?"

Fanshawe blushed bright red. "I say I'm a very lucky dog to have got myself such a beautiful and generous wife. Much better than I deserve."

"Just so long as you admit it," Lizzie said.

"Not him, then," Church said, moving to Richard Carrington. He stared up into the tall young man's face. "My goodness! Such an abundance of masculine charms."

"Yes, aren't we a stunning bunch?" Richard agreed. "You may stroke my hand all you like and whisper sweet words in my ear. I shan't object."

Church laughed and demurred. "Too eager, I'd say. You probably merely want to win the wager."

The others laughed. "Got you there, Dick," Andrew said.

Church looked from Verney to Pierce, noting Agatha on his arm, her swelling body and tender gaze, but still hesitating. He took the measure of Verney's athletic figure, the rich chestnut hair and strong, chiseled features, but shook his head. "You are not a marrying man, I think, any more than your friend there." He nodded in Monkton's direction. "Whereas you," he turned back to Pierce, radiant with joy and glowing from his fashionably barbered head to his Hessian boots with their gold tassels and mirrored surfaces. "You have all the marks of the impatient bridegroom. It appears to me that we have only half of a couple here. Perhaps there is another gentleman in the house."

"Well done," Andrew said over the others' congratulations and payment of forfeits. "Mr. George Witherspoon is upstairs. He and Pierce are not quite in sympathy at the moment, however."

"Oh, dear," Church said to Pierce. "Whatever may have come between you and your friend, I urge you, in the spirit of Christian love and forgiveness, to put it aside and seize the opportunity to be made one flesh."

"Damn it, I'm not quarreling with George," Pierce said. "He's the one quarreling with me."

"Now, now," Church said. "It takes two to quarrel. Perhaps I could accompany you upstairs and help you two on your way to making amends."

Lady David cleared her throat. "Don't mean to butt in on a parson's business," she said, "but I don't think that's a good idea just yet. Something I have to tell George. No, David." She put a masterful hand on her husband's arm. "Think he'll take it better coming from me."

GEORGE WITHERSPOON STUDIED THE LARGE canvas, gnawed a fingernail, nearly choked on the vermilion pigment, and ran his hand through his hair instead, streaking it a brilliant shade of pink. "I can't," he muttered. "Oh, God, I've lost it."

Lady David and the Reverend Church, knocking on the door and receiving no answer, entered quietly. "George?" Agatha said. "The minister is here. He wishes to speak with you."

Church stood arrested on the threshold, his eyes growing rounder and rounder and his jaw hanging open. "What a vision is this?" he asked in awed tones.

Witherspoon, startled by the voices, threw a concealing drape over his work and turned around. "Aggie," he said. "I didn't hear you knock. How was your honeymoon?" His normally mellifluous voice was dull and without resonance.

"Very nice, thank you, George," Agatha said. "David is downstairs. He'd like to see you."

"Well, I wouldn't like to see him," Witherspoon said.

"Come, come," Church said. "You seem a very kindhearted young man, not the sort to hold a grudge."

"I beg your pardon?" Witherspoon said. "Mr.—"

"The Reverend John Church," Agatha said. "He's here for the weddings tomorrow."

"Then I hope Carrington and Thornby are still willing," Witherspoon said, "otherwise he will have had a wasted journey."

Church chuckled as if Witherspoon had spoken a pleasantry. "That picture," he said. "Your wife?"

"Oh, no. That is Mrs. Carrington and her child."

"May I see it?" Church asked.

"No, I'm sorry," Witherspoon said. "It's hopeless. I can't let anyone see it."

"It can't be as bad as that," Church said. "The glimpse I had just now—"

Witherspoon shook his head. "You shouldn't have come in like that without warning. You shouldn't have glimpsed it at all. And as for David, do you know he waited until Aggie was almost showing before offering to marry her? I didn't know what to do."

"Is this true?" Church asked. "That is quite a serious matter."

"Now, about that," Lady David said. "I think there's something you ought to know."

"Truly?" Witherspoon asked, his face alight with anxiety and new hope after Agatha had sat him down and spent a good ten minutes expounding the same thought, forcefully expressed in two repeated sentences. "You're not just saying it to protect him?"

"For goodness' sake, George. David doesn't need my protection. I held off on agreeing to marry him because I wished to spare you from a very natural jealousy and sense of betrayal."

"I don't see how debauching my sister and not marrying her spares my feelings," Witherspoon said.

"It was just this sort of misunderstanding I hoped to avoid," Agatha said, patting her belly, "but as you see, nature had the last laugh."

"But that will be my nephew," George said in reverent tones. "Or niece. It's almost like being a father myself, the closest I can come to having Davey's child. I thought sometimes you cared for him, but I didn't dare say anything in case I was only imagining what I wanted to see. Oh, Aggie, I always hoped you'd marry someday, and I'd much rather you married Davey than anybody else, because then we couldn't all live together so easily."

The Reverend Church dropped the corner of drapery he had lifted and turned to smile his approval at the brother and sister, now embracing. As the three of them trooped downstairs, Church murmured, "Always the most beautiful are taken by another."

Pierce held out his arms. "Can you ever forgive me?"

Witherspoon ran into Pierce's embrace and kissed him on the lips. "Oh, Davey," he said. "I missed you so much. I just wanted to be certain you care for Aggie."

"You must know I do," Pierce said. "But I will never neglect you, my love."

"If I were you," Church whispered to Andrew under cover of the general acclamation, "I would seek counsel from Proverbs, chapter thirty-one, verse ten."

"I am most grateful," Andrew said, shaking Church's hand.

Church looked down with surprise at the coins that had materialized in his palm. "No, no, Mr. Carrington. Your fee for performing the ceremonies is more than generous." As Andrew refused to take back his offering, Church pocketed the money and said, "Charity is the greatest of virtues, after all. On behalf of the poor of my parish, I thank you."

Monkton lifted his quizzing glass again to observe the embracing couple. "Pink hair? Is Witherspoon playing the Lord of Misrule tomorrow?"

"What's that?" Fanshawe asked. "Lord who?"

"Twelfth Night," Verney said. "Very appropriate for madge weddings, don't you agree? The world turned upside down, and all that?"

LATE THE NEXT MORNING, the Reverend John Church stood at the rail, the two betrothed couples facing him. "Before we recite the familiar words of the sacrament," he said, "I think it in order that we understand what it is we do here." He looked up from the middle distance he had been addressing to focus on Andrew's and Matthew's solid forms, then turned to study elegant little Pierce and beautiful, ethereal Witherspoon. "Perhaps some of you are familiar with the words of the Gospel of Matthew. Jesus, when asked what was the highest commandment, answered first: to love the Lord thy God. Then he said, 'And the second is like unto it, thou shalt love thy neighbor as thyself.'

"And perhaps some of you are also familiar with the words of the Gospel of John. Jesus, at the Last Supper, said, 'A new commandment I give unto you, That ye love one another; as I have loved you, that ye also love one another. By this shall all men know that ye are my disciples, if ye have love one to another.'"

Church paused and looked out at his little congregation. "Jesus did not hesitate or hedge. He did not say, we should love our wife, or our children, or our patron or our landlord. No, he said *love ye one another.* And for some of us, there is one other that we love most in the world, one of our own kind, a man like ourselves.

"Now, the world would have us believe this is wrong, that some words of the Old Testament forbid such love. But I say unto you, as we are Christians, and follow not the old god of fire and brimstone, of plagues and the testing of Job, the god who demanded the foreskins of his enemies and the sacrifice of firstborn sons, but the new god, the god of love, his son, Jesus Christ, who died on the cross for our sins—as we follow him, so it is right that we follow *his* words above all others.

"Jesus did not say that our redemption requires the eating of this food but not that, or the wearing of this kind of cloth but not that, or the cutting of our foreskins or leaving them intact. Nor did he say that our love must be only of the spiritual kind and nothing of the flesh. No, my brothers and sisters, Jesus, the Lord of Christians, did not qualify. He said only that we must love one another. He left it to us, as rational beings who follow him out of love, not fear, to judge for ourselves if the love we feel in our hearts, whether expressed in the flesh or the mind, is true Christian love. And it is in matrimony that we find the purest expression, the blending of body and soul that binds us to our true love."

Andrew, who had been on the verge of pulling out his watch and announcing, as ten months ago, that he wished to enjoy the wedding breakfast while it was still a morning meal, felt himself touched by intense emotion, something he had not experienced in church since boyhood. He took Matthew's hand and squeezed it and was rewarded with an answering squeeze and the glimpse of wet cheeks, just as Pierce and Witherspoon exchanged a similar look and clasp of hands.

Phyllida sniffed noisily and blew her nose; Lady Fanshawe sighed;

and even Lady David Pierce was heard to mutter, "Very pretty speech indeed."

Only now did the Reverend Church open his prayer book and say, "Dearly beloved, we are gathered here in the sight of God, and in the face of this company, to join together these two couples in holy matrimony; which is an honorable estate, instituted of God, signifying unto us the mystical union that is betwixt Christ and His Church."

AFTER ALL THE REQUISITE PROMISES had been made, and rings and kisses exchanged—all being duly witnessed—having signed a little impromptu register, the four men were pronounced married and the Reverend John Church declared that they were now free to consummate the nuptials. He then looked around the spare chapel, denuded of its splendor during the Interregnum and not since restored, noticed the absence of couches or sofas, and exclaimed, "But how are the men to show their love?"

"Later, after the feast, in their own rooms," Verney explained.

"Oh, dear," Church said, crestfallen. "I was so looking forward to this part. In the White Swan, you know, it was customary for the married couples and their attendants—all who were inspired by the festive mood—to solemnize the ceremony right there. The chapel had a number of beds, and more could be brought in as needed. In fact, I had the impression I had seen you there once or twice, Sir Frederick."

"Possibly," Verney said, his eyes narrowing.

"I mean no harm by saying so," Church said, seeing Verney's misgivings. "I never have, nor ever will, betray a friend."

Verney smiled, more at ease. "Lucky we weren't there on the fatal day, though."

"Yes, indeed," Church agreed. "And it leads me to believe in fate, you know, for I remember how I had noticed your fine form and had often entertained a fond hope, never realized, that at one of those affairs you might have been persuaded—forgive me if I presume—"

"Not at all," Verney said. "Be my pleasure. It's just, you see, this is not a madge wedding per se. I mean, can't get down to it right here in front of the ladies."

"No, I suppose not," Church said. "Can't say I favor these mixed marriages."

"But, my dear man, I was under the impression that you are married yourself," Monkton said. "And a father, several times over."

"Yes, of course," Church replied. "I'm a man of the cloth."

Monkton shook his head. "Don't see what that has to do with anything."

"Have to set an example," Church said. "Can't father a lot of nameless children. I was a foundling myself, you know. I could never inflict that on any child of mine. Besides, I love my Emily and our little brood very much."

THE WEDDING FEAST WAS A merry affair that lasted through the afternoon, approached and passed the dinner hour, and carried on into the evening. In the spirit of Twelfth Night, when all hierarchy is overturned, the entire household participated, the ladies and the servants, with people working and eating in shifts to keep the plates and glasses filled. Many toasts were drunk to the happy couples and speeches were made, becoming less coherent as copious amounts of champagne were consumed. Phyllida took it on herself to perform the duty that would normally be that of the groomsman. She had prepared well in advance, and, in place of the typical witty and bawdy speech, gave a bravura performance, addressing an appropriate Shakespeare sonnet to each of the four newlyweds.

For George, she made the obvious choice: "Shall I compare thee to a summer's day?" For Lord David, she found an apt one: "O! never say that I was false of heart." ("As easy might I from myself depart / As from my soul, which in thy breast doth lie.") Its closing strophe was "For nothing this wide universe I call / Save thou, my rose; in it thou art my all."

Any incipient tears not yet shed were brought forth from the reunited couple at this point.

For Matthew, she recited "Let not my love be call'd idolatry," which contained a repeated phrase "Fair, kind, and true" and ended with the strophe "'Fair, kind, and true' have often liv'd alone, / Which three till now never kept seat in one."

The applause after this went on so long that the company was in danger of forgetting there was one more man to be serenaded.

"I know my verse," Andrew whispered, holding her hand. "'The expense of spirit in a waste of shame.'"

"Never!" Phyllida said, shaking her head and trying to free her hand.

"'Lust in action'?" Matthew said. "Perfect for you, my love."

"I suppose you're going to tell me you went to university, too," Andrew said. "Let me guess. Not Oxford—too royalist for an honest merchant's son. Cambridge, I presume."

"If you saw my application to the Brotherhood you already know the answer," Matthew said. "As Lord Isham would say, 'Humbug.'"

"Do you wish to hear your verse?" Phyllida inquired. "Or shall I read from *The Memories of Melisande*?" Once Andrew's groans had been stifled, Phyllida produced the crowd-pleasing "Let me not to the marriage of true minds / Admit impediments. Love is not love / Which alters when it alteration finds."

At the end, with her proud declamation—"If this be error, and upon me prov'd, / I never writ, nor no man ever lov'd"—Andrew was so moved he could only say, "You have written, and loved, truer than any man or woman." He pulled her down to sit on his lap and kissed her so long that Matthew considered reminding him just whose marriage they were celebrating this night.

It was Phyllida who put an end to the proceedings, saying she must go nurse Sophia. From Andrew's lap she shifted easily to Matthew's, kissing him on the mouth just as she had a minute ago kissed her husband, and causing the company to erupt with raucous cheers and beating of palms on the table. "He is my brother-in-law now," she said, looking up, eyes wide with innocence. "There can be nothing wrong in it."

Lady David Pierce followed her hostess out, and Lizzie Fanshawe attempted to drag her husband away, but he was too far gone in drink and insisted he would take his port with the other gentlemen. The household went about its business, and Richard Carrington, the one gentleman at the gathering with no partner for any sport later that night, decided to seek out the kitchen and, failing any joy there, the village, while he was still relatively steady on his pins.

"BUT I DON'T HAVE TO approve of it," Monkton said, continuing the interrupted discussion more or less where it had been left off at the departure of the ladies. "You may do as you please, only you can't force me to say I like it or wish to follow your example."

"How churlish," Verney said. "And on such a happy occasion."

"Is it?" Monkton said. "Why? Because two madge couples have

been coerced into aping the marital arrangements of society? I find it humiliating and sad. Of course I wish you joy, all of you." He raised his glass to each in turn. "But I do not see that there is anything to be gained for us sodomites in playing at husband and wife."

"But as a Christian," Church said, "don't you wish to join in holy matrimony with someone you love?"

"Not a Christian," Monkton said. "Whatever gave you the impression I am?"

"You're an Englishman, a gentleman," Church said.

"Yes to the former, and perhaps to the latter," Monkton said. "But I am first and foremost a man who prefers the company of his own sex. In short, a sinner and an outlaw. Says so in your Christian Bible. No getting around it, for all your clever obfuscation."

"That's not quite true," Church said. "It's a matter of interpretation."

"Bugger interpretation," Monkton said, to much laughter. "I consider myself a pagan, in the spirit of the ancient Greeks of blessed sodomitical memory, and of their estimable followers, the so practical and earthy Romans. Give me a good Horatian ode any day over anything in your Bible. Or a love poem by Catullus. Or, best of all, a Greek statue of a naked and perfectly proportioned athlete or a boyish, lithe Apollo. No problems of interpretation there."

"Hear, hear," Verney murmured.

"You understand my meaning," Monkton said.

"Yes, of course," Verney said. "Just think we ought to congratulate the others today and save our carping for later."

"Well, damn it," Monkton said, "I only said because I was asked."

"But, forgive me for interfering in what ain't my business," Fanshawe asked, emboldened by the plentiful champagne, "but doesn't it help your case if you show that you are like other men? That you wish to marry and be faithful and—"

"Yes," Monkton said. "You do have a valid point. None of your business."

Fanshawe looked so crushed even Monkton felt like a brute. "Mustn't be such a pansy, Fanshawe. Stand up to our verbal assaults like a man. The fact of the matter is, we are like other men. How many of you married men really *chose* to marry? Tell me that. Didn't you resign yourself to it as a necessary evil, because of needing an heir? Carrington? Or for wealth, and because the lady's family insists on her being supported in proper style? Fanshawe? How many of you would have married if society, Christian society, didn't insist on it? Pierce?"

"That silenced the wedding party," Matthew said after a long, thoughtful, and glum interval.

"I wished to be married," Fanshawe said. "Never had a moment's regret that I married my Lizzie."

"But would you have married her if you could have had her without marriage?" Monkton persisted.

"Couldn't," Fanshawe said. "No other way I could have had her."

"There you are." Monkton sat back in triumph. "Do you know, I sometimes think I should have studied law after all, as old Hearn wanted me to."

"There's one flaw in your argument, Monkton," Andrew said. "I was entirely of your mind until I submitted to my own marriages. Now I wouldn't be free for all the ganymedes in a Turkish paradise."

"Every tamed stallion enjoys his ration of oats," Monkton said with a sneer. "When they slip the bridle over his head, I'm sure the poor creature tells himself he chose it of his own free will."

Pierce rose and clenched his fists. "I'll have you know, Monkton—"

"Gentlemen," Matthew said, standing up, arms akimbo, and surveying his dining room with the lordly air of a landowner, "this is a friendly gathering. If you wish to participate in a more active discussion, the stables are out in the rear. As for me, it is time I fed my stallion his ration of oats."

"Foulmouthed beast," Andrew said, kissing Matthew on the way upstairs.

Church waited until the two married couples had retired to their rooms, before approaching the others. "That was a very interesting argument," he said to Monkton. "It requires a lot of thought. An idea that needs to be wrestled with."

"Is that an invitation?" Monkton said. "Wrestling, as the Greeks knew, is best done naked."

"Yes. That is," Church turned to Verney, "I know I made an appointment with you, Sir Frederick, and I am reluctant to renege in the face of such beauty. I only wish that there was a way—"

"You'd like to do some theological wrestling with both of us?" Verney asked. "Is that it?" He raised an eyebrow at Monkton. "How about it, Sylvester? Care to put your thoughts into action, as it were?"

Monkton bowed ironically. "Think I can't keep up my end of the debate against your too-solid flesh, Fred? I'm more than willing, if our Christian friend here doesn't object."

Church stared from the handsome, athletic squire to the slim, exquisite tulip of the *ton* and fell to his knees. "The Lord be praised," he said, lifting his hands in prayer. "My cup runneth over."

"Steady on," Verney said, lifting him to his feet.

"Yes," Monkton said, taking the other arm and helping to guide Church toward the stairs, "save the gutter talk for the bedroom where it belongs."

SOMETIME DURING THE NIGHT ANDREW woke up to find Matthew lying on his back, hands behind his head, contemplating the tester. "What is it, my love?" he asked. "Ready for more?"

"Always," Matthew said. "But I was just brooding, wondering what I'll do while you and Phyllida are busy getting a son."

"Perhaps you ought to have married Miss Swain after all."

"No, she was right to end it. I don't want a wife."

"Don't you want children? I've seen you with Sophie. You'd make an excellent father."

"No better than you, love. Anyway, I think of her as ours somehow."

"She is, as they all will be. But you ought to have an heir," Andrew said. "Who are you going to leave this estate to? And your hard-earned wealth?"

"As to that," Matthew said, "I was thinking, if you have more than one son, I'd choose the younger one for my heir. If you're agreeable and he doesn't object."

"No one objects to being rich, my dear. I am grateful in advance. But that's a long way off. Is that what you meant before? About while I'm with Phyllida?"

"Yes. Don't you see? I'm not jealous, but the situation is out of balance. What am I supposed to do when you're with her? Read the Bible? Bathe in ice water? I'm a man, in case you forget, not a monk."

"Ah." Andrew lay back and sighed. "I do see. And I could never forget you're a man. It's just that I've become used to thinking of you as *my* man."

"I am," Matthew said. "I always will be. That's what this marriage established."

"No," Andrew said. "That was for the world. You've belonged to me for much longer than that."

"Have I, Andrew?" Matthew said. "I don't recall the bill of sale."

"A certain auction at the Brotherhood," Andrew said to Matthew. "I think it was a left hook that settled the question."

"THERE IS ONE THING," ANDREW said later. "I owe a substantial debt. Perhaps you might like to work it off for me."

"Don't tell me you've lost your entire fortune on 'Change. And why should I work it off? Why not simply pay it?"

"Because it's not money I owe. More of a payment in kind. It's to Verney, for introducing me to Phyllida."

"Oh, I see. Sir Frederick likes backgammon, does he?"

"Likes every game I know. And best of all, he plays every position."

"You won't mind?"

"Damn it, I'm the one suggesting it. Just do me one favor, Matthew. Tell me everything."

"I won't do it at all if you're uncomfortable with it."

"You misunderstand, my dear. I like it very well. I simply wish to share the pleasure, however vicariously."

"You Eton boys always were a degenerate lot."

"No worse than you Harrovians. Only a lot more honest."

"THERE. WHAT DO YOU THINK?" Witherspoon pulled the drapery off his latest work and stood aside.

"It's indecent," Lizzie declared after a horrified stare.

"My word!" Agatha said.

"It's . . . different," Matthew said, attempting diplomacy.

"It's perfect," Phyllida said. "It's me. Really me. And Sophia. George, you possess true genius." She bestowed a kiss on his cheek as he blushed and turned his head.

"I've never painted anywhere except in my own attic," George said. "Or allowed any embellishment."

"But I insisted," Phyllida said. "When we started the sittings, just painting me, it didn't feel right. So I thought we should wait until after the birth to finish it. And I was right, wasn't I?"

"I didn't know if it would work," George said. "I had begun to think it was a mistake. Then I had to put it aside while I was married, and when I came back I saw that all it needed was knowing when to stop. And I stopped, and, well, here it is."

Andrew had to nerve himself for the pleasure of studying the large canvas. Unlike Witherspoon's other subjects, Phyllida was portrayed not standing but stretched full-length on the boudoir couch, propped up by several thick cushions and holding Sophia in her arms. She was naked, like the others; but where they were unadorned, Phyllida wore a necklace of large rubies around her white throat. The blood-red color of the stones blended into the deep rose of the nipple of her exposed breast and the warm pink of her daughter's mouth fastened onto the other. The colors shaded into one another, along with the ivory and peach and tawny of the naked flesh, in a palette of every variation of red. The soft brown of Phyllida's hair and the black fluff of her daughter's provided a welcome neutral contrast.

"I should have thought you'd have expired of cold, posing naked in the dead of winter," Agatha said. "And as for the baby, it's a wonder the poor thing survived."

"That's where we were very ingenious," Phyllida said. "I started posing last spring and summer, when it was warm."

"How did you know the right way to hold her?" Matthew asked.

"Phyllida thought of it," George said. "I tried painting her standing up, as I usually do, but it never worked."

"And I said let's paint me and the baby together."

"So we thought of how to pose a mother and baby," George said, "and we knew she wouldn't stand around naked holding a baby, but would sit or recline to nurse her."

"But surely you have to have both models here at some point, for the light," Matthew said.

"That's right," George said. "After Sophia was born, and after Phyllida was recovered, she posed with Sophia a few times, well wrapped, so I could see how the baby's face looked in the light. I judged the rest accordingly. Then, once or twice, we had the maids build up the fire and leave Sophia unwrapped, so I could see her skin tones. And that's when we got the idea of the rubies, because they'd complete the color scheme."

"Very clever," Agatha said. "I wish you'd let David see it. He'd be so proud of you."

"He won't look," George said. "He said it would not be proper to see a naked picture of another man's wife."

"Quite true," Matthew said. "It is kind of you to allow me to see it."

"You are one of the family," Phyllida said. "Not exactly a husband, but far more than a friend."

"I was under the impression," Andrew said, the first words he had spoken since viewing the painting, "that you considered Matthew a brother-in-law."

"Oh, that was only for the benefit of rest of the company," Phyllida said. "We are much closer than that artificial relationship." Ignoring her husband's dangerously hooded eyes, she added, "Do you know, Andrew, I think Sophia prefers being naked, because she was always so happy at those times, cooing and gurgling and reaching with her hands. Perhaps we can leave her unclothed, in her natural state, once the weather is warmer."

The noise emanating from Andrew's throat was difficult to interpret—not exactly a word, but neither so formless as a growl or a bark.

"What's that, Andrew?"

"I said that neither one of you will be showing yourselves in your natural state so long as you remain under my roof."

"Goodness! All that from such an inarticulate sound," Phyllida said. "Lady David, perhaps it is a new kind of cipher?"

Agatha shook her head, making a similar incoherent noise, which she clarified by muttering, "Not at liberty to discuss that sort of thing. Thought you knew that, Mrs. Carrington."

Phyllida left the lady in peace and said, "As Matthew has pointed out, it is his roof."

That worthy gentleman stepped back and held up his hands. "Nay, I'll not come between you two spitting cats."

"We are merely having a discussion," Andrew said.

"You haven't said how you like the picture," Phyllida reminded him.

Andrew shook his head. "Haven't I? I suppose I was overwhelmed, my dear. It is beautiful, like you, and like our daughter. And it is a pleasure to have the mystery solved of why you were so eager to wear the rubies."

"Do you mind?"

"Mind? I can't think of a better use for them. Don't you know what it says in the Bible?"

"The Bible?"

"Yes, the Reverend John Church is not the only one who can quote scripture." Andrew stood with his hands linked behind his back, like a schoolboy reciting a lesson:

> *Who can find a virtuous woman? for her price is far above rubies. The heart of her husband doth safely trust in her . . . Strength and honor are her clothing . . . Her children arise up, and call her blessed; her husband also, and he praiseth her. Many daughters have done virtuously, but thou excelleth them all.*

There was a deep silence when he finished, then a familiar scream. "Oh, Andrew!" Phyllida threw herself into her husband's arms, nearly knocking him over. "I am glad I married you."

Andrew's arms closed around the ample form of his wife. He drew her in against his chest, thrilling, as always, to the soft warmth of her vibrant flesh. His chin rested gently on her light brown curls as he locked eyes with his new-wedded husband. "Not half as glad," he said, "as I am to have married you—both."

THE HISTORY BEHIND THE STORY

The Story Behind *Phyllida and the Brotherhood of Philander*

Phyllida and the Brotherhood of Philander began life as a Regency romance novel. The first regencies, written by Georgette Heyer in the 1930s and '40s, are comedies of manners that take place in Great Britain between 1811 and 1820, when the future King George IV acted as Prince Regent because his father, George III, had become incapacitated. Heyer's prototypes established a popular subgenre of the historical romance: witty, lighthearted love stories between members of the wealthy and leisured upper classes, while the darkness of world conflict occurs mostly offstage in the final years and aftermath of the Napoleonic Wars.

Traditional regencies are courtship novels that end with a kiss and a marriage proposal. New generations of writers have updated the form with edgier plots and spicy sex, as most modern readers, myself included, prefer. But the mood of any Regency romance should be the same: blithe comedy with sparkling dialogue, set in a time when the titled aristocracy of England was the ultimate in glamorous sophistication and the dashing British forces, led by Lord (soon to be Duke of) Wellington, pushed the French out of Portugal and Spain in the Peninsular Wars of 1808–1814.

The Regency is a comic writer's dream, a delightfully awkward transition period between the Enlightenment and Victorian worlds. Coming near the end of the Georgian era—the long century (1714–1830) spanning the reigns of the first four Hanoverian kings, all conveniently named George—the Regency shared much of the coarse, matter-of-fact outlook of the previous century, but tempered with a new Romantic esthetic. The poets Wordsworth, Byron, and Shelley, soon to be joined by Coleridge and Keats, shocked readers and nonreaders alike with their wild verses and wilder lives. Perhaps Jane Austen's sharp satire might have completed its metamorphosis into sentimental realism if Austen hadn't died at forty-one in 1817. Even the clothing pushed the limits, favoring a slim silhouette for both sexes that left little to the imagination. Proper young debutantes wore figure-hugging gowns of sheer muslin, with sandals and hairstyles inspired by recently discovered Greek antiquities, while men showed off everything below the waist in cutaway coats, tight pantaloons, and Hessian boots.

Having found the perfect genre for my voice, I naturally wanted to put my unique spin on it. Like a growing number of women today, I enjoy a relatively new form of romance novel: the gay male story. It occurred to me that the only thing hotter than two sexy heroes falling in love with each other was an alpha male who finds that one special man to live with happily ever after *and* that special woman, too. My next question was, as my "authoress" heroine, Phyllida, wondered about her own gothic tale: "Could she possibly get away with writing that?" That is, could I tell it as a love story? This is how I came up with the idea of the "bisexual romance."

Many people have wondered if there really were "gay people" in 1812, and if a club like the Brotherhood of Philander could have existed. While people in the past may have defined themselves and their sexual behavior differently than we do today, often by avoiding categories altogether, most of us understand that sex wasn't literally "invented in 1963," as the poet Philip Larkin playfully declared. Human sexuality in its many permutations has existed for as long as there have been human beings to engage in it.

But the extent to which people could be open about their sexuality was far more limited in the past. During most of Western European history, various sexual acts, even between consenting adults, were considered immoral and sometimes made illegal. During the Regency, the sodomy law enacted in the sixteenth century was still in effect. Sodomy, defined as anal sex between men, was a capital crime punished by hanging. Because credible eyewitness testimony was required for conviction, executions were relatively rare, and men were more often found guilty of "attempted sodomy," although even this brought a fine, a stint in the pillory, and a jail sentence.

The pillory was not the innocuous little shame ritual some of us may imagine. Convicted offenders, men and women, were subjected to the abuse of the mob, pelted with rubble, dung and entrails from butchers' and fishmongers' shops nonstop for the length of their sentence, with the full encouragement of the authorities. In London, the pillory was set up like a turnstile with four projecting arms; the offenders were forced to walk around, giving the crowd equal access on all sides. Victims occasionally died from the stress, and could be blinded or disfigured by well-aimed rocks. Surviving jail was not easy, either. Filth and lack of adequate food almost ensured disease. Who knows how many "attempted sodomites" merely exchanged the slow strangulation of hanging, as it was then, for a slower death?

ONE OF THE REASONS I chose to write a historical romance was familiarity. If I were to "write what I know," as we're supposed to, what, besides my own uneventful life, did I know better than the sort of thing I had read so much of? The best training for any writer of fiction is reading, and my lighter choices had often led me to seek out more instructive works, such as history and biography. But once

I decided to write about "men who prefer the company of men," I knew some specific reading was required. The most useful source I discovered was Rictor Norton's *Mother Clap's Molly House: The Gay Subculture in England 1700–1830* (London: GMP Publishers, 1992), now out of print. An updated edition has just been published (Nonsuch, 2007).

As the subtitle of Norton's book implies, by the late seventeenth century there was the beginning of a subculture of men who identified as what we would recognize as gay—the "mollies" or, in Regency times, "madges." The "molly house" of the eighteenth century was like a combination of a modern gay bar and bathhouse. Men drank, danced, and flirted with each other, sometimes going upstairs to have sex in rooms with multiple beds and no doors, so as to provide vicarious pleasure to the audience. There were even "molly weddings," whether genuine commitment ceremonies or simply a way of ridiculing heterosexual marriage, impossible to know. My opinion is that men are men, in all cultures and times: a mixture of hilarity, raunchy sex, and a brief ritual is often the most meaningful observance.

The molly subculture was urban and primarily working-class. We know about it because, much like today, there were periodic attempts by the religious and political establishment to "clean up" London society. Informers posing as mollies infiltrated molly houses and viewed as much salacious activity as they dared, then reported back to a magistrate, leading to a raid and prosecutions of those unfortunate enough to be caught in the wrong place at the wrong time. It was the entertaining if often heartbreaking transcripts of these trials that Norton used to reconstruct the molly culture. In 1810, less than two years before the start of *Phyllida*, a club called the White Swan was raided, and six men served a horrific sentence in the pillory.

This incident was covered extensively in the newspapers, and the attorney for one of the club's owners wrote a lurid account of the trial and punishment of his client, sparing none of the stomach-turning details.

Norton points out what is obvious to most of us today, and was acknowledged by some people from the beginning: that such harsh penalties created a vicious circle. The laws have been called a "blackmailers' charter," as extortionists found a steady source of income in men who would pay anything to escape ruin or death. Men perceived as gay or suspected of having sex with other men were considered untrustworthy, their patriotism and loyalty questionable, because they were vulnerable to blackmail. In order to avoid the pillory, jail or hanging, many gay men gave in to blackmail. Full circle. It is this fatal weakness caused by the law of the land that the fictional characters Philip Turner/Philippe Tournière and Geoffrey Amberson exploit, Tournière in the service of his private demons, Amberson preying on his own kind, for pleasure and to further his work in British counterintelligence.

I had begun writing *Phyllida* before I discovered Norton's book, and had already decided that my gay and bisexual characters would belong to some sort of club. My original plan was modeled on other clubs I knew about: gambling clubs like White's and Brooks', where men diced, played cards and famously (at White's) kept a betting book in which they entered all wagers agreed on by members; groups formed around the members' mutual (and legal) inclinations, such as coffee houses or the many incarnations of the Beefsteak Club; and the later nineteenth-century tradition of the gentlemen's club in which crusty old aristocrats drank whiskey or brandy, nodded off in wing chairs while reading the newspaper, and grumbled about the immorality of the younger generation.

With the new information, I was able to incorporate features of the molly houses into my concept of the Brotherhood. The biggest problem was security. By charging expensive dues that paid for trustworthy bouncers, preferably former heavyweight boxers, and by limiting membership to a select few, unlike the molly houses open to anyone, the gentlemen of the Brotherhood could feel reasonably safe. What I most wanted, as a writer whose voice is inevitably humorous, was that perfect contrast between upper-class hauteur and gay exuberance, leading to the innuendo and sexual situations that could be expected to arise in any group of high-spirited young men.

Readers wondering if there could have been such a club are reminded that, despite Tournière's best efforts, the Brotherhood was never betrayed or raided, and no members were ever put on trial. There is no mention of it in the public record, and its existence can neither be proved nor disproved. I like to think of it as adapting to the changing tastes of society while remaining true to its origins as an upscale molly house, still the best-kept secret of twenty-first-century gay London.

For the writer of historical fiction, language is the ultimate challenge. Too much anachronism is obviously impossible, destroying a believable sense of time and place. But over-faithfulness can be a snare, confusing readers and turning what should be an effortless diversion into a scholarly slog requiring a dictionary and a stiff drink. Regency novels are often heavy with the thieves' cant and other slang that those rackety young gents loved, just as suburban kids today exhibit their high degree of cool by fluency in "gangsta" speech. I tried not to overdo it, seasoning the dialogue with just a pinch of period terms (bosom bow = confidante; loose fish = a sloppy, indiscriminate libertine; tommy = a lesbian or any "mannish woman), to prevent blandness, and trusting that context would resolve any minor obscurities. I also used one old device: the casual, jaunty, "incorrect" upper-class speech favored especially by the country huntin', shootin', and fishin' set. "He don't" and "ain't" were customary among this none-too-intellectual class, from a time before the adoption of the pedantic rules of the nineteenth century, such as demonizing a perfectly fine contraction of "am not."

When it came to the question of how "gay" men of 1812 would speak, I knew only that the words "homosexual" and "bisexual," like the concepts behind them, were coinages of the later nineteenth and twentieth centuries, and had no place in Regency narrative or dialogue. (I have sometimes used the word "bisexual" in writing about the story as a convenient way to describe it for modern readers.) In fact, it was by Googling "gay slang eighteenth century" that I discovered *Mother Clap's* and was delighted to learn, as Diana Gabaldon observed in the note to her book *Lord John and the Private Matter* (New York: Delacorte Press, 2003), that some expressions still in use today date back more than two hundred years, including "rough trade," "Miss Thing," and "Mary," a generic term for a gay man, from which both "molly" and "madge" are derived.

As the language endured, so did the culture. The gay world I encountered in Norton's description sounded surprisingly contemporary, reminding me of the glorious, freewheeling late 1970s, the days of disco and pre-AIDS sex. Men signaled each other with handkerchiefs and gestures, and cruised for "bargains" in the known pickup spots like parks, specific streets, and, yes, public toilets. The accounts of the raided molly houses are anything but sad, despite the consequences. Those mollies and madges were having fun, in the timeless way that any modern reader can appreciate: drinking and dancing, flirting and having sex, and "marrying" each other in ceremonies that, real or mock, allowed men to swear their love to each other and consummate it in front of witnesses.

When I imagined my "gay" and "bisexual" characters, I knew that they could not be any less in language and behavior than their confident, swaggering, virile counterparts in other Regency romances. The idea of same-sex attraction as a mental illness, along with the disciplines of psychology and psychiatry, was developed only in the later nineteenth century. Until then, gay men were considered to be merely lawbreakers. Is it perhaps less damaging to the psyche to see oneself as an outlaw, punished for a crime, than as sick, needing treatment for a disease?

And so I created my "Philanderers," free of the soul-destroying taints of self-disgust and a sense of inferiority. Above all else, they defined themselves as gentlemen—aristocrats, sons of peers or heirs to titles, men of leisure, the height of aspiration. They were masters of the universe at a time when, as the humorous—and truest—history of Great Britain, *1066 and All That,* by W. C. Sellar and R. J. Yeatman, first published in 1930 (London: Methuen), explains, Great Britain was about to become "top nation" with Wellington's victory at Waterloo (1815). These were the sort of people I wanted to write about: red-blooded, two-fisted gentlemen, who enjoy hot sex and witty conversation and are fun to be with—romantic heroes all.

As for the other facts in a work of fiction: The two owners of the White Swan were a Mr. James Cook and a Mr. Yardley (no first name listed). Since Yardley disappeared when the house was raided, I felt free to use his character as an offstage presence, and to give Andrew Carrington his (fictional) elderly uncle as a butler.

The story of Major George Scovell, who cracked the *grand chiffre*, the French military cipher that makes a brief appearance in *Phyllida*, is told in *The Man Who Broke Napoleon's Codes*, by Mark Urban (Harper Perennial, 2003; I used an earlier edition from Faber and Faber [London], 2001). My appropriation of the cipher for use in scenes of romantic comedy and sexual farce is in no way intended as denigration of the heroic and, until recently, unappreciated and unrecognized efforts of Major Scovell. Urban's book mentions a "little office . . . off Abchurch Street where the foreign secretary and the prime minister retained a few fellows skilled in the black arts of secret writing" (page 174 of the 2001 edition). Nothing more is said of it, since the focus of the action is the Iberian Peninsula, and it seemed an ideal location for my fictional cipherers, Amberson and Agatha Gatling, to practice their own black arts.

It is only to be expected that the most improbable character in the story, the Rev. John Church, really existed. Norton calls him the "molly chaplain." The clerical duty I had him perform is similar in substance to actual ceremonies he was reported to have carried out, admittedly in a rather different setting. The words I have given him to speak, while my own, are, I hope, true to his beliefs and personality.

Finally, the event involving Spencer Perceval and John Bellingham did occur on May 11, 1812.

On the Web . . .

For readers who wish to learn about the beginnings of the gay subculture in England, including the full account of John Church and the "molly weddings," I recommend Rictor Norton's Web site, which contains all of the information in *Mother Clap's,* as well as essays, trial excerpts and transcripts, quotations, and much more, covering centuries of gay history available at www.infopt.demon.co.uk/.

To see news of upcoming events, and for links to other sites of interest, please visit my Web site at www.annherendeen.com.

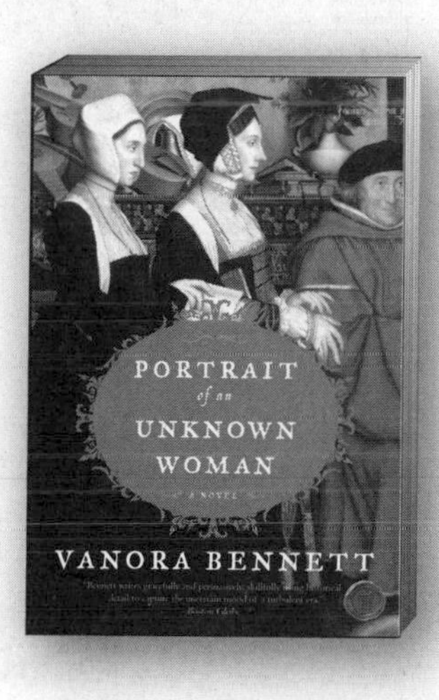

PORTRAIT
of an
UNKNOWN
WOMAN
A NOVEL
VANORA BENNETT

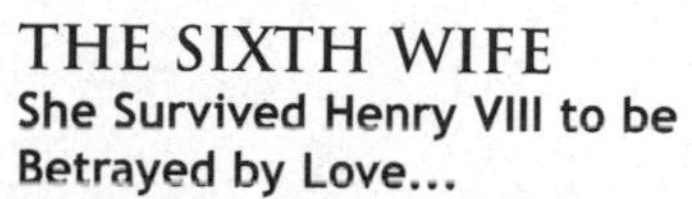

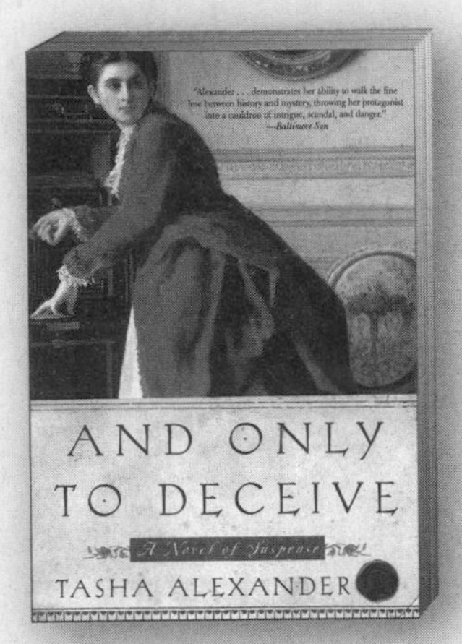

AND ONLY TO DECEIVE

A Novel of Suspense

by Tasha Alexander

978-0-06-114844-6 (paperback)

Discover the dangerous secrets kept by the strait-laced English of the Victorian era.

TO THE TOWER BORN

A Novel of the Lost Princes

by Robin Maxwell

978-0-06-058052-0 (paperback)

Join Nell Caxton in the search for the lost heirs to the throne of Tudor England.

CROSSED

A Tale of the Fourth Crusade

by Nicole Galland 978-0-06-084180-5 (paperback)

Under the banner of the Crusades, a pious knight and a British vagabond attempt a daring rescue.

THE SCROLL OF SEDUCTION

A Novel of Power, Madness, and Royalty

by Gioconda Belli 978-0-06-083313-8 (paperback)

A dual narrative of love, obsession, madness, and betrayal surrounding one of history's most controversial monarchs, Juana the Mad.

PILATE'S WIFE

A Novel of the Roman Empire

by Antoinette May 978-0-06-112866-0 (paperback)

Claudia foresaw the Romans' persecution of Christians, but even she could not stop the crucifixion.

ELIZABETH: THE GOLDEN AGE

by Tasha Alexander 978-0-06-143123-4 (paperback)

This novelization of the film starring Cate Blanchett is an eloquent exploration of the relationship between Queen Elizabeth I and Sir Walter Raleigh at the height of her power.

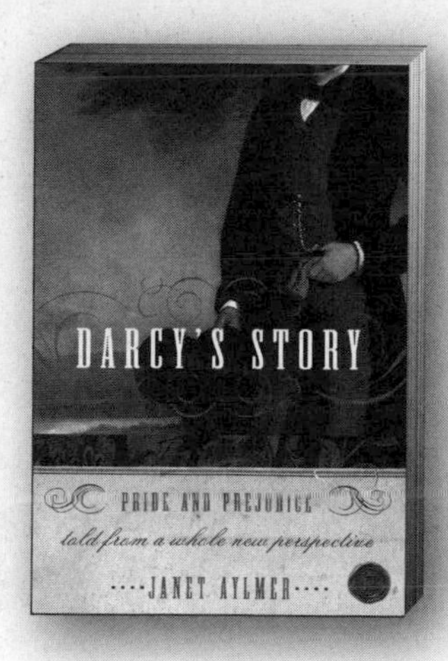

DARCY'S STORY

by Janet Aylmer
978-0-06-114870-5 (paperback)
Read Mr. Darcy's side of the story—*Pride and Prejudice* from a new perspective.

THE CANTERBURY PAPERS

A Novel

by Judith Healey
978-0-06-077332-8 (paperback)
Follow Princess Alais on a secret mission as she unlocks a long-held and dangerous secret.

THE FOOL'S TALE

A Novel

by Nicole Galland 978-0-06-072151-0 (paperback)
Travel back to Wales, 1198, a time of treachery, political unrest...and passion.

THE QUEEN OF SUBTLETIES

A Novel of Anne Boleyn

by Suzannah Dunn 978-0-06-059158-8 (paperback)
Untangle the web of fate surrounding Anne Boleyn in a tale narrated by the King's Confectioner.

REBECCA

The Classic Tale of Romantic Suspense

by Daphne Du Maurier 978-0-380-73040-7 (paperback)
Follow the second Mrs. Maxim de Winter down the lonely drive to Manderley, where Rebecca once ruled.

REBECCA'S TALE

A Novel

by Sally Beauman 978-0-06-117467-4 (paperback)
Unlock the dark secrets and old worlds of Rebecca de Winter's life with investigator Colonel Julyan.

REVENGE OF THE ROSE

A Novel

by Nicole Galland

978-0-06-084179-9 (paperback)

In the court of the Holy Roman Emperor, not even a knight is safe from gossip, schemes, and secrets.

A SUNDIAL IN A GRAVE: 1610

A Novel of Intrigue, Secret Societies, and the Race to Save History

by Mary Gentle

978-0-380-82041-2 (paperback)

Renaissance Europe comes alive in this dazzling tale of love, murder, and blackmail.

THORNFIELD HALL

Jane Eyre's Hidden Story

by Emma Tennant 978-0-06-000455-2 (paperback)

Watch the romance of Jane Eyre and Mr. Rochester unfold in this breathtaking sequel.

THE WIDOW'S WAR

A Novel

by Sally Gunning 978-0-06-079158-2 (paperback)

Tread the shores of colonial Cape Cod with a lonely whaler's widow as she tries to build a new life.

THE WILD IRISH

A Novel of Elizabeth I & the Pirate O'Malley

by Robin Maxwell 978-0-06-009143-9 (paperback)

Hoist a sail with the Irish pirate and clan chief Grace O'Malley.

Available wherever books are sold, or call 1-800-331-3761 to order.